Dead Beneath the Water

Sonia Suedfeld

Dead Beneath the Water

ISBN: 978-0-9731052-4-7

In memory of
my teacher, mentor and friend:
Marlene Pruesse
(1940 - 2002)

&

For the special guys in my life:
Michael, Kaleb and Jordan,
You've inspired me beyond words.

Prologue

THE BOY CROUCHED by the doorway into the living room, his small body shrinking into the shadows gathering in the corner. His hands pushed against the sides of his head, but still the sounds that were all around him slipped through his fingers and into his ears. Silent tears coursed over his cheeks and he rubbed his face roughly over his drawn-up knees, his fingers pulling out clumps of hair as they dug into his head. He didn't feel the pain, but the screams coming from the living room pierced through him like arrows of poison.

Another shrill, terrorized scream rose above the roar of the television as the woman was thrown against the wall. Her thin body slid to a heap on the wooden floor, strewn with broken glass and upturned furniture. Her moan of pain turned into another scream as big hands grabbed strands of her long, pale hair and pulled her upright.

"Shut up!" Spittle flew from the man's snarled lips as he smashed his fist into the side of her face again. Blood intermingled with tears as she turned saucer-like eyes to him.

"Please," she begged, "please stop."

A laugh bellowed out of his wide mouth, and then a vicious slap split her lip wide open. Blood dripped down her chin and her neck throbbed under the pressure of his hands as they circled around it. She gasped for air, her body smashing into the sofa as his hands pressed down, choking off the flow of air to her lungs. She feebly struggled but blackness washed over her in waves and her eyes fluttered closed.

Suddenly she was pushed to the floor and kicked in the stomach.

Her eyes flew open and another scream clawed its way out of her parched, burning throat as she struggled to breathe. He kicked her again and again, pain flaring anew in every part of her, a thin river of blood skating from her open mouth. She saw darkness once more.

"Wake up, you bitch!" he yelled, shaking her body back and forth, her head lolling from side to side. "Don't you dare die on me now!"

He cursed steadily, his voice ragged with rage as he whipped her around, slapping and punching her face with renewed vigour. He pounded her head into the floor over and over again, and the crunch of bone was deafening even above the roar of the TV set.

Letting her body slither to the floor, he threw his head back and howled, his bloodied hands finally falling at his sides as he knelt beside her lifeless body. He laid his head on her back and the sounds of his laughter bounced madly around the room.

Then there was pounding at the door and the sound of wood splintering apart as a battering ram was hurled against it. Uniformed bodies rushed into the apartment, weapons raised. They moved carefully into the living room, eyes drawn to the macabre scene just visible from the doorway. Dark, glistening blood puddled on the floor, streaked the sofa, and spattered the walls. They advanced slowly, their guns drawn, until they surrounded the man bent double over the body of a woman, his face pressed into her, his laughter muffled against her back. One drew nearer, and making sure the man was unarmed, swiftly handcuffed his bloodied hands behind his back and loudly recited section seven of the Canadian Charter of Rights, placing him under arrest. The others quickly checked over the still warm body for any signs of life. Finding none, they worked to secure the scene, while uniformed officers dragged the still-cackling man down two flights of steep stairs into a snowy night pulsating with the blue and red lights of police vehicles parked haphazardly in the street.

In the chaos that remained, someone mercifully turned the television off and silence settled over the room. It was then that a soft whimper was heard coming from the hallway leading to the kitchen. There, in the corner, the boy still crouched, ensconced in shadows so deep they almost swallowed him. His scalp bled where his dark hair had been torn out, and his eyes were vacant mirrors. Someone cradled him in a strong pair of arms, his tiny body curling into the fetal position, and took him into another room. A blanket was tucked around him; a woman's voice softly sang a lullaby in his ears.

But the boy didn't hear it. The laughter still echoed and the screams still rose and fell, rose and fell inside his shattered mind as the parade of uniformed and plainclothes bodies crowded into the apartment, dusting surfaces, photographing the body, and measuring blood splatters on the walls.

All he could hear in his mind were his mother's screams and his father's laughter.

Chapter One

THE FIRST STORM of the summer came like a stranger in the night, arriving on the wings of fierce winds barrelling across the bay. Sheets of rain fell hard to the ground. A zigzag of lightning streaked across blackened afternoon skies and thunder grumbled somewhere in the distance.

Hanna Laurence slowed her aging Honda around a rain-washed bend in the highway, her eyes straining through the downpour for the sign of the road she was looking for. Finally, just past a grove of cedar and pine trees and boulders of massive grey rock, it loomed out at her. She turned left onto Muskoka District Road 5, following its narrow curves as it snaked down to the shore of Georgian Bay, and then left again on a side road.

Almost immediately, she spotted a dozen police and emergency vehicles parked a couple of hundred metres away at the dead end of the road, their lights pulsing like faint heart beats in the rain.

An offshoot sprouted in both directions. It was little more than a gravel path, the first road running parallel to the shoreline of Georgian Bay. To her left, Hanna could see grey, tumbling water through gaps in gangly pines and wooden cottages newly opened for the season. Flowers grew in window boxes and in planters on decks, their colours bleached in the rain. On the other side, a small marina with several outbuildings and docks jutting out into the bay operated next to a variety store. She glimpsed boats through the wrought iron fence surrounding the marina and extending all the way to the beach.

A lone officer stood in the rain just in front of the vehicles, guarding the path running the length of the fence down to the shore. The large hood of his raincoat was drawn over his head and yellow crime scene tape flapped in the wind behind him.

Hanna noticed a couple of local news stations' vans and several other unmarked cars parked along the road as she pulled in behind a blue Chevy pick-up and turned off the engine. Rain immediately covered the windshield in rivulets.

Hanna glanced at the camera bag on the passenger seat beside her, her stomach knotting up with dread. It was the same feeling she got every time she had to cover a story like this, every time a body was found.

Please God, don't let it be Lydia Tomlinson.

But before the thought was fully formed, another more terrifying took its place - it could very well be her. Ten days was a long time to be missing, an eternity, and Hanna knew the chances of finding the 19-year-old alive and well were slim if non-existent.

She shivered in her silver vinyl raincoat as she thought of the missing girl's family. A picture of her parents formed unbidden in her mind - Albert and Cynthia Tomlinson on a white leather sofa in their living room, sitting so close together they seemed sown at their sides, their faces wrung with worry, their eyes deadened with desperation as days turned into a week and then 10 days and still their daughter was missing. How could this happen? How could she just disappear like that? They asked these questions again and again and they did not know the answers.

No one did.

And now there's a body, Hanna thought, and knew she was about to find out a lot of those answers if it was Lydia they had found. She felt the place below her rib cage harden like a fist.

Reaching in the back seat for the rubber boots she kept there for those times when she had to brave inclement weather to cover a story, Hanna kicked off her loafers and put them on. Following the officer's lead, she pulled the hood of her own raincoat over her head. She slipped her digital camera around her neck and under her coat to avoid getting it wet, and tucked the tools of her trade - press card, notebook, a pen, and a micro-recorder - into the deep pockets of the coat.

It was now or never. She took a deep breath and stepped out into the rain.

"Hold on," called the officer guarding the pathway as she trudged down the road to him. "You can't go down there. Police business, ma'am."

Hanna identified herself, flashing her press card, and went to stand near a group of local television and newspaper journalists milling about close to the path, talking to each other as they set up their camera equipment. She nodded to a few she recognized and watched a photographer she didn't know trying to hold an umbrella in one hand while loading film into his camera with the other. A small group of people, most of them huddling under umbrellas, stood on the road a few feet away and watched quietly.

Hanna looked down the path to the beach and was stunned to see the number of police officers and other emergency personnel crowding around a blanketed form lying on sand stained dark with rain. One officer stood off to the side, a cell phone clasped to his ear, gesturing animatedly with his hands. Another was stuffing something into a plastic evidence bag, and Hanna made out the letters FIS on the back of his jacket. Forensic Identification Services. More officers shuffled their feet as they stood talking to each other.

Beyond the commotion on the beach, a couple of divers up on a dock were helping a colleague climb out of the water, his black body suit clinging to him like a second skin.

Hanna watched them until movement at the corner of her eye made her turn back to the beach. An officer wearing a black raincoat with the hood pulled up over his head was walking up the path, but she didn't recognize his frowning features until he was only a few feet from her. Recently promoted, Tim Bennett was now a Detective-Inspector with the Criminal Investigation

Branch of the Ontario Provincial Police at Central Region general headquarters in Orillia. He had formerly worked at the Midland detachment of the OPP as a detective-sergeant and as the unit's public relations officer, and Hanna had gotten to know him well in the 14 months she'd worked for the small daily in Midland. He was intelligent, sensitive and dedicated to his work, and his promotion to headquarters a few months before had come as no surprise to her. A reliable source in the past, he continued to be happy to talk to her whenever she called now and again for a quote or a question. He was tall and well-built, with a quick, warm smile and the most beautiful eyes she'd ever seen on a man. Every time she looked into them she was reminded of the deep pools of sulphuric water she had once bathed in while traveling across Mexico a few years back. They were the exact same hue of jade, and Hanna felt her heart skip a beat looking into them now.

But it was more than the striking colour of his eyes that had her heart galloping as she looked down the path at the covered body again. The involvement of the divers and the other units were formidable enough on their own, but combined with the presence of the Ontario Provincial Police's Criminal Investigation Branch, Hanna knew the situation did not bode well at all.

Drownings were tragically common on Georgian Bay during the summer months, but she knew a simple drowning wouldn't bring the CIB out here. She'd done a story not long ago when the new superintendent of the branch had taken over, and knew the CIB provided case management support and specialized investigative assistance in major cases involving homicides, suspicious deaths and other serious criminal matters occurring in the province of Ontario.

It had to be a homicide, Hanna thought, although she knew they were virtually unheard of in this part of Muskoka, a district encompassing thousands of square miles across the crust of the Canadian Shield in central Ontario. The nearest town from the scene, Honey Harbour, was a small tourist hamlet whose population consisted mainly of cottagers and boaters in summer, and local police had worked very few homicides over the years.

But this had to be a suspicious death or else all these OPP units wouldn't be here, she thought, and fought a sense of dread.

"Tim? Detective-Inspector Tim Bennett?" she called just as he was about to walk past her. "I almost didn't recognize you under that hood. How are you?" She pulled her own hood back to reveal her face.

"Hanna. Hi. Long time no see," he said, smiling. "Damn this lousy rain, eh?"

"Lousy describes it pretty well," she agreed, smiling back. Then inclining her head towards the beach, she asked, "Did you catch this one?"

He nodded. As a detective-inspector with the OPP's Criminal Investigation Branch, he would act as case manager, overseeing the investigation with the assistance of the lead investigator and a file co-ordinator from the Midland detachment, whose jurisdiction included Honey Harbour.

"What's going on? Anything you can tell me?"

"We just pulled the body from out there," he said, indicating the docks where the divers were still huddling. "We're now securing the scene and the divers are scouring the area where the body was found for any evidence."

Hanna followed his gaze, her boots sinking into wet gravel. "When was the body found?"

"Just shortly before the storm hit, around eleven this morning, according to the guys who found it. They'd been fishing around those docks over there for a couple of hours. Apparently, one of them cast his reel and you might as well know, it hooked on to the back of a human hand."

Hanna's eyes widened. "A hand? You're not serious?" But she could see that he was and she shuddered as she looked up into his face. "Jesus. Who are they?"

"Brad and Joseph Tillmore. The father, Brad, owns the cottage next to the marina and the son was visiting for the week. That's them over there," he said, inclining his head towards a small group of four men - two wearing rubber boots, hip-waders and fishing caps - standing near the fence at the shoreline. "They're still pretty shook up about it."

Hanna made a mental note to talk to the anglers later as she gathered information about the various units of the OPP on the scene. A minute later, flashing lights cut through the downpour and she turned to see an ambulance approaching. It pulled a tight u-turn in the fork of the road and backed up between police cruisers, parking close to the edge of the pathway. Two paramedics, a man and a woman wearing white uniforms under hooded coats, hopped out, slamming doors behind them. Bennett excused himself to go talk with them and they returned to their vehicle, sliding out a stretcher. They lifted it up by its ends - there was no way to wheel it down in the wet sand - and started down the path.

Bennett came back, rain dripping from his chin.

"I know you probably don't have an I.D. yet, but what about the victim? Is it a woman?"

"Yes."

"Not a drowning?" She leaned over to see his profile against the rain.

He swung his gaze straight ahead, looking out at Georgian Bay tossing and turning in the rain-driven wind. When he looked back at her again, a drop of rain hung from his nose and his eyes were deep emeralds in his pale face.

"It doesn't look like it, Hanna. I'm sorry, but you know how it is... that's all I can say right now. We've got a lot of work to do, but we should know more in a short while."

Hanna could see the rotund form of Dr. Lucien Bergeron, the area's Regional Coroner, squatting near the body on the sand. "Will Bergeron be doing the autopsy?"

A shake of the head.

She raised an eyebrow. "Then she'll be taken to Toronto?"

"Yes."

Taking the body to the Office of the Chief Coroner in Toronto for the autopsy spoke volumes. There was little doubt left in Hanna's mind now that the woman they had found near the docks of the marina had been the victim of murder and she thought of Lydia again.

"So it's a homi-" she started to say and stopped as another vehicle pulled up. She made out white lettering surrounding a crest on the doors as they swung open. The OPP's Investigative Support Bureau, Behavioural Sciences Section. Her mouth went dry as two men wearing suits stepped out of the car and flicked open umbrellas.

Seeing these men wiped out any remaining hope that the body lying on the sand had not been the victim of murder. More than all the others put together, the arrival of this unit of the Ontario Provincial Police at the scene unsettled her. The BSS was the OPP's equivalent to the FBI's Special Crimes Unit, and their job was to study the behavioural and psychological aspects of cases involving homicide, attempted murder, sexual crimes, non-parental abductions, missing persons and found human remains.

She watched them approach, aware of the buzz of voices around her. Reporters had caught on, as she had, and they swarmed as Bennett joined the two suited men.

"What's the Behavioural Sciences Section doing here?"

"Do you suspect foul play? Can you confirm this is a homicide?"

"Is the victim the missing girl? Lydia Tomlinson?"

"Inspector Bennett, is it true the body was mutilated?"

The questions went on and on, but Hanna had frozen when she'd heard the word 'mutilated'. Oh please God, she prayed, Lydia's pretty face swimming up to the surface of her mind, let that be only a rumour and nothing else.

Bennett raised a hand for silence and identified himself. "We have an idea who the victim is, but until the family has been notified we will not be releasing her identity. I'm sure all of you can understand... her loved ones don't need to find out about this senseless tragedy on television or in the papers." He looked down the path towards the beach. "All I can say now is that we are launching a murder investigation into this young woman's death. There'll be a press conference... as soon as we can hold one, probably tomorrow. We'll be releasing some details at that time. Thank you."

A murder investigation. Reporters pounced with questions, but

Bennett turned his back and ducked under the yellow tape. Hanna watched him walk down the path to the water's edge, and felt a familiar tightening in her stomach. This would be the first murder investigation she'd have to cover since leaving Toronto almost a year and a half before. The first murder investigation the area had seen in at least twice that time.

The rain continued to fall in sheets from overcast skies and Hanna shuffled her feet on the muddy gravel of the road, waiting with everyone else for the body to be brought up the path. She made use of the time by talking to the anglers who had snagged the body while fishing that morning, as well as some of the other reporters and a few of the people watching the scene, most of them vacationers. An hour crept by, and puddles in the road soon grew into small lakes.

Finally she could see a procession moving up the path from the beach. A couple of uniformed officers led the way, followed by the paramedics carrying the stretcher, now heavy with the body. Other officers, Bennett and the regional coroner brought up the rear. Reporters jostled each other for space, their cameras dripping in the rain, just in front of the yellow crime tape. She moved slightly off to the side and turned on her digital. Through the LCD monitor, she watched an officer catch up to the stretcher and lift a corner near the bottom of the body bag to insert a clipboard beneath it. The metal clip along the top ripped open a long gash in the black plastic and the gusting wind immediately blew into the hole, forcing the flaps to gape. She caught a glimpse of a foot, mottled like old, brittle china, and a dark, square patch just above the ankle.

The wound looked exactly like an area of skin had been cut away from the leg and Hanna felt nausea roll in her stomach.

She saw the purple, chipped polish on the toenails in the split second before the officer closed the flaps in his fist, and the camera slipped in her wet fingers as she swallowed around a lump in her throat.

Someone lifted the police tape and the procession moved onto the road. The officer guarding the pathway called to everyone to please stand back, and she could hear the whir of automatic shutters as reporters took shot after shot of the scene. Their shouted questions were a cacophony of sound distorted in the howl of the wind.

A violent or suspicious death is always a public event, and Hanna felt a twinge of shame being a part of the media circus as she watched the paramedics move into the fray with the stretcher. There was no dignity and privacy left for this victim, whether she was the missing young woman or someone else. She looked down at the shape as it passed in front of her and knew that from now on, this woman would become a case number, a piece of evidence, a statistic. No longer a person, but a pile of bones and teeth and hair.

The stretcher was laid down on the gravel, rain pummelling the body bag and splashing up, as the paramedics hurriedly opened the back doors of the ambulance, its lights still sweeping in wide arcs. Hanna watched them lift up the stretcher, one on either side, and saw something long and pale trapped inside the zipper towards the head of the stretcher.

A clump of the victim's hair.

Lydia Tomlinson had long blonde hair like that.

Hanna shuddered inside her raincoat as she snapped pictures of the paramedics sliding the stretcher inside the ambulance. Two uniformed officers climbed in and she knew their job would be to guard the body while en route to Toronto, to preserve the chain of evidence. The doors were shut and latched, and after the ambulance drove off down the road, followed by a CIB vehicle, reporters resumed their interviews with residents and police before they could get away.

Catching up on some notes under the cover of a nearby pine tree, Hanna glanced at the piers where the divers had been joined by the two Behavioural Sciences Section officers. She wondered what they were talking about.

A few minutes later, Bennett walked over to her. "I'll be glad to get out of this rain," he said as tiny rivers of water coursed down his cheeks and dripped from his chin.

She nodded, but the rain was the farthest thing on her mind.

"It's bad, isn't it?" she asked, indicating the activity at the docks. "That's why the BSS is here."

He said nothing for a moment, but held her gaze. "Bad doesn't begin to describe it, Hanna," was all he said as he wiped his face with a hand.

She shuffled her feet on the gravel. "Is it her, Tim? Is it Lydia? You know I won't print anything you tell me, unless you say so. I just... I don't know. I just have this god-awful feeling."

Fatigue rimmed his eyes when he turned to look at her. He sighed and scratched at the stubble on his jaw. "You know I can't confirm or deny anything on the record, not until next of kin has been notified."

"Off the record then."

He gave her a little wave, as if dismissing her, and walked to his unmarked vehicle. When he had the driver's door open, he turned and looked back at her.

And nodded, just once.

Chapter Two

By HANNA LAURENCE
THE POST staff writer

HONEY HARBOUR — *The Criminal Investigation Branch (CIB)
of the Ontario Provincial Police has launched a murder investigation
into the death of a young woman found in the waters of Georgian
Bay on Thursday morning near this small town in the heart of cottage
country.*

*Detective-Inspector Tim Bennett of the CIB, who will be in charge
of the investigation, said the victim remains unidentified at this time
pending notification of kin. There is speculation the body is that of
Waubaushene resident Lydia Tomlinson, the 19-year-old Sheridan
College student who went missing 10 days ago after a camping
trip with friends on nearby Beausoleil Island, but there has been no
confirmation as of yet.*

*The body was discovered around 11 a.m. Thursday when Brad
Tillmore, a resident out for a morning of fishing by the docks of
Bayhaven Marina with his visiting son, Joseph, got his line hooked into
the back of a human hand.*

*"Thought I'd finally gotten me a big one at first, it seemed so heavy,"
the retired lawyer said, "but then, oh God, when I saw the hand, I just
freaked out."*

Tillmore ran to his cottage and dialled 9-1-1.

*Local police responded within minutes. First-at-the-scene officers
were quickly joined by neighbouring department forces and several*

Ontario Provincial Police branches, including the Underwater Search and Rescue Unit, employed primarily in the search for evidence and the recovery of drowning victims and sometimes in occurrences of marine disasters and plane crashes. Also at the scene were the OPP's Forensic Identification Services Section, the Emergency Response Team, and the Investigation Support Bureau's Behavioural Sciences Section.

Divers pulled the body out of six feet of water from under a pier after it was freed from rocks and debris. The body was examined for forensic evidence, photographed by analysts and transported by ambulance to the Office of the Chief Coroner in Toronto where an autopsy will be performed to determine the cause of death. Investigators believe the victim may have met with foul play.

The victim is described as a white female, age 18-23, 5"6 in height, weighing approximately 120 lbs, with long blonde hair and blue eyes. Anyone with information is urged to contact his or her local police detachment or Crime Stoppers.

The discovery of the body has shocked permanent and seasonal residents of Honey Harbour, a small tourist town located on the south eastern shores of Georgian Bay in the Muskoka region.

"Nothing like this has ever happened here," said resident Nora Stevens. "There are drownings every year, you know, but this, well, this is truly awful. I still can't believe it."

Hanna flexed her fingers over the keyboard, hit SAVE and dropped her neck into a roll. Her shoulders were bunched up from tension and the beginnings of a nasty headache was forming behind her eyelids, proof that she'd had nothing to eat all day but a granola bar and too much coffee. She rinsed and filled her cup with water at the fountain, drank greedily, and returned to her desk.

Her copy deadline had been pushed back an hour to accommodate the story and it was now almost 6 p.m. The only sounds she heard were a toilet flushing and laughter drifting from the pressroom. Everyone in editorial had left by the time she'd returned; only the managing editor, Jake Belmont, was around to edit her story and finish the last of the front pages before press deadline.

Hanna glanced at the photograph they'd chosen earlier. It was already laid in next to the text on the front page and showed the victim, shrouded in the rain-spattered body bag, being lifted into the ambulance. Flashing blue and red lights were reflected in pools of rain. Strands of long hair were trapped in the zipper.

Hair that belonged to Lydia Tomlinson, Hanna reminded herself as she thought of Bennett standing by the opened door of his unmarked car, nodding in answer to her question. She trusted him enough to know that he would never have done so had he not been absolutely sure that the victim was in fact Lydia. But it was unofficial and she could not confirm it in her story.

Her poor, poor parents, she thought and placed two Tylenol tablets on her tongue, swallowing them down with a gulp of water.

Jake Belmont shuffled out of the men's room, his big belly proceeding him as he dried his large hands on a square of paper towel. "How's it going? Almost done?" he asked in his usual growl, perching his behind on the edge of her desk and pitching the crumpled towel in her wastebasket.

"I think so," Hanna said. "Have a read."

She got up, and Belmont slid into her chair. He pushed the keyboard aside and rested his elbows on the desk, tenting his fingers under a goatee-covered chin.

Hanna turned to the window and looked out into the rain-splattered parking lot. Her head pounded in rhythm to the rain as she rested her forehead against the cool glass.

Belmont, she knew, always read the entire story first, never slashed and deleted unless necessary. With her work, more often than not, only the headline remained to be added, and she watched him draw the keyboard closer. He'd told her, somewhat grudgingly after she'd been at the paper for a few weeks, that she was a natural with great instincts for where the real story was. But after years of covering the news, more than seven as a crime reporter in Toronto, it had become second nature to her.

"This is great, by the way," he called without looking up.

Hanna said nothing, but she wondered if the word 'hook' and how it could be played in the headline was flashing in his mind.

She knew other editors wouldn't hesitate to use it, giving no thought to how the victim's family might feel reading it in the paper.

"Go on home, Hanna," he went on, looking up at her. "And get some sleep, for Christ's sake. You look like death warmed over. And have a drink. You did fantastic work today, kiddo. This is a great story."

That was the problem with this profession, Hanna thought. Everything was a story. Child abuse, terrorism, drive-by shootings. The finding of a body in a watery grave.

A body that belonged to a young woman who was dead and lying on a cold, stainless steel table tonight. It wasn't a great story and it never would be.

"More like a goddamn nightmare," Hanna muttered out loud, surprised to hear the rage in her voice.

She turned from the window, but Belmont appeared not to have heard her. He was still reading her story, but looked up when he sensed her eyes on him.

"Good work, kiddo," he said, shooing his hands at her. "Now you can go home and forget about it. And don't come in until noon tomorrow. Okay?"

Why were editors always like this? Placating, even condescending? Hanna wondered if Belmont would feel the same way if he'd been out there covering the story himself. And calling her kiddo. What was up with that? She hadn't been a kid in a decade. But she was too drained, both physically and mentally, to make an issue out of it now. All she wanted was to go home and sleep through until the next morning.

She watched Belmont type MURDER VICTIM FOUND in 48-point Helvetica Bold, and underneath in smaller caps, INVESTIGATION LAUNCHED AFTER BODY PULLED FROM GEORGIAN BAY.

"All right, Jake, I'm out of here," Hanna said, giving him a ghost of a smile as she gathered her belongings together. "I'll see you tomorrow."

Belmont nodded, smiling back, waving her away.

Her raincoat was still sopping wet when she put it on again and headed out into the rain to her car.

Hanna stood in the light of her refrigerator, holding the door open with a foot, her raincoat dripping puddles on the linoleum floor. She uncorked the bottle of red wine she had received as a birthday present from Belmont months ago and, without bothering with a glass, took several, long swallows. She made a face, the bitter liquid burning its way down to her stomach.

She kicked the door shut and took the bottle into her small living room, shrugging out of the raincoat before plopping down onto the sofa. Pistachio, her long-haired year-old grey cat, rubbed up against her legs and she picked him up. He twitched his whiskers at her, his wet nose wrinkling as he sniffed her. He can probably smell death on me, she thought, stroking his soft ears. Soon the purring began and he curled himself on her lap, tucking his front paws under his chin.

Her small house, usually drenched in sunlight during the day, was dark and dreary as the rain continued to fall. Shadows were forming against the walls as her body slouched against the cushions and her eyelids drooped with sleep.

She suddenly sat bolt upright, startling Pistachio to the floor. She was surprised to realize she had fallen asleep. She glanced at the digital clock on her DVD player, and saw that it was already almost 11 p.m.

The after-image of an old dream lingered, and Hanna squeezed her eyes shut, her palms pressing against the sides of her head. It was always the same. The dream would burst from the shadows of her mind, filling her with images as sharp as shards of broken glass. And then, as always after the dream, she was powerless to stop the memories from elbowing their way in and the tears that flowed down her face.

Fourteen years this summer, she thought as she wiped her cheeks with shaking fingers, and it still feels like it just happened yesterday. *Goddamn it to hell.*

She blew her nose and punched a cushion several times, her eyes dry now and hard with old hate.

Throwing the cushion away, she leaned back and clicked on the TV to the local news. The shrouded body was being lifted up by paramedics, carefully and slowly, and then the gurney itself into the back of an ambulance with its lights rotating in the rain.

"The recovered body has been taken to the Office of the Chief Coroner in Toronto," a sober female voice broke over the image, "where an autopsy will be conducted to determine the cause of death."

Hanna turned off the TV with a click of the remote and picked up the bottle of wine. She took a long swallow and thought about all the horror, violence and suffering she had seen on a daily basis in Toronto where she had worked as a crime reporter until a year and a few months ago. Moving 150 kilometres back to her hometown had seemed to offer the perfect escape, but now she wasn't so sure. Violence knew no limits or boundaries, and it took root in remote places as well as it did in crowded ones, like a pugnacious weed that chokes everything in sight.

She wandered around her house, drinking too much, and after a while found herself in her small lavender bathroom where she undressed in front of the full-length mirror hanging on the back of the closet door. She ran her fingers through her dark honey-coloured hair, cut short like a boy's, and peered at her reflection in the mirror. Her chocolate eyes were fringed with long lashes, her nose was small and upturned at the tip and she had been blessed with high cheekbones, shapely lips and a chin that was dented with a small cleft.

Hanna stuck out her tongue at herself in the mirror and stepped under the needle-sharp spray of the shower. She scrubbed herself raw with the soap, letting the hot water pummel her head and back for a long time without moving.

On her way to bed later, a towel wrapped around her body, she sat with her laptop, accessed the Internet and logged on to her mail server. She downloaded two new messages, and opened the first, chuckling as she read her brother's short note describing how his roofing business in the city and new girlfriend kept him too busy to call. Deleting the message, she went on to open the second, sent to her at 11:55 a.m. that day, from someone whose address was *tatler@ Zebra.net*. She clicked to open it.

The message was only one word long, PAMIDONEGOG, all in upper case letters, and the file contained a .jpg attachment. A picture?

She double-clicked on the icon and waited as the file was downloaded and decompressed. Then an image began to appear on her screen, one band of pixels at a time.

Before the black-and-white photograph was even half revealed, Hanna shot out of her chair, her breath coming in short little spurts as she stared in disbelief at the image on her computer.

She now knew how it felt to be chilled to the bone.

Chapter Three

HANNA WAS FROZEN to the spot behind her chair as if invisible hands chained her ankles to the floor. She couldn't tear her eyes from the image on her screen.

Although the resolution was poor and details were grainy especially around the edges, the photograph clearly showed a dark-haired, naked man bending over the prostrate form of an obviously deceased young woman. Her eyes were fixed and open, her arms splayed out on both sides of a table, her light hair pooling around her head. The man was aiming a large, erect penis between her open legs, his features hidden in shadows.

Wrenching her eyes away from the photograph, Hanna felt nausea rise in her throat. Running to the bathroom, both hands clamped across her mouth, she collapsed in front of the toilet, but only a thin stream of reddish spittle came out. An ache bloomed in the deepest parts of her, and Hanna knew she would never forget the image as long as she lived.

Pushing herself away from the toilet, she raised herself on wobbly legs, turned on the tap in the sink and threw handfuls of cold water on her face and neck.

Soaked and shivering, she looked at her reflection in the mirror and felt sweat drip down from her armpits, icy as Arctic glaciers against her skin. She stared into her own eyes and forced herself to be calm, to breathe slowly and evenly, to think through the repulsion and the fear and the desperation the image had evoked in her.

Necrophilia.

There was something wretched about the word, something perverse and dirty lying at its core, and Hanna thought of what it meant. *Sex with the dead.* A shudder rocked her body; her skin crawled.

Gripping the sides of the sink, she forced herself to see past the image.

Was this someone's idea of a sick joke?

Possible. Some of the mail she'd received over the years fell into one of two categories: strange at best or deranged at worst. But mostly these were few and far between and the bulk of her e-mail consisted of letters from readers who responded to the stories she wrote in the paper or to her weekly column on women's issues. She wasn't hard to find. Anyone with access to the web could send her messages; her e-mail address was always printed at the bottom of her column.

But this went far beyond anything she had ever been sent in the past. And try as she might, she could not imagine who or why someone would send her something like this in the first place.

Could it be a mistake? Could the picture have been meant for someone else?

Intent on finding out, she returned to her computer and, averting her eyes from the depraved image, saved the file on her hard drive. Then she went into the message's properties and studied the information printed there. Looking closely, she was baffled to notice that the sender's address contained an upper case letter, the Z. It was something she had never actually seen before but she knew it meant the address was likely bogus. But the message had been meant for her all right; her e-mail address stared out at her from the 'envelope to' field.

Someone had deliberately sent her this image, using what probably amounted to a fake address. Hanna had no idea how someone could manage the latter; she was no expert when it came to computers although she wrote on one practically every day. Pondering how someone would go about doing this, she was struck by a bolt of unease. She saw Lydia Tomlinson's beautiful face in the photograph her parents had given her for the stories she had written and all of a sudden, she wondered if it could all be connected.

Her murder, the e-mail.

"My God," she muttered, rubbing at the gooseflesh covering her arms.

Could it be connected? But if it was, then who was *tatler*? The killer? Hanna felt her heart hammering against her rib cage as the thought took hold in her mind. Fuelled by a sudden and irrational fear that someone was watching her through the windows, she went from room to room checking the locks on her doors and windows. She was relieved to find that everything was secure and that no one was lurking outside in the shadows. But it did little to make her feel safe, and she attacked the hallway closet next, tossing its contents aside as she searched for her old wooden baseball bat. Finally, her hand closed around its neck and she pulled it out. She would take it to bed with her, place it within easy reach.

Just in case.

She stood staring at the phone as the image rose in her mind again, and she wondered if she should call the police. But it was already past midnight and after deliberating a few moments, she decided to deal with the whole mess in the morning and made her way to her bedroom.

Hanna placed the bat close by, crawled into bed and closed her eyes, willing sleep to come and erase the vile image that had been branded into her mind. But she was up most of the night, tossing and turning in her big, soft bed, and only fell asleep as the grey light of dawn appeared like a ghost at her window.

Wisps of white clouds drifted by in the sky when she woke, pieces of a hazy dream clinging to her like after-images. She was immediately aware of two things. One was the pain of a headache mushrooming in the back of her head and the other was the clock on her bedside table. It read 7:36 a.m.

She groaned, knowing she wouldn't be able to return to sleep even if she tried. Just her luck, especially when she had lain awake most of the night and didn't even have to be at the office until noon. She groaned again and Pistachio gave her a one-eyed stare from his spot at the foot of the bed. Holding her head gingerly, she tossed the blankets aside, sat up and stroked the cat under the chin.

On her way to the bathroom, she remembered with a jolt the chilling e-mail message she had opened the night before. The image rose in her mind and she shuddered as she shook out two Tylenol tablets and swallowed them with a handful of cold water.

Pushing the image to the back of her mind, she put on a pot of coffee in the kitchen and thought of the sender's user name, *tatler*. Immediately, the phrase "tattle tale" came to mind and she wondered if the sender had not known the correct spelling of the word 'tattler' or if the extra *t* had been omitted on purpose because the user name *tattler* had already been selected by someone else. Whatever the case, the name sent a shiver of unease crawling along her back. As for 'pamidonegog', she thought it was obviously an Indian word or name, perhaps Ojibway or Huron. But she had no idea what it could possibly mean and wondered how she would go about finding out.

She then showered and dressed in worn jeans and a mauve tee shirt and took a cup of coffee over to her laptop. She copied the file onto her memory stick and stuffed it inside her shoulder bag, reminding herself to call Bennett at the CIB and to talk to Matthew Henry, another reporter at the paper, when she got to the office later. If anyone could find out who had sent her the message, it was Matt. He knew his way around computers better than some people knew their way around their own homes.

Sipping coffee, Hanna flipped through her notebook and read over the interviews she had conducted the day before with the investigators and the anglers who had found the woman's body. She thought of Bennett nodding in confirmation when she'd asked if it had been Lydia Tomlinson's body they'd pulled from the bay and she saw again the unnatural colour and mottled look of the girl's foot. The polish on the nails. The dark patch on the leg that looked as if a square of skin had been cut off.

Hanna felt reasonably sure that the autopsy would have

been done as soon as the body arrived in Toronto late yesterday afternoon, especially if the situation was as bad as Bennett had said it was. She thought of Dr. Francesca Ellis, a forensic pathologist who'd been a reliable contact at the Office of the Chief Coroner in Toronto during the years she'd worked in the city, and wondered if a call to her might yield some answers. Of course, it was entirely likely that Dr. Ellis would know nothing about the case – she was only one of many forensic pathologists working there and this case was only one of dozens coming in every week. But it was worth a try.

Scrawled on a card she kept in her Rolodex, she found what she was looking for – the direct number for Dr. Ellis. But it was much too early to call; the building wouldn't even open its doors for another hour.

Her headache was slowly receding to a dull ache around her ears and suddenly ravenous, Hanna went into her small kitchen in search of breakfast. She inserted a frozen waffle in the toaster, took out a carton of raspberry yoghurt and a peach out of the fridge, and settled to eat on the sofa in the living room.

Licking a spoonful of yoghurt, she wished she could just drive down and visit Dr. Ellis instead of calling her. Not only because she missed the straight-forward, eccentric pathologist but also because she had always believed that phone interviews were poor substitutes for face-to-face talks - there was nothing to rely on other than timing and tone, perhaps the choice of words. Hanna placed a lot of value on a person's demeanour, facial expressions and body language, and tended to avoid the phone whenever she could. But there was no getting around this one - Toronto was almost a two-hour drive away.

Hanna returned to the kitchen, poured herself another cup of coffee and slipped into her sneakers. Then she went outside to do a little gardening before calling Dr. Ellis.

The rain had tapered off during the night and sunshine filtered through the remaining pockets of fog as she knelt in front of a flowerbed. She smelled wet earth mixing with the heady scent of the peonies growing along the edge of the fence and saw a toad hop out of sight under drooping leaves.

She remembered the last time she'd been to the Office of the Chief Coroner, just a few days before she'd decided to pack it all in and head back to Midland. Hard to believe almost a year and a half had since gone by. She'd been one of perhaps 50 reporters cramming the lobby of the massive building that day, while somewhere inside, the battered and chopped-up body of a four-year-old child revealed the unspeakable horrors of parental abuse.

And right now inside that building, she thought as she tugged on stubborn weeds with both hands, Lydia's body lies on a cold stainless steel table, her torso slit in the usual Y-incision of autopsy. The image of her bloated foot with the chipped polish on the nails rose in her mind again and Hanna pulled harder at the weeds.

She thought of Albert and Cynthia Tomlinson, remembering the pain etched on their faces. She couldn't begin to imagine what they were going through this morning, if they were at this very moment receiving the terrible news that their daughter was dead.

Murdered.

Hanna stabbed the earth with her hand trowel, anger flushing her face.

She finally threw it down, grabbed the weeds she had pulled and dumped them in the compost bin she kept at the back of her property. Then she went back inside her cottage, dialled Dr. Ellis' direct line to her office, and was surprised when the phone was answered after the first ring.

"Yes?"

Her voice was as Hanna remembered it - deep and rich and booming like a man's, with more than a hint of an Italian accent. Anyone hearing it for the first time did a double-take - how could such a manly voice belong to such a petite, middle-aged Italian woman?

"Dr. Ellis? Hi, it's Hanna Laurence. How have you been?"

There was a pause. "Oh dear God," Dr. Ellis finally said, surprise in her voice, "is that really you, Hanna?"

"The one and the same."

"Are you still up there, in cottage country? How is your job?"

"Good... coming back here was the best decision I ever made, Dr. Ellis."

"What is it with this Dr. Ellis stuff, Hanna? How many times do I have to tell you to call me Frank, like everyone else?" she chided in her perfect English, and she had never used a contraction in all the years Hanna had known her. "You make me feel old and tired."

She pictured the pathologist's youthful face, her long black tresses wound around her head and secured with dozens of bobby pins. "You may be tired, but you're not old, Frank. There. I called you by your first name. Is that better?"

"Oh, much. And you are right. I will be 50 next month, that is not so old. But I am tired... you are right about that."

"How could you not be? You're still doing autopsies, aren't you?"

"Oh yes. Those never end, you know. There is so much death in this city."

And Hanna didn't doubt Dr. Ellis had seen every manner of it in her long career as a forensic pathologist in the city. Shootings, strangulations, stabbings, she'd seen everything. Death had been her business for 24 years, almost as long as she'd been in the country.

"There's death here, too," Hanna said and her mind filled with Lydia's pretty face again. "Have you heard about the young woman found yesterday just a few miles from here, up near Honey Harbour? She was dumped in Georgian Bay."

A deep sigh filled the line. "Yes, yes. Of course. You must be covering the story up there for your newspaper. That poor girl. The chief himself took her case, you know. He completed the examination last night."

Hanna was genuinely surprised - Dr. Terrence Mullen, the chief coroner for the province of Ontario, didn't often take cases himself because of a gruelling schedule and frequent travel. In all the years she had known him while working in Toronto, he'd done perhaps a half dozen cases, including the one of the four-year-old boy that had been the emotional cataclysm for her move back to her hometown.

"Must be highly sensitive if Dr. Mullen himself took it."

"Yes. It is one of the more gruesome ones. The police were all over the place."

Hanna swallowed hard. "Can you tell me anything, Dr. Ellis?"

"Oh Hanna, you know how it is. I can't give you any details that could compromise the police investigation. I am very sorry."

"I don't mean to compromise you in any way, Frank. You know it's the last thing I'd want to do."

There was another pause and Hanna imagined her staring out her tiny office window at pedestrians passing by. She remembered the mountains of paper and case folders covering the doctor's desk, chairs and the top of her computer, the gun-metal grey file cabinets on either side of the window, the framed degrees adorning the wall space behind her desk, the wastebasket overflowing with paper. The last time she'd been in Dr. Ellis' office, the only personal touches had been a plant with yellow leaves on the windowsill and a framed picture of a tall, gaunt man standing next to a bicycle – her late husband. But most of all, she remembered the smell of formaldehyde settling over everything like a fine mist.

"Of course. But I am surprised. You did not say the public has a right to know."

Hanna laughed. "I haven't used that argument in years, Frank. But it's true, you know. The public does have a right to know... some things."

There was the sound of a tongue clicking against teeth. "You really believe that? What about the fact that the public also includes the one person with the whole story?"

Hanna knew there was more than just a grain of truth in Dr. Ellis' words. The public did include the one person with the whole story – the killer. Too much information could tell him just how close the police were to catching him and could, quite possibly, prompt him to change his habits or cover his tracks, even drive him underground. On the other hand, she also knew just how crucial the media could be in helping the police catch him. And whether she liked it or not, a violent death was a public event, and it was her job to write about it. A messenger of the worst news society could produce; she was well aware of what some people thought of her and all those who did what she did for a living. And while it was true that sometimes the message could be painful, even brutal to the living, it was a message Hanna believed had to be told over and over again.

"Of course, you're right, Frank. But I'm a lot more concerned about the countless young women out there. Young girls who need to be aware... who need to know how to protect themselves. Forewarned is forearmed, isn't that what they say?"

"Yes... but sometimes, even that is not enough." Dr. Ellis cleared her throat. "I said this case was very disturbing, Hanna, and I will say it again. Very, very disturbing. It has been a long time since I saw anything like this."

"You worked on her?"

"No. But I saw her yesterday when she was brought in to the morgue. Before the autopsy. This young woman was healthy, with no abnormalities and no disease before she died." She sighed loudly, the air whistling across the line. "It is unbelievable what some people can do to another human being."

"It was bad then?"

"This is off the record? Nothing goes in the paper, Hanna. But yes, it was very bad. Terrible." She paused again. "There is not one inch of her that is not covered in bruises and cuts and wounds."

Hanna squeezed her eyes closed. "Cuts? Do you mean to say she was stabbed?"

"Yes. With something small, sharp. Like a steak knife... something like that."

"Oh God, Frank. That's awful."

"Yes, but that is not all, Hanna. Her face was mutilated, too."

"Jesus." Having worked with the police for so many years, she knew that mutilating a face meant the attack might have been personal. Typically, when killers have a relationship with their victims, whether real or perceived, they direct much of their violence at the face because it represents the person. She wondered if Lydia had known her killer.

The image of the patch of missing skin on the girl's leg rose in Hanna's mind. Her breakfast churned in her stomach like clothes in a washing machine on the spin cycle. "She also had a tattoo and he removed it, didn't he? Just above her right ankle."

There was total silence, then another sigh. "I will not ask how you know this, but yes."

"And she was ra-," Hanna started, then stopped, unable to get the ugly word past her lips. She took a deep breath and tried again. "Was she sexually assaulted?"

Another silence, briefer this time. "Yes…although we found no vital reaction to injuries of the genitalia. And… well, that is all I can tell you."

"And?"

"There are some things the police want to hold back, Hanna, you understand. But I can tell you there was evidence that she had been pregnant before. In the not-too-distant past."

"Oh." Hanna put a question mark beside the word pregnancy and thought of something else. "Was there evidence of a struggle?"

"No. She had a broken fingernail on her right hand, but you know that does not necessarily mean anything. And unfortunately, any trace evidence we might have found, like hairs or fibres, were washed away by the water."

"How long was she under water?"

"Maybe a day or two, no more than that."

"And you're sure she didn't drown?"

"Absolutely. If she had drowned, the alveoli would have been much more dilated and there should have been more pronounced pulmonary edema. That is a build-up of fluid in the lungs, if you remember, Hanna," Dr. Ellis explained. "Simply put, if she had drowned she would have been exposed to fresh water and her lungs would have begun decomposing more rapidly than other tissues. Plus, we would have seen some hemorrhaging in her brain. But that was not the case with this one, although to be frank, her lungs were a bit on the heavy side when they were weighed." The doctor paused a moment and when she spoke again, her voice had developed an edge. "There is reason to believe she was already dead when she was dumped in the bay, Hanna. Long dead."

The image she had been sent the night before flitted across her mind in graphic detail and Hanna shuddered. "How long?"

"More than likely a week or longer. Maybe 10 days. When victims are recovered from water, you know, it is always difficult to determine when they died."

A week or longer. Maybe 10 days. That would mean Lydia had been killed on or shortly after the day she went missing on June 1st, a Sunday, taking into account the two days she'd been under water. Hanna didn't want to think about what the killer had done with her body in all that time before he dumped her in the bay, but the image she'd been sent the night before surfaced in her mind again and she felt a cold fist lodge in her gut.

"Jesus, Frank. You're saying she was dead when he stabbed her and mutilated her face? When he assaulted her?"

The doctor sighed again. "Yes, all of her injuries, except one, are postmortem."

"Except one?" she repeated dumbly. "What do you mean?"

"We found a small injection site high up on her left thigh, on the outside. We almost missed it completely with all the cuts and bruises on her skin."

Hanna could feel her eyebrows climb up into her forehead. "You think she was injected with something? Was that the cause of death? An overdose of some drug?"

"It is quite possible... but you know how long it takes for toxicology tests to come back. We put a rush on this one, Hanna," the doctor said. "We should know in a week or so what killed her."

Chapter Four

NAUSEA RIPPLED LIKE a wave in Hanna's stomach as phrases – *postmortem, covered in wounds, dead more than week* – kept rising out of the fog that swirled inside her head. She could not get past the idea of someone doing such heinous things to another human being.

The world had long spawned its share of psychopaths – Jack the Ripper, Ted Bundy, Andrei Chikatilo, Gary Ridgway, the list went on. And let's not forget Canada's own monsters such as Paul Bernardo, the infamous "Scarborough Rapist" who had also raped, tortured, murdered and dismembered two teenage schoolgirls in the early 90s in the St-Catharines area, and Canada's worst serial killer to date, Robert "Willy" Pickton, the BC pig farmer who had murdered women from Vancouver's seedy East Side over a span of decades, and fed their remains to his pigs. Police spent almost two years excavating human remains on his farm in Port Coquitlam, just outside of Vancouver.

But it was entirely something else to know that one lived and breathed here, not halfway around the world or across the border or even a few hours away, but right here in this small area known as Huronia, in honour of the Huron people who first inhabited its land and shores.

Bile rose in her throat and she forced herself to breathe slowly, concentrating on inhaling and exhaling, feeling the air expand beneath her rib cage.

Hanna recalled reading somewhere that at least one per cent

of the population was psychopathic. These people were antisocial, but medically sane. Some committed heinous crimes for which they felt no remorse and assumed no blame. They were dangerous because they didn't have a moral code, and blurred lines existed where only black and white should. In all likelihood, whoever had killed Lydia was not a mental misfit with damage to his frontal lobe, nor was he psychotic. But it was likely that he was a sexual sadist like Bernardo, someone with above normal intelligence who was able to function very well in society, enough anyway to maintain an acceptable public image. He probably worked somewhere in the region, and he might be anything from a caterer to a computer analyst.

He was the guy cutting his lawn next door, the mechanic changing the oil in your car, the teacher explaining sentence structure to nine-year-old kids. He could be anyone and he probably looked no different than a thousand other men.

Few monsters look like what they do, Hanna thought, bumps rising along her arms. She would never be able to understand how a person could derive any kind of satisfaction, and certainly not sexual pleasure, out of causing any living creature pain and suffering. She could not comprehend any of it and thought something horrendous must have happened to this killer in his childhood for him to have been able to do what he did to Lydia.

Thank God her injuries were postmortem, Hanna thought. She hoped the 19-year-old had died instantly after the killer had injected her with whatever drug or poison he had used. At least she would have suffered little. But the thought provided little comfort and it sure as hell didn't erase or even lessen the brutality that had been inflicted on her corpse.

She fought another shudder as she thought of what might have happened to Lydia. She'd been young and healthy with no signs of disease and no abnormalities, Dr. Ellis had said. Then that Sunday almost two weeks ago while camping with friends at popular Beausoleil Island in the heart of Ontario's playland, she had met her killer. Had he employed some sort of ruse to approach her? Had he been sweet, charming and full of invitations? And then, after he had gotten her alone somewhere, he had injected a lethal dose of a powerful drug into her leg, killing her. Had she known in that moment that she was going to die? Or had the drug obliterated all ability to feel, to fear?

Hanna swallowed hard, tears welling up in her eyes. What had that monster done to Lydia after he killed her? She saw again the photograph she had received the night before and she could not stop the images coming at her from the dark recesses of her brain.

Who was *tatler* and why had the photograph been sent to her? Was it connected to the murder? Or was it just a coincidence? And what did Pamidonegog mean?

Hanna picked up her cell to call the paper. An automated voice message greeted her and she entered her editor's extension number. He picked up on the second ring.

"Newsroom."

"Jake, it's me."

"Hanna, who in the hell were you on the phone with? I've been trying to get a hold of you for over an hour. Is everything all right?"

No, Jake, she thought, nothing will ever be all right again. "Yes," she lied. "Sorry I was on the phone so long. I just finished talking with an old contact at the Office of the Chief Coroner."

There was a pause. "You're something, you know that?" he said, a note of admiration in his voice. "Now, if only I could get the others to show half as much initiative..."

Hanna ignored him and came right to the point. "Jake, it's not good. She was stabbed, her face was mutilated and it looks like he cut off a tattoo on her leg. She was also sexually assaulted and they found an injection site on a thigh. Toxicology tests won't be known for at least a week, but my contact says the victim may have been killed with an overdose of some unknown drug."

A low whistle blew in her ear. "Christ."

"Yeah, and it seems the killer mutilated her after she was dead. All of her injuries, except the injection site, are postmortem."

"Postmortem?" he repeated, sounding just like her when she'd found out. "Jesus."

Hanna's fists balled in her lap as she saw again the image she had opened the night before. "There's something else, too, Jake. I was sent a really disturbing e-mail last night."

"Like what?"

"A photograph. Really sick stuff. I copied it on my stick so I could show you."

"Look, Hanna, are you all right?"

"Yeah," she assured him, but she wondered. "Were you trying to call me about the press conference?"

"Yes. It's set to go for 11 a.m. at the office of the OPP's Criminal Investigation Branch. The press release said they had identified the body."

Hanna thought of Lydia and her parents again and wished with all her heart that Bennett was wrong and the body they'd recovered the day before would not be the missing teen's. But she knew better.

"Consider it done."

"Thanks. And when you get back, I'm taking you out for a drink."

She laughed, the sound strained and phony to her own ears. "Better make it two. Or three. God knows I'm going to need it."

Hanna thought of Lydia as she took the ramp leading to Highway 12 and followed a lumbering transport truck all the way to Orillia, a town of 27,000 located on the shores of Lakes Couchiching and Simcoe about 40 minutes east of Midland and an hour's drive north of Toronto. Her nerves were like tightly strung guitar strings as she drove, and her head was filled with thoughts and images she couldn't escape.

Exiting the highway into the Sunshine City, home of famous humourist Stephen Leacock, she took the ramp to Memorial Avenue. She drove along the commercial strip to Ontario Provincial Police general headquarters, parked in the crowded visitor's lot and got out of her car.

She'd been inside the massive brick and glass structure once before, for the interview she had done with the new superintendent of the Criminal Investigation Branch a few months ago. But like the first time, she found herself awed by its curved stone architecture and sheer imposing size - every inch of which was needed, she knew, as the OPP provided service to over one million square kilometres of land and water throughout the province of Ontario, rendering it one of the largest deployed police agencies in all of North America.

Hanna entered the building through tall, glass doors and reported to the information desk in the spacious lobby, where potted trees rose up towards the 30-foot glass ceilings.

The receptionist, her eyes heavily lined in charcoal, bobbed her platinum curls towards Hanna. "Let me guess… the press conference, right?" She smiled as she pushed a visitor card across the counter. "Take the elevator to the second floor. Go through the door at the top, then turn right. It'll be the last door on the left." She offered a half smile, then turned back to her desk.

Camera crews were setting up and a couple dozen reporters and photographers - some sporting national logos - were crowding around the middle of the room chatting when Hanna entered, her pass card clipped to the hem of her blouse. She nodded and smiled to those she knew, and chose a seat near the front where a table and three chairs had been set up next to an empty easel off to the side.

At exactly 11 o'clock, Detective-Inspector Tim Bennett entered the room from a side door, accompanied by the investigators from the Midland department. His handsome face held no hint of a smile as his emerald eyes briefly met Hanna's dark ones. They nodded to each other. She watched him set some folders down on the table and remove the light grey jacket of his suit, folding it neatly on the back of a chair. He tapped the microphone in front of him and looked up at the reporters.

"Ladies and gentlemen," he started, "as you all know, the body of a young woman was found yesterday just a couple of kilometres south of Honey Harbour. We called this press conference as soon as possible because we were able to identify the victim through Missing Persons, and through the positive identification of her body by a family member. It appears she is Lydia Janice Tomlinson, age 19, of Waubaushene, Ontario, the teen who went missing 10 days ago after camping with friends at Beausoleil Island." He paused to clip a blown-up photograph to the easel, and flashes of light burst around the room as photographers snapped their shutters again and again. "She was a first-year Engineering student at Sheridan College in Mississauga who just recently moved back home for the summer."

Even though he had confirmed at the recovery scene that the victim was Lydia, Hanna was nevertheless troubled. There was no doubt left now, no more room for hope. She thought of the girl's parents as she snapped several pictures of Bennett fidgeting with the poster. She couldn't begin to imagine what they were feeling now.

"She was reported missing on Monday, June 2nd by her parents after friends called to inform them that their daughter had disappeared," Bennett continued.

Hanna stared at the photograph mounted on the easel. It was the same graduation portrait the girl's mother had shown her during the interview at her home the week before, and a sick feeling washed over her. Lydia Tomlinson had been a beautiful girl with wide blue eyes and long blonde hair the colour of corn silk drying up in the heat of an August sun. In the picture, her head was tilted to one side and her smile showed two rows of perfect, white teeth. She was wearing a white blouse under her graduation robe, her tasselled cap askew on her head. An image of the girl's mutilated body lying in the cold dark of the cooler at the morgue surfaced in her mind, and Hanna shivered in the hot room.

"The autopsy was performed late yesterday by the Chief Coroner for the province of Ontario, Dr. Terrence Mullen. A cause of death is not expected for at least a week, pending results from toxicology tests, but preliminary findings indicate Lydia Tomlinson was without a doubt the victim of a brutal murder."

There was a split second of silence, then the sound of chairs scraping across linoleum was all but drowned as questions erupted around the room.

"What evidence have you found to support this?" yelled a balding man wearing an untucked shirt over baggy pants.

"Can you confirm rumours the body was mutilated?"

"How did the family react to the news?"

"Any ideas as to who might have killed her?"

Bennett held up a hand to stem the flow of questions as he sipped water from a glass. He shuffled through his folder, taking his time, then raised his eyes again. "One at a time please... You should all know that there are aspects of this case that we will not be discussing with the media at this or any other time, but we can confirm that we have launched a murder investigation into her death and are working around the clock. Not only are we trying to trace the victim's last movements, but we are also re-interviewing her friends and family, as well as employees at Beausoleil Island. We are also trying to locate as many of the campers and day-trippers to the island in the hopes someone saw something out of the ordinary around the time the victim went missing. We have also started interviews with staff at Bayhaven Marina where she was found, as well as boaters who have used the marina since the beginning of the season and local residents. It's still very early in the investigation, but let me assure you, we are doing everything we can."

"Any leads yet?" asked a small brunette, waving her hand like a school girl.

Bennett looked up from under the hot camera lights and wiped sweat from his forehead. "Nothing definite, but we are investigating any and all avenues opening up. Identifying the victim was the first step and now we are concentrating on solving this murder. We will find out what happened to her."

"Any suspects?" another reporter asked.

"None at this time. But we are leaving no stone unturned." He flipped through a page in his folder and raised a finger in the air. "Also, before I forget, our investigation will be named Project Georgian Bay. We've also established a special, direct phone line and we're appealing to the public to phone in any information that may seem relevant to this investigation. Even information that may seem insignificant should be called in."

Bennett recited the number and made sure everyone got it right. Then he pointed at Lydia's photograph, his face hardening. Hanna thought his eyes, when they came to rest on hers a long moment, were the midnight green of a dark, haunted forest.

"We'll need all the help we can get with this one... because this murder," he said, his voice soft in the light-flooded room, "is one of the most brutal I've come across in a long time."

Chapter Five

THE LAST CHORDS of a Nickelback song were being drowned out by the opening bars of Tracy Chapman's "Fast Car" when Hanna and Belmont made their way past the entrance of The Loon into the bar. It was almost five-thirty.

Spying Karen O'Malley, the lifestyles writer, Matthew Henry and David Lakefield, two general assignment reporters, and Justin Turner, the sports editor, sitting at a table near the back of the bar, Hanna and Belmont joined them, pulling up chairs. She ordered a gin and tonic and Belmont an imported beer from the waitress who materialized at their elbows, snapping her gum.

Although meeting at The Loon was a long-established Friday afternoon ritual, it was a rare occasion to have the entire newsroom present. There were always stories to cover or sporting events to photograph, and one or two of the gang was usually missing. Hanna and Belmont had barely made it. After the press conference, she had driven back to the office and spent almost two hours writing the story for the weekend paper, weaving in some of the details she had tracked down in the days since she had taken on the story of the missing teen. She wrote that Lydia Tomlinson had been an honours student at Midland Secondary School, that her father, Albert, was the owner of the new country club which had opened at the beginning of the year on the outskirts of town, and that her mother, Cynthia, was a hairdresser at a local beauty shop. The family had one other child, a 10-year-old girl who was a student at Waubaushene Public School and Hanna made sure to include her name, as well as her parents', on the card accompanying a wreath of sweetheart roses and baby's breath she sent to the family.

But it wasn't until after her story had been edited and the front page sent off to the composing room for processing that Hanna had a chance to talk to Belmont and Matthew Henry, the newsroom's own computer expert, and privately show them the photograph she had received the night before. They reacted in much the same way she had and expressed disgust with a few choice words. She told Belmont she had already arranged a meeting with Tim Bennett to give him a copy of the image the next day, the only time he had available. The more she thought about all the things she had learned while talking with Dr. Ellis, the more she was convinced that the message was somehow connected to Lydia's murder.

Thinking of her now brought a stab of pain for her poor parents and Hanna took a large sip of her drink, the liquid burning down her throat. She had called to offer her heartfelt condolences after returning to Midland, and she could still hear the sound of Mrs. Tomlinson's wailing on the phone, her words all but lost in her grief and sorrow.

"I can't... believe... she's gone. Oh God... please... this can't be happening," she'd stammered through her tears and Hanna had cried along with her, her insides twisting with hate for the monster who had killed a beautiful girl with her whole life ahead of her.

She downed the rest of her drink in one swallow. It eased some of the tension in her shoulders and a little of the ache in her heart, but it would take a lot more than one drink to numb her mind, she knew.

It didn't help to know that Matthew had gotten nowhere in trying to trace the e-mail she'd received. He had kept at it, but he'd only been able to trace it through a couple of Internet "nodes", whatever they were, in Ontario to eastern Canada, through a transatlantic satellite to London, England and back into the country again. Matthew explained that the unknown sender was using an anonymous remailer for his e-mail.

"With regular e-mail, you can trace it," he'd said, "because regular e-mail has a packet header. From there, you can get a user name or at least take back-bearings, and get a location. But not this guy. He's using an anonymous remailer who's stripping off his real address and putting in a fake or random one in its place. That's why I can't trace it."

Hanna wondered if the police would have better luck and if, thanks to a precedent for getting cooperation in some cases, they would be able to get information from the remailing service, wherever it was located. But she seriously doubted it. She vaguely recalled that this only happened in some countries and only in extreme cases. And not only that, but these remailing services were usually run by anarchist types – people who'd rather destroy all their files than provide police with one iota of information on one of their clients. Which was, she reasoned unhappily, the whole point of the service in the first place.

Hanna sighed and forced herself to look around. At five in the afternoon, the bar was practically deserted except for a couple of guys shooting pool in the back and a few regulars sitting at the horseshoe-shaped bar. A noisy group of factory employees came in a little later, laughing boisterously.

"--impossible to believe this kind of thing can happen around here," she heard Justin Turner say as he adjusted his big body in his chair. "But statistically, it happens more often than you might think. Even in small towns. Most people believe murders are an urban phenomenon, but really, if you consider population demographics, they're just as often committed in small towns as they are in big cities."

Everyone around the table groaned. Karen rolled her eyes towards the ceiling and Hanna smiled. Justin was famous around the paper for putting in his two-cents worth and voicing his little-known facts and most people affectionately called him "Cliff" from the Cheers sitcom. He didn't seem to mind much.

"You know, you have a point there," David Lakefield piped up. At 24, he was the rookie of the group and the adopted son of Dr. Thomas Lakefield, owner of the area's best veterinary clinic where

Hanna had brought Pistachio for his annual shot just a couple of weeks before. David had only been a reporter at the paper for less than two months, having been hired straight after graduation to help out over the summer.

"I'm reminded of that girl's murder in the early 80s," he went on, and Hanna was struck not for the first time by the intensity of his dark, cerulean eyes as they rested on hers for a moment, then moved on, "the one who was backed over with a car. Remember that one? I heard about it growing up. And the one in the 90s where they found that teenage girl decapitated in the woods? Now, that was weird."

"That was probably one of the most baffling cases the local cops here had ever worked," Belmont joined in. "One cop I talked to at the time said it was the most savage thing he'd ever seen... I'd just come on board as the new editor right around the same time."

"And that case is still unsolved to this day," Hanna added as she remembered, from somewhere in the recesses of her mind, that the girl's first name had been Cindy.

"A cold case." David took a swallow of his drink and looked at Hanna over the rim of his glass, flashing her a smile. "Isn't that what they call it when a crime doesn't get solved after a certain amount of time?" His eyes moved around the table and came to rest back on hers. "Cold. Case. Sounds so final... so hopeless. I hope that's not what's going to happen with the Tomlinson girl. Do they have anything yet?"

Hanna gave him and the others a brief run-down of what Bennett had said at the press conference and added, "So, no, they don't have much. So far."

David inclined his beer bottle at her. "Well, if you ever get bogged down or need some help covering the story, Hanna, I'll be happy to tag along and lend a hand... even if it's just to do some research or whatever. That would be all right, wouldn't it, Jake? It'd be a great opportunity for me... I've never covered anything like this before."

But Hanna had and for his sake, she wished he never would. She remembered every one of the more brutal cases she had covered during the course of her career and often saw the faces of the victims in her nightmares, even years later. She would wake in the dead of night with tears on her cheeks, her body bathed in sweat. So many faces, so much pain.

"Thanks, I appreciate that, David," she said, "and I might need some help later, but right now, this is a one-person job."

The conversation soon drifted to major-league baseball, and the guys batted ERAs and WHIPs back and forth across the table. Hanna took the opportunity to go to the ladies room. Her face was pale and drawn in the mirror, dark crescents rested below her eyes and lines drew down the corners of her mouth. She splashed cold water on her cheeks and blotted her face with a paper towel, but it did little to improve her looks. She sighed and threw the crumpled towel at the wastebasket, missing it by a foot.

Making her way out, she walked past the bar and decided to order another drink while she was there. She climbed on a high stool and drummed her fingernails on the hard wooden surface of the counter while she waited for the bartender to finish serving two guys sitting a few bar stools away. Young and handsome with bulging muscles in all the right places, the bartender moved down towards her, cracking a smile.

"What'll it be?" he asked, swiping at the counter with a rag.

"Gin and tonic," she replied, smiling back.

He nodded and set to work mixing the drink. Hanna's attention wandered, and she looked over at the two men sitting down a few feet from her. She'd never seen the blond, skinny guy before but the big, red-haired one looked vaguely familiar. She racked her brains trying to place him, but came up empty. She'd probably interviewed him before, she was almost sure.

"It's sick," the skinny one was saying, bringing the beer bottle to his lips.

"You got that right, man," the red-haired guy replied in a slurred voice. "What kind of twisted bastard does something like this?"

Intrigued, Hanna pretended not to be listening. She kept her head straight ahead, smiling her thanks at the bartender when he placed her drink before her. She dropped a twenty on the bar, left him a nice tip and pocketed the rest of her money. He nodded and moved down to the other end of the bar.

"I've never heard anything like it, James. A goddamn snake! A rattler or something, can you imagine?" the red-haired one was saying, his eyes bloodshot. "I thought I was going to be sick all over the goddamn floor when I heard about it. Jesus Christ!"

The one named James clapped a hand on his friend's shoulder and ordered him a whiskey on the rocks. The bartender swiftly poured the drink.

"I still can't believe it! It was all coiled up in there, you know, like a goddamn garden hose. And the bastard stitched her up, too." The red-haired man downed his whiskey in one swallow and wiped his mouth with the back of his hand.

Hanna stared into her drink, her stomach lurching acid into her throat. Her fingernails dug into her palms and she swallowed hard. She had never heard anything so horrible in her whole life. And she'd heard plenty of vile things already today – her mind still reeled from the shocking details Dr. Ellis had told her about the case.

Was this something totally unrelated or could they possibly be talking about Lydia Tomlinson? Was this some of the hold back information Dr. Ellis had alluded to? Hanna knew that some murderers inserted foreign objects such as cutlery or tools into their victims - recently one in Florida had rammed a pair of pliers into his victim's rectum after killing him - and almost always into orifices other than their mouths. It was designed to be sexually degrading. But a snake stitched up inside a vagina?

Oh God, oh my God. There were no words to describe this horror and Hanna felt her bowels tighten painfully. Her hands shaking, she could hardly pick up her glass and bring it to her mouth.

"Nice name," the one named James said, turning to his friend.

"What?"

"That lady's name, Lydia. It's nice, you know, kind of pretty."

Hanna's breath clogged in her throat. Oh God, they *were* talking about her. Christ, this couldn't be real. She swayed on the stool, her vision blurring, her head spinning.

"You know, funny thing is, Irene and I were thinking about it for the baby, if it's a girl," James said. "But not now, no goddamn way."

Hanna stumbled off the stool, her drink sloshing over her hand. She glanced over her shoulder at the men and it hit her all of a sudden. The red-haired guy, he was a cop with the Midland OPP. She couldn't remember his name but she recalled interviewing him a few months before about a series of break and enters that had left residents along the beach feeling unnerved and angry. He'd talked about what owners could do to protect their homes and cottages from burglars, and Hanna had followed some of his advice herself, installing a double security lock on her front door and replacing some of the locks on her windows.

When she got back to the table, Karen gasped at the sight of her. "Oh my God, Hanna. Are you all right? You look like you've seen a ghost."

Everyone stared at her, but she couldn't speak. She set her glass down on the table and took a step backward. She stumbled and nearly fell over a chair.

"I just need some air, I think," she mumbled and Matthew Henry hurried around the table to help her. "I don't feel so good."

Outside, the sun was still blazing in the sky, its heat coming off the parking lot in undulating waves. Hanna leaned against the wall, fighting tears springing to her eyes. But she wouldn't cry. Not now, damn it. Not here in a parking lot with traffic just yards away.

"I'm going home."

"What's wrong? Are you okay?"

"I'll be fine… I just don't feel very good right now."

"Do you need a ride home? You're looking pretty pale."

"Thanks, Matt, but I'll be all right."

He was still standing where she'd left him, staring after her, as she drove out of the parking lot and headed for home.

Hanna had never felt so miserable in her life. She was hurting all over; nausea rolled in her stomach. But she was hurting most in places she'd never known existed before, way down deep past even her own wounded soul, and the horror, sharp and icy, moved through her like a giant glacier under black water.

Oh God, what is this thing? This freak, this monster? This is beyond human.

She wondered at what point evil could become so acute that the human brain simply refused to accept it. Hers had shut down, numbed with the chilling images playing on like an endless movie montage in her head and she wanted to scream.

A snake. *Oh please God.*

Breathe, she commanded herself, slow and easy, one-two-three, count to 10. But she couldn't stop thinking about Lydia and her family, couldn't stop seeing images in her mind like a horror movie she couldn't turn off. She wondered how much the Tomlinsons had been told, if they knew what their daughter's killer had done to her. How would they ever go on with their lives, knowing what had happened to her?

Hanna had always known that evil existed in the world, she'd seen it time and again, had even experienced it herself once before, the kind that scars for life. But not evil this monstrous.

She felt a hot rush of tears flood her eyes and brushed angrily at them, her fingers shaking. Damn it, she thought, this story is going to kill me.

She thought again of the e-mail and wondered what the word Pamidonegog meant. She decided she would contact the chief on Christian Island, the First Nations reserve located northwest of the paper's coverage area in Georgian Bay, and see if he could point her in the right direction. She also wondered what Bennett would think when she told him about it the next day at their meeting.

She felt her stomach flutter, and knew it wasn't just in anticipation of his reaction. She found herself thinking of his eyes, those mesmerizing green eyes, and the way his blond, wavy hair curled over his forehead. She remembered meeting him for the first time, all those months ago, how she'd fumbled for words and dropped her notebook after just one look into his eyes. She remembered thinking: A man shouldn't be this beautiful.

At home, Hanna went straight to the freezer, took out the Absolut and went to sit on the couch in the dark. The more she drank, the more she berated herself. Drinking had always been one of her crutches, one of the ways she dealt with stress. For others, it was drugs or cigarettes. Or sex.

A little smile twisted on her lips. Who was she kidding? There'd been a time in her life - and not that long ago - when she had indulged more than a little in all of the above, a time when she had been searching for escape, for ways to erase parts of herself and reinvent others. Drunk, stoned on pot, chain-smoking cigarettes and lying in bed with some guy, she thought. How many nights of her life had been spent like that?

Too many.

But she thought she had put it all behind her since she'd moved back to the area. She had quit smoking almost a year ago, joints were the things that held her bones together these days, and sex had only taken place in the fantasies of her mind.

Unfortunately, she thought as she crawled into bed and felt the cold emptiness of the pillow next to hers.

Chapter Six

HANNA WAS STILL thinking about Tim Bennett the following afternoon as she waited for him to show up for their meeting. He was more than ten minutes late.

She looked around at her surroundings. Maple and cedar trees grew in clusters around her, edging the gravel path as it dipped down a small incline to the bay. Tiffin Park, jammed with teenagers groping each other in their cars on weekend nights, was deserted at this late hour on Saturday afternoon. A breeze carried the scent of summer into the car and Hanna breathed it in, filling her lungs to the brim.

She hated to admit it, but she was nervous. When they had set up this meeting, she had given him the address to her house but he had suggested they meet at the park in Midland instead because it was close to where he lived. Hanna knew she'd be in the area visiting her parents on Saturday afternoon anyway, and had agreed. But this would be the first time they met outside of a crime scene or his office, and she tried to quiet the flutter of butterflies inside her stomach as a green Toyota swung into the entrance to the park. She watched Bennett get out of his car, dressed neatly in navy slacks and a short-sleeved light blue shirt, a paisley tie loosened around his neck.

"Hey," he greeted her as he climbed into her car, "how're you doing?"

His deep green eyes flicked her way. The car filled with the spicy scent of his after-shave and Hanna sucked in a breath. Tim

Bennett, she thought for the umpteenth time, was easily one of the best-looking and sexiest men she had ever laid her eyes on. He was at least ten years older than her, in his late thirties, and tall, with beautiful hands that now rested on his lap. Her heart ached just to look at him, and she wondered why she had never noticed before that he looked a little like Kevin Costner. There was the same softness about the eyes, the same sensual curve of the mouth when he smiled.

Hanna caught herself staring. For God's sake, she admonished herself silently, Tim's a friend, a cop, a good source. And a married man, she added grudgingly. Get a grip.

"Fine. How about you?"

"Same." He fingered the tiny, triangular scar above his eyebrow – a parting gift from a scuffle with a drunk offender yielding a knife, he'd told her, a long time ago when he had been a rookie cop in Toronto. "Look, Hanna, I'm sorry, but I don't have much time. Belinda's expecting me."

Hanna stared out the windshield at the slice of water she could see between the trunks of tall trees. How many times had her thoughts turned to him during all those long, quiet evenings she spent alone in her little cottage? Often when she was reading a novel, listening to music or watching TV, she'd find herself wondering what he was doing at that very same moment, trying to imagine what kind of food he liked, what type of music he listened to… what he would be like in bed. She wondered if something could have developed between them had things been different. If he hadn't been married. Hanna had met his wife at the police association's banquet last year, and she pictured her now, thin and wispy, her blonde hair pulled into a severe bun at the nape of her neck. They had been married almost as long as he had been a police officer, but they had never had children. She wondered if he was trapped in a loveless marriage, and she felt a sudden need to touch him.

"So, what's up?" he said, turning towards her in the seat.

She cleared her throat, deciding there wasn't a good way to come out and say what she had to. She looked up at him and caught the glint of silver in his light hair as the sun poured in through the windshield. Licking her lips, she plunged ahead. "There are a couple of things I need to talk to you about, Tim. It's about the investigation."

"All right," he said, nodding. "Shoot."

Hanna looked down at her hands. "I need to confirm something, and I thought since you're heading Project Georgian Bay, you'd know." She looked up into his eyes and came right out with it. "Is it true there was a snake inside her?"

Bennett's head snapped forward and his green eyes flashed. So it is true, she thought, her gut twisting inside her.

"Where the hell did you hear that?" he asked, his voice tight with fury.

"I overheard a conversation at The Loon yesterday between two guys. One was a cop, I've interviewed him before."

"Jesus Christ," he mumbled, squeezing his eyes shut. He raked his fingers through his short blond curls and let out a loud breath. "Who was it?"

Hanna shrugged. "I can't remember his name. Tall, big shoulders, red hair. I talked to him after that rash of break and enters last winter."

"That's Ted Pierce," Bennett said, disgust thick in his voice. "Goddamn drunk. Can't keep his mouth shut." His hands fisted as he stared at her. "Tell me you won't use it."

Hanna started to say something, but he cut her off with a wave of his hand.

"C'mon, Hanna. I've never asked you not to use information before, but I'm asking you now. I'm begging you. Hell, I'm *ordering* you. You write about this and not only will I make sure no one in the OPP ever gives you the time of day again, but I'll personally hold you responsible for screwing up this investigation and I could even get you for obstruction of justice. No one outside of the investigation knows about this and we need to keep it that way to flush out the real killer. This bit of information is the ace up our sleeve."

She swallowed a biting retort; she had never taken kindly to being told what to do or what not to do. Especially by a man, sexy or not. But she knew keeping the peace was more important at the moment since she had an ulterior motive.

"Don't worry," she said, touching his arm. "I never had any intention of using it."

He looked into her eyes. "Are you sure? What about your editor? He'll want to splash it all over the front page, I bet."

"He doesn't know, I didn't tell him. I haven't told anyone."

He relaxed visibly in his seat. "Thanks. You don't know what this means to me. To the team," he said, looking at his hands. "Sorry about coming down so strong on you there."

She indicated there were no hard feelings with a smile. "But I want to be kept in the loop, Tim. I want to know what you know, I want details, I want in. Do you think we could work something out?"

His eyes flashed with renewed anger. "Or what? You'll use it, after all?"

Hanna shook her head. "Tim, for a smart guy, you can be pretty dense sometimes." He narrowed his eyes at her and she held up a hand. "Just listen to me, all right? We've known each other for what? Almost a year and a half? In all that time when you were here with the OPP in Midland, I must have interviewed you a dozen times or more. And not once did I ever go over your head with anything you asked me to keep under my hat. Right?"

She waited until he'd nodded before going on. "You should know by now that I keep my promises, Tim. And I promise you I will never write a word about this investigation unless you tell me it's all right. Okay? Do we have a deal?"

"Why is this so important to you?"

There was a short answer and a long answer to that question, and Hanna chose the short one. "It's personal," she said simply, and counted to twenty in her head before she turned to look at him. There was a mix of concern and confusion in his eyes and she swallowed around a lump in her throat. "So," she said, "do we have a deal or not?"

By way of an answer, he simply nodded and they were both quiet a long moment.

"Do you know what type of snake it is?" she finally asked, breaking the silence.

Bennett hesitated, then shook his head. "A couple of our guys have been assigned to talk to experts. Once we know what type it is, we may be able to pinpoint its habitat as well. That could lead us right to the killer. At least, we hope." He raked a hand through his hair again, sighing heavily. "Sixteen and a half inches long. Unbelievable."

Hanna squirmed, her pelvic muscles tightening as if protesting this horror. She was afraid she might throw up. "Oh God."

"Looked like it had some kind of rattle thing on its tail."

She clenched her teeth. "A rattlesnake?"

He caught the tremor in her voice, gave her a concerned look. "It could be, but no one's sure yet. We're looking into it."

"Jesus. What kind of sick person does something like this, Tim?"

"A psychopath. He sutured her, too. Did that bastard Pierce mention that?"

"He did."

"Damn it. Then you probably know it was professional."

"What was?"

"This is just between the two of us, okay? Nothing goes in the paper."

"Agreed."

"The suturing material, it's professional. The kind used by doctors."

A knot of unease tightened under her rib cage. "Silk?"

"Yes. At first we thought it might have been fishing line or dental floss. But silk, well, that raises a whole new set of questions. Like, where did he get it? You can't just walk into a store and buy a roll of this stuff." Bennett flashed her a look. "But the job, that wasn't professional."

"The job?"

"The suturing. He didn't do a very good job. In fact, it was pretty lousy."

Hanna said nothing, staring at the slice of water she could see down the incline and trying to stop her mind from conjuring up too many disturbing images. She failed miserably. "So what do you think?"

"Well, bear in mind that I'm no profiler, but you've got professional suturing material and a drug overdose as the probable murder weapon," he said, his eyes narrow and hard as he looked her way again. "I'd say our guy has some knowledge of medical procedures and drugs, maybe not very much but enough to know how deadly any drug can be in high doses. Enough to know what it can do." He scratched his chin. "He might even have access to a medical facility of some sort. He might work at a hospital, but I wouldn't say he's a doctor. That suturing job wasn't clean enough for him to be a doctor. Unless..." He stopped, didn't finish what he started to say.

"Unless he did a lousy job on purpose?"

He shot her a sidelong glance. "You have to admit, it's plausible."

Hanna was silent as she absorbed the information she had just learned, her insides still churning. "What about Beausoleil Island? Any luck so far?"

"No. But there's a lot of people to talk to," he said.

She recalled camping on the island with a friend's family when she'd been a kid. They'd taken the ferry from Honey Harbour to the island, which she remembered from a map was vaguely shaped like a giant hammer. The campground had always been popular, attracting thousands of campers each year.

"Did you talk to her friends again?" Hanna had interviewed a few of them after Lydia disappeared and wondered if Bennett had learned anything new.

"Yeah, but it was just more of the same. She met up with some guy, who may or may not be the killer, and said she was going to a party on the island. That's it. We don't know if she ever did meet up with him or what happened after that, but her friends say that's the last they saw of her. She never came back. You know all the rest."

Hanna thought of Lydia's parents again, imagining her own. Empathy filled her to the point of pain. "What do you think happened to her that night? What's your theory?"

"Well, we know she was at the beach by herself that afternoon and that she met someone who invited her to a party on the island that night. She described this guy as 'tall, dark and handsome' and 'really hot' to her friends and she seemed excited. She told them not to worry about her, she'd be fine." His jaw tightened. "That's as much as we know. The rest is pure speculation at this point. But this guy, he had to be real smooth for her to feel safe enough to go off by herself to a party with him. And who knows about this party? Maybe that was all bullshit, all part of the line he fed her. No one we've talked to so far remembers a party and the rangers all said it had been a quiet night for a change. No parties bigger than a dozen or so people at any one camp site."

"For a change?"

"This is a popular campground, lots of people are there to party. Most nights, they usually have to deal with fights breaking out, and the usual problems that go with that. Drunks stumbling around. Excessive noise. On occasion, there's even a fire, or God forbid, a missing child. Plus, all the other stuff, like toilets overflowing and the local wildlife getting into garbage. But that night, they said everything was quiet."

"So you don't believe there was a party?"

Bennett raked his fingers through his hair. "No. Someone would have remembered if there had been one that night. The way I see it she went out to meet with him and he convinced her to go with him to his boat. He had to have one. She wasn't killed on Beausoleil. What he did to her… Jesus. It would have taken time and privacy. He would have wanted to get her alone somewhere. My guess is he has a cottage or some place nearby, maybe on another island somewhere in the 30,000 island group or even on the mainland. The point is he couldn't have done what he did to her on Beausoleil. Too many people, too much going on."

Hanna swallowed hard, pressure grating behind her eyelids. "I know there's only been one victim, but these guys, these monsters who get into heavy duty sex crimes, they don't just start by killing and mutilating their victims, do they? They start off by torturing animals, working their way to sexual assaults…" She let her voice trail off.

"I don't know." The green of his eyes deepened as he stared at her. "All I know is that we're dealing with everyone's worst nightmare. A sexual killer. Sadistic, violent. She was raped and mutilated, Hanna, her face slashed and he even took a souvenir. Not to mention the snake. And the fact that she was found naked, dumped in the bay." He shook his head, turned up his hands. "He does this kind of thing once... We'll have to see what ViCLAS turns up."

The Violent Crime Linkage Analysis System, or ViCLAS, is a program used by law agencies in Canada and other countries around the world to track and link cases.

"You think he's killed before or will again?" Hanna asked.

"What do you think?" Bennett sighed and looked at his watch. "You said there were two things you wanted to talk about. What's the other one?"

She handed him the memory stick on which she had saved a copy of the image she'd been sent. "This was sent to me by e-mail Thursday, the day Lydia was found. Could you have a look and tell me what you think?"

"Sure, what is it?"

Hanna twisted the silver ring she wore on her right hand and looked up into his eyes. "A picture of a man about to perform an act of necrophilia on a dead woman."

"What?" His eyes widened to the size of silver dollars.

"Someone calling himself or herself *tatler* sent me an e-mail containing a photograph of some guy about to have sex with a woman who looked very much dead," Hanna repeated. "Totally repulsive."

Bennett rubbed at his chin. "And you say it was sent to you Thursday? When?"

"I think around lunchtime. I didn't download my messages until after eleven o'clock that night." She debated telling him that she thought the message was connected to Lydia's murder, but then rejected the idea. "I don't know what to make of it."

"Have you ever gotten messages from this sender before? What did you say the name was again?"

"*Tatler*." She spelled it for him. "And no, I've never received anything from this sender before." She grimaced, her features scrunching up in disgust. "I'm positive I would have remembered something like that. Trust me."

"Did you try to trace it?"

"I got another reporter at the paper to check it out yesterday and he said he'd traced it through a couple of Internet nodes – don't ask me what those are - in Canada through a transatlantic satellite to England and back here again. The damn thing is Matt thinks this sender's using an anonymous remailer."

Bennett raised an eyebrow. "Is that where they shield some guy's real address and put in a fake one?"

"Exactly. Which means it might be all but impossible to find him, unless you've got any ideas."

"None off the top of my head." He rubbed his bare chin as if smoothing down a beard. "But leave it with me and I'll pass it along to the guys at the E-Crimes Unit. If anyone can get a lead on this, it'll be them."

Chapter Seven

THE SUN WAS a golden disk in the sky on Monday morning as Hanna drove up Fueller Avenue towards Penetanguishene.

It wasn't yet 10 o'clock but already she had interviewed a group of unionized employees picketing outside a local seatbelt manufacturing plant and taken pictures as they waved placards demanding wage increases and job security. Her shoulders were bunched up around her neck, her wrist was sore from taking down comments for the better part of an hour, and her eyes felt grainy from lack of sleep. She had tossed until the wee hours of the morning again and when she had finally drifted into sleep, her dreams had been filled with images of slithering snakes and hacked-off body parts and Bennett's green eyes on hers.

Not especially restful, considering the kind of day she was already having and what still lay in store.

The street narrowed above a slight incline as she drove past the almost new 1200-bed super jail, sporting twelve interconnecting pods of cells. Since its doors had opened several years before, inmates serving sentences of up to two years less a day had been transferred here from older, dilapidated jails around the province, some of which had since been visited by the wrecking ball. Hanna drove on past high chain-link fences topped with rolls of sharp barbed wire silhouetted against a cloudless sky.

Rolling Sands, Ontario's only maximum-security psychiatric hospital for the criminally insane, loomed into view. Constructed of maroon brick, the building seemed ancient and cold in appearance after the sleek newness of its neighbour. It was shaped like a capital H, with four two-storey wings, running east to west, that were connected like a bridge by a long corridor in the centre. She counted 28 barred windows on each of the lower and upper levels, and recalled that at the end of each was a sunroom where "patients", as they were called here, spent their days. She spotted a security camera under an eave of the building as she came to the stop sign just before the entrance and remembered that movement sensors were also spaced strategically around the compound.

Hanna drove through the open electronic gate and parked in the visitor lot off the side of the main entrance. She studied the building's intimidating façade as she got out of her car and locked up.

Overlooking the shores of Georgian Bay and situated just steps away from Discovery Harbour, the site of the area's first British naval base in the 1800s and a tourist attraction today, Rolling Sands had been built during the Depression by the Ontario government. It wasn't long before the name of Penetanguishene, her hometown of 7,000 located just five minutes from Midland and about 150 kilometres north of Toronto, became synonymous with the word 'nuthouse'.

Just close enough to be convenient, yet far enough away to be out of sight, she thought. She supposed it was human to want to keep the monsters locked up as far away as possible, but it was her town which had inherited the house of horrors, her community which had been forced to live with its notoriety. Economically sound for the area or not, the institution *was* home to some of Canada's most violently insane criminals - the majority of its current "patients" were murderers and serial killers found not guilty by reason of insanity. And flanked on one side by the area's Mental Health Centre and on the other by the super jail, Rolling Sands was the stuff of Hitchcock movies.

Hanna made her way to the entrance, passing through the first in a set of steel barred doors. Like most residents of the area, she had never actually been inside Rolling Sands. She jumped when the door buzzed shut behind her, locking electronically, and felt a faint claustrophobic stirring in the pit of her stomach.

Opening the next heavy steel door, Hanna emerged into a small room where two uniformed guards were talking behind a small counter. They looked her over from head to toe as she identified herself and one of them, his name tag identifying him simply as Robert for security reasons, scanned through a list, located her name, and placed a check beside it. Tall with piercing grey eyes, he came around the counter and pushed a logbook towards her. Hanna wrote in her name and the date and he initialled her entry. He pinned a plastic VISITOR card to her magenta silk blouse, taking pains not to poke her. Next, he made her go through a metal detector and examined the contents of her purse while he droned on in a bored voice about the dangers of taking in contraband. In addition to the usual - guns, knives, explosives and street drugs - the list also included cough medication, glass bottles, plastic utensils, even Rolaids.

His job over, he pushed a button near the locked door leading into the rest of the hospital and a female nurse-attendant materialized almost instantly on the other side. Silently, she escorted Hanna down a long corridor; concrete blocks painted a pale institutional green, into a large, bright room with floor to ceiling barred windows on one wall. Several people occupied the tables around the open space. It was impossible to tell the "patients" from the visitors -- inmates wore street clothes they or their families provided for them. Only the guards were easily identified by their uniforms of dark pants, light blue shirts and navy ties. Two of them lounged by the doors as Hanna walked past.

Giving her a wry smile, her escort pointed to a table in the far back of the visitors' centre and left. Hanna licked dry lips and wiped damp palms on the sides of her short grey skirt as her eyes made contact with those of the man sitting at the table near the windows. She carefully wove her way around tables, her heels clicking on the white linoleum floor, all the while studying him.

Raymond Fortin was one of two patients who had agreed to be interviewed for a feature Jake Belmont had assigned to her just a couple of days before Lydia Tomlinson had gone missing. It was to be a feature about their academic achievements through the hospital's Education Centre - both were completing high school equivalency correspondence courses - as well as a profile of their lives before and after Rolling Sands that would appear in the next issue of *The Post*'s special monthly magazine, Reflections. Good for them, Hanna had said, but the idea of giving these guys the time of day never mind news space had seemed preposterous to her. Belmont had disagreed, waving a recent reader survey under her nose. She had been shocked to learn that 79 per cent of readers indicated they would like to see more stories of a celebrity nature, with an unbelievable 66 per cent requesting more true crime stories. Unfortunately, the Huronia region being what it is – small, mostly rural and far from the city – not many natives had legitimately achieved celebrity status, the exceptions being curling pro Russ Howard, skating champion Brian Orser and baseball idol Phil "Babe" Marchildon, plus a few others. But true crime? Not a problem. Rolling Sands was teeming with celebrities of its very own - true-life serial killers, mass murderers, pedophiles and arsonists, take your pick. Hanna still hadn't forgiven Belmont for assigning the story to her and feeling Raymond's eyes roam over her now, she wondered if she ever would.

Most of the information she'd been able to find about him through old news accounts centred around the reason he was in Rolling Sands in the first place, and she briefly went over what she had read in her head. Two decades ago, he had been charged and tried for the brutal murder of his common-law wife in the mid-80s, found not guilty by reason of insanity and sentenced indefinitely to the maximum-security hospital. Raymond Fortin was what they called a mentally disordered sex offender.

She was looking forward to doing this story about as much as she looked forward to her Pap smear each year. Especially considering the other patient to be interviewed was a serial arsonist who had burned an entire family in their home while they slept and landed here after being found incompetent to stand trial. Just the thought of it made her grimace.

As Hanna pulled up a chair and sat down across the table from him, Raymond Fortin's eyes bore into hers, dark and opaque, the colour of pewter. He had a high forehead, long black hair – peppered with grey and pulled into a ponytail at the nape of his neck – and a ruddy, pockmarked complexion. He was of medium height and slight of build with prominent cheekbones that seemed chiselled of granite.

His eyes undressed her, and Hanna quelled the impulse to flee.

"Soooo," he drawled, interlocking his long fingers like the teeth of a zipper under his chin. "We finally meet. You know, that picture of yours in the paper doesn't do you justice. You're a lot more beautiful… *en personne.*"

He spoke with a hint of a French Canadian accent like her parents did and rolled his r's the way she sometimes did.

"You know, you and I have something in common," he went on. "We're writers. You write stories for the paper… I write poems." His teeth, yellowed like the pages of a newspaper left out in the sun too long, peeked from between moist lips. "Here's one… I just made it up." His nostrils flared slightly as he sniffed the air. "Sweet Hanna, wearing Lily of the Valley, but no pantyhose on legs so lovely. Makes me so very hard and… horny."

She stiffened against the plastic backing of the chair.

"I bet you're the type to wear lacy panties, am I right? No sensible cotton undies for you." He smirked, thoroughly enjoying himself.

She felt her face flush. "Look, Mr. Fortin, this has gone on far enough," she said, struggling not to let her impatience creep into her voice. "Could we get on with the interview, if you don't mind?"

"All good things come to those who wait," he said, tilting his head to the side. "And one more thing. Call me Raymond." He pronounced it Raymon, the 'd' silent.

Hanna sighed. "All right, Raymond, let's get started then. Tell me about your –"

"Wait," he interrupted, raising a hand to silence her. He turned his hands palms up on the table. His eyes fluttered closed then flew open, the black of his pupils fixed on a point just beyond her head. "In school, you were the shy one. You took great pains not to stand out in the playground. You never raised your hand in class even though you always knew the answers. You didn't play like other children, you dreamed."

The words tumbled from his mouth, each sentence a statement spoken with a current of urgency as Hanna stared at him. His eyes were as still as pools of water under windless skies, and she was flooded with memories of the little girl she'd been – a flash of herself at eight in the second grade, red-faced with shame, her desk pushed up to the front of the class as punishment for staring out the window at the clouds drifting by.

"Ever since you learned to read, you always had your nose stuck in a book," he continued in the same hurried, clipped voice. "You read everything you could get your hands on and the library soon became your window to the world."

That's true, Hanna thought, feeling disoriented, as if she had just woken up in a strange place. *What's going on? What's he doing to me?*

"I bet you even read the dictionary."

She couldn't hide a smile. "I did," she said. "Webster's and even Roget's Pocket Thesaurus. From cover to cover. How did you know that?"

He laughed. "I can read you, Hanna, *comme un livre.*"

She offered him a brief, tight smile. "All right, Raymond. You have amazing insight, but enough about me. Let's talk about the course you're taking at the Education Centre. Is getting your high school diploma something you always wanted to do?"

She leaned forward across the table and pressed PLAY on the recorder.

"Sure, why not? It beats sitting around all day."

Great, she thought. If all his answers were going to be as scintillating as that last one, it was going to be one of the longest interviews of her life. Not to mention the worst.

"What was your education level before you began the course and when do you think you'll be finished?" she tried again.

Raymond shrugged. "Grade eight, I think. And I started back in January… so I guess I still have a few months left."

Hanna jotted this down. "And what do you do when you're not

studying?"

"Watch movies and TV, read, exercise, eat and sleep. *C'est tout*."

"What kinds of movies do you watch?"

He smiled, a slight pulling of his lips at the corners, and his eyebrows wiggled like caterpillars above his eyes. "I subscribe to PayTV so I watch that a lot but I also like westerns. A good comedy once in a while, too."

So it's lots of porn and a little cowboy-and-Indian action on the side with a few laughs thrown in, she thought. What did I expect? A diehard Chainsaw Massacre fan? A Freddy Krueger devotee? She almost laughed out loud.

The real issue here, she knew, was that he was able to pay for these luxuries out of the comfort allowance most patients received from the province, a couple of hundred dollars a month to spend as they pleased. Others also collected Canada Pension Plan disability cheques as well, some receiving as much as $800 a month or more. Many spent their money on take-out food from nearby restaurants while others owned televisions, DVDs, compact disc players, computers and exercise equipment. There were no rules concerning what they could or couldn't watch or read, and at one time an inmate ran a profitable bootleg movie video rental business out of the building's basement for several years, offering everything from X-rated porn and slaughter films to kids' movies. But the one thing they didn't have was access to the Internet. She couldn't imagine a guy like Raymond surfing the Internet for any of the reasons 'normal' people did, but she could see him preying on young, naive minds under whatever guise he could make up for himself. The phrase 'homicidal cybersurfer' flashed in her mind.

She dragged herself back. "What's your biggest complaint about Rolling Sands?"

He smiled again, showing his yellowed teeth. "*La nourriture*." His face puckered.

"The food? Tell me about it."

"Well, let's just say it ain't gourmet cuisine by any stretch of the imagination," he said and Hanna felt something like pity for him, realizing the man hadn't eaten an unsupervised meal anywhere outside of the psychiatric institution in twenty years.

"What else bothers you?"

"*L'ennui*. After the food, I'd have to say boredom is the worst. If you don't know how to keep your mind busy, you can go crazy in here," he said.

Hanna smiled at the irony of his statement – weren't all inmates in Rolling Sands insane to begin with? But it was a good quote and she thought she understood where he was coming from. No one is compelled to work or take part in rehabilitative programs at Rolling Sands – psychiatrists had long given up on the notion that psychopaths were curable, although at one time, lobotomies and shock treatments were handed out like candy at Halloween. These days, most inmates drifted in a haze of acute apathy, staring out windows for hours on end, seven days a week, month after month, year after year.

"Okay, Raymond, can we talk a little about your childhood?"

He glanced out the window. When he turned back to her, his eyes had gone flat. "Well, let me see. I was born the fourth of seven children in a poor community way up near James Bay where it's so cold in the winter that even poking your face out the door will freeze your nostrils together," he said, pinching his nose shut to demonstrate. "I was six when my father shot himself in the bushes behind our house. It was summer and I remember my mother screaming at his dead body that day after my older brother, Vincent, found him in the grass. She never snapped out of it and was committed to an asylum after that. All of us kids were taken by child welfare and placed into foster homes."

He smiled, his eyes fixed on hers. There was fierceness in their depths and Hanna wanted to look anywhere but into those mad, calm eyes.

"So they sent me off to live in another little place near Thunder Bay and I ended up living with this family. They had only one child, *une fille*. She was quiet and terribly ugly with big teeth spilling out of her mouth. And one day, I found out why Abbi never said a word. I saw her father raping her when her mother was out of the house. He always threw her nightgown over her head, I guess so he wouldn't have to see her face. She was only eight or nine, I think. And then one day, he caught me watching, marched me to the back of the property and threw me face down in the leaves. He tied up my hands behind my back, kicked me everywhere, pulled down my pants and then… then he raped me."

Hanna again fought the urge to look away. She winced inwardly, knowing the suffering he had caused others throughout his life was a projection of his own misery, the result of the nightmare childhood he had endured.

"It happened so many times over the next few years," he continued, shrugging his thin shoulders, "that I guess you could say I developed a taste for it myself and I raped Abbi one day. I must have been 11 or 12, I don't remember."

His smile pushed up the corners of his mouth and Hanna felt the pit of her stomach knot with revulsion.

"She was the first, you know, but certainly not the last. But you know that, don't you, Hanna? You're smart; you did your research. You know why I'm in here."

"Yes. Tell me what happened after that."

He laughed and the sound chilled her to the bone. "My foster father," he said in a low voice, bringing his head close to hers. "I tried to kill the son-of-a-bitch with my bare hands one night when he was sleeping."

Hanna reeled back as if slapped. Of course, she hadn't read anything about this - juvenile records were sealed. But still, she was shocked and knew it showed in her face.

"I was never charged, but I was sent to a reformatory and kicked out about a year later. I ended up living on the streets, breaking into houses to steal whatever I could find. I eventually hitched to Toronto and by this time, I was seventeen. I did some time for rape and for aggravated assault with a deadly weapon. When I wasn't in jail, I found work in construction. I hated it, but the money was good. And so life just went on."

"Until you committed murder."

A strange, fleeting light shone in his dark eyes and then it was gone. The shadows returned and he laughed, a rattling sound rising from the depths of his chest.

"Murder," he said as if savouring the name of a loved one on his tongue. "That bitch got exactly what she deserved."

Hanna felt a bolt of anger rise to the surface. "You claimed you couldn't remember any details about what happened that night. You said you blacked out. Is that true?"

"What do you think?" he asked, locking his hands behind his head.

"I think you never expected to be found not guilty by reason of insanity and brought here to spend the remainder of your days. You've been here how long? Twenty years? You must know that you would have been eligible for parole a few years ago had you stood trial and been given twenty-five to life. How does that make you feel?"

Abruptly, he leaned forward and stared at her. His eyes were ablaze with fury and a sneer distorted his face. He reached out and touched the place where her collarbones met, his fingertips pressing down hard against her skin. Instinctively, Hanna lashed out and he roughly grabbed her wrist, pinning her arm down on the table.

"So Hanna, tell me, do I repulse you?" The lecherous smile was back and she struggled to free her arm, anger roiling through her as she glanced back at the guards standing by the door. He immediately loosened his grip and she snatched her arm away.

"You're not the first man who's ever repulsed me, Raymond," she said, her teeth clenched to control the tremor in her voice, "and I'm sure you won't be the last."

He laughed boisterously, throwing his salt-and-pepper head back. "Quid pro quo, Hanna," he said. "*C'est mon tour.* Tell me, why is it that the light fades from your eyes when you hear the word 'rape'?"

She felt her stomach somersault but said nothing.

"You can't even say the word, can you?" he pressed on, licking his lips with the tip of his tongue. "I've seen that look before. They all have it, you know."

Her hands shaking, she willed her heart to stop hammering.

"What did he do, Hanna? Did he stick it in you hard? Did he

fuck you but good?"

She leapt from her chair. *This is too much, goddamn him to hell.* Her face burned with humiliation and anger and she stared at him with rage blackening her eyes.

"This interview is over," she spat out, grabbing her recorder.

Striding across the room to the exit, she didn't look back once.

Chapter Eight

THE WORLD AND everything in it was tinted red as Hanna tore out of Rolling Sands, the automatic lock of the door snapping behind her. The sky was a giant crimson sea tumbling towards her and she stumbled on the steps, grabbing the metal railing to keep from falling. She gripped it like someone clinging to a life preserver, sucking air in huge, gasping gulps.

A click.

Like a shutter going off, it was almost inaudible over the rush of blood in her ears, and abruptly she was there again, floating above it all, watching it happen.

The truck is parked just inside a dirt road on government property, hidden from the highway by rows of tall pines growing near maples and oaks. Sun-dappled leaves stir in the summer breeze and John Cougar Mellencamp sings on the radio about holding on to 16 as long as you can, the volume turned down low.

He towers over her, the Swiss Army knife just inches from her neck, and she's crying, fat tears trickling down the sides of her face into her ears. Her eyes are wide open with terror, her back sticky with sweat against the vinyl seat. Her hands are pinned in his damp fist and she smells stale beer on his breath.

She presses her face into the hard plastic of the door, the handle cutting into her cheek, but he roughly grabs her chin, his lips touching hers. She clamps her mouth shut, but his tongue is wet and insistent. "Kiss me for Christ's sake," he hisses at her. She presses her face into the door again. She gasps when he hits her across the face and she makes herself smaller, cowering on the seat like a kitten under the heel of a heavy boot.

She's shaking now, and he's fumbling with his free hand at the zipper of her shorts, yanking them down roughly over her legs. She tries bucking her hips, but he jams a knee into her thigh to hold her still and presses the blade of the knife against her neck.

She's crying harder, mascara running into her eyes, and she sobs "No!" again and again, but his hands are pulling at her panties, ripping them off her. Then he's frantically jerking down his jeans, grabbing himself, and he's huge and purple, ropey with veins. He jabs her with his penis, trying to hold her legs open at the same time, and he swears at her, tearing a fistful of her hair. He forces himself into her finally and she cries out with pain and shock and shame. He groans as he rips into her again and again, and it seems to go on forever, but only seconds later, he gives a grunt as he ejaculates into her. It's finally over.

She hastens to pull on her clothes as soon as he pulls out, his wet penis sliding along the vinyl of the seat, like a snail. A trickle of blood runs down her leg and he's watching her, laughing, and she can't stop the tears from cascading down her cheeks.

A car swung through the gate and snap, the film playing on the screen of her mind came to an abrupt stop. Trees were once again green, the sky blue, the pavement black under her feet. Hanna wiped tears with her hand as she hurried to her car.

Sagging like a rag doll against the seat, she felt sweat bead her forehead, and there was a taste like dry chalk in the back of her throat. She caught a glimpse of her eyes in the rear-view mirror and she thought of wild, windswept fields in late November, of cracked brown earth under a weak sun. She hated seeing it there, that gaping emptiness like a rat gnawing at her soul, bit by bit, year after year.

Hanna wiped her tears, squared her shoulders and drove out of the parking lot. She stopped to pick up a large coffee and was back at the office in less than 15 minutes. It was almost lunchtime and the building was quiet when she walked in through the back door to the newsroom. David Lakefield was busy typing on his keyboard, a tinny voice coming out of the mini recorder on the desk beside him, and Jake Belmont had the phone glued to his ear as usual. She sat down at her desk and booted up her computer.

The next three hours were spent returning phone calls, writing the story on the strike and finishing others she had put on hold. At three, she called one of Lydia Tomlinson's childhood friends, Kirk Andrews, and after offering him her condolences, explained that she wanted to do an interview with him and as many of Lydia's friends as possible following her funeral the next day. Not only did he agree to hold the meeting at his parents' house, but he also promised to contact her friends himself.

After thanking him, she hung up and attacked the pile of press releases overflowing her in-basket, rewriting the information into short news briefs that would appear in the paper when space allowed. It was practically mindless, routine work but with the funeral looming heavily on her mind, Hanna made little headway.

A half hour later, the phone rang.

"Ms Laurence? I'm sorry to disturb you," a soft male voice said. "My name is George Jackson, I'm the superintendent of Georgian Bay Islands National Park. I got a call this morning from the chief of Christian Island. Tom Monague thought I might be able to help you with a definition for a word?"

The e-mail message, Hanna thought. *Pamidonegog.* She had contacted the chief early that morning before going out to cover the strike.

"Yes, Mr. Jackson, it's so kind of you to phone me directly."

"No problem," he said. "The chief said it had something to do with an e-mail?"

"Yes. It contained only one word. I don't know if you'll be able to translate it or not, but it was spelled P-A-M-I-D-O-N-E-G-O-G. Is that Ojibway?"

"As a matter of fact, it is," he answered. "It's not very well known, but pamidonegog is an easy one to translate. It means 'an island in the centre of a channel, a shelter offering protection from the open sea'."

"Oh," she said. "It's the name of an island?"

His answer was only two words long, but it was enough to set her heart galloping at full speed in her chest.

Chapter Nine

BEAUSOLEIL ISLAND.

"It used to be the area's native reserve about 150 years ago, before it was moved to Christian Island," Jackson went on. "The first settlers tried to make a go of it here, but the soil is infertile and most of them relocated just a few years later to Christian Island."

He went on about the island's history, but Hanna's mind had stuck on the island's name and she barely heard the rest of what he said. All she could think of was that Lydia Tomlinson and her friends had been camping on Beausoleil Island when she disappeared.

Her mind whirled with questions as she struggled to understand the significance of the message. It couldn't be a coincidence or someone's idea of a sick joke. She felt more certain than ever that it had to be directly related to the investigation.

She felt a trickle of sweat run down her back as she tucked the receiver between her ear and shoulder, freeing her hands to jot down information in her notebook.

"If I understand correctly, Pamidonegog was Beausoleil's original name?"

"According to the Ojibway or Chippewa, yes. But it's been called many other names by other peoples over the years."

"Such as? Can you give me an example?"

"Well, the Hurons called it Schiondekiaria, meaning 'this land to appear floating afar', and the French had several names for it as well, like St. Ignace, and later Ile de Traverse, because the fur traders passed by its shores on their way back and forth along the Nipissing trade route."

"Why is it known as Beausoleil today?"

"In 1819, a French Canadian fur trader and fisherman by the name of William Beausoleil came to the island and made his home on its southern tip." He chuckled. "I guess the name just stuck."

"Mr. Jackson, what's your reaction to the fact that the girl found near Honey Harbour last Thursday was camping on Beausoleil with friends when she went missing?"

"I'm horrified, of course. It's just terrible to think that something like this could happen here. We get thousands of campers each year... something like this has never happened before."

"And Beausoleil Island is part of a national park, isn't that right?"

"Georgian Bay Islands National Park. It was formed in 1929 and originally included 29 of Georgian Bay's 30,000 islands. Now there are more than 59 islands in the park, and Beausoleil is the largest of them. Most of the park services are offered here, such as camping, guided tours, etc. The other islands are just too small."

Hanna leaned back in her chair, her mind whirling. Who was *tatler* and how had he known about the island's original name? Could someone who worked there, a guide or a maintenance person have murdered Lydia? Someone who knew the history of the island? And what about the snake?

"Mr. Jackson, would you know of reptile species being indigenous to Beausoleil?"

"Sure. The island is home to a wide variety of reptiles and amphibians. In fact, we've designated four of these, including the Eastern Massasauga rattlesnake, as priority species requiring special protection."

Hanna pulled her notebook closer towards her, and after asking him to spell the name for her, jotted it down.

"It's the only snake found in Ontario that is poisonous and potentially dangerous to humans. It's seldom seen here but we still warn everyone to watch out for it."

"So this species only lives on the island?"

"No. Their range extends from central Ontario down to

Western New York, and south to eastern Iowa and extreme eastern Missouri," he said. "They're becoming increasingly rare and are now considered endangered in much of their range."

"Mr. Jackson, thank you so much for calling. You've been very helpful," Hanna said, drawing the conversation to a close.

"I'm glad to be of help. If there's anything else I can do, don't hesitate to call," he said and left her his home and office numbers. She thanked him again and hung up.

Many of her questions had now been answered, but the two most baffling still plagued her: Who had sent her the message? And why?

Other questions rose from the back of her mind, tumbling around and around inside her head like too many wet clothes in a dryer. Was the message directly related to the Tomlinson case? And scariest of all, could it have been sent by the killer?

Tim Bennett, when she reached him later at the CIB office at headquarters in Orillia, could only spare a few minutes.

"We're getting jammed with calls. It seems every loony bin for miles around is calling to tell us he did it," he complained good-naturedly. "It's been hell."

"Sounds like you have your work cut out for you," Hanna commiserated. "I won't keep you long, but I wanted to tell you that Canadian Press picked up my story and it's been in some of the national papers already."

"Thanks for the heads-up, but I already know." He paused, clearing his throat. "And Hanna, about this picture that was sent to you, we didn't get anywhere trying to trace it. I know it's disgusting, but there are no laws against sending this kind of stuff, unfortunately. Whoever sent it is probably some wacko who gets off on this kind of sick thing. And as for that Ojibway word, we've got a historian digging up some information."

"Don't bother. I already found out what it means." She told him about her conversation with Jackson.

There was dead silence on the line and then a low whistle blew in her ear. "Holy Christ. This changes everything. Listen, can you meet me in an hour?"

"Sure. Where?"

"You know that roadside diner in Coldwater? On the highway? The one that's painted blue and has fish nets over the windows?"

"Yeah, I know the one you're talking about."

"Good. Meet me there at 5:30."

Halfway between Midland and Orillia on Highway 12, Coldwater is a small village built on a winding river by the same name, with lots of century-old homes on tree-lined streets and country charm in shop windows. The Coldwater Grist Mill, once the town's general store and wheat milling plant, perches precariously close to the river, watching over the main street like a sentinel from bygone days.

Hanna pulled into the parking lot of The Fish Net and hurried inside. She spotted Bennett, dressed in a lightweight grey suit, sitting at a table in the back and made her way past hand-painted waves on walls and seashells clinging to sturdy fish nets strung across windows overlooking the highway. She slid across the worn vinyl bench opposite him, smelling his after-shave and thinking how gorgeous he was.

"Hi. Sorry about all this," he said, "but I thought it would be best to meet."

"That's all right," she answered. "It's good to get out of the office."

A matronly waitress shuffled tired feet over to their table and Bennett ordered coffee and a slice of apple pie a la mode. Hanna wasn't hungry and asked only for some hot tea.

When the waitress had brought their food and moved away, Hanna stirred cream and sugar into her cup. "What did you mean when you said this changes everything?"

"Well," Bennett said around a mouthful of pie, "it's not just the fact that this sender knew about Beausoleil Island's original native name that we've decided to check into this. It can't be that hard to find out things like that, it's probably a recorded historical fact. It's more a combination of things."

"There's something else, isn't there?"

He pushed his empty plate to the side and Hanna noticed the network of fine lines at the corners of his eyes, the paleness of his skin, the weariness in his green eyes.

"Yes, but you have to give me your word this won't go any farther than this room. It could be my ass on the line."

She nodded, crossed her fingers over her chest. "You've got it."

"We got the entomology report back this morning."

Hanna nodded, swallowing, her mind filling with images of large-winged insects and creepy crawly things.

"So it's official. We've got a necrophile on our hands."

Hanna thought of the image she'd been sent and something Dr. Ellis had said came rushing back to her – *this young woman had been dead more than a week before she was placed in the bay.*

"Hanna? You okay?"

She heard his voice underneath the rush of blood in her head and nodded, aware of something shifting deep in her mind like a reflection on the surface of water.

"I don't know what you know about entomology, but it goes something like this: blowflies arrive minutes after death and lay their eggs on the mucous membranes of a dead body, such as the mouth, the eyes, the nostrils, the anus, the vagina… you get the picture. And at the same time, if there are wounds and blood, the flesh flies go to work."

"And they lay eggs in the wounds?"

"Larvae. First instar larvae. Except the coroner didn't find any insect activity. Blowflies or flesh flies."

Hanna shuddered. "He kept her for a while. Preserved her for as long as he could."

He shot her a look. "Yes. He probably stored her in a freezer when he wasn't using her. To slow down decomposition. Also explains why the usual signs of rape weren't there. There was no bruising and tearing to the genital area. That's because dead tissue doesn't really react to violence such as rape. He only raped her after she was dead."

Poor, poor Lydia. Hanna felt revulsion like a fist in her gut.

"Killing isn't the thrill for this guy," Bennett went on, shaking his head. "I think that's why he killed her with an injection. It's quick, clean, and it leaves the victim whole. No mess, no fuss. Killing is just a means to an end. The corpse is what he's after."

"I don't think I can hear any more of this."

Bennett appeared not to have heard her. "This guy prefers his victim dead. His fantasy isn't the classic rape-kill scenario most killers embrace. What's important to him happens after he's killed, then he rapes and mutilates to his heart's content. I would guess he dumps the body into the bay after it becomes too mangled for him to use or after the thrill with that particular one wears off."

The dead beneath the water.

The words appeared to float across her mind's eye and Hanna imagined a nude, ravaged body tumbling in a cold, watery grave.

But it's what the killer had done prior to dumping Lydia's body that Hanna couldn't stop seeing in her mind. Every image was more vile than the last and she knew there was nothing she could do to stop them. Terrible sights, the kind she could never unimagine. The kind that came out to haunt her in the dead of night.

"If the Tomlinson victim was his first, then she won't be his last. Guys like that, they develop a taste for this kind of thing. And he'll be young, in his mid to late 20s. Just old enough to have started down this road, but not old enough to have left 20 or more victims behind." Bennett looked out the window and then back across the table. "But that's how many we'll have in a few years' time if he isn't caught."

"Then hurry up and catch him already."

"Yes, ma'am," he said and saluted her. "And before I forget, let's talk about the e-mail. When we first took a look at it we decided it was probably just some pervert trying to scare the hell out of you. But after you told me what that word meant, warning bells went off. So we took another look at it, just before I came out here to meet you. And this is what is putting the screws to us. The picture was sent to you at 11:55 a.m. on Thursday, around the same time we pulled Lydia Tomlinson out of the bay. Think about that for a minute. At that point, no one knew about the killer being a necrophile. Not even us, no one. The post hadn't even been done yet, of course. So you tell me. How did this *tatler* know about it?"

A chill passed through Hanna as she thought of the implications of what Bennett was telling her. It made sense that the killer or someone involved in the crime had sent her the photograph. No one else could possibly have known then that Lydia Tomlinson's killer was a necrophile.

"Jesus," she whispered, the hairs at the back of her neck prickling. "But what I don't understand is why it was sent to me. Of all the reporters he could have picked."

Bennett leaned back against the vinyl seat. "Maybe he's a fan of yours. Could be he feels some sort of connection with you. Who knows? There's no logic to these kinds of people. They just do whatever they feel like whenever they feel like it."

Hanna swallowed a sip of tea. "I don't understand what his motivation would be for doing something like this. It serves no purpose, Tim."

"Maybe not to you," he answered, "or to me, for that matter, but to this person, this must make perfect sense."

"Not if *tatler* is the killer. Why would he want to draw attention to himself? Especially when it's so early in the investigation and there's so little to go on. Why wouldn't he want to stay hidden so he's free to continue his evil?"

"But he is. By using a remailer, the guy is as anonymous as they come."

"That's a good point, but I still don't think *tatler* is the killer." Hanna shook her head and sighed. "Maybe *tatler* is someone with a lot of inside information in the case, an accomplice, or perhaps even a confidant."

"That may very well be."

"So how do we catch someone like this?"

Bennett shrugged. "The guys at the E-Crimes Unit are good, but they don't know much more than what your friend at work told you. We tracked down the remailing service in England, but no go. So short of a warrant, and we really don't have enough at this point to get one, we're not holding much hope of getting anywhere using this route."

"So where does that leave us?"

"I don't know, but leave it to E-Crimes. They're working on it."

"What if I sent him back a reply? Any attempt on my part to contact him would probably get him to bite. Then maybe I could arrange to have him meet me in a chat room or something… then you could trace him, couldn't you?"

Bennett shook his head vehemently. "No, Hanna. Do you have any idea how dangerous that could be? Let E-Crimes do their jobs. The last thing I want is for you to get involved."

She smiled wryly. "It seems to me that I already am."

"Don't be a smart-ass," he said, smiling back. "You know what I mean."

Hanna told Bennett what she had learned about the Massasauga rattlesnake and he told her he hoped it would lead to some kind of break "so we can nail this bastard."

"Amen to that," she said, briefly closing her eyes. "I have to cover Lydia's funeral tomorrow, and to tell you the truth, I'd just as soon not have to cover anymore."

Bennett nodded, swallowing the last of his coffee. "I guess I'll see you there then. A few of us are going to pay our respects. And check out the crowd, 'cause you know how some killers like to show up at their victims' funerals."

Hanna shuddered, knowing it was true - some perverse killers relished the burial of their victims and fed off the grief of those who mourned them. "Cheery thought."

He nodded, glancing at his watch. "Sorry, Hanna, but I have to hit the road."

"I have to go, too," she said.

"About the photograph. We're trying to determine its authenticity… you know, if the picture is real or just something he downloaded off the 'Net," he said, sliding out of the booth and dropping some money on the table. "I'll let you know how that pans out. In the meantime, let me know right away if you get anything else from this pervert."

"Okay."

"And Hanna? I know this is hitting you pretty hard. Hell, it's hard enough when you're a cop," he said, opening the door for her. "But sooner or later, this guy will get what's coming to him. It's just a matter of time."

Hanna fervently hoped it would be sooner rather than later as they walked out of the restaurant to the parking lot and parted ways to their respective cars. She watched Bennett head back out on the highway towards Orillia, praying he was right and that they would be able to catch this monster before he took another innocent, young life.

But somehow, she didn't think so.

Chapter Ten

THE STREET IN front of the First Presbyterian Church was jammed with vehicles, as were many side streets when Hanna drove through the hamlet of Waubaushene in search of a parking space the next day. She went past the small stone structure with its bell steeple and bronze crosses on the entrance doors, circled around the block and found a space almost directly behind the church. She sat staring at a small cemetery where mounds of earth indicated a freshly dug grave that would become Lydia Tomlinson's final resting place.

The last plot in a row about midway down, the grave bordered the wrought iron fence surrounding the cemetery. Two lush maples provided shade over it and the fence was choked with twisting summer vines, white daisies, purple loosestrife and wild sage.

Hanna entered the cemetery, walking past curving rows of headstones. Butterflies danced in the sunlight, yellow and blue and white, their wings gentle flutters in air redolent with the smells of summer. Apple and cherry blossom trees scattered their petals over everything, blanketing the ground like a fine dusting of snow.

Hanna finally came to the new grave. She stood in the midday shadows of the maples, staring down into the rectangular hole, shivering despite the heat swirling around her. She picked a handful of daisies growing in a clump by the fence, brought the bouquet to her nose and let it fall from her fingers into the grave.

I will always remember you, Lydia, she thought, although I never knew you.

She wiped a tear from the corner of her eye and made her way around the side of the church. The funeral hearse was stationed in front and two attendants leaned against it, arms folded, watching people hurry up the flower-edged walkway to the church entrance. Men wore dark suits over starched white shirts and striped ties; women wore dresses in sombre colours. Hanna was glad she had chosen to wear her only sensible dress – a dark grey coatdress trimmed with black velvet around the collar and sleeves. It buttoned like a jacket and fell to just above the knee. Dark pantyhose and black wedge heels completed the outfit. She blended in with the crowd surging through the doors into the church.

With every pew full, ushers were directing people to the side sacristy where additional chairs had been set up. Hanna went to stand at the back of the church instead, knowing she would have a much better view there than she would in the sacristy with only the doorway to see through to the front of the church.

The service had not yet started. A closed white casket overflowing with bouquets of flowers took centre stage in front of the altar; a framed portrait of Lydia was set on top amid the pink and white blossoms. Even from the back of the church, the intense blue of her smiling eyes and the brilliant whiteness of her teeth struck Hanna. In this pose, Lydia's hands were folded in her lap and she wore a yellow sundress. Her shoulders were covered with her pale blonde hair, which fell straight down on either side of her head.

Scanning the crowd, she spotted Bennett in a dark suit standing next to the lead investigator from the Midland OPP about halfway up the church. Here to pay their respects, she thought, and make sure the killer isn't lurking somewhere, getting his last jollies while everyone else is crying their eyes out.

Organ music swelled from the loft above her and she turned to watch the minister lead a procession of altar children up the centre aisle, followed by the family and friends of the deceased. Lydia's mother walked past, her tear-streaked face framed by ash-blonde hair, her tall body clothed in a loose black dress. She clung to her husband and a small blonde girl of about 10, as they sat in the first pews reserved for the family. Their pain was so plainly visible on their faces, and Hanna felt her heart go out to them.

The music reached a crescendo and in the lull that followed, the minister stepped up to the pulpit, flanked by two small girls holding candles. His full head of black hair contrasted sharply with the paleness of his face. He shuffled his feet, cleared his throat and began the service with a small prayer. The congregation joined in and the church filled with the sound of voices raised in unison. When it was over, the minister placed his hands on either side of the wooden pulpit and looked out over the assembly.

"'But now is Christ risen from the dead, and become the first fruits of them that slept. For since by man came death, by man came also the resurrection of the dead. For as in Adam all die, even so in Christ shall all be made alive'." He paused a moment, his eyes scanning the room. "Let us find comfort in these words from the Book of Corinthians as we are gathered here today to mourn the loss of Lydia Janice Tomlinson, beloved daughter of Albert and Cynthia, dear sister of Emily, friend and member of this church. The entire community shares in your grief today and we turn to God in this moment of great sorrow."

Another prayer followed and then a group of children, Emily's classmates at Waubaushene Public School, rose from their seats to sing a heart-wrenching rendition of *Ave Maria*. Several people dabbed at their eyes with tissue and Hanna heard a choking sob from up near the front of the church. Then Emily herself, pink ribbons in her braided hair, stood up and turned to face the assembly. She was a small girl, short and skinny for her age, with a dusting of pale freckles across her nose. Her little face was wrung with sadness.

"My big sister was beautiful and friendly and kind. She was the best sister in the whole world and I loved her. I've got this special place here," she said, tapping her heart while tears spilled down her little face, "and I'll always remember her. I hope she's in heaven where no one can ever hurt her again."

Hanna fished around for a tissue and wiped her wet cheeks. That poor little girl had already known more pain in her young life than some people would ever know in a lifetime.

Others followed Emily's eulogy to her sister. Lydia's best friend in high school spoke briefly, stopping often to wipe tears from her eyes. Then a group of her friends from Sheridan College made a circle around the casket, joining hands as they bowed their heads and took turns placing a pink rose on the casket.

The last person to address the assembly was Lydia's aunt, Clara Harding. She was tall and painfully thin, and Hanna felt sure she was Lydia's mother's younger sister. Her hair was permed, but it was silvery blonde like Cynthia's, and her eyes appeared red-rimmed but dry as she took her place behind the podium.

"Standing here today is the hardest thing I've ever had to do," she began and her voice was soft in the silence of the church. "Even harder than identifying her body or learning that she had been murdered. Saying good-bye to my niece is the hardest thing I will ever have to do if I live to be 95. She was like another sister to me, a best friend, a daughter, and I will miss her for the rest of my life."

She looked towards her sister and Emily, offering them a weak smile.

"Lydia was full of life and full of dreams. She was studying to become an engineer, and she wanted to work for the city after she graduated from the four-year program at Sheridan College. She worked so hard to get to where she was. I was so proud of her, we all were. She was warm, intelligent, sensitive, and beautiful like an angel. And then, just like that," she snapped her fingers, "a very sick person took her away from us forever. We will never see her accept her diploma or thrive in her career, we will never see her fall in love or grow old. But we will never accept that the act of violence that took her life will have the power of obliteration because her body, our bodies, are just the outfits we wear. We are so much more than flesh and blood, brains and bones. We are heart and soul, and as such we are eternal. Lydia will live on in our hearts and in our souls forever."

She paused, rubbing furiously at her eyes, but the tears still came. "She was only 19, had just turned 19 in April. How can she be gone when she'd only just started living?"

Tears running down her face, Clara shakily sat down next to her sister who immediately enveloped her in a bear hug. Emily threw an arm around her aunt, too, and their sobs reached all the way to the rear of the church.

Hanna squeezed her eyes closed, two tears slipping out of the corners, and leaned against the wall. How eloquent and truthful her words had been. No disease or accident or act of violence could have absolute power of eradication of a human life - we continue to live on in the hearts and souls of loved ones, long after death.

Awed by the depth of feeling Clara Harding's words had evoked in her, Hanna blinked wet eyes and for the hundredth time, wondered how one family could bear so much pain. How would they ever go on living knowing what had happened to Lydia? How could they even set foot in a church after all that had happened? She was angry, too, not only at the monster who had destroyed such a young life, but also at a callous God who had dealt the cards of fate with the indifference of a blackjack dealer at a sleazy casino.

The rest of the service included more prayers and songs, and Hanna slipped out just before it was over. Local newspaper and TV station reporters were setting up their cameras, waiting for the casket and family to emerge from the church, and she wasn't surprised to see quite a few more whose microphones sported national news logos.

Hanna nodded to those she knew and sat down on a nearby bench. She was glad she and Jake had seen the wisdom of not taking along her notebook and camera – she couldn't imagine intruding on this family's pain and adding to their suffering on this day. She ignored the reporters and concentrated on organizing her thoughts. She wanted her story to be a tribute to Lydia, a last encomium to a young woman whose life had been snuffed in the most violent of ways. She was only here as an observer, nothing more.

A shadow moved across her and Hanna glanced over her shoulder. A tall, lanky young man with a reddish moustache and matching hair was approaching and he sat down beside her at the opposite end of the bench. He looked at her, offered a half smile, and began studying his hands. He wrung them this way and that and finally turned to her.

"You're Hanna Laurence, right?" He held out his hand. "I'm Kirk Andrews."

She'd talked to him on the phone twice - once after Lydia disappeared and again the day before to set up the interview with her friends - but she had never met him in person. She noted the expensive camera slung around his neck.

"It's nice to meet you," she said, shaking his hand. "I'm so sorry for your loss."

He waved her condolence away and shrugged. "So it's all set for the interview," he said. "Is two o'clock at my folks' place okay? It's 176 Pinecrest Drive."

"That's great, thanks. I'll be there," she said.

The front doors of the church opened then and the minister and the altar children emerged, followed by the pallbearers carrying the casket. Lydia's family and friends were close behind, and Kirk excused himself to join them. Reporters wasted no time jumping into the fray, some with cameras up to their faces and others with microphones outstretched in their hands. The minister tried shielding the family with his arms, but it was to no avail. Automatic shutters whirred and asinine questions - How does it feel to say a final good-bye? Are you confident the police will get her killer? - were shouted as the procession rounded the corner of the church. Cynthia Tomlinson let out a strangled cry and buried her face in her husband's neck. Hanna shook her head at the media's lack of discretion and respect for the family. How are they supposed to feel? she wondered, passing the group of reporters and shooting them a dirty look. What a bunch of idiots. Jesus.

The rest of the mourners poured out next and followed, heading towards the cemetery, and Hanna merged into the crowd.

It wasn't until everyone had gathered around the new grave and the minister had started his final prayers that she made eye contact with Bennett as his watchful eyes roamed over the crowd. Standing off to the side near the pine trees, he cut a striking figure in his navy suit. When his green gaze alighted on hers, he gave her a lingering look and a wink. Hanna felt a flutter of butterflies in her stomach as she smiled and winked back from the other side of the grave. His eyes moved over her and then shifted to the crowd.

The sealed casket was being lowered into the ground when she looked back. Lydia's family was locked in an embrace, and she could see tears in their eyes. The minister sprinkled holy water over the casket and made the sign of the cross, bringing the service to an end. He moved over to the family, whispering condolences and shaking hands, before assembling the altar children and returning to the church. Many of the mourners began to leave and Hanna heard car engines start up in the street.

She waited until Lydia's family was alone before approaching them. Albert and Cynthia stood at the lip of the grave, supporting each other as if they might fall if they let go of one another, and Clara Harding held Emily's hand tightly in her own. Albert stood stiffly erect, his suit hanging off his bony frame, his face slack and pale in the sunlight. Silent tears coursed down Cynthia's lined face and her lips seemed to be moving. Perhaps she was praying or simply saying good-bye to her first-born daughter. Hanna felt an ache tighten inside and push all the way to her toes.

She swallowed around the lump in her throat. "Mr. and Mrs. Tomlinson?"

They turned wet eyes towards her and Cynthia smiled through her tears when she recognized her. "Hanna. How nice of you to come."

"I'm sorry for intruding, but I wanted to offer you my deepest sympathies," she said, extending her hand. Albert shook it limply and Cynthia pulled her close for a hug. Hanna smelled lavender and shampoo in the brief contact, and then Clara Harding was introducing herself and shaking her hand. The blue of her eyes, so deep they were almost violet, startled Hanna as she again offered condolences and complimented the woman on her touching eulogy. Then she lowered herself to a crouch in front of Emily, took her small hand in hers and told her she had never heard such a beautiful speech before.

The little girl blushed. "I wrote it all by myself," she said.

Hanna smiled. "Your sister would have been so proud. It was perfect."

It wasn't until she had walked back across the cemetery to her car that she finally gave in to tears that coursed hotly down her face.

Chapter Eleven

KIRK ANDREWS' HOUSE was a huge Victorian with a wrap-around veranda and gingerbread trim along the edges of the shingled roof. It sat in the middle of a well-manicured property that was full of ancient oak and chestnut trees. Waves of purple petunias cascaded down from painted pots on each of the steps leading up to the wooden front door.

Hanna parked across from the house. A grey Toyota pickup and several cars were crammed in the driveway in front of a detached garage, with more spilling out into the street. She checked her reflection in the rear-view mirror and noticed that most of her eye makeup had washed away with her tears. She rubbed the skin under her eyes with a wet finger to remove traces of smeared mascara, applied some lipstick and ran a hand through her hair. Then she grabbed her purse and started towards the house.

Kirk opened the door before she could knock and led her down a hallway past a large living room decorated with tasteful furniture. He opened a door, and she followed him down wooden stairs into a finished family room that was comfortable and roomy with mismatched sofas and chairs facing a pine entertainment centre. The flat-screen television was tuned into Much Music; the sound turned down low.

Lydia's friends stopped their conversations as Hanna entered. Kirk introduced her and she smiled a greeting, offering her condolences to the group. They thanked her and made room for her on the sofa, pushing aside clothing, magazines and cushions, and

offered her a drink. She accepted a Coke and told them why she
was there as she took out a notebook and pen from her purse.

"I thought it would be a nice gesture to share some of your
thoughts and feelings about Lydia, some insight about the kind of
person she was," she explained.

They all started talking at once, then stopped and laughed. It
was a welcome icebreaker and they relaxed a little as Kirk sat down
beside Hanna and suggested they go around the circle, one at a
time. He elected to go first.

"Well, you already know my name and all I have to say about
Lydia is that she was one of the best friends I ever had. I knew her
a long time. I was a year older but we did everything together. We
caught frogs in the summer; we built snowmen in the winter. Our
families were friends, too, and sometimes her parents would hang
out with mine and play cards. We drifted in high school, she had
new friends and all, but we still got together once in a while and
went to parties and stuff. I think what I'm going to remember most
about Lydia is that she was always trying to make everyone laugh.
She was such a joker."

Heads nodded and the girl sitting next to Kirk patted his back.
Hanna recognized her from the church; she had been Lydia's best
friend in high school.

"My name's Robin McIntyre," she started in a voice strained
with tears, "and I remember the day I first met Lydia. I was new at
Midland Secondary School and didn't know anyone; my family had
just moved here from Ottawa. But that first day, she came up to me
in the cafeteria and said something like 'I hope you don't mind, but
it looks as though you could use a friend'. I said sure and from that
day on, we did everything together. After high school, she went to
Sheridan and I went to the University of Toronto, but we always
kept in touch. She was a great person and I'm going to miss her so
much."

She stopped, wiping her eyes with a tissue, and gestured to the
dark-haired guy sitting next to her on the floor. He wore three
studs on each ear and his arms were covered with tattoos. His black
hair was tied in a ponytail and his chin was dark with stubble.

"Jay Connors," he said in a deeply rich voice, extending a hand to Hanna. "I only met Lydia a few months ago when I transferred into the Engineering program from another college but I found out pretty quick that she was smart and funny. All the profs liked her. Hell, everyone liked her. She had a great sense of humour and she was always doing little things for people. I remember once her roommate had missed a few classes so Lydia cancelled her plans one night to help her study. She really was nice that way."

A good-looking blond named Terry Banks was next and Hanna listened as he eulogized his friend, taking notes when something struck her as interesting. She allowed everyone time to talk, knowing it was important for them to say what they wanted about their friend. This process was as much about healing as it was about reminiscing.

When the last of them, a college classmate named Suzanne Tremblay, had finished talking, Hanna explained that she had several questions she needed to ask, some of which might be a little painful. She also asked if there was a picture of Lydia she could borrow to go along with the story, since she had not taken any at the funeral. Kirk offered to find one for her and disappeared up the stairs.

"I don't know how much you know about the details of what happened to your friend," she began, looking into their eyes in turn, "but you were all questioned by the police about what happened?"

Heads bobbed up and down and they all started talking at once again.

"They told us she was beaten pretty badly, and cut up, too," Terry said and Suzanne let out a sob. He reached across the table and squeezed her hand. "They said her face was all smashed up and that she was... raped."

"That fucking bastard," Jay exploded, the venom thick in his voice. "I don't have to tell you what I'd do to that animal if I ever got my hands on him. Sorry about the swearing, but the psycho wouldn't last an hour. I'd kill him with my bare hands."

"Too bad we don't have the death penalty here," Robin said, moving to Suzanne's side and rubbing her back in soothing strokes.

"It's the least this sick guy deserves."

Images of a battered body floating in water tore at Hanna's mind. She couldn't have agreed more. Even the death penalty would never be enough punishment for someone who had been capable of doing what he had done to Lydia. She hoped none of the grieving faces in front of her knew any more than they absolutely had to, and that they would never know the true extent of an evil so fetid it could never be fully grasped, never mind understood.

Kirk returned with a head shot of Lydia. Her pale hair pooled on her tanned shoulders and her smile lit up the blue of her eyes. It was perfect and Hanna thanked him, carefully tucking the photograph in her purse.

Then she asked them to relate in their own words what had happened that weekend on the camping trip.

"It was the greatest weekend… until Monday morning." Suzanne swiped at her nose with a tissue. "I remember Lydia telling me she'd met this guy, when was that? Sunday afternoon? Yeah, she'd been swimming and when she came back, she said she'd met this guy and that he had invited her to a party that night. She was so excited… she said he was a dream come true. Tall, dark and handsome. She went on and on about him. I told her way to go and wished her luck." She stopped, her bottom lip quivering, and wrapped her arms around herself as tears ran down her face. "I didn't even offer to go with her."

"It's not your fault, Suze," Jay said, passing her a tissue. "None of us went with her… it wasn't just you."

"What happened Monday morning when you realized she wasn't back?"

Terry cleared his throat, raking his fingers through his blond spikes. "We freaked, man. We didn't know what the hell was going on; she knew we were supposed to leave on the 10 o'clock ferry. Jay figured she'd either passed out at the party or spent the night with this guy, but the later it got and there was still no sign of her, the more pissed off we got. Then, when we realized she wasn't coming, we thought something could be wrong, so Jay and I went looking for her, but we didn't have the first clue about where she could be on the island. After a while, we just went down to the camp office. They got as much information as they could from us about what she looked like, you know, and they started a search party right away. We helped them look for her, but it was like she just disappeared into thin air."

"That's when the cops got involved," Jay said. "The camp people called the police in Midland and they spent a couple of hours searching, but it was totally useless."

"Did Lydia ever experiment with drugs, specifically the kind that are available at clubs? Like Ecstasy? Anything like that?"

Jay looked down at his toes and Suzanne shot Terry a worried look. "You can't put this in the paper, OK? But yeah, everyone does," she said with a shrug of her thin shoulders. "Nothing too heavy, a little pot once in a while, maybe some E if we were out at a club or something. But nothing major. Lydia wasn't really into drugs, she didn't like being out of it, you know. She only tried it a couple of times that I know of. But please don't put that in the story, her parents didn't know anything about her doing any drugs."

Hanna assured them her goal wasn't to cause Lydia's family further pain, but to help her gain a better understanding of what Lydia was really like.

That brought her to her last question. "Did any of you know anything about Lydia being pregnant sometime in the past?"

Silence settled over the room and they all looked at each other with shocked expressions on their faces. Sitting beside her, Kirk fidgeted with the sleeves of his shirt and across from her, Suzanne looked confused.

"You did know she was pregnant not long ago, right?" Hanna tried again, clearly puzzled by the reactions around her. Hadn't the police questioned them about this?

Finally, after another brief moment of silence, Robin spoke up. "This is the first I've heard of any pregnancy. She never told me anything like that." She sounded almost angry or perhaps it was hurt that made her voice shrill.

Terry, Jay and Suzanne all shrugged, looking surprised and

shocked.

"The police didn't ask any of you about this? The medical examiner was positive she'd been pregnant not long ago…"

"I guess it's possible," Suzanne said, and her voice was too loud in the quiet of the room. "She was dating this guy for a while last year. I think his name was Ryan. But I find it hard to believe she was pregnant. She was real careful about things like that."

Hanna surreptitiously glanced at her watch and saw that it almost three o'clock. She felt a familiar tightening in her stomach, the same feeling she always got when she was nearing a deadline. Seven years she'd written for newspapers, seven years she'd faced deadlines almost every day of her life. Yet, they still had the power to make her sweat.

She flipped her notebook closed, thanked everyone for their comments and once again expressed how sorry she was for their loss. She left business cards on the coffee table, asking them to call her anytime if they thought of anything else that might be important.

Kirk stood when Hanna did and, after she'd shook hands with everyone, escorted her back up the stairs into the kitchen.

"Kirk, would you mind if I used your bathroom? That Coke went right through me, I'm afraid," she asked as he closed the door to the basement.

"Sure, no problem. It's upstairs. I'll show you."

Kirk was nowhere to be found when she came out of the bathroom a minute later. She continued down the hall back towards the stairs, passing two more doors. The first was firmly shut but the second was ajar, and Hanna glimpsed a rumpled bed and walls completely covered in posters and pictures. She thought she saw Lydia's smiling face in one of the pictures and hesitated, looking over her shoulder. The hallway was deserted and she pushed the door open with a finger, unable to quell her curiosity.

The first thing she noticed was that the floor was entirely strewn with clothes and sports equipment, the desk hidden underneath mounds of books and papers. She stuck her head inside the opening of the door and was assaulted by the ripe odour of sweat.

She quickly took a step back. Her eyes lifted up to the walls and she couldn't tell what colour they had originally been painted – hundreds upon hundreds of posters, some of rock stars and others of half-naked women, overlapped each other all the way around the room. Hanna was almost dizzy as her eyes swept past again and that's when she noticed it.

Lydia's picture.

Except it wasn't just one picture. More like a shrine. Dozens of photographs covered the entire space above the desk. Every one featured Lydia. She was riding a horse in one, holding a bouquet of flowers in another. She had her arms wrapped around a long-haired dog in yet another. Hanna let her eyes wander over the photographs to the desk, piled high with papers, books and video cassettes. She was drawn to what looked like a photo album lying on top of a tower of books, a giant, hairy tarantula on the cover.

"Yuck," she couldn't help mumbling in response to her aversion to anything resembling a spider as she flipped open the cover. And gasped.

The first photograph she saw featured Lydia kneeling on a carpet, wearing nothing but a tight pair of unbuttoned cut-off denim shorts, her arms crisscrossed over her naked breasts. Hanna quickly flipped through the pages, counting over two dozen similar photographs. Most showed Lydia in various forms of undress, a sexy pout on her face as she smiled for the camera. But the one that shocked Hanna to her core showed Lydia lounging completely nude on a bed, a hand on each of her round breasts, her legs open to reveal a triangular patch of blonde pubic hair. A tattoo of a butterfly could be seen just above her ankle - the tattoo that had been removed by the killer.

Hanna was stunned. Not so much because she was naked, but because she had recognized the bed Lydia had been lying on when the picture was taken.

It was the one in this room.

And it was obvious this room was Kirk's, and it was plain as day that a lot had been left unsaid down in that basement, and that in many respects, Lydia had been just another regular girl with all the same desires and problems of young people everywhere. Sex, drugs and rock 'n roll, she thought.

And a pregnancy that no one seems to know anything about, she reminded herself as she closed the photo album and replaced it exactly as she had found it.

She didn't need to wonder if Kirk and Lydia had been more than friends; the evidence was staring her in the face. People didn't usually strip down to their birthday suits so their friends could take pictures of them in the buff. It just wasn't done. So what was going on here? Had Kirk been Lydia's lover? And if he had been, why hadn't he said anything about it? To the police, to her? And what about this mysterious pregnancy? Could Kirk have gotten Lydia pregnant sometime in the past?

Her mind reeling with questions, Hanna quickly made her way out the front door where blinding rays of sunshine assaulted her eyes. She hurried to her car, turned around in a neighbour's driveway and sped down the street, her thoughts whirling.

Chapter Twelve

SWOLLEN RAIN CLOUDS scuttled low on the western horizon outside the window when Hanna finally looked up from her computer screen. She had just finished importing her story into the text box next to Lydia's photograph, just above the fold of the front page. On the radio, weather forecasts were predicting rain and a possible thunderstorm overnight, with hotter than average temperatures for the next several days.

When she had typed in a cutline under the picture, Hanna glanced at her watch. She was surprised to see that there were still 20 minutes left before her copy deadline, and she was immensely pleased with her efforts.

The layout was simple yet striking in its design, with the headline 'bleeding' into the top of the picture. Jake Belmont had already typed in the headline earlier. A FINAL GOOD-BYE seemed to capture the essence of the story, and the subhead HUNDREDS ATTEND FUNERAL OF LOCAL WOMAN AS MURDER INVESTIGATION CONTINUES was informative without being sensational. She silently thanked Belmont, knowing some of the other papers wouldn't be so kind in their choice of headlines.

Sensational rags every one of them, she thought. She had always abhorred journalism that was calculated to excite and cater to vulgar tastes, and she had always made it a point to work for newspapers of good repute. Those that didn't go out of their way to publish gruesome accident photographs and stories recounting every heinous detail of a killer's work. Those that showed respect for the dead and the families that were left in the wake of such misfortune and evil.

And it was for that very reason she had not taken any photos at the funeral. A picture of Lydia's family weeping around her grave would have been the epitome of poor taste, not to mention blatant disregard for parents who had suffered their worst nightmare - the murder of a child.

Far better to remember Lydia as she had been in the photograph Kirk Andrews had lent her - beautiful and whole, her eyes the sparkling blue of Caribbean seas in her smiling face. There was light and hope in her gaze and Hanna was troubled to think that Lydia had never once in her worst nightmares believed that anything like this could ever happen to her.

Wrenching her eyes from the picture, Hanna reread her story with a critical eye, the editor in her taking over now that the words were up there, black on white. The power and permanence of the written word seized her, as it often had in the past, and she stepped out of herself a little, trying to read the words through the eyes of Lydia's mother.

There was no mention of Lydia's missing patch of skin, no allusion to the horror Dr. Mullen had found stitched inside her body. Not only didn't her parents need any more reminders of the atrocities inflicted on their daughter's body after her death, but she was also determined to do everything she could to help investigators catch her killer. She knew that restricting certain details, especially what the police call 'hold back' or 'key fact' details, could help weed out ninety-nine per cent of nuisance calls. In other words, that bit of information - in this case, the insertion of the snake - was the sieve in which to sift the real killer from all the cranks calling to claim they had done it.

It didn't matter that this was the biggest story to hit this quiet little area of the province in years; it didn't matter that she was the only reporter with knowledge of what the killer had done to Lydia. Other reporters might have thought nothing of writing about this gruesome detail, no doubt driven by self-servitude. But Hanna didn't give a damn about any of it, least of all objectivity, and would have flipped her middle finger to her old journalism professor had she been able. To hell with being a reporter first and a person second, and all of his grandiose expositions on the merits of good journalism. What a crock of shit, she thought. Good journalism was about being able to look people in the eye, and maybe more importantly, it was about being able to live with yourself after all was said and done.

She pushed her chair back and wheeled herself over to Belmont's corner. He lowered *The Star* he'd been reading and glanced at his watch.

"Made it," he said, "with 15 minutes to spare. Way to go."

"It wasn't really hard," she replied, and felt just a twinge of guilt for not letting him know about the hold-back information she had learned. It wasn't that she didn't trust him. But she believed that if he didn't know about it, he couldn't force her to include it in the story. "Most of it was already written, up here." She tapped a finger against her temple.

He smiled, gave her a thumbs-up and set to work. He called up the front page on his computer, perched a pair of glasses on the bridge of his nose and began reading.

Hanna watched him a moment longer, then headed out to the parking lot.

The scent of rain was heavy in the air when she pulled in her driveway twenty minutes later. Her little house, a five-room winterized cottage, had been built in the 1930s on a wooded lot. It was located near the harbour down at the end of a side road in Victoria Harbour, a picturesque little town overlooking the shores of Georgian Bay just minutes east of Midland.

Dusky blue siding and white shutters peeked from among pines and cedars as she walked up the stone path to her front door, flanked on either side by big clay pots full of geraniums, dwarf daisies and cascading petunias.

It was good to be home.

Hanna let herself in, congratulating herself once again on her luck at finding this small gem of a house with its original stone hearth in the livingroom and claw-footed tub in the bathroom. She had bought it for a song and dance, as her father was fond of saying, just four months ago. An estate sale, the children of the deceased owners had been in a hurry to sell. They accepted the first offer she put to them, almost 10 grand below the asking price, and Hanna had dipped into her savings for the down payment. She was still amazed that her mortgage was cheaper than the rent she had paid in Toronto.

There were many other pluses as well - the beach was a five-minute walk away, her neighbours were occasional weekend visitors in the summer, and the only sounds were those of squirrels and birds as they flitted among the trees in her backyard.

She still found it hard to believe that just 14 months ago she had been living on the sixth floor of a high rise in downtown Toronto. Strangers, smog and noise had been her constant companions for five years, not to mention the violence she saw daily in her job as a crime reporter. By the time she'd worked in the field only a few years, she had known every cruel thing that people did to one another. She had done stories on violent home invasions, murdered or abducted children, fatal hit and runs, and boyfriends and husbands stalking and stabbing their estranged girlfriends and wives to death with long butcher knives. She had interviewed teenagers who had killed their parents with stolen guns, mothers who had shaken the life out of their newborns because they wouldn't stop crying, teens who had shot store clerks for little more than pocket change. She had covered car wrecks and highway pile-ups, bank bombings and carjackings, and more fires and drownings than she cared to remember.

Burnout had been inevitable. But it hadn't completely consumed her until the particularly gruesome murder of that four-year-old child, that little boy found dismembered in a popular city park. That had broken her, made her rethink her entire life. She had decided to head north, back to her roots so to speak, and she had answered an ad for a general assignment reporter at *The Midland Post*. She wasn't surprised when Jake Belmont had hired her on the spot, not 10 minutes into an interview, and she had quit her job at *The Star* and moved out of her apartment in the city two days later. The decision to start over had been the right one, but she had not counted on violence following her, certainly not the kind she was facing now – brutal, unexplainable, nightmarish.

Dropping her purse on the oak floor near the door, she kicked off her heels, locked and secured the deadbolt on her door, and went around the house checking windows and drawing curtains closed against a day that had grown prematurely dark with the threat of another storm. A severe weather watch had been called for most of Simcoe County and other parts of southern Ontario overnight, and Hanna made sure she had candles nearby in case the power went out.

She turned on lamps as she headed to her bedroom, unbuttoning her dress and rolling pantyhose down her legs. She slipped into black leggings and a roomy tee shirt, and went to inspect the contents of her refrigerator.

Deciding on a simple omelette and salad for dinner, she grated cheese into lightly beaten eggs and sliced tomatoes and cucumber over shredded lettuce. She blended olive oil, lemon juice and herbs as dressing for the salad and poured the egg mixture into a buttered frying pan. When it was all ready, she carried the food into her living room and settled on the sofa with the television as company. She avoided news shows, clicked past sitcoms and pop videos and sports highlights, finally settling for a movie that had already started.

A panoramic shot of Las Vegas at night, lights and neon glowing from a distance, followed by a slow pan of a Dodge Caravan parked on a lookout. Inside, a boy and a girl are lying on the backseat, making love in the soft glow of the moon peering at the windows. They are young, beautiful and obviously in love, and they move as if it were their first time. Slowly, tenderly.

Hanna clicked the TV off, a lump in her throat. Her first time should have been slow and tender like that and with someone special; she had dreamed the same fairy tale fantasies as young girls the world over. Instead, it had been sudden and terrifying, and it still hurt to think of how naive and innocent she had been at fifteen, how unprepared for the harshness of life, the cruelty of others.

But she wasn't alone. Every day, women get raped by men the world over. Sometimes by strangers, but most often by friends, dates, colleagues, even lovers. That's what had happened to her. Acquaintance rape. Committed in circumstances of privacy and supposed safety and trust, these attacks are the most personal and cut the deepest. Victims often blame themselves and question their judgement.

No wonder it was the most under-reported crime in the country - only a very small percentage of women, something like five or six per cent, report acquaintance or date rape to the police. Hanna herself had never done so, although she had often thought of it over the years. Mostly out of fear that no one would believe her - hadn't her own parents, when she had finally disclosed what had happened to her two years after the fact, swept the whole ugly matter under the rug never to bring it up again?

And, of course, later it was the knowledge that it would have been she, and not her rapist, who would have been put on trial, judged and in many ways, violated all over again.

She wiped a hand over her dry face, relieved that she had managed not to shed a tear while ruminating over the past. But she was feeling edgy and angry as she switched on her computer and opened her e-mail messages.

There were eight, all from readers expressing shock and outrage over Lydia's murder or complaining about the lack of police results. "This man, this killer, should be behind bars already!" read one message, but only one was from a reader who nailed the issue squarely on the head when she wrote that what had happened to Lydia was "a sick power trip for this madman". The operative word here, of course, was power.

All sex crimes, and Lydia's was most definitely that if not more, were about the abuse of power by someone over another. And power, when it came right down to it, was the root of all evil. Not money, or materialism or anything else in the world.

It was time to write her column for the weekend paper, while all of this was fresh on her mind. Her fingers flew over the keys and before an hour had elapsed, Hanna had written more than eighteen inches of copy and the pads of her fingertips tingled.

She was reaching to turn off her computer when the first thunder bolt split the night sky and the rain started its staccato beat against the roof of her house.

Chapter Thirteen

HANNA WOKE TO the sound of her own voice screaming or had it just been the wind howling at her window? She couldn't be sure. And then she heard it again, a shrill ringing right on the heels of another thunderclap, and her heart galloped inside her chest like a racehorse nearing the finish line.

Her cell phone on the bedside table was ringing; the glowing numerals on her alarm clock read 7:02 a.m.

"What the hell?" she mumbled, sitting up and groping for the phone. "Hello?"

"Hanna, I'm so sorry, did I wake you?"

At the sound of Bennett's voice, her eyes snapped wide open and she sat up in bed, throwing the blankets aside. He had never called her at home before and her mind raced ahead, barrelling down dark roads of despair.

"Oh God," she said, "you've found another one."

He filled the line with a long, tired sigh and she could only imagine what new horrors he had come to know. The monster had now struck twice. Did two bodies make him a serial killer? Had he climbed up another step in the echelon of evil?

"Yeah, another one."

Her jaws clenched, Hanna stared out her bedroom window at the dull light of dawn. "Tell me what happened, Tim. I promise, off the record."

He sighed again and when he spoke, his voice was low and quiet. "A bunch of people found her, coming back from an evening of boating. One of the women noticed a shape in the water as they were pulling in to moor the boat at Bob's Marina, just around the corner from the other one. Turns out it was a pair of legs. She called 9-1-1, this was about 10:30 last night, and the next thing you know, we're out in the rain again, pulling another body from the water. Another young woman, someone who could be the Tomlinson girl's twin sister. They look that much alike. Same long blonde hair, blue eyes, build, everything. Same M.O., too. It looks like she was cut up and raped after she was killed. Her face was beaten and there was a snake inside her, too, stitched up. Only difference is that she's been dead longer, Dr. Mullen thinks a month or so."

"Oh my God," Hanna choked out. "She was the first then?"

"Yeah. She's pretty badly decomposed; Dr. Mullen had a hard time with her. He thinks she must have been in the water at least a couple of weeks or longer, so you can imagine how horribly bloated by gas the body was."

"They did the autopsy already?"

"Part of it, the external examination. I had to be there, just got back a while ago."

"What did Dr. Mullen say? Was there an injection site?"

"Yes. I think they'll find this one was also killed with an overdose of something."

"Jesus, Tim, this is so awful." Hanna pressed a hand to her throat, her heart thumping in her chest. "Have you identified her yet?"

"No. We'll have to do it through dental records, I think. The body's too far gone."

Hanna got out of bed, went to her living room and drew the curtains open. Thunder was a faint rumble off into the distance, but rain continued to fall in sheets to the ground. She noticed her front yard was littered with bits of branches and gutted with puddles of muddy water, and she felt like smashing something.

"So this maniac kills and mutilates two women in the space of a month or so, and you guys have got nothing."

He didn't answer.

She sighed hard. "Are you getting anywhere with the employees at Beausoleil?"

"There are a lot of people to talk to, Hanna."

"What about visitors? Day trippers? Campers?"

"Do you have any idea how many people visit that island on any given day? Hundreds, according to Jackson. And they don't all take the ferry. Plenty of boaters use the island, too; they just get up close and drop anchor. Plus, I didn't know this, but many of those little islands all around Beausoleil are privately owned."

"So it could be an employee, a camper, a boater, someone who lives on a private island? Who else? The pope? This is so goddamn frustrating," she exploded.

"It's like looking for a needle in a haystack."

"What about the semen that was found on Lydia? Anything there?"

"Just trace amounts. What little we recovered has been sent for DNA profiling. But with our luck so far, he'll turn out to be a non-secreter."

Only 20 per cent of the population enjoyed the distinction of being a nonsecretor. Hanna had read up on the subject for a column on DNA profiling she had written a couple of months back. If the killer was a nonsecretor, it meant that his blood type antigens could not be found in his other bodily fluids, such as saliva or sweat. It also meant that without a blood sample, his blood type couldn't be determined. Once upon a time, this status would have meant a dead end for the forensic investigation. But with DNA profiling, an assailant could now be identified to the exclusion of all other human beings, provided of course he was caught first and biological samples obtained and compared.

With a start, Hanna found herself abruptly thinking of the photograph she had been sent by *tatler* and she wondered if she would receive another message now that a second body had been recovered. It seemed likely, given that the first had been connected to Lydia's murder. Trepidation flooded through her.

"I wonder if he'll send me another e-mail."

"Damn, I'd forgotten about that. But let's hope he does, Hanna.

If he follows the same format as before with the first e-mail, it just might provide us with a clue as to this victim's identity or at least where she was abducted from." A glimmer of excitement had crept into his voice. "Check your e-mail often throughout the day, all right? And if you get anything from this pervert, let me know as soon as possible."

"I'll check now," she said, moving to her desk. She was relieved and, at the same time, disappointed to see there was no new mail waiting for her. "Nothing." She stared out the window again and felt caught in a maelstrom of frustration. "So what happens now?"

"We're going to give ViCLAS a shot," he answered. "Who knows? Maybe we'll get lucky and get a match."

Pioneered by RCMP Inspector Ron MacKay in the early 1990s, the Violent Crime Linkage Analysis System (ViCLAS) is used by Canadian law enforcement agencies such as the Ontario Provincial Police, the Royal Canadian Mounted Police and the Surete du Quebec, as well as many others in countries throughout the world. The computer program collates and compares data on victimology, suspect profiles, modus operandi, and forensic and behavioural information in all cases of homicide, attempted murder, sexual crimes, non-parental abductions, missing persons and what they were presently dealing with, found human remains where foul play is suspected.

"I don't know if you remember this," Bennett went on, "but two years ago when we had the murder of that doctor in Orillia, ViCLAS linked the case to another in Winnipeg, Manitoba where an unidentified person had killed another doctor in a similar fashion a few months before. That's how we were able to combine our efforts and finally catch him."

"I remember reading about that story. He killed them by bombing their cars, right?"

"Yeah. A homemade bomb under the driver's seat. Ka-boom. If it hadn't been for ViCLAS, the guy might have gone on bombing his way across Canada."

ViCLAS establishes a cross-jurisdictional database on a regional and national level, which means that a sexual assault or any other major crime committed by an offender in Vancouver can be compared against those committed in Toronto, Montreal or anywhere. One of the most important facets of ViCLAS, Hanna knew, was that moving from place to place, or crossing police jurisdictions, was no longer an advantage for the offender. Serial killer Ted Bundy had once said that jurisdictional boundaries and the inability of law enforcement agencies to communicate with each other is what allowed transient killers like himself to avoid identification and capture for so long.

ViCLAS performs two jobs. Step one is tracking. Cops investigating violent crimes complete a crime analysis report containing 263 questions, each of which has a specific purpose, ranging from establishing victimology to developing offender behavioural traits to determining geographical similarities.

Step two involves linking. When all the questions are answered, ViCLAS searches the database for patterns that reveal a serial offender at work. Police can then compare their cases with others throughout the country for links.

The largest ViCLAS centre in the world is located at OPP headquarters in Orillia, housed within the OPP's Behavioural Sciences Section, along with Criminal Profiling, Geographic Profiling, the Sex Offender Registry and others.

"Do you think you'll get a link with this one?" Hanna asked now.

"If he committed a similar crime out there, ViCLAS will find it."

A thought suddenly occurred to her. "It's interesting that both Lydia and this other victim were blonde and blue-eyed. Do you think there could be some connection there? Did Dr. Mullen say anything about this new victim having been pregnant, like Lydia?"

Hanna heard Bennett sigh long and hard and she knew before he told her anything that the news was going to be bad. She felt her body stiffen.

"It's worse than that," he finally said, his voice flat. "I didn't want to tell you until we had more information, but it's going to get out eventually. She was three months pregnant at the time of her death."

Hanna absorbed this information silently, rage burning in the pit of her stomach. She couldn't speak, no words came to mind.

"Fifteen years on the job and I've never seen anything like it," Bennett continued, his voice so low she had to strain to make out his words. "Never had a chance, that poor little baby. Jesus Christ."

Images came at her from the recesses of her mind and Hanna squeezed her eyes shut. Had the madman known she'd been pregnant? Had he deliberately picked her because she *had* been pregnant? *Oh God.*

She found herself thinking about the album of lewd photographs she'd seen in Kirk Andrews's room the day before and let Bennett in on her suspicions that he and Lydia had been more than friends. He agreed that a closer look at Kirk was warranted.

Slumping against the cushions of her sofa, Hanna couldn't get the image of a monster killing a pregnant woman out of her head. "What kind of madman does this kind of thing, Tim? What kind of psycho are we dealing with here?"

"The worst. I don't know much about necrophilia, except what I've read about Jeffrey Dahmer after they found all those bodies in his apartment, but I'm hoping the profile the Criminal Profiling Unit is putting together will give us more to work with."

"What do you hope to learn?"

He explained that an Unknown Offender Profile could be a valuable tool in describing the personality, as well as the behavioural and motivational characteristics of an unidentified offender or unknown suspect – an UNSUB in police speak. As part of the Behavioural Sciences Section, the Criminal Profiling Unit's job was to look beyond the crimes themselves and put the offender's motivations and behaviours under a microscope. He explained that profiling took into account the offender's method of approach, the amount of force he may have used and any precautionary acts he may have taken, like wearing gloves to conceal fingerprints, as well as any patterns in victimology, sequence of acts, trophies he may have taken, and the dump sites themselves.

"Dump sites," Hanna repeated as she thought of Lydia's body

floating beneath water and freed from under a pier at Bay Haven Marina. Now another young woman had been found, her watery grave yet another marina just three kilometres south of Bay Haven. "What can they tell you?"

"In this case? Water's important to him; he's very familiar with Georgian Bay. And, he wanted them found eventually. Otherwise, he would have buried them in some shallow grave, I would imagine."

Hanna found herself thinking about necrophilia again and realized she didn't know much beyond the obvious. What could drive someone to kill another human being for the purposes of raping and mutilating their corpses? She didn't have the first clue.

"Oh hell," Bennett said. "It's a quarter to eight. I've got to get going."

"Me, too. I have to be at the office in an hour."

"Don't forget the press conference later today. The releases are going out this morning."

"Thanks, Tim. I guess I'll see you later, then."

After she hung up, Hanna took a hurried shower and made a mental note to research necrophilia on the Internet later. Just the thought made her nauseous, but she knew it was her best bet in trying to understand something that defied comprehension – a dark and twisted obsession that lived inside the mind of a killer.

Chapter Fourteen

THE WEEKLY WEDNESDAY morning editorial meeting was well underway when Hanna snuck into the lunchroom and sank into a chair. She was 10 minutes late.

Belmont fixed smouldering grey eyes on her. "Nice of you to finally join us."

"Sorry, I've had one hell of a morning."

"So have I. Ran out of hot water right in the middle of my shower and then the stupid dog pissed on my shoes. Can you beat that?"

Hanna took out her notebook and a pen out of her purse. "Yeah, I think I can. They've found another body."

Five pairs of eyes stared at her. The only sounds were the hum of the refrigerator in the corner and the tick-tick-tick of the clock on the wall.

"Jesus," Belmont finally said, passing a hand through his thinning hair. "How do you know this? There's been nothing."

"The body was found really late last night… at another marina," Hanna answered, avoiding his question. She told them only the details she was sure Project Georgian Bay would be releasing later on – the time and place the body was found and the fact that the victim had been dead at least a month. The rest she kept to herself. "There'll be a press conference later today."

Belmont gave her a long, curious look before turning back to his notepad. He scribbled something down, assigned two new human interest stories to Karen, handed Matthew a press release about council's plan to install a bike path around town, and reminded Justin Turner they needed a photo spread for the sports pages.

Then he looked up at Hanna. "I want the whole story by five today… everything they've got. And your column is due, by the way." Flipping his notepad closed, he stood. "Well, that's it, guys. And be *careful* out there," he joked, borrowing the famous line from the show Hill Street Blues, as he did every week when the meetings wrapped up.

Hanna went directly to the fax machine, rifled through the pages in the tray, and retrieved one that had just been sent from OPP headquarters to every newspaper and news outlet in central and southern Ontario. The press conference was scheduled for 1 p.m.

At her desk, she spent several minutes getting herself organized before attacking a pile of phone messages. The first one she saw was from Kirk Andrews. His call had been logged at 8:53 a.m., and included the phone number where he worked. Lakefield Animal Clinic. She had taken Pistachio there for his shots just a few weeks before, after David had told her about his dad's clinic.

She saw again in her mind's eye all the pictures Kirk had taken of Lydia, and she decided she would drop by and talk with him in person before driving to Orillia. She would return the photograph, slip in a few well-placed questions, and see what she could learn.

She designed a page for the front section, cropped photos, and checked her e-mail. Nothing from *tatler* was waiting for her. At eleven, she let Belmont in on her plans for the rest of the day, grabbed her shoulder bag with digital camera, recorder, notepad and the picture of Lydia she had borrowed from Kirk tucked inside, and went out.

Hanna was immediately assaulted by the faint odours of animal feces and antiseptic cleanser when she walked inside Lakefield's Animal Clinic. A pretty, chubby blonde girl of about eighteen was talking on the phone as she typed on her keyboard. She smiled, looked up at Hanna with huge blue eyes, and indicated she would be with her in just a moment.

Hanging up the phone, she swivelled her chair forward. "Can I help you?" The tag she wore pinned to her tee shirt read "Hi! My name is Ingrid".

Hanna asked for Kirk Andrews and the girl told her to take a seat while she went to get him. She disappeared through a door marked PRIVATE, and Hanna glimpsed a sheep dog with mournful brown eyes lying on an examination table before the door swung shut.

A minute later, the girl returned with Kirk in tow. He smiled in surprise when he saw her. "Hanna, what are you doing here?" he asked as he peeled off his lab jacket and hung it up on a peg by the door.

"I just wanted to come by and drop off the picture you lent me. And check on you to see how you're doing."

He grimaced. "Not too well, but I know it's going to take some time."

He took the envelope from her and asked Ingrid to hold it for him. When he turned back to her, Hanna asked him if he had time to talk and he nodded. He led the way outside through a side door and sat down on a lawn chair, waving Hanna into another.

"I read your story this morning. That's why I called you. I just wanted to say thanks, it was great. And I'm sorry I wasn't around to see you out after the interview yesterday. My dog had gotten into some trouble with the garbage out in the backyard."

"That's okay, Kirk, and thanks." She smiled. "I didn't know you worked here."

"Going on three years. I just finished my second year at Guelph University." He shrugged, his palms turned out. "I'm studying to become a vet."

"That's great. Are you also into photography? I noticed your camera yesterday."

"I dabble."

"Me, too. Nature mostly, when I'm not shooting for the paper. Sunsets, flowers, wildlife. What about you?"

"This and that."

"Did you and Lydia stay in touch after she went to college, Kirk?"

The question surprised him. "Sure, we talked on the phone once in a while and I saw her over the holidays last Christmas."

"Did you know she was going camping on Beausoleil that weekend?"

His frown deepened. "She told me the last time I talked to her. I guess that must have been the weekend before she went."

Hanna wondered if he'd been upset or jealous about not being included in the trip, but decided on another course of action. "Kirk, I need to ask you something," she said in a soft voice, "you and Lydia dated at one time, am I right?"

He quickly glanced at her, then away. "Where did you get that idea?"

She shrugged. "I don't know. Just a feeling."

"Well, the answer is no. We were friends, that's all."

"You're sure?"

He stared at her, then looked away again. "Yes. Why wouldn't I be?"

She said nothing for a long moment, looking over the weeds in the adjacent lot. Then she turned and stared him in the eye. "Because friends don't usually take nude pictures of their friends."

"I don't know what you're talking about," he said, his eyes wild as he looked everywhere but at her.

"I'm sorry I looked at them, Kirk, when I was upstairs at your house. I didn't mean to invade your privacy, but-"

"You had no right. No goddamn right." He stood up, his fists clenched at his sides. "I loved her, all right? I took some pictures of her. Big deal. Are you happy? Can I get back to work now?"

"Why didn't you just admit it in the first place? What happened?"

He wiped his eyes with the back of his hand. "It just didn't work out, okay?"

"Did she get pregnant, Kirk?"

He didn't answer. Instead, he wrenched open the door and went back to work.

After lunch at McDonald's, Hanna drove along Highway 12

to Orillia and arrived at OPP headquarters with a few minutes to spare. The visitor parking lot was overflowing with cars and media vans and she had to park in another lot behind the building.

Unlike the last press conference, this one was held on the first floor in a huge boardroom and Hanna wasn't surprised to see the number of media people present. In addition to local newspaper and television reporters from around Simcoe County and the District of Muskoka, there were dozens of others. They represented many of the national newspapers and television stations from Toronto and as far away as Ottawa, and she recognized many – *CBC, CTV, Global News, National Post,* and the paper she'd worked for in the city, *The Toronto Star.* It had to be the biggest gathering of news media in the area since Pope John Paul II's 1984 visit to the venerated Martyrs' Shrine in Midland, Hanna thought, doing a head count. More than fifty men and women, some in suits and others in jeans, crowded around a podium set up on a slightly elevated platform at the front of the room. Dozens of microphones littered the top of it and coloured wires spilled like tentacles to the floor. Camera lights bathed the room in white-hot unreality.

As she always did when the crowds were big, Hanna hung back on the fringes, content to watch and listen. It was amazing how much she could learn that way, so much more than if she were right in the middle of the pack, shouting to be heard above the din of raised voices and jostling for space in front of the podium.

Pandemonium ensued as soon as Bennett appeared through a side door with a small entourage of investigators, and made his way to the podium. Bodies pressed in on each other, feet trampling over wires and other feet. Voices were a confusion of shouted words and only the loudest rose above the cacophony of sound. Hanna watched it all from her spot against the wall, feeling sorry for Bennett. He looked exhausted.

Wearing a double-breasted navy suit with a white dress shirt and a muted blue and grey striped tie, he took his place and silently surveyed the media circus in front of him. After a few minutes of his steely stare, reporters and camera operators gradually pushed back from the podium, fanning out like a deck of cards, and fell silent.

"Thank you. For the purposes of this conference, I will have to ask you to abide by a few simple rules. I will first issue a statement, then we will open the floor to questions. At that time, I would ask you to identify yourselves and your organization before asking questions."

He slipped a finger inside his shirt collar and cleared his throat. He placed both hands on the sides of the podium and began.

"Ladies and gentlemen. As you all know, we recovered a second victim last night at about 11 p.m. after two local couples, returning from an evening of boating, spotted a body floating under the docks at Bob's Marina, located about three kilometres from Bayhaven Marina in Honey Harbour where Lydia Tomlinson's body was found on June 12th. They called 9-1-1 and within minutes our team was on the scene. The body was taken to the Office of the Chief Coroner in Toronto and a full autopsy is scheduled for today."

Bennett glanced down at some notes he had written. "Due to the extent of decomposition of this victim, the Chief Coroner for the province of Ontario, Dr. Terrence Mullen, has determined that this young woman was killed about a month ago, around the Victoria Day weekend, and was three months pregnant at the time of –"

He was interrupted by shouts as reporters, shocked by this information and fuelled on adrenaline, surged forward in a maelstrom of tangled limbs and extended microphones.

"How far along was she? What was the baby's sex?" yelled a petite woman although she was less than three feet away from the podium.

Bennett sighed. "Please, everyone, I will again remind all of you to reserve your questions until the end of my statement." His eyes were green stones in his face as he looked around the room. "As I was saying, Dr. Mullen estimates the woman found last night was about 12 or 13 weeks along. The fetus she was carrying was male. We are asking for your help in publishing the following details in the hopes of identifying this victim and her movements prior to her death: she has blonde hair, about shoulder length, blue eyes, fair skin, and is approximately five feet four inches tall. Determining–"

"You could be describing the first victim, Lydia Tomlinson," interrupted a woman. "What other similarities are there? And are these deaths related?"

"At this time, all I can tell you is that both victims share similar physical characteristics. They were also both savagely beaten, stabbed and sexually mutilated, and found at marinas, but so far, we have not found a connection between their deaths."

He paused again and cleared his throat. "As I was saying, determining weight is never easy, especially when a body has been in water for any length of time, but after examining and weighing her internal organs during autopsy, Dr. Mullen estimates the victim weighed between 105 and 120 pounds. We are hoping the fact that she was pregnant will bring forward someone who knew her, such as a doctor, boyfriend or spouse, or family member. At the present time, dental impressions are being made and missing persons reports around the province are being checked to see if there is a match. So far, we have had no luck but we hope that with your help, we will soon have a name."

The camera lights bore down on him and he loosened his shirt collar again, pulling on his striped tie as a trickle of sweat coursed down the side of his face.

"As of this morning, more than 950 calls have been logged since Lydia Tomlinson's body was recovered last Thursday, June 12th, and detectives are checking every tip. The only clue we have so far in this case is the description Ms Tomlinson gave to her friends of the man she had met the day she went missing. She described him as 'tall, dark and handsome'. We are questioning all employees, from office staff to maintenance personnel, at Beausoleil Island and we're presently working our way down a long list of campers who had signed in at the office the weekend Ms Tomlinson went missing. It's been a long, tedious process involving hundreds of man hours spent on the phone as many of the people who camped on Beausoleil Island that weekend are from out of town, some are even from out of the country. For that weekend alone, more than 180 people signed in, not including their guests. As well, this number by no means includes boaters who visited the island on their own that weekend nor any day trippers, people who rode the ferry across to spend a few hours there. It's been estimated by officials at Georgian Bay National Parks that approximately 150 to 200 people took the ferry across each day of that weekend. However, since they are not required to register their names to board the ferry, it is impossible to track these people down. But we are appealing to anyone who traveled to Beausoleil that weekend either by boat or by ferry and who may have noticed anything or anyone suspicious, to please contact their local detachment or Crime Stoppers."

Bennett produced a tissue from a pocket and wiped his brow. "As with the two men who found Ms Tomlinson's body, we have questioned the two couples who spotted this latest victim, as well as staff and boaters at both Bayhaven and Bob's marinas and residents who live close by. So far, no one we talked to has reported any suspicious activity around the time of the Victoria Day weekend, which is when we believe the killer may have dumped the body of the latest victim, nor the following days after the first weekend of June when the body of Ms Tomlinson may have been disposed of."

The floor was then opened up to questions and reporters once again crowded around the podium, holding up recorders and microphones in the air.

"Mark Truscott, *CTV News*. It seems like the victims shared a lot of similarities. Is there a serial killer on the loose in cottage country?" asked a tall guy with a ponytail.

Bennett held up a hand. "First of all, according to FBI protocol and our own, it takes three victims to be classified as a serial killer. And yes, there are similarities between the two victims, but at this time we can't say with any degree of certainty that they were killed by the same offender." He pointed at someone else.

"Hal Johnson, *CBC*. Can you elaborate on the mutilations you mentioned earlier?" asked a bearded man with a shiny, bald pate.

"At this time," Bennett said, "we are withholding certain key fact evidence of the crimes in an effort to help us flush out the real killer. As you all know, notorious crime investigations often generate what we call the 'nutbar factor' – people who feel compel to confess to the crimes although they are innocent. We have had several of these types of calls already, as well as many from psychics and clairvoyants who claim to know where the victims were killed. One even went so far as to offer the services of his goat," he said, cracking a smile, "which he claimed possessed rare powers of ESP."

Guffaws and chuckles erupted around the room.

"You still haven't answered my question," the same man persisted when the laughter died out.

"I'm sorry. All I can say is that both victims were brutally, sexually mutilated." It was obvious he was having a hard time; his face reddened a little more with each word and his tone grew hard.

"Jean Montagne, *The Ottawa Citizen*. In an earlier press release, it was mentioned that sperm had been found in the first girl. Have the results become available?" asked a young reporter, his *accent quebecois* like a melody to Hanna's French-Canadian ears.

"Not yet. Trace amounts of semen were collected and what little we were able to recover has been sent for DNA profiling. It will prove invaluable once we have a suspect in custody. We will then be able to compare his biological samples."

"Excuse me, monsieur," piped up the same reporter, "but how is it possible that semen was recovered when the victim was found in water? Wouldn't the water have washed it away, no?"

A muscle twitched in Bennett's jaw and Hanna sympathized with his obvious dilemma. She had pondered that same question herself and had surmised that trace amounts of semen could only have been preserved as a result of the snake essentially acting as a plug, thus sealing the vagina and preserving evidence. The fact that Lydia had also been stitched shut would have further contributed to this factor. She shuddered, aware she was the only reporter in the room with knowledge of this brutal and heinous indignity.

"I can't answer your question," Bennett was saying, "because it concerns the mutilations I spoke about earlier."

"Doesn't the public have a right to know?" persisted the reporter.

"Absolutely not. Releasing these details could seriously hamper our investigation," Bennett replied, an edge to his voice. He turned to someone else and the reporter mumbled something that sounded a lot like *'mange de la merde'* under his breath. Thinking how fortunate she was to be fluently bilingual and smiling to herself, Hanna sincerely hoped Bennett didn't know any French. He had just been told to eat shit.

A woman who had already asked a question earlier waved her arm in the air. "Do you have a profile of the killer?"

"No, but our Criminal Profiling Unit here at headquarters is presently working on an unknown suspect profile. The report won't be ready for a couple of days."

Hanna stepped forward. "Hanna Laurence from *The Midland Post*. What's your advice to women? How can we protect ourselves?"

"My advice is to exercise extreme caution, especially when meeting or being approached by strangers. Don't take unnecessary risks. This is a very sadistic killer we are dealing with here, so follow your gut instincts and report suspicious persons or activity to the police immediately."

"Thank you."

The conference wrapped up after several more questions and reporters soon packed up their cameras and assorted gear. One of the first to leave, Hanna was soon following a long line of traffic on the highway heading back to Midland.

Chapter Fifteen

RAIN BURST FROM swollen clouds, drenching the highway and pounding on the windshield. Hanna eased up on the accelerator, switched on her wipers, and saw a zigzag of lightning split apart the sky as she neared the exit to Waubaushene.

On a whim, she took the ramp and drove through the quiet hamlet to Albert and Cynthia Tomlinson's home, a comfortable split-level bungalow located just seven doors down from Kirk Andrews's house in the middle of a cul-de-sac. English ivy clung to the pale brick, covering the entire east and south sides of the house. Cedar trees formed a hedge around the property and peonies in full bloom spilled out of flowerbeds, their giant fuchsia heads bent from the weight of heavy rains.

Hanna parked in the driveway behind a Jeep Cherokee and made a dash to the front door. Rain fell on her head, plastering her hair to her skull. She blinked water out of her eyes and pressed the bell.

The door opened slowly and Cynthia Tomlinson stood in the entryway, dressed in a tattered housecoat. Her hair stood up on end on one side of her head and her grey eyes were lined with dark smudges, the trademarks of little or no sleep. They lit up briefly when recognition dawned and she motioned Hanna inside.

"What a surprise! What are you doing here?" she asked, ducking into the guest bathroom to her left and grabbing a towel.

"Thank you," Hanna said, moping her face with it. "I was driving back from Orillia and thought I'd stop by to see how you were doing. I hope this isn't a bad time?"

"No, no. Not at all. It's just been a slow day," Cynthia said, indicating her housecoat and patting her hair down. "Albert took Emily to her grandmother's. Can I get you something? I've got some coffee made."

Hanna accepted and Lydia's mother led her through the hallway to the kitchen. She busied herself with pouring coffee into two mugs, and Hanna glanced around the cozy green and white kitchen. A picture on the wall near the refrigerator caught her eye, a framed black-and-white photograph of the Tomlinson family laughing as they splashed each other at the beach. Lydia, in a one-piece swimsuit, couldn't have been more than 14 or 15, her little sister four or five. She felt an ache spread across her chest.

Mugs in hand, Cynthia led the way into the living room. Hanna sat in the same flowered chintz chair she had sat on two weeks before when Cynthia and her husband had been frantic with worry over the disappearance of their eldest daughter and had turned to the media for help. Cynthia perched on her white leather sofa and Hanna remembered how she and Albert had sat there during that first interview, clinging so tightly to each other they had seemed sown together like Siamese twins. But she remembered their tears most of all and the dread she had seen leeching their faces of colour and hope.

"They called me this morning, about the other girl they found. I can't believe this. What kind of monster does this? I've been walking around the house in a daze."

The kind who kills for his own sick pleasure, Hanna thought. The kind without a shred of conscience or remorse. "I'm so sorry, Mrs. Tomlinson," she said, reaching over to place her hand on the woman's arm.

"I don't know how much more I can take," Cynthia said, her voice faltering. "They didn't tell me much when they called. What did they say at the press conference?"

"Not a lot, I'm afraid. They still have no suspects, no leads, just a lot of questions. And they still don't know who she is. They said they were working on missing persons reports and taking dental impressions."

Cynthia clenched her hands in her lap. Her eyes filled with tears and when she blinked, they coursed down her cheeks like the rain against the windows overlooking the street. "Do they think it's the same guy? How many others will die before they catch him? I'm going out of my mind... I can't sleep, I can't eat. It's all I can think about."

Hanna moved to the sofa and Cynthia buried her face against her shoulder, sobbing without making a sound. Hanna swallowed around a lump in her throat, her own eyes wet and her heart breaking with sorrow for this woman who had lost so much.

Cynthia straightened herself up, grabbing tissues from a box on the coffee table to blot Hanna's wet shoulder. "I'm so sorry. I ruined your blouse and made you cry."

Hanna smiled as best as she could. "It's okay, Mrs. Tomlinson. It's just an old blouse. But I am worried about you. Is there anything I can do?"

Cynthia shook her head. "You're so kind and sweet. Thanks for asking."

Hanna took a deep breath. "Can I ask you something? It's about Kirk Andrews."

Cynthia's face hardened and her eyes narrowed to slits. "What about him?"

"You don't like him."

"No, never did. There was just something about him that didn't feel right, even when he was a little boy," she said and her hand found its way to her throat.

"Did the police talk to you about Lydia's pregnancy?"

She nodded, her hand scrunching and releasing the material of her housecoat. "I was shocked when they told me. I'd had no idea."

"Do you know when this might have been? Did she have any boyfriends?"

Cynthia slowly shook her head. "Lydia didn't bring a lot of her boyfriends home."

Hanna's mind flashed on the pictures in Kirk's album. "What about Kirk?"

Cynthia's eyes widened. "You mean Kirk and Lydia? I don't think so. They were friends, but I don't think Lydia would have been interested in him in that way."

As gently as she could, Hanna told Cynthia about her conversation with Kirk Andrews that morning at Lakefield's Animal Clinic. She decided not to tell her about the photos Kirk had taken of Lydia. The woman had suffered enough.

"That's what he said? That they were dating?" The expression on her face was incredulous. "I find that hard to believe." Abruptly, she stood and began pacing.

After a moment, she stopped in front of the mantel and picked up a framed picture of a younger Lydia. She turned back to Hanna, the frame bobbing in her hand. "He took this picture of her." She studied it closely, then bent her lips to the glass, her eyes filling with tears. "He was always running around with that camera of his, taking pictures of everything and everyone whether you wanted to have your picture taken or not."

Hanna remembered the camera slung around his neck at the funeral as she watched Cynthia replace the frame on the mantel and step up to the window.

"For her eighteenth birthday, he gave Lydia an album full of pictures he had taken of her. Some were actually quite good, but then again, Lydia was very photogenic."

"Would you still have it?"

"It's in the desk drawer in her room. Do you want to see it?"

"If it's not too much trouble."

"None at all. I'll show you," she said and Hanna followed her down the hall. Cynthia hovered in the open doorway to Lydia's room, and she braced a hand against the doorframe, tiny sounds bubbling out of her.

"Mrs. Tomlinson? Are you all right?"

She swallowed hard and blinked back tears as she looked at Hanna. "I'm sorry, I just can't go in... I haven't set foot in here since all this happened."

"It's okay. I don't need to see the album."

"No, no. Go ahead, take your time. It's in the top drawer of her desk. I'll just wait in the kitchen." She walked back down the hall towards the opposite end of the house.

Hanna hesitated at the threshold, her eyes roaming around the small room. A canopied double bed with a ruffled bedspread held an assortment of white stuffed animals and a spacious window seat featured plush cushions and billowing lace curtains. A book by one of her own favourite authors rested face down on the carpet near the window – *The Body Farm* by Patricia Cornwell - and she imagined Lydia sitting there, curled up against the cushions, and the ache in her chest expanded a little more.

Walking in, Hanna spun around in a circle. She had wanted to visit Lydia's room the first time she had been here to interview Albert and Cynthia, but she had not wanted to add to their pain by asking. She took everything in now – the posters of Robert Pattinson from the Twilight saga and the Jonas brothers tacked up to the walls, the chest of drawers painted purple and stencilled with tiny flowers, the basket with its assortment of makeup compacts and perfume bottles on a bedside table, the desk with a pile of textbooks on one side and a television set on the other.

She opened the top drawer of the desk and pulled out a photo album with a sunflower on the cover. She sat down on the bed to look at it and was struck by the quality of Kirk's photography – Lydia breathed life in every picture. It poured from her soul through her eyes and her smile, and Hanna could not look away from the beauty she saw in each of the photographs. She had to admit, Kirk had more than a little talent.

Closing the album, she opened the drawer to put it back inside and glimpsed something shoved way in the back. She reached in and pulled out a music box. A tiny ballerina spun to tinny music when she lifted the satin-lined lid. Some of the material had frayed at the edges of a corner and she peeled it back, surprised to see a folded piece of paper tucked in behind the lining. Curious, she took it out and unfolded a poem.

REMEMBER

I was running in the spring mist, far away from our fiery kiss.

I remember looking into your eyes. Now, I hear the echo of my cries.
I was running in the summer rain, far away from our words of pain.
I remember holding your body tight. Now, I hear the silence of the night.
I was standing in the autumn sunset, far away from the place where we
had met.
I remember your touch on my hair, and I know in my heart that I still
care.
I was walking in the winter snow, far away from our love, once aglow.
I remember...

It was signed "I'll always love you, Kirk". Hanna turned the piece of paper over and noticed something written down near the bottom. A phone number next to the letters DRT. She frowned as she scribbled the number and letters on her palm, noticing that the handwriting on both sides of the paper was the same. She replaced the folded piece of paper inside the lining and pushed the music box to the back of the drawer.

In the kitchen, she found Cynthia staring out the window at the rain, her eyes vacant like the boarded-up house across the street.

"Mrs. Tomlinson?"

She jumped in her chair, a hand splayed across her chest. "Oh! You scared me."

"I'm sorry," Hanna said. "Thanks for letting me look at the pictures. They're beautiful."

"Would you like some more coffee?" Cynthia asked, getting up from her chair.

"Thank you, but I should be getting back to the office."

Cynthia nodded. She walked Hanna to her front door and hugged her tightly, thanking her for stopping by.

Hanna wrote her home number on the back of a business card and pressed it into Cynthia's hand. "Please, Mrs. Tomlinson, if there's anything I can do, let me know. Anytime, day or night."

Hanna hugged her again and dashed through the rain to her car. She waved as she backed out of the driveway, her heart breaking again at the sight of the woman standing on her veranda, rain and tears streaking her face.

The conversation she'd had with Kirk that morning tumbled around inside her head all the way back to the office. But despite the nude photographs of Lydia he had taken, the lies he had told her that morning, and the obvious dislike Cynthia had shown for him, Hanna could not imagine him killing anyone, let alone mutilating a corpse. She had to admit the idea seemed absurd - Kirk Andrews reminded her of a puppy begging for scraps at the table. His was not the face of a killer.

Still, she was quick to remind herself that not all killers looked like what they did. Ted Bundy and Paul Bernardo were perfect examples.

It was almost four o'clock when she parked her car in the office lot and rounded the corner into the newsroom. All she could hear was the clickety-clack of fingers hitting keyboards – a sure sign deadline was looming.

She wasted no time getting started. It took a couple of tries, but once she was satisfied with her lead, the rest of the story flowed easily enough. In no time, she was filing her story over to Jake's desk. Then she called Bennett, reaching him on his cell.

"Hanna, hi. Sorry, but you got me at a bad time. I'm right in the middle of a meeting now," he said.

She told him she had some interesting information concerning Kirk Andrews and asked him to call her back when he had a moment. He surprised her by suggesting that he drop by her place around eight instead, on his way home.

"Great," she said through a big grin, pleased that she would be seeing him again in a couple of hours.

Returning to her desk, she rummaged around in her bag for her memory stick and plugged it into her computer. She was only vaguely aware that the newsroom had emptied as she opened her column and set to work finishing the piece. She added information concerning the latest victim found and was just about to write the concluding paragraph when she remembered she wanted to watch the news.

She walked over to Belmont's desk and turned on the television mounted on a platform on the wall. She found a national news show and stood listening as the anchorwoman lead off with the top story, entitled "Cottage Country Murders". As soon as she was done introducing the piece, the screen filled with a beautiful aerial shot of Beausoleil Island and the many smaller islands dotting Georgian Bay's shoreline around the area of Honey Harbour. A man's voice broke over the image.

"This is cottage country in beautiful Georgian Bay, an area that draws thousands and thousands of visitors, cottagers and campers each year. It seems impossible to reconcile this picturesque setting with anything but boating, sunbathing and camping, yet the Ontario Provincial Police's Criminal Investigation Branch has doubled its efforts in a massive manhunt for a killer who may be responsible for two deaths in this region.

"A second body was recovered last night from under the docks at Bob's Marina, just three kilometres from the location where the first victim, who has since been identified as 19-year-old Lydia Janice Tomlinson, was found by anglers five days ago."

The aerial shot disappeared and the screen filled with Lydia's graduation photograph. Hanna's jaw tightened as she listened to the horrible details of her murder and watched footage of her parents clinging to each other at her gravesite.

Then they were gone and Detective-Inspector Tim Bennett appeared, his face grim as he stood in front of the podium at the press conference held earlier at OPP headquarters. He described the physical characteristics of the latest victim found, including the fact that she had been pregnant, and made an appeal to the public for any information that could lead to her identity or to the apprehension of her killer.

Hanna clicked the television off and caught a glimpse of something scribbled on her palm. Instantly, she remembered the letters and number she'd seen written on the back of the poem she'd found in Lydia's music box. She grabbed her phone and dialled.

After three rings, an automated voice message came on. She listened intently, her brow furrowing, and then replaced the receiver in its cradle.

"Jesus," she mumbled. "I should have known. DRT. Of course. Dr. T. Why didn't I think of that?"

She had just reached the office of Dr. Timon, obstetrician and gynecologist.

Chapter Sixteen

HANNA FOUND HERSELF thinking about her conversation with Kirk again as she drove home. She thought of how he had denied that there had been anything more than friendship between himself and Lydia. She thought about the poem he had written to her and the information he had scribbled on the back of it.

Had he gotten Lydia pregnant and she'd decided to get an abortion? Had he lied and avoided Hanna's questions because he was terrified of being found out? By his parents, his friends, his employer? Or was his motivation more complicated, more sinister than that?

She continued to ponder these questions as she followed slow-moving traffic along Highway 12 to Victoria Harbour and made the left-hand turn into the village.

Pulling in her driveway, Hanna groaned out loud. Her front yard was a swampy mess of broken branches and soggy patches of grass. Stalks of hollyhocks growing along the fence had been snapped like brittle bones, their blossoms now bathing in mud, and several shingles on her roof had come loose. She kicked her car door shut, muttering a string of expletives, and made her way to her front door.

Pistachio rubbed his body against her legs as soon as she came inside and drew the deadbolt. She dropped her shoulder bag on the floor and picked him up. Rubbing the cat's chin, she suddenly remembered that she had not checked her e-mail since that morning.

Sitting in her swivel chair at her desk, she turned on her computer and logged on to the Internet. She knew details of the second body found had already been reported on radio stations and the local and national six o'clock news, but she was still amazed at how fast news traveled in a small town. It seemed everyone had heard the news already and she counted thirty-nine new messages in her inbox, a record for her.

When she went through the list, Hanna was startled to see the same address as before appear in her inbox, tatler@Zebra.net. She froze, her finger lifting off the mouse as an image of the first photograph she'd been sent flashed in her mind. Her heart sped up; her palms grew clammy.

Oh God, she thought, *here we go again.*

Like the first, this message contained only one word, AMIKWANDAG, all in upper case letters, and included an attachment. She hesitated, the arrow flashing endlessly on the icon. Would the word point to the location where the second victim found had been abducted from? Would the attachment feature another depraved photograph of a necrophile defiling a young corpse?

Sweat beaded on her forehead as she clicked on the attachment. An image began to appear on her screen and she shifted in her chair, every muscle in her body tense as she mentally prepared herself for what she was about to see. Pistachio sensed her anxiety and scurried off her lap, meowing loudly in protest.

The picture was different than the first, but the theme was certainly the same. It showed a side view of a man, fully clothed except for the zipper of his trousers undone, standing at the head of what looked like an autopsy table on which lay a nude female corpse. She had been laid on her stomach, her head positioned at the level of the man's crotch. It wasn't hard to imagine what was going on.

Wishing Bennett was already there, Hanna saved the image and tried to make sense of it all. Was the killer sending her these messages? Was he toying with her? Or was *tatler* someone with a lot of inside information, as she had mentioned to Bennett?

As she was thinking of him, a knock sounded on her front door. She leapt from her chair and went to her bay window to look out. Tim Bennett stood on her front stoop, still wearing his navy suit, and she smiled as she unfastened the deadbolt and opened the door.

Hanna let him in and wasted no time in telling him about the message she had just received. Leading him to her computer, she opened the attachment on her screen.

Bennett grimaced and took a step back as the image appeared. "Christ. Can I see the first one again, too?" he asked as he peered at the screen over her shoulder. She felt his peppermint breath fan her skin and forced her mind to concentrate as she searched through dozens of messages to locate the first one. She finally did and proceeded to open it.

"This is some sick, twisted stuff. Jesus." He pursed his lips, an expression of disgust on his face, as he studied the photographs, clicking from one to the other. "And look… it was sent to you around the same time as the last one."

Hanna checked and sure enough, the message had been sent to her at 12:04 p.m. "Do you think that's significant?"

"Maybe, maybe not," he said, helping himself to her phone and punching in a number. Waiting for the connection to go through, he covered the mouthpiece and turned to her. "I'm going to need you to send this up to E-Crimes. You can do that, right?"

She nodded. "How're they doing with tracing, by the way?"

"Not well, I don't think. They keep hitting a brick wall no matter what they do, but they did determine that the first image you got wasn't an actual photograph of Lydia. Probably something the bastard downloaded off the 'Net."

Hanna stood by her window, staring at the mess on her front lawn while he talked to someone named Terry on the phone. A minute later, he hung up.

"All right, Hanna, they're waiting for it." He gave her the e-mail address and within seconds the image was in Orillia.

He moved to the sofa and sat down, passing a hand through his hair. "Well, I have to admit, this is getting worrisome." He looked at her, his eyes deepening in colour, like pools of water under night skies and the concern she saw in them and heard in his voice slammed a bolt of fear through the core of her body. Reality hit home. This was no joke anymore. Not that it had ever been, but now she could almost smell the scent of danger and she bit her lip as she took one of the wing chairs flanking her stone hearth. She didn't trust herself to sit too close to Bennett, not when she was feeling so vulnerable and afraid.

He sighed long and loudly and she noticed for the first time the shadows beneath his eyes, the lines around his mouth. Something stirred in her heart.

"If this turns out to be a clue to this latest victim's disappearance, Hanna, we're not going to be able to discount the possibility that these messages are being sent to you by the killer or someone involved in some way, like you said before. Who else would know all these details?"

"I don't know, Tim, but I'm going to call George Jackson." Hanna went to her desk, found her notebook and located the man's home number. An answering machine picked up and she left a brief message and her cell number.

"So what's this interesting information about Kirk Andrews?" he asked when she hung up and returned to her chair.

She told him about the conversation she'd had with him that morning. "Plus, I stopped in to visit Mrs. Tomlinson after the press conference—"

"How is she making out?"

"For a woman who's lost a daughter to a maniac and buried her just yesterday, I'd have to say better than expected. But you should have seen her face when I mentioned Kirk. No love lost between those two."

Hanna went on to tell him about the conversation she'd had with Cynthia and mentioned finding the poem with the phone number scribbled on the back of the page. "So I called the number when I got back. And get this, it turned out to be the office of a Dr. Timon. An obstetrician and gynecologist."

Bennett stared at her, his brows climbing up his forehead.

"Interesting."

"It was signed 'I'll always love you, Kirk'. I think she got herself an abortion."

"Good detective work, Hanna. We'll check it out."

"Thanks. So what do you think? Is the guy suspicious or what?"

He shrugged. "Suspicious, yes. But that doesn't make him guilty, Hanna. We interviewed him twice, like all her friends, but nothing stood out. He doesn't fit the profile we're working on. Plus, his alibi for the weekend she went missing is airtight. His parents swear he was home with them and didn't go anywhere."

"Do we know if Kirk's parents own a boat? He would have needed one to get to Beausoleil Island if he's the one."

"Way ahead of you. They own a small aluminum fishing boat, moored down at Wright's Marina in Waubaushene. But they haven't been out in it since early May."

"Well… there goes that idea," she said and stood. "You don't have to rush home, do you? Want a beer? Or some wine?"

A look she couldn't decipher crossed his face. "No, no. A beer would be great. No mug, just out of the bottle."

Hanna started towards her kitchen. She returned with two Coors Lights and handed Bennett one, twisting the cap off hers. "So, Tim, are you up for a little surfing?" she asked, nodding towards the computer. "I thought I'd search the web for some information on necrophilia."

Bennett drank half his beer and wiped his mouth with the back of his hand, making a face. "You're serious, aren't you?"

"Of course I am," she replied, pulling up another chair next to hers at the desk.

"Oh God," he groaned as he settled in beside her. "Something tells me I'm not going to like this one bit."

"Well, that makes two of us, then." She was acutely aware of his body mere inches away as she 'googled' the word necrophilia. A small list of sites appeared and Hanna clicked on one promising a historical and social overview.

The page opened immediately. A full-screen image of a man lying on top of a young female corpse made them both wince and Hanna was reminded of the photographs *tatler* had sent her. Transposed over the picture were the perverse lines: "Fresh from the crypt into my waiting arms, I unleash upon you all my charms".

They grimaced at each other as Hanna scrolled down the page to a block of text. The owner of the site had written an interesting introduction to the topic, namely that human beings were as much products of their environments as they were of their genetic makeup. Nature, he went on to say, provides humans with the various abilities to survive but it is our personal experiences and our interpretations of those experiences that make us who we are.

True enough, Hanna thought as she scrolled down past another picture of a necrophile desecrating a corpse, gravestones leaning in the background. She shuddered, unable to stop her mind from imagining the killer with Lydia's dead body, as she found another block of text further down. This one explored the history of necrophilia and how it had been celebrated in ancient cultures as a spiritual connection to the dead. She learned that magic and cult worship had long been fascinated with death and had often contained elements of necrophilia.

One of history's most memorable necrophiles, she read, was Sergeant Bertrand, a handsome ladies' man active in the mid 19th century, whose passion for young female corpses was so intense that he once swam across a lake in winter to get to a cemetery. And while the fetish is generally limited to men, Hanna read about a real American woman who made national headlines in the mid-90s after she stole a hearse with a body inside and disappeared for two days. Hanna vaguely remembered the case and was shocked to read that the woman had been imprisoned eleven days, fined $255 and sent for psychiatric counselling. She wasn't charged with abuse of a corpse, a simple misdemeanour in some states, although she had freely admitted to breaking into funeral parlours and performing various sex acts with close to 40 young male corpses over the years.

"This is sick," Bennett said, his face pale as he read over Hanna's shoulder.

"You can say that again, but I'm sure we haven't seen anything yet."

True to her word, the next section explained that clinically, necrophilia was simply one fetish in a long list of paraphilias ranging from abasiophilia, sex with a lame or crippled partner, to zoophilia, sex with animals. Hanna grimaced and Bennett looked over at her and she noticed his face was getting greener with every word he read.

"Are you all right?"

"Yeah, I think so. But I could use another beer. Or something stronger. Whatever you have."

Hanna sent him to the kitchen to get two more beers. When he returned, she scrolled down to the next section. Necrophilia, they learned, wasn't limited to sociopaths, psychopaths or serial killers. Killing for the sake of having sex with dead bodies, while sensationalized by infamous serial killers such as Jeffery Dahmer, was not the norm. The various professions dealing with the preparation and handling of corpses, the owner noted, have the highest incidence of necrophilic activity. He wrote that the funeral parlour or mortuary is perhaps the "center-most icon representing all contemporary necrophilic activity" today.

"Oh God," she said, squirming. "That's it, I'm being cremated when I die. No way some fat, smelly funeral director is having his way with my body after I'm dead."

Bennett grumbled something and she scrolled down past more noxious pictures, stopping at the next block of text. The owner, describing himself as a self-professed necrophile, attempted to explain the reasoning behind necrophilia, saying that the most Freudian of theories involved the ultimate submission of the body. For the dead person? Hanna wondered, feeling revulsion settle in her stomach.

She had always been open to the concept of 'live and let live', had always tried to be open-minded and tolerant of other people no matter what their preferences were in or out of the bedroom. She wasn't in the habit of judging others and knew that ignorance led to fear and fear to hatred. She believed in free expression and intellectual openness; she believed in choices. But there were limits to what she could accept.

Hanna felt soiled from the inside out as she read the words of a necrophile who described his errant, salacious behaviour as "eroticism of a different sort". Bullshit, she thought, exiting the site and disconnecting. She'd had more than enough and knew Bennett would have logged off long ago.

"My mind just can't get around it," she said, after they had both finished their beers in silence and stared at the jungle animals of her screen saver a long time.

"Me neither." His voice was edged with steel and she watched him get up to go stand by the window. He looked out, and Hanna felt his pain in the drawn lines of his face and saw the hardness in his eyes when he turned to look at her.

"Jesus," he muttered, his voice low. "I know what I said at the conference today, Hanna, but I have no doubt that we're looking for one guy. And I can tell you he's not some screwed-up mortician getting off with a dead body in an embalming room somewhere. He's much worse than that, he's a thousand times worse, because he kills for his own sick pleasure. He killed those girls, used them for as long as he wanted, and then dumped them. In Georgian Bay. In the debris and seaweed under those docks. Like garbage. Their bodies bloated and a goddamn snake inside of them."

He squeezed his eyes closed and opened them again, and gave a tight shake of his head. "We've got the worse kind there is on our hands, a psychopath. We've looked at every sex offender in the county, hell, even in the province, and we've got nothing. No clues, no suspects, no leads."

He suddenly barked out a harsh laugh. "I mean no disrespect to the victims when I say this, Hanna, but we're dead in the water. Just like they were. And there's not a goddamn thing we can do about it."

A muscle flexed in his cheek as he turned back to the window. Hanna knew exactly how he was feeling. She went to stand beside him, close enough to touch him.

"I'm sorry," he muttered, "I didn't mean to blow up like that."

"It's okay, Tim. You have every right to be angry. I'm angry, too, and I can't stop imagining all the unspeakable things this monster did to those girls. But he'll get caught, I have to believe that," she said, her eyes shining with unshed tears.

He stared at her for a long time, and it seemed to her that he was searching for something in her eyes.

In the next moment, his lips brushed against hers so softly she feared she had imagined it. Her heart pounded in her chest as he pulled her closer, moulding his body to hers, backing her against the wall. There were plenty of reasons why she should stop him, right now, before something happened that would change everything between them. He was a cop hunting down a madman; she was a reporter caught in the middle. But her mind was empty, filled only with his sounds, his scent, his touch, and she sank her fingers into his soft hair as they kissed, tongues curling and tasting and sucking. Lust enveloped them like a blanket and she wrapped herself in it, lost in sensation.

He smelled of rain and apples and peppermint, and Hanna felt her legs tremble as he pressed his hard body into hers and let his hands caress her shoulders and cup her breasts. It had been so long since a man had touched her. Every nerve in her body was on fire, every cell alive. Oh God, she wasn't thinking; she wanted him a thousand times more than in her fantasies. She moaned deep in her throat, her eyes tightly closed.

As suddenly as he had kissed her, Bennett pulled away. Confused, Hanna opened her eyes to see him reaching for the suit jacket he had taken off.

"I'm sorry, I don't know what came over me," he said, looking everywhere but at her. "I can't believe I just did that. I'm sorry... I have to go."

Anger flushing her face, Hanna strode to her front door and opened it wide.

Bennett stopped in front of her. "Hanna?"

"Thanks for coming by, Tim. I'll call tomorrow to get an update on the case." Her voice was colder than winds sweeping off the bay in January.

He winced. "Would it matter if I told you I always wanted to kiss you like that?"

She said nothing, but her heart fluttered in her chest.

"It's true. Remember the first time you came to interview me? I wanted to kiss you right then and there. But things are… complicated right now."

A lump formed in her throat. "Go home to your wife, Tim."

He winced again, his green eyes filling with pain. He started to say something, changed his mind, and instead, brushed his thumb across her lips briefly before walking to his car.

Shivering at the touch, Hanna stood in the open doorway and watched him drive away until his red taillights were just dots in the night sky.

Chapter Seventeen

HANNA WOKE TO stifling heat, a stuffy head and skin that felt clammy and feverish to the touch. First heat wave of the season, she thought. Summer's finally here.

Heat waves are not only common in Ontario, they often signal the official start of the summer season. Temperatures soar into the high nineties; the air becomes saturated with humidity. Forecasters use words like 'hot', 'hazy' and 'humid' and encourage people to practice 'safe sun' – on scorching days, it takes less than ten minutes for unprotected skin to burn. But for those lucky enough to live and vacation on Georgian Bay, escape is only as far as the many beaches that surround this great body of water.

Thinking longingly of her favourite beach, Hanna peeled off her damp shirt and traded her usual hot shower for a tepid one. But by the time she drove to the office, her clothes were already stuck to her skin and a moustache of sweat beaded her upper lip.

When she got to the office she stood a few moments under an air-conditioning vent, letting the cool air fan her hot skin. Then she made her way to her desk and looked up George Jackson's numbers again. She dialled the one for his office and was patched through without delay. He picked up on the second ring.

"George Jackson here."

"Mr. Jackson, it's Hanna Laurence from *The Midland Post*. I left a message on-"

"Yes, Ms Laurence," he interrupted. "I'm sorry I didn't return your call… I didn't get home until almost one o'clock in the morning. How are you?"

"Fine, thanks. And you?"

"A little overwhelmed, as you can imagine. The island has been invaded, so to speak, by investigators and the last couple of days have been extremely busy."

"I won't take up too much of your time, but the reason I'm calling is because I received another e-mail. This one spelled A-M-I-K-W-A-N-D-A-G. I wondered if you would happen to know what this word meant since you were so help--"

"Amikwandag? You're sure? What's the spelling again?"

She told him and asked if the word was Ojibway.

"Yes, I think so... but let me check something. Hold on." A plunk sounded in her ear as the phone was dropped on a hard surface. A moment later, he was back. "Sorry I took so long... I had to consult The Dictionary of the Ojibway Language by Frederic Baraga. Great tool. Have you heard of it? Of all the hundreds of studies of North American languages that European missionaries compiled over the years, this one continues to be a useful reference for teachers and students even today. Did you know Baraga was a Catholic priest who came to the new land in the 1820s? He was appointed the first bishop for Upper Michigan... I'm sorry. I seem to be getting off track here."

"That's okay."

"The dictionary lists the word amikwandag as meaning 'white pine'."

"White pine? Like a tree?"

"Yes. But the word specifically means 'white pine'. Let me see.... ah, here it is. The word for 'tree' is mitig."

Hanna jotted this information in her notebook, thanked him for his time and retreated to the picnic table area, her shoulder bag in hand. She was sweating almost as soon as she was out the door; heat rose from the asphalt in shimmering waves only to melt into air that felt laden with moisture against her skin. The only shade was under a great big pine tree whose lower branches bowed to the ground to form a misshapen tepee. This was where she came when she was at work and needed a little time to think or to hide out for a few minutes; no one could see her from the outside. She ducked inside a gap and sat up against the trunk on ground made spongy by thick layers of needles.

So many things were looming in her mind, especially what had happened with Bennett the night before. But she didn't want to think about it now. Instead, she concentrated on what Jackson had told her. She had assumed that the word 'amikwandag' would also point to a specific location, like Pamidonegog had with Beausoleil Island. But while that seemed not to be the case this time, she continued to believe that the word was a clue pointing to the location where the newest victim had vanished from. There was no doubt in her mind that the messages were linked to the murders and that in all likelihood, the killer or someone linked to the killer had sent them to her. She felt a tremor of fear as she stared at the pattern of sunlight dancing on the ground. She needed to call Bennett, but couldn't bring herself to actually do it.

She replayed the kiss in her mind, felt the hardness of his body against hers, smelled the scent of rain and apples on his skin. Why had he kissed her? Why had she let him? He was married, for God's sake. He was a cop, one of her best sources, and a friend. Now everything would change between them, and she could hardly bear it.

Her cell chirped inside her bag and Hanna was jarred as if from a dream.

"Hello?"

"Hanna, it's me," Bennett's familiar voice filled her ear, and her heart lurched. "You got a few minutes?"

"Sure. What's up?"

"A few things… but first I wanted to apologize for last night. I had no right to do what I did and I don't blame you for being angry with me. This case is driving me up the wall and well, there's some other stuff, too, but I had no right and I'm sorry. Can you forgive me and pretend it never happened?"

No, she couldn't pretend it hadn't happened, couldn't deny she had wanted him with every fibre of her being and would have happily taken him to her bed if he hadn't pulled away. She thought of his wife and felt guilty, but it was the truth.

"There's nothing to forgive, Tim," she finally said. "I'm not angry anymore, but I can't pretend it never happened either."

Silence on the other end. Then, softly, "Me, neither."

Oh God, she thought as her heart hammered, what's he doing to me?

"Hanna? You still there?"

"Yes," she said, her voice cracking. "I'm here."

"We should get together and talk about this, but right now isn't a good time. I'm sorry. We got a hit with ViCLAS. The unsolved murder of a 17-year-old girl in North Bay. No buried treasure, if you know what I mean, but the coroner's report listed several stab wounds and mutilations, all postmortem, and guess what? The only antemortem wound was an injection site found on one of her thighs… just like the Tomlinson victim."

"Oh God. No." Her hand tightened around the miniature phone. "When was this?"

"She was last seen on April 4th of this year, almost three months ago. Her nude body was found in a river by a couple of hikers on, hang on a minute… fifteen days after she went missing. April 19th. She was badly decomposed, the ME estimated she'd been dead at least that long."

She shivered in the heat as she pulled a notebook and a pen from her bag and wrote down the information. "What was the cause of death?"

"Respiratory depression due to a massive dose of ketamine hydrochloride," Bennett said. "You're familiar with this drug? You've probably heard it called Special K or Vitamin K or kit kat, even cat valium."

"The date rape drug?" Hanna remembered a story she had done three or four years ago after a rash of rapes at high schools and university campuses in Toronto. The victims had all been drugged with what are known as 'club drugs' - Ecstasy, GHB or gamma hydroxybutyrate, and Special K or ketamine hydrochloride - and then viciously raped. The drugs had started appearing on the scene in the 1980s and had steadily grown wildly in popularity ever since.

Kids "tripping" on "E", or Ecstasy, was now as common a sight at parties, clubs and concerts everywhere as it had been to see kids twisting to Elvis Presley in high school gymnasiums in the 1950s.

"Uh-huh. Did you know it's actually a synthetic chemical? I'm reading from the report now… it's a rapid-acting dissociative anesthetic mostly used by vets to put animals under during surgery. It paralyses the patient from the neck down. In lethal doses or in conjunction with other drugs including alcohol, it causes cardiovascular toxicity, convulsions, asphyxiation, and eventually, the person stops breathing."

Hanna's skin crawled with goosebumps. "You know… Kirk Andrews works at a veterinary clinic."

"Yeah… it's the first thing I thought of, too. We plan on picking him up for further questioning. With this new information and what we already know about him, we have to consider him a suspect now."

"Are you going to arrest him?"

"We have motive and means… but no opportunity. His alibi for the Sunday night Lydia disappeared is airtight, so we'll have to see how things shake up."

"I wonder what he was doing around the time this victim in North Bay disappeared. What was her name?"

Hanna heard him shuffle some papers. "Her name was Marianne Legault. She was a senior at Ecole Secondaire St. Agnes in North Bay. You know where that is, don't you? About two hours north from Orillia, straight up Highway 11."

"I know, Tim. I've lived there before."

He went on as if he hadn't heard her. "Her mother was the last one to have seen her alive. That was April 4th, a Friday, right after dinner. She said Marianne was going to the public library to do some research for an essay. She never made it."

"Jesus. This is getting worse and worse." Hanna squeezed her eyes shut, her thoughts racing along endless dark tunnels. Another victim, another step up the ladder of evil. The words 'serial killer' flitted across the surface of her mind and she felt the hairs on the back of her neck stand straight up. "You think the same guy killed all three?"

"I don't want to say for sure, but after reading the North Bay police report and the coroner's findings, I'm starting to lean that way big time. Too many parallels there. It's got to be the same UNSUB. I sent two of our guys up there to talk to the investigating officers and the girl's friends and family. Or what's left of it, I should say. The father committed suicide a couple of weeks after his daughter was found and the mother's been in and out of mental institutions since all this happened."

"Jesus," she said again, a lump in her throat. A violent death causes hardships no one sees in movies or reads in newspapers. Those left behind are often the true victims of violent crime - the parents, siblings and friends of those who are murdered and must now go on with their lives. "So if it's the same guy, that's... what? About six weeks between her and the time he took the victim you recovered last night?"

"Give or take a few days."

Hanna swallowed. "And if I'm correct, about three weeks between that one and Lydia Tomlinson, right?"

"About that, yes. Or less."

She bit her lip, her mind jumping ahead trying to find an explanation for the decreasing time span between murders. One theory was that serial offenders developed a taste for their work and as their confidence grew, they tried to fulfill their fantasies more and more frequently. Another says that they begin to decompensate, that the neuroses driving them begin to fracture their minds, pushing them toward capture or even death, and murdering more and more frequently is the path they choose.

"You're thinking he's decompensating," Bennett said.

"Either that or he's enjoying himself so much, the sick son-of-a-bitch, he's got to do it more and more often."

"Yeah, that could be."

Hanna would have given a lot for a cigarette at that very moment; she could almost taste the tobacco on her tongue. "So he should be due for another one then. Soon."

Bennett's silence was affirmation enough and after a moment, he cleared his throat. "There's something else you should know."

"What?"

"We got a call last night from a woman who said the victim we found Tuesday night at Bob's Marina might be someone she worked with. She wasn't sure, all she had was the description we made public yesterday. This woman who called, her name's Jody Adamson, she said her friend took off about a month ago, just before the Victoria Day weekend, and hasn't been heard from since."

Hanna's hand was cramping from writing so fast. "And how do we know this information is authentic?"

"She said her friend was three months pregnant at the time she took off."

"Holy shit."

"Yeah, exactly. Adamson said she assumed her friend had returned home to her parents, at least that's what she thought her friend would do."

"What's her name?"

"Hang on," he said, and she could hear the rustle of paper as he searched for the information. "Ah, here it is. Tina Joliet."

"Can you spell that? Her last name, I mean."

He did and went on to tell her that he and another detective were on their way to question the woman who had called. Since she worked at a resort on a private island in the 30,000 Islands archipelago and didn't have transportation to the mainland until the weekend, the OPP Marine Unit was providing a boat.

"A resort? In the 30,000 Islands? I didn't know there were any."

"Apparently, this resort is more like a spa," Bennett said. "She described it as a vacation retreat offering everything from accommodations and traditional cuisine to kayak excursions and guided boat tours. Some really pricey little place tucked away in the wilds somewhere. And get this, it's called The White Pine Inn at the Bay."

It didn't even register at first. Then her mind kicked in high gear and Hanna clamped a hand across her mouth. "Oh God... did you just say The *White Pine* Inn?"

"Yeah. The White Pine Inn at the Bay." Bennett chuckled. "Quite the name... it sounds almost, I don't know, a bit much. Why?"

But Hanna wasn't listening. Her mind whirled as she thought about the word amikwandag and its meaning. And now a woman had called to say she had worked with the victim at a resort on a private island until about a month ago. A private island that just happened to be called The White Pine Inn at the Bay. She fought mounting trepidation as her mind made connections that seemed all too obvious. She didn't believe in coincidences. She had learned long ago to trust her instincts and she clung to them now.

"Jesus, Tim. Listen to me," she said, sweat dripping from her forehead. "I was just talking to George Jackson, and I know you won't believe this, but he said the word amikwandag means white pine."

Silence.

"Tim? Do you understand what I'm trying to tell you?" she asked after a long moment. "This island where the resort is located is called The White Pine Inn. And this word, amikwandag... it's the Ojibway word for white pine. Do you understand? It's the place where this woman was taken from."

More silence followed and Hanna could only imagine the look on his face as he processed this news.

"You're serious, aren't you? Holy Christ," he finally said, biting down hard on the last word. "He's absolutely one hundred per cent sure this word means white pine?"

"He said he looked it up in A Dictionary of the Ojibway Language."

"Jesus. Who is this asshole sending you these messages? How does he know so much? I'm starting to get worried. Really worried. There's no telling what else this sender might know about you."

Hanna's breath clogged in her throat. "If you're trying to scare me, you're doing a good job, Tim."

"I'm sorry, but I don't like this at all." There was a catch in his voice.

"You and me both."

"Oh damn, I'm late for a meeting, Hanna. I'll call you later, all right?"

"Okay, bye."

She disconnected and stared off into the distance, thinking of everything Bennett had told her. Three victims now. She imagined them struggling to breathe, terrified and utterly helpless, and felt rage rise up in her chest at the thought of one killer responsible for all their deaths. A serial killer. A madman.

A few minutes later, Hanna returned to her desk, having made two decisions. One, she wouldn't let some unknown person sending her disturbing messages get the best of her, and two, she would contact the woman who had called the police about her pregnant friend and arrange an interview.

This would be her chance to do a little digging around of her own; an opportunity to satisfy her curiosity about the resort. Besides, she couldn't think of a better way to spend an afternoon than on the sparkling waters of Georgian Bay, also known as the Sixth Great Lake because of its enormous size - 120 miles long and 50 miles wide - almost as large as Lake Ontario. She suddenly remembered something learned long ago in school – the French explorer, Samuel de Champlain, had called it "La Mer Douce", the Sweet Water Sea, the first time he'd ever laid eyes on the bay, sometime in the early 1600s.

The only problem was that she didn't have a boat, but she knew someone who did.

She looked around for Belmont and found him in the lunchroom, stuffing the last bite of a burrito into his mouth. She filled him in on the latest developments with the story and told him about the interview she wanted to do with Jody Adamson at the resort.

Belmont smiled. "You're in luck, Hanna. Trish is on holidays this week and she's been bugging me to go boating. I was planning on cutting out early tomorrow to take her out, anyway, so why don't you come along and we'll head up there in the afternoon. How's that sound?"

"Great. I'll call the resort and set it up, then. Do you need directions?"

"No, I know where it is. And make the interview for about three in the afternoon, if you can. We'll set out about noon, stop somewhere along the way to eat, have a beer, and enjoy some sun, then head up there with lots of time to spare. Just bring your swimsuit. We'll have lunch and everything else covered."

"No, no," Hanna protested. "Let me bring something. I make a pretty good batch of brownies. Or I can bring some wine."

He licked his lips. "Do you make yours with walnut pieces on top?" he asked and when she nodded, he patted his rounded belly and made drooling noises like Homer on The Simpsons. "Then you're bringing brownies. And don't you dare skimp on the nuts."

Chapter Eighteen

THE REST OF the day was filled with writing, interviews and phone calls but Hanna's concentration was shot. She couldn't focus on what she was doing for more than a few minutes at a time and caught herself staring out the window into the middle distance more than once, Bennett's voice like an echo in her head.

There's no telling what else the sender knows about you.

At four, she gathered her things and headed out to the parking lot into broiling heat. The short walk to her car made her feel like she was wading through thick sludge.

Hanna decided to drop in and visit her parents before driving home. She hadn't seen them in over a week and wondered how they were doing. They still lived in the same house she had grown up in, just outside of Midland on a rural concession. Her father had built it himself, log by log, and she still remembered summer afternoons helping him fetch tools and mix cement while her mother cooked and baked in the kitchen.

Pulling in the driveway, she looked up at the house and recalled all the strangers who had stopped to ask if it was for sale over the years. Her father had always laughed, and she knew he would never sell as long as he lived.

Heat hung in the air, thick and heavy, as Hanna got out of her car and made her way to the front door. It opened before she could knock and her father stood there, holding a bottle of the dark, rich beer he liked. His hair was white and thinning on top, and his smiling face was deeply tanned from working outside.

"Come in, come in," he urged in French. "Can you believe this heat? Must be El Nino or something."

"Hi, Dad," she said, giving him a hug. "Thought I'd stop by and see how you guys were doing. Where's Mom?"

Her mother appeared in the doorway to the kitchen, wiping her hands on a tea towel. She was dark and small, barely 4'11, and Hanna still found it hard to believe she had carried and given birth to four kids.

"Well, don't just stand there," she scolded with a smile, her arms akimbo. "Come on in and give me a hand in here."

Hugging her, Hanna helped her finish preparing dinner as they caught up on family news and other gossip. Her mother insisted she stay for dinner and an hour later, they sat down to platters of barbecued chicken, salad and herbed rice.

"So, how's work?" her father asked, cutting into his meat.

"Fine."

"You're not covering the story of those girls being murdered, are you?" her mother asked, giving her a searching look.

"Actually, I am."

"I don't know how you do that job of yours, Hanna. All those murders, all that misery. Why couldn't you have gone into nursing or teaching, like your sister?"

Hanna put down her napkin. "Like my sister? Don't you mean like my married sister? I don't know why you just can't accept me for who I am, Mom."

"Damn it, Hanna, you're twenty-nine years old. I just want you to be happy."

"I am happy. See?" She plastered a big smile on her face, but her mom would have none of it. "C'mon, Mom. Just because I'm not married and don't have a bunch of kids running around doesn't mean I'm not happy."

Her mother just stared at her. "I don't know how you can be happy when you're so lonely. Look at you."

Hanna pushed her plate away, her appetite gone. They finished the rest of dinner in near silence and after the dishes were done, her father walked her out to her car.

"Don't let your Mom get to you, Hanna," he said, opening the door for her. "She doesn't mean to get on your case. She just wants the best for you. We both do."

"I know, Dad." She hugged him, tears in her eyes. "I'll talk to you soon, okay?"

Hanna got in her car, started the engine and backed out of the driveway. In the rear-view mirror, she could see her father standing where she'd left him, staring after her.

She deliberately avoided thinking about what her mother had said as she settled on her sofa with Pistachio curled up on her lap. She thought instead about the conversation she'd had with Bennett earlier, and the e-mails she had received. The photographs loomed larger than life in her mind's eye and she couldn't understand why they had been sent to her. She thought of the victims, all killed by the same butchering, filthy hands. The hands of a monster. And he was out there somewhere; she could sense him as if he was close.

Turning inward, searching the recesses of her mind, she tried to make sense of all the things that had happened in the last few days, but nothing was working.

She turned on the television just as the 10 o'clock national news was starting. The atrocious murders being committed locally were the top story. If it bleeds, it leads, she couldn't help thinking, and she was again astounded at how quickly the news media flocked to any situation that held the promise of gore and misery. Her heart broke again as she watched footage of Albert and Cynthia Tomlinson standing at the edge of their eldest daughter's grave, clutching each other in their grief and sorrow.

This was now a high profile case receiving national attention. The media was having a field day; some reporters had even started referring to the murderer as The Bay Killer. Tourists to the region were getting nervous; retailers complained of a slow start to the summer season. The public was deeply outraged, demanding action of police, while at the same time, watching and reading everything on the case with morbid fascination. It was the topic of choice at water coolers and coffee shops across the province, perhaps even the country. And through it all, the CIB investigators plugged along, leaving no stone unturned. They tracked down and interviewed hundreds of campers, boaters and employees at Beausoleil Island. They pursued every lead and checked and rechecked for links between Lydia Tomlinson and the teen murdered in North Bay, and now the new victim. They had even hauled in every known sexual offender who lived around the region, checking their alibis for the time of the murders and questioning their friends, families and fellow workers for any leads, clues or suspicions. And so far, all that work and effort had led nowhere.

But there were a lot of challenges hampering the investigation, not the least of which happened to be the fact that no one knew where the murders had actually taken place. The abduction and recovery sites, what the police call secondary crime scenes, were all they had. And the e-mails, Hanna reminded herself.

When the story was over, she clicked the TV off and placed an old Blue Rodeo disk on the CD player. Standing at the window, she looked out to see stars glittering like diamonds in the darkening sky. She closed her eyes and let the plaintive country-blues rhythm of *Til I Am Myself Again* wash over her like waves dancing across the bay.

That thought reminded her of the interview she had set up with Jody Adamson, the woman from the resort, the next day at three o'clock. She was looking forward to feeling the wind in her hair and the sun on her face, and couldn't wait to tour the archipelago known as the 30,000 Islands. Having grown up in the region, she knew all sorts of interesting tidbits of information about the islands and how they were formed millions of years ago. She could almost imagine the great hands of glaciers scraping and gouging the landscape during the retreat of the Ice Age, leaving in its wake a rugged, treacherous maze of shoals and islands in this eastern part of the bay.

The ring of her cell phone snapped her back to the present.

It was Bennett, his voice sounding far away. "I'm sorry I didn't call earlier, but I was wondering if you were feeling up for a drink. I just got back a little while ago."

Her heart did a little flip inside her chest as she glanced at her watch. It was half past 10. "Sure, yeah. You can come here or we can meet somewhere."

"I was thinking of The Lion's Heart. Can you meet me there?"

"I'm already on my way," she said, ending the call and making a dash to her bedroom. She changed into her favourite jeans, a white cotton sweater and high-heeled sandals, and quickly fixed her hair and applied some lipstick.

Ready at last, she locked up and drove once more into town, unable to stop a smile from spreading across her face.

She couldn't wait to see Bennett again.

Chapter Nineteen

A GROUP OF teenage boys stood on the sidewalk across King Street where Hanna parked a few minutes later. They stopped talking and feigning jabs at each other when she climbed out of her car, and she could feel their eyes roaming over her as she hurried up the sidewalk and turned down a dark alley. The Lion's Heart was just up ahead.

The sound of an accordion touched her ear as she stepped through the foyer into the main part of the pub. A couple of older guys wearing plaid shirts over worn jeans sat a small table in the middle of the place. One held a harmonica to his lips, thin wisps of a moustache hanging down on both sides, while the other, rounder around the middle and older with a shock of white hair hanging over his forehead, balanced a black accordion on his lap. He winked at Hanna as she walked by and she gave him a smile.

Upstairs, it took her eyes a minute to adjust to the near darkness. Strands of tiny, white Christmas lights had been strung all along the plate rail at the top of the walls, curling around pottery and baskets and threading through plants in corners. Aside from a few neon signs at the bar and some candles glowing on a couple of occupied tables, they provided the only illumination as she walked all the way to the back of the narrow room to a small table for two in the far corner and sank into an overstuffed chair.

A man about her age with a blond goatee and a tiny white apron tied around his hips appeared at her side and Hanna ordered a Corona just as Bennett arrived, wearing jeans and a black tee shirt and carrying a thin leather satchel under one arm. Stubble threw the bottom of his face in shadow and Hanna noticed tired lines circling his eyes as she watched him sit down across from her and order a pint from the waiter.

"How're you doing?" he asked when the waiter had returned to the bar.

"Good. Great idea meeting here. I've always loved this place."

"Me, too." He moved his elbows off the table when the waiter appeared with their beers, paid for both, and looked up at her. "You look… beautiful."

Hanna blushed and busied her fingers with her slice of lime. "Thanks." She took a sip, squeezed in more lime. "So, what's up?"

He drank from his beer. "I wanted to talk to you about the resort we visited today… and about what happened between us last night."

Though she wanted to talk about their kiss, she was curious about the resort. "I think we should leave the personal stuff until later."

"All right. The resort it is then." He sipped more beer and licked foam off his upper lip. "It's built on one of the largest islands after Beausoleil. Rocks and pines and gorgeous views no matter which way you look. I can understand why people come from all over to visit this place; it's like a postcard. It has guest cottages and a huge lodge that houses the reception area, dining room, bar, gift shop, small library, recreation centre, and health spa. There's a swimming pool in back with a sauna and hot tub, as well as sandy beaches. Guests can go cruising around the islands on a 20-passenger boat or do some canoeing, snorkelling and hiking, as well as take part in workshops. There's even stuff for kids and there are counsellors available to look after them, if the parents want a break."

"How many guests can they accommodate?"

"Up to 120. And they have a choice of staying two days, four days or a full week." Bennett unzipped his satchel, removed a glossy brochure and slid it over the table. "There's a ferry service that runs six times a day from Honey Harbour to the retreat or vice versa, something like what Beausoleil offers, except the ferry's a lot smaller."

The picture on the front of the brochure took Hanna's breath away. Surrounded by windswept pines and wildflower gardens, the two-storey pine lodge with its many windows and covered verandas featured two wings jutting out on either side. The words 'White Pine Inn at the Bay' were superimposed over the top of the picture in a sweeping arc.

"Wow," she said, looking up at Bennett. "It's beautiful."

Hanna opened the brochure, spreading it out on the table. A photograph of a spectacular sunset over Georgian Bay dominated the centre of the layout, with several smaller ones of the dining room, the pool area, the beach, the guest cottages and the ferry boat scattered around small blocks of text providing descriptions of the resort's many services and amenities. She flipped to the back page, where a mission statement was printed. "At The White Pine Inn at the Bay," she read, "nature's beauty, the area's history and five-star accommodations ensure a unique experience for each of our guests." She tapped the price list with the tip of a fingernail. "It'd better for what they're charging."

"Tell me about it."

Hanna stuffed the brochure in her shoulder bag. "So what else did you find out?"

"The island was bought six years ago for $1.1 million and the resort was built over the next two years. It grossed a massive profit in the first season, due to aggressive marketing in this country, across the border and overseas. They've got 60 full-time people, including desk clerks, chefs, waiters, housekeepers, gardeners, counsellors, ferry operators, etc. Everyone works four days and gets three off, on a rotation basis, and they stay in small cottages on the other side of the island when they're working."

"Who owns it?"

He smiled. "Ah, now we get to the good part. You won't believe this, but the owner is Victor Lachance. Ever heard of him?"

Hanna stared at him. Lachance was a Canadian legend; the name was synonymous with search engines and great food. "You're kidding me."

"Nope. He also owns another island not far from the retreat where he built himself a summer home. What's his chain of restaurants called? I can't pronounce it."

"Le Grand Gourmet," Hanna said. "I've eaten there once. Great food."

Bennett swilled back the rest of his beer and motioned to the waiter for another. "Never had the pleasure myself, but I hear it started with one restaurant in Montreal back in the 70s and just grew. Now the chain includes more than 15 and he's branching into the States. The latest one just opened up in Chicago a couple of months ago."

"Didn't he just get married again, too? "

"Yeah, for the third time. His first wife apparently died of cancer just a few years after they were married. Two kids... something interesting there, but I'll get to that in a minute. His second wife divorced him after a few years, took him to the cleaners."

"Figures. Typical Don Juan."

"Yeah, but he's been lucky. Bounced right back and started making another load of money. I hear he's worth somewhere in the $100 million range. Not bad. Not bad at all for a guy who grew up in a four-room farmhouse in rural Quebec."

"Whereabouts?"

"Three hours north of Quebec City. A little place called St-Honore."

"Really? My mother's from Chicoutimi. St-Honore is right by there."

"I hear it's just a couple of houses on the way to nowhere."

"Well, maybe a few more than a couple but, yeah, blink and you miss it."

"Vic was the youngest of ten kids," Bennett continued. "What is it about the French anyway? All these families could have opened up their own baby factories."

"Catholicism. Birth control is against the religion."

"And stupidity is against mine. I can't imagine having ten kids. Jesus."

"Me, neither. But my grandmother had ten, and she was one of the sweetest, smartest women I've ever known. I think it's just the way things were back then."

The waiter returned and Bennett paid and thanked him for his beer, taking a long swallow. "Luck must have been on his side," he said, wiping his mouth with the back of his hand. "Most people aren't so lucky. Like Tina Joliet."

Hanna sat up straighter. "You've positively identified her?"

He shook his head. "Not yet. Only dental records will be able to do that, considering the shape she's in. But there's little doubt. I talked to her father in North Bay after I got back today." He sighed deeply. "That's got to be the worse part of my job. Shit."

He'd been a cop for fifteen years, eleven of which had been spent working patrol, vice and then homicide in Toronto before moving to the Midland area, and Hanna knew he had delivered his share of bad news to people over the years. She doubted he had ever gotten used to the despair he heard in the voices of family members and friends, and she wondered about the kinds of nightmares that must keep him awake at night sometimes.

"His name's Marc Joliet. He's a contractor and he sits on council, second term. He started crying on the phone when I told him we had a victim who fit his daughter's description. He said he hadn't spoken to her in weeks, ever since she left to go work at the resort. He said she was so excited about this job; it was her first real job in the field after graduating from the Tourism & Hospitality program at the local college up there in North Bay. Candore it's called... something like that."

"Canadore."

"What?"

"The name of the college. It's Canadore. I went to J-school there two years before I enrolled at Carlton University in Ottawa." She fondly remembered the sprawling complex on the hill just at the north-eastern edge of the small city located two and a half hours' drive from Midland – it housed both the college she'd attended and tiny Nipissing University.

"Really? I didn't know that's where you went to college," Bennett said and took another swallow of beer. "Anyway, Mr. Joliet gave me the name of their family dentist. Her records will be sent by express courier in the morning."

Hanna felt her heart go out to this man, and she thought of Albert Tomlinson standing at his daughter's grave, his suit hanging off his bony frame. Did they wake up screaming in the night, tortured by images no father should ever have to see?

"Did he know she was pregnant?"

"No. I don't think she knew herself until after she started working at The White Pine Inn. Jody said Tina told her she'd just found out and didn't know what she was going to do. She even talked about going back home to her folks. Then a few days later, Tina disappears. Jody said she didn't think too much of it at the time; it was a weekend and she just assumed that Tina had gone back to North Bay."

"Didn't she start worrying when Tina didn't come back? She never called Tina's parents or anything? To check on her?"

"No, they only knew each other for about three weeks before Tina went missing. Jody said Tina was very quiet and shy. Plus, she told me it's not the first time this kind of thing has happened. Apparently, lots of people come and go at these kinds of places."

"If they weren't close, why would Tina tell Jody about her pregnancy?"

"I asked her about that. Jody said the employees are bunked six to a cottage, girls with girls and guys with guys. She and Tina shared a cottage with four other women and she said she woke up one night and heard someone crying. It was Tina. When Jody asked her what was wrong, Tina told her she was pregnant."

"And because she was three months along, it couldn't have been-"

"Anyone from the resort. Tina told Jody she didn't know who the father was… she'd been seeing a couple of different guys in North Bay. We're tracking that down."

"How old was she?"

"I think Jody said she was twenty."

"God, that's so young. Did she say anything else?"

"Just that she was concerned when Tina didn't return. She was scheduled to have the Thursday, Friday and Saturday off of the long weekend, but when she didn't show up on Sunday, Jody was concerned and spoke to her supervisor, Bonnie Gray. She told her that Tina had left a note on her desk saying she wasn't returning. Something about an emergency and that she was going home to North Bay. It was signed with her name."

"You realize anyone could have left that note."

He nodded. "And the most likely suspect would be the killer. To make sure no one would be alarmed when she didn't come back."

There was nothing random about this likely scenario and a chill shot up Hanna's spine. "Jesus. It's like he planned the whole thing."

"Right down to the last detail." He passed a hand over his face and dropped his voice down a notch. "The profile's in, by the way."

Hanna leaned forward on her elbows. "How does he profile? Were we even close when we talked about him the other day?"

"Bang on, but there's a lot more." He sighed, his hand resting on top of his satchel. "And I have to tell you, Hanna, this UNSUB's scarier than hell."

"You wouldn't happen to have that report in there now, would you?" she asked, eyeing his satchel with wide, eager eyes.

He smiled, but kept his hand where it was and his eyes locked on hers. "I do. But I have to warn you, it's for your eyes only. Okay?"

Hanna laid her hand on top of his and gave his fingers a gentle squeeze. "Tim, have I ever given you cause to worry before? No one will see it but me."

"You better make sure of that." He took out a stapled document from the satchel and slid it to her. "The coroner's report is there, too, from Lydia Tomlinson's autopsy. You can go ahead and use that, if you want. It'll be made public tomorrow."

Hanna stifled the urge to dive into the report immediately. Instead, she folded her hands on top of it and glanced up at Bennett. "They have a cause of death?"

"Respiratory depression. It's like we suspected…a massive overdose of ketamine hydrochloride. Just like Marianne Legault."

"Jesus." Hanna shivered, thinking of the terror the victims must have felt as the drug coursed through their systems and they found themselves unable to draw a breath.

"And, I'll bet you a hundred bucks, just like Tina Joliet, too."

She suddenly remembered something he had said at the beginning of their conversation. "What's this interesting thing you mentioned earlier? About Victor's kids?"

"Oh. *That*." He leaned forward, his eyes bright in the candlelight, and lowered his voice. "A second possible suspect."

Hanna's eyebrows arched. "One of his kids? Really? Why?"

"This stays between you and I, okay? Good. Victor and his first wife adopted two kids within a year of each other when they first got married... a boy and a girl. Jenna, now 28, was adopted when she was five, and Benjamin, who's almost 25, was adopted when he was four. They both work at the resort. He's a chef, she does the bookkeeping."

"A chef. What makes you suspect him?"

Bennett raised an eyebrow. "What makes you think it's him we're looking at?"

Hanna gave him a get-real look. "Because most psychos are men, Tim, and you know it. What makes you suspect him?"

He shrugged. "We don't... yet. Let's just say... we're taking a very, very close look at Benjamin Lachance."

"What's he done?"

"Nothing." He buried his fingers in his hair. "That we can prove, at least at the moment. But unlike Kirk, who's got motive and means, this guy had means and opportunity... if the victim turns out to be Tina Joliet. Haven't come up with a motive yet, but he had to have known her. Jody Adamson said they both worked in the kitchen/dining area. She was one of a dozen servers, he's one of four chefs who rotate shifts. Plus, here's where it gets interesting... he has access to his father's boats and to both Bayhaven and Bob's marinas through his father's memberships and was actually placed at those marinas around the time Dr. Mullen estimated the girls' bodies were dumped under the piers. And we have some corroborating statements from witnesses who saw him. Of course, it might not mean anything... the guy does work at a resort that ferries guests back and forth from the island to the mainland... but it's not in his job description."

Hanna frowned. "Still, it doesn't sound like much."

"Oh, but there's more." He grinned, looking a lot like the cat who ate the canary. "A whole slew of other things. Little things that don't necessarily mean much on their own, but string them together and maybe you've got something." He held up three fingers and started ticking off points. "He fits the description Lydia Tomlinson gave her friends of the man she'd met that afternoon - tall, dark and handsome. I mean, like Lou Diamond Phillips handsome. Which brings me to my second point – and I'm sure you'll find this very interesting, Hanna - he's native. First Nations. His sister is, too."

The Ojibway words that had accompanied the sick photographs she'd been sent surfaced in her mind. *Pamidonegog. Amikwandag.* Clues to the victims' murders. Something crawled in her guts as she absently rubbed at goosebumps on her arms.

"You don't think he could be *tatler*, do you?"

He raised a shoulder. "Who knows?"

"And the third thing?"

He bent the last finger. "His step-mom, Victor's second wife, lives in North Bay."

Hanna leaned back in her chair and let her mind wander where it wanted to go. Tina Joliet was from North Bay. Marianne Legault had lived in North Bay. What was the connection there? How was that city of about 52,000 in Northern Ontario where she'd lived and studied ten years ago tied in to what was happening here?

"So now you have two suspects. What happened to the theory of a serial killer?" she asked after a while. "I thought the murders were so similar in MO and ritual, it could only be the work of one guy."

He nodded. "We still think that. But right now, we have to take a hard look at anyone who had means, opportunity and motive. It's still early in the investigation and we're working with North Bay on it. Who knows what we might still dig up?"

Or recover from watery graves. She shivered and asked if they had picked up Kirk Andrews for further questioning yet.

"Yeah… but he swears he's never been to North Bay in his

life and says he's not the only one with access to ketamine hydrochloride at Lakefield's Animal Clinic… there are 16 employees who could have taken the drug, including Kirk and Dr. Lakefield himself. We're now interviewing everyone there… but it's not looking real good so far."

Hanna told him about her plans to interview Jody Adamson for a story the next day, and then they both fell silent, looking at each other.

"So," Bennett finally said, "I guess we should talk about what happened."

She finished the last of her beer. "Look, Tim, I don't know what it is, but something has been eating at you this week, and it's not just the case. I can't deny that I didn't enjoy that kiss. I can't even deny that I wouldn't have let things go a lot farther." She blushed and looked down at the table. "But for God's sake, you're married, Tim."

He lifted her chin with a finger and looked into her eyes. "Belinda left me."

A rush of feeling flooded through her. "Oh, Tim. I'm so sorry. What happened?"

He shrugged. "I'll tell you all about it some time, Hanna, but you're right. Things have been eating at me this week… I'm a mess right now, but I want you to know that I have some strong feelings for you. Okay?"

She folded her hand over his and smiled. "Okay."

A few minutes later, they made their way down the stairs to the first floor. Most of the tables were still full of people drinking and singing old English ballads despite the late hour, but the accordion player and his friend were nowhere to be seen.

Outside, the air smelled earthy and moist as they walked to their cars, the moon hanging like a bright silver coin over the silhouettes of buildings along the main street. The teenagers who had ogled her earlier had long since gone and the abandoned movie theatre on the corner was shut tight, its windows and billboards black squares against the night sky.

They crossed the street to Hanna's car. She unlocked the driver's door and climbed in, rolling down the window. Bennett bent his head, peering in at her.

He reached out, his fingers brushing a strand of hair back from her forehead. She shivered from his touch, her eyes fixed on his.

"Drive safely and lock up when you get home, okay?"

"I will." She watched him walk to his car parked up the block. He waved to her before getting in, turned his engine over, and took off down the street.

Hanna drove all the way home with a smile on her face.

Chapter Twenty

THE WORD 'SIGNATURE' jumped off the page and Hanna stabbed the air with a finger. That's it, she thought. That's how the bastard is going to get caught.

She was sitting up in bed, the profile report open on her lap. Pistachio twitched in his sleep beside her and she absently petted his soft fur as she glanced at the clock on her beside table. It was two o'clock in the morning and outside her window, a fat moon played a game of hide and seek with clouds rolling across the night sky.

Hanna turned the page and resumed reading. Also known as a calling card, a signature is what links the common threads that extend from crime to crime. It can reveal a lot more than a killer's modus operandi ever could. And while similarities in MO can be useful, differences are extremely common. Hanna recalled a story she had done on a serial rapist who had gagged one victim, tied up another and slashed at a third.

A criminal's MO is never static, she continued reading. Most perpetrators develop a modus operandi in the first place because they discover that a plan works. They gain confidence in it and believe using the same plan will lower their chances of getting caught. There's always a learning curve and as with everything else, practice makes perfect. Killers get better with every murder - they learn what works and what doesn't. They're continually improving their techniques and they are good at avoiding detection.

But it's a killer's ritual or signature that may prove to be his undoing. With violent, repeat offenders, something deadlier is at work. They are driven by rage, which leads them to fantasize about violence and eventually they act out their fantasies. Violence itself often isn't enough. They need rituals for expressing their anger.

For most killers, rituals usually involve a need to control, perhaps even to humiliate the victim. For many, the victim herself isn't important. Her age, her appearance, what she does for a living, are irrelevant. Often, a victim is chosen out of convenience. But not always. Sometimes killers require a certain victim, someone who figures in their fantasies. That sounds like our madman, Hanna thought. In this case, the victims' appearances seemed to be extremely relevant to him. Both Lydia Tomlinson and Tina Joliet, if it was her, had been young, healthy, blonde-haired, blue-eyed, slim and of average height. Marianne Legault, the teenager murdered in North Bay in April, had also shared those same characteristics - she had been petite, blonde, blue-eyed and young. This suggested the killer carefully selected his victims as opposed to randomly picking them out of the crowd.

A shiver worked its way across her spine as she wondered how he did it. How did he encounter them? He wouldn't jump them, attack them or scare them in any way. No, this monster had brains; he would know that honey attracts more flies than vinegar. He would ask for the time or directions to somewhere. He would thank them, smiling, and lavish compliments on them. He would be charming, friendly, the perfect gentleman.

Shuddering, Hanna learned that signature killers, the largest subcategory of serial killers, don't just want to kill, they need to exert control over their victims and that control manifests itself through their signature. These fall into one or more of the basic traits of sexual sadism - humiliation, bondage, picquerism, posing, torture, overkill, necrophilia and cannibalism. And each is a clue not only to what the murderer does, but what he wants, what he seeks and what drives him from victim to victim.

At the far end of the violence continuum is necrophilia, a most extreme form of control where the murder itself is an obligatory process to the killer's real goal: the completely submissive body of a dead victim. Hanna thought of Ted Bundy and Jeffrey Dahmer, real-life necrophiles whose crimes not only violated the law but some of society's most secret taboos. And the Bay Killer, who quickly dispatched his victims with a fatal dose of ketamine before preying on their corpses for sexual gratification, seemed to be following in their bloody footsteps. These killers have a dire need for unconditional and unresponsive acceptance; they crave the ultimate power trip – owning the victim.

Necrophilic killers are also compelled to keep victim memorabilia, which can include clothing, jewellery and body parts. Is that what the Bay Killer had done with the tattoo he had cut off from Lydia's leg? Was it a souvenir he brought out to help feed his sick fantasies? Did he also love his own press and keep records such as articles, maps, diaries, videos, tapes, and pictures of his murders, like so many other killers did?

In conclusion, the criminal investigative analysts had written that Lydia Tomlinson's killer, the same man who had probably also killed Marianne Legault and Tina Joliet, was classified as a necrophile, male, white, in his late 20s or early 30s. He would be educated beyond the secondary level with a career in a professional field. He might have an adolescent history of nuisance sexual offences, such as peeping, obscene phone calls and indecent exposure, as well as possible animal torture in childhood. He would be a careful planner and meticulous about details. He would probably use a ruse to approach his victims and would prepare the murder location well in advance. He either owned or had access to a boat and a cottage or property somewhere in the area. He would harbour deep-seated rage against women, obsess over pregnancy or abortion issues and nurture a morbid interest in death. Possible revenge orientation. Probable access to ketamine hydrochloride through hospital/veterinary clinic. Knowledge of reptiles.

The short-term forecast indicated that the killer showed an insatiable need to kill, extreme boldness, and a decreasing time span between murders. Underlined were the words "Will Kill Again Soon".

Hanna was horrified to think there would soon be another

victim - it was already nearing three weeks since Lydia's murder. If the analysts were right - if the killer was on a roll - then it would just be a matter of time until another young woman's battered body was found, like the others, floating under the pier of a marina.

An ungodly urge to scream filled Hanna's throat. Lydia. Tina. Marianne. Their names were a litany in her head, an endless refrain. She had not known them, yet she grieved over their senseless deaths and ached to think of their fear and helplessness in the face of such madness. She couldn't wait to see the son-of-a-bitch caged behind steel bars.

Turning to the coroner's report, she learned that Lydia Tomlinson had died almost instantly from respiratory depression due to an overdose of ketamine hydrochloride injected intra-muscularly in her left thigh. However, due to a number of complicating factors in postmortem toxicology, scientists were unable to determine the actual amount injected, but estimated a fatal blood concentration of Lydia's blood taken from her heart at autopsy to be above seven milligrams of ketamine per litre of blood. Cardiovascular toxicity as well as pulmonary edema had also been detected at autopsy.

The report described ketamine hydrochloride as a central nervous system depressant with sedative-hypnotic, analgesic and hallucinogenic properties that was marketed as Ketalar in Canada and in other countries for use as a general anesthetic in both animal and human medical practice. Known as one of several 'date rape drugs', the report noted that ketamine used alone or in conjunction with other drugs or alcohol had been responsible for a number of overdose deaths here in Canada and in the United States in recent years.

She also learned that ketamine was often diverted from legitimate sources, such as vet clinics and hospitals, and sold on the street because the drug is difficult to synthesize. It comes in liquid form, and is odourless, colourless and tasteless.

Hanna stared off into space after she had finished reading, haunted by everything she had learned. The monster was starting to take shape in her mind. Tall, dark and handsome. In his twenties or early thirties. Someone very familiar with Georgian Bay and how to navigate its rebellious waters, someone who had a boat and a place somewhere in the area remote enough to allow him to indulge in his depraved appetites. Someone with access to a hospital or a vet clinic, and she thought of Kirk Andrews again.

The killer was out there, she thought, somewhere close. Was he awake and staring into space like she was right now? Or was he at this very moment taking a corpse out of his freezer? She shuddered, and her need for a cigarette nearly bowled her over.

Something nagged at the back of her mind, some flutter of a feeling. Some piece of the puzzle. But the more she tried to bring it into focus, the more it danced just out of her reach. She cursed under her breath, her voice a ghostlike whisper in the dead of night.

She ran through the woods, her feet silent on the thick blanket of fallen leaves that was the forest floor. Moving stealthily among the trees, she watched her breath cloud the air. Like a greedy child, November had already come to steal the last warmth of an Indian summer, forcing the leaves to turn rust and gold and the winds to blow from the north.

Over the treetops, a corpulent moon showed a face with steel edges as her legs pumped like automatic machines.

She suddenly stopped when she came to the clearing. Hundreds of dead tree stumps sat like sentinels in the glow of the moon, waiting and watching. And then they were moving, inching closer and closer, their decaying tongues twisting to form sounds. She screamed, frantically pushing them away, but they only crowded in closer, shrilling noises rising up from the depths of their rotting throats.

Gasping, her arms flailing the air, Hanna sat bolt upright. Her eyes encountered darkness when she opened them and she let out a short scream as the shrilling pierced the silence again. Her heart clambered as if it wanted to climb out of her chest.

It's the phone, she told herself, it's only the phone.

Rummaging around her night table, her hand closed around

the receiver. She shoved the instrument up to her ear, but there was only the sound of the dial tone. Replacing it on its cradle, she noticed her bedside clock's green numbers read 4:21 a.m. She'd been asleep maybe an hour and a half, tops. She clicked on the lamp and watched feeble light push shadows into the corners of the room.

Who had been trying to call her at this ungodly hour, she wondered? Or had it just been a wrong number? The directory only listed the number as unknown.

Wide awake now, Hanna knew it would be hopeless to try to get back to sleep. She got out of bed, went into the living room and turned on a floor lamp next to the sofa. She sat down at her desk, thinking she'd at least get some work done if she couldn't sleep.

Ten messages had been sent to her since she had checked her mail that morning. She scrolled down the list, her eyes scanning the senders' names carefully. Finally, at the bottom, she found a message from *tatler*, and her heart slammed in her chest.

Was *tatler* Benjamin Lachance? Could he be the one sending her these messages?

Another thought cut in and Hanna felt a wrenching in her stomach. Had there been another victim and she had yet to hear about it? She looked at the entry again and noticed that the message had been sent to her the day before - the time logged read 12:20 p.m. - and contained no attachment.

The last two messages had both included attachments. Her scalp contracted as the photographs *tatler* had sent her flitted across the surface of her mind.

She was afraid to open the message.

After several seconds of staring at her screen, she double-clicked on the message.

Rearrange them to form a new one.

She read the sentence over and over, puzzled. What did it mean?

Rearrange what? she wondered. And then it hit her. Letters. An anagram. It was the only thing that made any sense. But figuring out what word to rearrange was proving much more difficult, no matter how hard she wracked her brains or how long she stared at the words on her computer.

By the time the sun had rusted the tops of the trees in her backyard, Hanna had cleaned her cottage, eaten breakfast and baked a double batch of her chocolate brownies, making sure to generously sprinkle the top with walnuts. When the minute timer beeped, she set the pans to cool on top of her stove, laced up her running shoes and went outside.

It would still be too early to call Bennett, she decided, as she made a beeline for her small garden shed. Armed with a wheelbarrow and a rake, she spent the next hour picking up broken branches around her property and pushing her second-hand lawn mower over the grass. Next, she climbed a ladder and nailed some left-over shingles over the bald patches on her roof.

That done, she went back inside and turned on the shower. She stayed under the spray until the hot water ran out, trying to keep her eyes open. Already, fatigue was settling in and she wondered how she would make it through the rest of the day on so little sleep.

After towelling herself dry, she dressed in a long, narrow black skirt and a scoop-neck burgundy tee shirt, and slipped black sandals on her feet. A little blush, mascara and lipstick added some colour to her pale face, and she used her fingers to brush her short, wavy hair back from her forehead and around her ears.

Then she grabbed the duffel bag she had already packed, and remembered to include her camera, a notepad and her micro-recorder. The brownies, placed in a Tupperware container, went in on top.

Ready at last, Hanna fed her cat, locked up her house and threw her duffel bag into the back seat of her car. Setting off, she pecked Bennett's home number on her cell.

"Hello?" He sounded breathless.

"Tim, it's me. I'm sorry for calling you at home. Is this a bad time?" she asked as she passed the majestic Martyrs' Shrine overlooking a dozen sprawling factories lining both sides of the highway just outside of Midland.

"No, no. It's okay. I just came back from a run."

An image of him clad in nothing but shorts formed in her mind and she had to shake her head to clear it. "I stayed up most of the night reading the stuff you gave me."

"Pretty sick, eh?"

"I'll be having nightmares until I'm 80. But I didn't call about that. I wanted to let you know I got another message from *tatler*."

"Did he send you another picture?"

"No, just a message this time. It said 'Rearrange them to form a new one.'"

"What?"

"That's what I thought, too, at first. But I think he means an anagram."

"That's when you have a word and you move the letters around to make a new word, right?"

"Right. Now all I have to do is figure out what word he wants me to rearrange."

"This is crazy. I have to get going now, Hanna, but can you call me tonight when you get back? You're interviewing Jody Adamson today, right?"

"Yeah. I'll call." She pulled up alongside the entrance to Rolling Sands.

"Better yet, why don't you just come over?"

Hanna felt her heart beat too fast. He had never invited her to his place before and she wondered if it was only because he wanted to hear all about her interview with Jody that afternoon. The thought of being alone with him gave her goosebumps.

"Might be pretty late when we get back."

"Doesn't matter." He gave her his address.

"In that case," she said, her heart racing even faster, "I'll see you tonight."

Chapter Twenty-One

HANNA PICKED OUT the serial arsonist at once. He was the only Rolling Sands patient with blaze orange hair in the visitor's centre, and he was sitting alone at a table, staring out the windows. Strands of silver were in his hair, and he was short with rounded shoulders. A double chin waggled under thin lips, a paunch sat on his lap and his skin was the colour and texture of porridge left out on the stove too long.

When she was standing on the other side of the table in front of him, Hanna called his name and he turned his head quickly, swinging beady eyes up to her, his kinky hair sticking up a good five inches from his forehead straight up in the air. She was reminded of Kramer's unruly mop on the 90s hit sitcom, Seinfeld, as she introduced herself, shook his outstretched hand and sat down on a vinyl chair across from him.

"How ya doin'? Hanna Laurence, isn't it?" he drawled, his accent thick with the cadences of the Irish. " 'Tis a French name that?"

She nodded. Many people pronounced it Lawrence, the English version, but it was a French name and she had always pronounced it Lorence.

"Aye. 'Tis a hot one out there?"

"Yes, we seem to be having a bit of a heat wave," she said, taking out her recorder and placing it on the table. "It's supposed to be up in the 30s today."

"Och, aye," he said, nodding his head, his hair bobbing with the motion. "Reminds me of Ireland in the summer. 'Twas hotter than a furnace going full blast."

Hanna smiled and activated her recorder. "Which part of Ireland are you from?"

"Limerick, the holiest place in all o' Ireland."

"How old were you when you came to Canada?"

"Just a young lad, 'bout 18 years old I was, with me brothers and sister, Angelina, and me parents, o' course. Came 'cross on the boat, landed in Montreal. Dad worked in the shipyards and Mam, she was a skivvy for 'em rich folks up there on the hill."

"A skivvy?"

"A charwoman, a maid. Cleaning up after 'em, 'twas what she did."

"Can you tell me a little about your childhood, Mr. Keating?"

He pinched the bridge of his nose. "'Twasn't pretty. We were dirt poor. Me and Tom and Paul and Peter, me brothers, but not Malachy, he died when he was seven of the consumption, we went out after dark to the coal mines to pick up all the bits lying around. Tough times, they were. Mam was always raging that it was all me father's fault. He was from the north, and she said he had a bit of the odd manner and a sour gob to match."

"A sour gob?"

"Y' know, a long face. He drank up his wages when he had a job in the flour mills or the coal mines, and then he drank up the dole money when there was no work. And Mam took to the bed a lot, sick with the cough. We blamed the rain and the River Shannon, always bringing the cold. Aye, 'twas enough to kill many an old folk and the little babies, like our sister Margaret, who died in the night before she even walked."

Hanna tried to imagine what it would have been like growing up poor in Ireland with a sick mother and an alcoholic father and death coming to steal little sisters in the cold dark of night. Her own childhood had been a sunny day in the park compared to his, and she felt a stab of pity for the man. "When did you first became attracted to fire?"

His pudgy face broke out in a gleeful grin and he rubbed his hands together like Scrooge over his piles of money. "'Tis a beautiful thing, fire. So strong, hot and 'tis useful to no end. 'Twas the candles that started me, I think. I used to watch the flames dancing in the night. Mam used to say, 'Get away from those candles, Mickey, ye'll burn the whole place down, not that's it worth the dirt it's built on.' One day, me and me brother Paul, we were playing inside and Mam and our other brothers was at the St. Vincent de Paul, and by accident, Paul knocked the candle and it fell on Mam's bed. Soon the flames were burning up everything in sight, not that we had a lot, mind ye. Even after Paul ran out to get some help, I stared at that fire and no pack of wild wolves could have taken me away. It was the most powerful thing I had ever seen with me two eyes and I could not believe how fast it burned. Finally help came and I was pulled out of the house, with only a burn or two, but that was the beginning, I think. Couldn't stop me after that, I stole matches and things to burn and I would go out whenever I could to light fires and stare at the flames."

Hanna had done her research and knew that his obsession had escalated from starting fires in sheds and garages to burning a house in which an old man died. Although it was never proven that Mick was responsible for the death, his family was shamed and scorned by suspicious neighbours. One month later, the Keatings borrowed money from relatives and boarded a boat for the Americas in the hopes of putting all their troubles behind them. But it was only the beginning.

"Two years after you moved to Montreal, there was another fire and another death, wasn't there? What happened?"

He raised his eyes to hers briefly, then swung his gaze down at the tabletop. "I was walking home one night after working in the restaurant and some drunk homeless man accused me of stealing his things and started beating me. I hit him and he fell to the pavement, bleeding. I didn't know if he was dead or not, I just lifted him up into a garbage bin that was there in the alley and I set a fire in it. Then I ran all the way home. The next day, there was a mention of it in the paper and a few days later, a man came forward to say that he had seen someone running from the alley that night and the description fit me well enough. The police came to the door and Mam broke down crying. They questioned me a long time and it was only by the grace of God that I wasn't charged, you see, the owner of the restaurant where I worked was convinced I had left that night later than I actually had. Between what he said and what the witness said, there was a good two hours' discrepancy and it made all the difference in the end. It saved me."

But it didn't stop him from starting fires. In fact, the next time he lit a match, an entire family died in their home while they were sleeping. Three small children, all under the age of seven, and their parents. It was the reason he was here now.

Hanna watched him pull at a hangnail, ripping the flesh of his thumb, and a bright dot of blood appeared. He sucked at the wound for a moment, his black gaze fixed on a point just beyond her shoulder. She turned and spotted Raymond Fortin sitting alone at a table several feet behind them. Every muscle in her body tensed.

Raymond fluttered the fingers of his right hand at her, a wide grin turning up the corners of his mouth. His long salt-and-pepper hair hung loosely on his shoulders and his eyes, even from a distance of several feet, shone darkly as he stared at her.

Hanna sucked in a breath, then turned back to look at Mick Keating. "Did you know Raymond before you took the high school equivalency course?"

"Aye, we've known each other a long time."

A shadow fell across the table and Hanna looked up into Raymond's face.

"You don't mind, do you?" he drawled as he pulled up a chair close to her and sat down, crossing his arms. "Go on with what you were doing. Just pretend I'm not here."

Hanna clamped her teeth together. "I would appreciate it if you would leave."

His grin grew wider, the crows' feet around his eyes fanning out across his temples. "It's good to see you, too, Hanna. You're looking well, a little tired and stressed, but otherwise, just as lovely as you were the other day."

"Please-"

"Do you know how sexy you look when you're pissed off,

Hanna? Look," he said, gesturing at his crotch, "you're making me all hard and horny."

"Enough," she hissed, staring daggers at him. "Or I'll call the guards." She looked behind her at the entrance where two of them stood, talking quietly.

He grinned, lifting a hand. "Not another word. Cross my heart and hope to die."

True to his promise, he remained silent as she continued her interview with Mick. She asked him why he had decided to get his high school diploma, what his likes and dislikes were about the institution, and how he spent his time from sunup to sundown.

"Aye, with my nose in a book, most of the time," he said, shrugging. "I read everything about history I can get my hands on."

"And not just Ireland's history, right, Mick?" Raymond leaned forward and stared at Hanna with his opaque eyes. "He knows more history, including local history, than anyone in this entire place. Don't you, Mick?"

"Och, aye. 'Tis so."

"The man's a walking encyclopedia of historical facts," Raymond enthused.

Hanna had run out of questions. She stopped the recorder and extended her hand across the table, smiling. "Mr. Keating, thanks for your time."

He shook her hand, mumbling something in return and then shuffled towards the entrance of the visitor centre.

Raymond fixed his gaze on her. "You know, we never did finish our interview."

Hanna dropped her recorder in her handbag and stood. "I'm sorry, Raymond, I can't. I have piles of work waiting for me at the office."

His eyes narrowed and he stood up abruptly, his chair skidding across the floor. "The murder story, right?" he growled, his hand snaking out to encircle her wrist. "Can't it wait? It's not like these dead girls are going anywhere."

Hanna felt a burst of anger as she looked down at his fingers tightening on her arm. "Neither are you, as I recall," she said, shooting him a murderous look.

"Bitch," he hissed at her, loosening his fingers and slowly trailing them down across the back of her hand and along the length of her fingers. Hanna flinched at the contact, her skin crawling. He leaned so close to her, she could see tiny flecks of yellow in his dark eyes and smell the sourness on his breath. "I'll make you pay for that."

She froze as she was snatching her arm away, her hand poised to grab her handbag. "Are you threatening me?"

"Threat, promise... it's all the same to me. I know where you live, Hanna. One hundred and eighty-nine Shore Lane, isn't it? Can't say I would have chosen Victoria Harbour myself, but it must be nice... little place right by the water. Quiet, isolated."

He hissed the words in her ear, and Hanna felt the hairs at the back of her neck stand straight up. Grabbing her handbag, she stumbled backyards, her eyes fixed on his, and then she turned away, almost running to the exit.

His laughter followed her down the corridor, stinging like a slap.

It wasn't until she was safely inside her car that Hanna was able to force herself to breathe calmly, drawing air that was still hot and muggy into her lungs and expelling it slowly through her mouth. After a few seconds, the tremor in her hands stilled and her heart slowed its staccato beat against her ribs. She rested her forehead against the steering wheel, a hollow feeling in the pit of her stomach.

Only a handful of people knew her exact address - her family, a few close friends, her editor and Bennett. Even her personal mail was delivered to a rented box at the post office in the village; her home number was unlisted. So how had Raymond known where she lived? She had never mentioned him to any of her friends and family; only Belmont at the paper knew she was doing a story on Rolling Sands patients. But she strongly doubted he would even talk to Raymond Fortin, let alone provide sensitive information concerning one of his reporters. So how had he known?

With an hour left to go before it would be time to head out to the marina, Hanna pushed all thoughts of Raymond Fortin to the back of her mind and drove to the office.

What she needed now was work and she pulled out the coroner's report Bennett had given her, read through it again and dialled Dr. Frank Ellis' direct line at the Office of the Chief Coroner in Toronto.

"Do you happen to know if an injection site was also detected on the second victim found up here?" she asked after the pleasantries of catching up were over.

"Yes." Dr. Ellis sighed in her deep voice. "It might not be the same cause of death, though. None of the tests are back yet, of course."

"But?" Hanna prompted, sensing that the doctor was holding something back.

"But... it's very likely. That's all I can say, Hanna."

"Thank you, Frank."

Three victims. Three beautiful girls. All likely killed the same way with a fatal dose of ketamine hydrochloride. Hanna felt a sickening weight in her stomach as she started writing an update to the murder story for the weekend edition.

Working like a demon, she was surprised to find she wrote the story in half an hour and still had time to design the layout for one of the weekend paper's pages.

At noon, she shut down her computer, changed into shorts and a tee shirt, and went in search of her editor. She found him at the picnic table smoking a cigarette.

Belmont looked at her. "You look like death warmed over."

"Thanks." She told him what had happened with Raymond Fortin that morning.

"I wouldn't worry about it too much, Hanna. The guy's locked up. He ain't going nowhere."

"I guess you're right." She stifled a yawn as they walked over to his utility vehicle. She climbed in, put her duffel bag on the back seat, and buckled her seatbelt.

Belmont settled in the driver's seat. "Did you sleep at all last night?"

She yawned again. "Not really... but I'm okay," she said and promptly fell asleep, her head lolling against his shoulder.

Chapter Twenty-Two

THE EARLY AFTERNOON sun, high up in the cloudless azure sky, sprinkled the surface of Midland Bay with glittering diamonds of light.

Refreshed from her nap, Hanna sat up on the bridge of Belmont's 27-foot Bayliner and watched the marina recede behind her, the wind a gentle caress on her skin.

Belmont's wife, Trish, emerged from the aft-cabin, her dark tanned skin in sharp contrast to her white shorts and blouse. She smiled at Hanna and came to stand behind her husband, massaging the back of his neck as he manoeuvred the steering wheel.

Hanna leaned back and watched them. She envied their domesticity, their easy way of being with one another even after 25 years of marriage and two children, grown and gone now. Wondering if she would ever find that same kind of enduring love, she thought of Bennett and closed her eyes. She remembered the feel of his lips on hers, the touch of his hands on her body, the scent of rain and apples on his skin.

Opening her eyes, she turned her attention to the scenery speeding by her. They were leaving Midland Bay behind as they crossed into the vast expanse of water that was Georgian Bay. Sailboats and a sleek yacht dotted its shimmering surface and a small island rose out of the water on the right, its shoreline an artist's palette of summer greens.

"Present Island," Belmont shouted, cocking a thumb at the island as *The Joyride* skimmed across open water that sprayed up behind it in twin arching plumes.

Hanna leaned over the edge, letting the fine mist cool her skin as she watched the wake churn water the colour of dusky skies. She felt her chest swell with something like pride and belonging - this was the place she called home. It wasn't difficult to understand why tens of thousands of tourists flocked to cottage country each summer or why boating was a billion-dollar industry here - Georgian Bay was simply breathtaking with its sandy beaches and cool, refreshing waters for miles in any direction.

"There's Beausoleil," Belmont announced and she turned to see him pointing at an immense island directly ahead and to her left. He guided the boat along its east side and she noted the mixed coniferous and hardwood forest which she knew was part of the Great Lakes - St. Lawrence Forest Region, a transition zone between the hardwood forests extending into the United States and the boreal forests of the Canadian north. Along this side, a beautiful sandy beach stretched all the way up to the island's curving north-eastern tip. Several campers were making use of the beach as they passed, and the Georgian Bay Islands Day Tripper ferry was letting out tourists at the main dock.

Continuing along, they passed Roberts Island and Little Beausoleil Island on the right, and moved up the narrow Little Dog Channel. They glided past Deer Island as they entered Honeymoon Bay at the northern tip of Beausoleil Island.

Hardwood trees gave way to barren, glacier-scraped rock and more windswept pines as they moved further north, and Hanna spied several outer islands breaking the surface of the water. Resembling surfacing whales, they were sometimes called "whalebacks" and were essentially banks of submerged shoals. On some of the larger ones, dwarfed white pines and willow trees twisted up from rocky outcrops and several varieties of lichens and grasses grew on rock faces and between crevices. Fierce, icy winds and crashing waves during winter prevented little else from surviving on these barren islands.

She was fascinated to note that many of the smaller shoals were entirely made up of rocks with alternating colours of pink, white and grey that appeared swirled across their surface. She remembered learning in school that these rocks were the roots of a billion-year-old mountain range that had once towered as high as the Himalayas. The range was believed to have been formed millions of years ago when two continental plates collided, forcing the rocks 20 to 30 kilometres underground and exposing them to temperatures as high as 700 degrees Centigrade. The swirling was evidence that at one time, these rocks had flowed like molten lava.

Hanna saw patches of pale yellow and pink blooms growing out of several crevices and further on, a carpet of nodding red flowers around a stand of tall grasses. On a rock, a map turtle lay with its large, flat shell turned to the sun.

Moving into the heart of the archipelago known as the 30,000 Islands, she was awed by landscape so hauntingly beautiful, she finally understood why the famous Group of Seven artists had painted it over and over again. Summer on the islands is a time of stunning contrasts and the sun brings out the richest colours of the landscape. She was swept away by the cobalt blue of Georgian Bay forming a striking counterpart to the light blue of the sky, the pinkish-grey of the rocks and the midnight green of the white pines.

"We're stopping here for lunch," Belmont shouted as they approached a small cove lined with a row of cottages set back from a sandy beach. Docks grew like fingers into the bay. Tiny stick figures walked along the beach and even smaller ones played at the edge of the water. Belmont cut the engine and Hanna heard a child shriek in delight as she chased a seagull across the sand.

Dropping the anchor, Belmont stepped back from the steering wheel and growled like a bear. "I'm starving," he announced. "Bring on the food, mama."

Trish laughed. "Can you hang on a minute? I wanted to take Hanna on a tour of the aft-cabin first, okay?"

"Just don't take all day, all right? A man's got to eat, you know."

Hanna and Trish both laughed as they started down steep stairs. The head was immediately to the right, a cramped space with a pump-action toilet, a tiny sink and an overhead shower.

Directly ahead, a small kitchen was designed to make the most of tight space with cupboards tucked into nooks and crannies. There was a tiny stove, a sink below a curtained window, a hotel-sized refrigerator with freezer and a table that folded down into an extra bed. A door led into a small bedroom where a double bed took up most of the space. Shelves and a closet were built into the walls, drawers lined the space under the bed and a handmade quilt covered the top of it. A framed colour photograph of a quaint wooden cottage on an island adorned the wall just under another small window.

Hanna indicated the picture. "Did Jake take this?"

Trish pushed her sunglasses up on her head and nodded. "It was his parents' cottage until about 15 years ago. Then it was sold as part of the estate when his dad died."

"It's so beautiful," Hanna said, following Trish out of the bedroom and through the kitchen. "Where is it located?"

"Around here, I think. Jake would know."

A few minutes later, they were back up on the bridge with a platter of salmon and egg salad sandwiches, vegetables and dip, barbecue corn chips, Hanna's brownies piled high on a plate, and three chilled cans of Heineken.

"Can you show Hanna where your dad's cottage is?" Trish asked Belmont as he popped the top off his can of beer. "She was admiring the picture in the bedroom."

"Ah, yes. The cottage," he said and smiled wistfully. "God, I loved that place. We spent every summer there. It's a damn shame we had to sell it." He unfolded a map and pointed at a tiny cluster of islets near Tomahawk Island. "There. One of those."

"Is it on the way to the resort?"

"I'll point it out to you when we pass it."

When lunch was over, Belmont set about turning on the boat's blower while Trish and Hanna carried the platters and empty cans to the kitchen. Soon the rumble of the engine came to life and they returned to the bridge in time to see him pull out the anchor.

Seconds later, the boat picked up speed as they continued on their way.

"There it is," Belmont shouted minutes later, pointing to his right.

The cottage his family had once owned sat on a tiny islet no bigger than an acre. Surrounded by pines and swirled boulders, it had been built to face south and had several large shuttered windows along its front. A rocky path ended at a single, empty dock bobbing in the water at the foot of the cottage.

"It's beautiful, but it looks abandoned."

"Probably hasn't been opened up for the season yet," Belmont yelled as he manoeuvred his boat around the tiny island's eastern side.

Hanna got out her camera and snapped a shot of the cottage. She noticed the island was the biggest of a dozen smaller isles surrounding it and the only one that had a cottage built on it. She closed her eyes as they sped away and imagined herself sitting on that little dock enjoying the quiet and the solitude, hearing the water lap at the rocks and the seagulls circling in the sky.

A few minutes later, she spotted a large island rising up in the distance. But it wasn't until they were passing its southern tip that she realized that this had to be the island on which The White Pine Inn had been built. Small log cabins could be seen among the pines and Hanna guessed they were the employee cottages.

They passed a sandy beach and just around a small finger of land jutting out into the bay, a huge pine lodge broke the line of trees at the shoreline. Built on a sloping hill of windswept pines, the massive wood and glass structure rose up to meet the sky, its enormous windows reflecting the surrounding landscape like framed oil paintings on a wall. On either side of the windowed A-frame sprawled two long wings with covered verandas lining the entire length of each. A large stone patio with deck chairs and tables artfully arranged in groupings here and there dominated the space in front of the main entrance. Flowers spilled out of hanging baskets and clay pots every couple of feet; tiered wildflower gardens meandered up along each side of the wide, stone steps leading up to the front doors.

Hanna had to admit The White Pine Inn was several times

more beautiful than in the photograph on the front of the brochure Bennett had given her. It seemed impossible that a woman could have been abducted from these picturesque surroundings and then murdered in cold blood, her ravaged body dumped a few kilometres away in the bay.

Fighting a chill creeping up her spine, Hanna was brought face to face with the reason she was here in the first place. It had been easy not to think about the murders on the way up. The scenery had captivated her, made her forget the reason for the trip itself. But now as they approached a private marina lying at the foot of the lodge, it all came rushing to the surface and she found herself thinking of *tatler*'s latest bizarre message.

Belmont slowed *The Joyride* to a crawl and Hanna counted over forty sleek yachts, sailboats and speedboats moored around eight floating docks as he steered his boat into an empty space. She noticed a couple sitting on their yacht sipping blue drinks from long glasses. Raking her fingers through her wind-blown hair, she grabbed her shoulder bag and glanced at her watch. It was just after three o'clock.

Belmont and Trish finished tying up the boat and gathering items for the beach, and the three of them made their way up to the marina office where Jake registered his boat and paid the dockage fee. Then, according to their plan, they headed towards the beach while Hanna started up the stone steps to the main entrance. She would meet them for a swim later when she was finished interviewing Jody Adamson.

Pulling open the glass door, she entered an immense foyer bathed in sunlight pouring in from windows and skylights cut out of the 30-foot cathedral ceiling. Hanna passed several people sitting on plush couches and chairs arranged in front of a massive stone fireplace. A dozen tree-sized plants growing out of large clay pots gave her the feeling of being outdoors and a beautiful Indian rug caught her eye as she approached the registration area.

"May I help you?" A woman's face followed her voice as she stepped out of an office directly behind the registration desk. She had short hair the colour of ripe plums and was wearing a navy blouse and skirt that set off the light blue of her slanted eyes.

"Yes, I'm looking for Jody Adamson," Hanna said, pulling out her press pass.

"That's me," the woman answered. "You're Hanna Laurence from the paper, right?"

Nodding, Hanna smiled. "Nice to meet you," she said as she gripped Jody's hand. "Would it be all right if I took some pictures first before we do the interview?"

"Sure." Jody came around the desk and they headed out to the stone patio where Hanna took several shots of her standing on the steps, the pine lodge rising up behind her. When she was finished, they retraced their steps through the foyer and out glass doors to the rambling back patio. A giant, kidney-shaped swimming pool lay directly ahead with several bath houses, an elevated stage, a dining area and a covered bar arranged around it. As in front, flowers provided a brilliant backdrop to the dark green of the pines surrounding the patio. Through the foliage at the end of the pool area, Hanna spied two rows of large log cabins extending into the heart of the island, each with its own open-air front porch, hanging baskets of flowers and table with umbrella.

Jody led her to a table near the pool. Sitting down, she raised her hand towards the bar and asked Hanna what she would like to drink.

"A Coke would be fine," she said as a young waiter approached them, a small white apron tied around his waist.

"Hey, Jimmy. Could you get us a couple of Cokes, please?"

"Coming right up." He went back to the bar.

Hanna swept her arm in the air. "This is a really beautiful place. How long have you worked here?"

"This is my second summer. I worked in the dining hall last year, but I like working in reception better." Jody smiled and gave a little shrug. "Easier on the feet."

"You don't mind if I tape this?" Hanna asked as she retrieved her recorder, as well as her notepad and pen. She rarely counted on the recorder alone - too many things could go wrong. She remembered the time she had interviewed a top FBI profiler when she'd been working at *The Star* several years ago only to discover - to her horror - after he had already left the city, that she had forgotten to put a cassette in the recorder. It remained to date the biggest gaffe of her career.

"Go ahead," Jody replied as the waiter placed two glasses of Coke in front of them. A slice of lemon and a tiny, yellow umbrella decorated each glass. "Thanks, Jimmy."

"Can you tell me a little about Tina? How did the two of you meet?" Hanna asked after the waiter left, pressing PLAY on her recorder.

"She started working here at the beginning of May, like everyone else. It's a real busy time, everybody's trying to get the place ready for when it opens on the May long weekend. I met Tina the first day back on the job; she was working in the dining hall and stopped me to ask a question. She seemed really nice. But it wasn't until that night when I went to my cottage that I found out I was sharing it with her and four other women. We introduced ourselves and decided to share a bunk."

Hanna lifted her pen from her pad. "What was she like?"

"Shy and quiet." Jody twirled the umbrella in her glass. "She kept to herself a lot, but she was really nice once you got to know her a little. She had a funny laugh and I know a couple of the guys who work here thought she was cute."

"What did you think when you found out she was pregnant?"

Jody shook her head. "I felt really bad for her. She was so young, you know? And she was scared, who wouldn't be? She had no idea what she was going to do… she told me she'd probably have to go home."

"Is that why you didn't think it was unusual when she didn't return from her time off that long weekend?"

Tears sprung in her eyes. "God, I feel so awful about it. I keep thinking there should have been something I could have done."

Hanna slid her chair closer. "There's nothing anyone could have done, Jody. You had no way of knowing."

"I know," she said, dabbing at the corners of her eyes with the sleeve of her blouse. "But I keep thinking about her baby… and I can't get past what happened. I've been trying to forget about it and just do my job, but it's so hard."

"What did you do after you realized she wasn't coming back?"

"I went to talk with Bonnie Gray. She's the general manager here," Jody said, taking a sip of her Coke. "She told me Tina had left a note on her desk, saying there was an emergency and she was returning to North Bay. It made me feel better at the time, thinking that she had gone home where she could at least get some help and support."

"When did you start thinking that maybe she hadn't gone home?"

Jody briefly closed her eyes. "I was watching the news a few nights ago and they were saying another body had been found in the bay not far from here. I'd been following the news ever since that other girl was found and I remember thinking this couldn't be happening. Not another girl. But it wasn't until they described her that alarm bells went off. Even then, I thought I had to be wrong. There are plenty of girls out there who fit that description, you know? What were the odds that it would be her?" Pausing, Jody slowly shook her head. "But then they mentioned that this girl had been pregnant and all of a sudden, I knew it was her. I just had a feeling. I can't describe it exactly, but I just knew."

Hanna scribbled in her shorthand, looking up at the same time. "How have people reacted to the news here at the resort?"

"It's been kept as low-key as possible for our guests. The last thing this place needs is that kind of publicity… but it's been hard for everyone who works here. You know, she was only here about three weeks before she disappeared, but everyone seemed to like her. I know I did. She was a really sweet person… she didn't deserve what happened to her." She pulled a Polaroid out of her skirt pocket and put it on the table. "That's her there. On the right in the yellow shirt."

One look and Hanna felt nausea settle like a stone in the pit of her stomach.

There had to be a mistake, she thought, swallowing hard, her mouth dry as a desert sandscape. But she knew there wasn't.

Her fingers shook as she picked up the Polaroid of Jody and Tina with their arms around each other's shoulders, standing in front of a white boat. Bennett had not been exaggerating when he'd said that Tina and Lydia could have been twins. The resemblance was startling - they shared the same long, blonde hair cascading past slim shoulders, the same laughing blue eyes, the same heart-shaped face, the same carefree smile.

It was only after she had stared at the picture for a few seconds more that subtle differences began to emerge – Tina had a tiny beauty mark above her lip, her nose pointed down at the tip. Lydia's features had been softer, rounder.

Unsettled and troubled at heart, Hanna looked up at Jody. "I can't believe the similarities… could I take a picture of you holding this?"

"Sure."

She took a shot of Jody looking at the picture while holding it at chest level and returned her camera to her shoulder bag as two men walked by, laughing at a joke one had told the other. She and Jody both turned to look at them and Jody waved to catch their attention. One of them, in a navy shirt and matching pants, waved back and turned to say something to his friend.

Jody leaned towards Hanna. "The tall one there? With the gorgeous face? I'm pretty sure he knew Tina. His name's Benjamin Lachance, he's a chef here."

Chapter Twenty-Three

HANNA STARED AT Jody. Had she heard her correctly? Had she just said Benjamin *Lachance*? The guy the CIB was taking a very, very close look at?

"The owner's son?"

"You know about that?" Jody asked, looking curiously at her.

Hanna nodded and wiped damp palms on her shorts. Craning her neck to take another look at the men, she saw they were approaching their table. She turned off her recorder and stared up into the most beautiful Indian face she had ever seen.

Tall, dark and handsome. The description Lydia had given her friends popped unbidden into her head and Hanna saw that Benjamin Lachance was certainly all three, although the word handsome didn't come close to describing his looks. Six feet tall with black hair and smooth skin the colour of dark, golden honey, he was simply beautiful.

Based on that generic description, Benjamin Lachance could certainly be the killer. But so could half of the area's male population, she knew, including the man standing next to Benjamin, a few of the guys who worked at the paper, even her own two brothers. The world was full of tall, dark and handsome men. Still, she couldn't help recalling all the things Bennett had told her about Benjamin.

Jody took care of introductions. "This is Ryan. He works on our ferry," she said, gesturing toward the man at Benjamin's side, "and this is Benjamin, one of our best chefs. Guys, meet Hanna

Laurence. She's a reporter at *The Midland Post*."

Ryan stuck out a hand in front of Hanna's face. "So what brings you out here? That murder?" he asked, pumping her hand as he pulled up a chair and sat down next to her. He didn't look a day over twenty, and still had faint traces of acne on his chin and forehead.

Before Hanna could reply, Benjamin laughed. "Forgive my friend. He's got no manners whatsoever," he said with a smile as he took Hanna's hand between both of his. "It's always a pleasure to meet such a beautiful woman with an equally beautiful name."

Aware of a blush staining her cheeks, Hanna watched as he bent his dark head and planted a feathery kiss on the back of her hand. "Thank you," was all she could think of saying as she stared up at him, sunlight giving his short, black hair an almost violet tint.

Smiling broadly, he turned to Ryan. "Aren't you supposed to be at the docks?" he asked, glancing at his watch. "The ferry won't drive itself across the bay, you know."

"Damn," Ryan said as he stood up and turned to Hanna. "Gotta go, but it was real nice to meet you," he added, and inclined his head toward Benjamin. "Just don't let this guy fool you. Underneath all those manners is a first-class idiot."

"Takes one to know one," Benjamin shot back, laughing. Ryan rolled his eyes and then hurried into the foyer of the lodge.

"So Jody," Benjamin said with a twinkle in his eyes, "you never did say why you were being interviewed by this beautiful creature here."

"Don't mind Benjamin, Hanna. He's just showing off," Jody said and turned her blue eyes in his direction. "Hanna's interviewing me about Tina."

He pursed his lips. "That poor girl. I can't believe what happened to her. One day she's fine and the next she's dead. It's unbelievable."

Hanna watched him for signs of nervousness, but saw none. "Would you mind if I asked you a couple of questions?"

Benjamin smiled. "Not at all. I'd be delighted."

"Was there anything else you needed from me?" Jody asked, standing up and glancing at her watch. "I need to finish up some work in the office."

Hanna felt a moment of unease at being left alone with Benjamin but shook her head. "Thanks for everything, Jody. If there's anything else you remember, feel free to give me a call." She fished out one of her business cards and handed it to her.

"Sure thing." With a little wave and a smile in Benjamin's direction, Jody left.

As soon as she was out of sight, Benjamin turned his dark eyes on Hanna. "Looks like I'm all yours now. Fire away."

"I'll need to tape your answers, if that's okay."

"No problem." He folded his hands on the table and Hanna saw that he had long, tapered fingers and nails that were neatly trimmed. A chef's hands. Clean, beautiful, well cared for. Could these be the hands of a killer?

She decided the best way to approach this was to pretend to know nothing. "Why don't we start with a little information about you?" she asked, activating the recorder.

He leaned closer to her, conspiratorially, as if what he was about to say held great importance. "My name's Benjamin Lachance. That's L-a-c-h-a-n-c-e. My father owns this place." He leaned back in his chair again, a broad smile on his face.

Hanna plastered what she hoped was a genuinely surprised smile on her own face. "Really?" was all she said, her tone interested.

He nodded. "You've probably heard of him. Victor Lachance? He owns Netchance, the Internet search engine, and a chain of restaurants called Le Grand Gourmet, plus about a billion other things, " he said, beaming another smile at her. "And I'm the head chef here."

She wrote in her notebook and stared at him out of the corner of her eye. He did look a little like Lou Diamond Phillips back in his younger days, but he was even more beautiful. What did he remind her of? And then the image came to her. A peacock. With all of his feathers gorgeously fanned out around him, strutting around the yard.

She smiled at the thought. "So tell me about yourself, Benjamin. What made you decide to become a chef and work here for your dad?"

He swept his arm at his surroundings. "Look at this place, Hanna. You don't mind if I call you Hanna, do you? Good. This is one of the most beautiful places in the world, and I've traveled to a few truly gorgeous places over the years - Nepal, Australia, Indonesia, Greece. Why would I want to be anywhere else? I can do everything I love right here."

Including murdering young, innocent women? Hanna couldn't help thinking. But she had to admit that she was touched by his answer; she had not expected sentimentality.

"And cooking is what you love?"

He nodded. "And boating, snorkelling, soaking up the sun. But cooking is my first love. I don't know what it is about it exactly, but there's something relaxing about cooking. It's a great feeling. Do you cook?"

"Sometimes."

"There's nothing like it. My father was a cook, you know, before he became rich. He used to work at a little family restaurant up north where I grew up and sometimes he would bring me along. I was fascinated watching him cut up vegetables. He was so fast; the blade of his knife was just a blur. Chop, chop, chop."

He made the motion of a knife cutting, smiling at the memory, and Hanna could not help but feel a cold hand clamp around her heart. Both Lydia and Tina had been slashed and stabbed - especially their faces.

"Where up north did you grow up?"

"Little place between North Bay and Sudbury... you wouldn't have heard of it." He shrugged. "But watching my dad... I think that's when I decided that's what I wanted to do when I grew up, too. So here I am. What about you? Did you always want to be a reporter?"

Hanna smiled. "No, but I always wanted to write."

Benjamin laughed. "Like what? A book?"

"A bestseller, sure. But a steady paycheque won out in the end, I'm afraid." She surreptitiously glanced at her watch and saw that it was already past four. "How many chefs work in the dining hall here?"

He brought his hands up on the tabletop. "We're four altogether. Always two in the kitchen at a time and we rotate shifts."

"Did everyone know Tina?"

"Not everyone. Most people working the dining room did, but not very well. She was only here three weeks before she disappeared."

"Did you ever talk to her?"

"Sure, a few times. She came to me with a question or two. But that was it. We exchanged, I don't know, a few dozen words altogether. I didn't really know anything about her, except that she was from North Bay."

"What did you think when she didn't come back?"

"Not much, actually. I don't mean to sound callous, but it wasn't the first time someone had left without notice or anything. I just thought maybe she didn't like it here."

"Did you know she was pregnant?"

"No. We barely talked. I only found out yesterday," he said and shook his head. "I was shocked. And disgusted. Who would want to hurt a pregnant woman?"

She wrote down his comments and turned off her recorder. "Thanks for talking with me, Benjamin. I hope I didn't take too much of your time."

"Not at all. It was my pleasure."

Hanna stood, automatically offering him her hand and he rose and took it, his palm soft against her own.

He bestowed a last, bright smile on her and then he was gone.

Putting her recorder back into her shoulder bag, Hanna couldn't believe she had just talked with a possible suspect in a heinous murder case. A man who was tall, dark and handsome; a man who knew his way around knives; a man who had known Tina Joliet; a man who was the adopted native son of the resort's owner; a man whose step-mom lived in North Bay. A man who could be a killer?

Hanna started down the stone steps to the beach where she spotted Jake and Trish lying on towels near the water's edge. They were both asleep, their skin reddening under a broiling sun. She repositioned the beach umbrella to create more shade over their bodies, peeled off her tee shirt and shorts and kicked off her shoes.

It was good to be alive. To feel warm air brush her skin, cool water lap at her feet. There wasn't a place in the world she'd rather be - Georgian Bay at the pinnacle of summer was a treat for the senses. She had missed everything about the area when she'd been living in the city, but like most things in life, she'd had no idea just how much until she had returned. This was the place she called home, the place that had drawn her back after all these years. She never wanted to leave again, at least for the time being.

Benjamin's right, she thought as she followed a sleek sailboat's progress across the bay with her eyes. This is one of the most beautiful places in the world.

Hanna waded into the water, careful not to cut her feet on sharp pebbles.

Clink. Belmont tapped his fork on the side of his beer bottle and Hanna and Trish looked across the table at him. His balding pate, face and arms were the colour of the pasta lying alongside the thick steak on his plate, but if he was in pain he didn't show it.

He smiled broadly as he lifted his beer. "Here's to a great day, a fabulous start to the summer and good company," he toasted and touched his bottle to their glasses.

Hanna took a long swallow of her wine. "I couldn't have said it better myself, Jake. Thanks for today. It was a real treat."

"Anytime." He forked a huge piece of steak into his mouth.

A seagull flew past the window and Hanna looked out at the bay, rosy as the sun started its descent to the horizon. They had decided to have dinner together at The Harbourview Bar & Grill after mooring *The Joyride* at the marina.

"So tell me, did you find out anything interesting?" Belmont asked.

Hanna told him and Trish about her interviews with Jody and Benjamin.

"Sounds like you've got enough for a good story, Hanna," he said, reaching for his pager on his belt and squinting at the message. "Ah shit. I wonder what the hell he wants now. Can I use your cell? I'll just be a minute."

Hanna passed it to him and watched him punch in a few numbers. "David, it's Jake. What's up?" then, "Oh Christ!" followed by silence for a minute, and then, "I'll be right there."

Hanna felt her gut clench like a fist. "What is it? What happened?"

The sunburn slowly bleached from his face as Hanna watched.

Had they found another body? Had the Bay Killer struck again? She felt nausea rise in her throat and she gripped his forearm. "Jake! What's going on? What is it?"

He blinked. "There might be another one. Another girl. Missing."

"Oh Jesus."

"It gets worse," he said and ground the heel of his palms into his eyes. "It's the mayor's daughter."

Chapter Twenty-Four

HANNA HAD NEVER run so fast in her life. The soles of her shoes pounded on the sidewalk as she rushed the 15 blocks from The Harbourview to *The Post* building, heat glazing her skin with sweat. She passed storefronts and houses without seeing them, and she met none of the curious stares from people stopped in the streets to watch her stream by.

She kept remembering the interview she had done with Evan Marshall and his wife, Maxine, after he had won the mayoral race almost a year ago. Nice, cultured people, the mayor was a well-respected lawyer in town and his wife, a former nurse, was heavily involved with the hospital's fundraising board. Hanna had never met their children, but knew they had two older daughters, both married, and another who would be graduating from high school in a couple of weeks. The baby of the family.

And now she might be missing, Hanna thought as she rounded the parking lot and burst through the employee entrance. She couldn't help fearing the worst. Could the Bay Killer have struck again?

She lunged down the hall into the newsroom. The television mounted up on the wall showed a rerun of a Law & Order episode, the volume jacked up loud. Phones rang, stopped, then rang again. The fax machine spit pages into its tray. Computers hummed.

David Lakefield stopped pacing as soon as he saw her. "Hanna! What are you doing here? Where's Jake?"

"We were having dinner," she panted and wiped beads of sweat from her forehead. "He'll be here in a minute... just had to take his wife home first. God, I think I'm dying." She couldn't seem to get enough air into her lungs. "Okay, give me the rundown."

"The rundown?"

She frowned at him. "Yeah, you know, the rundown, David. Details. Like what happened? And turn everything down a bit, I can't think with all this racket."

He did as she asked, saying nothing, and Hanna moved into the room to her desk. "So what happened, David?" she asked again when the noise level was bearable.

He raked long fingers through his dark curls. "I got a call from some woman a little while ago. Said she was a neighbour and that there was a big commotion at the mayor's house, cops all over the place. She said his daughter might be missing. So I paged Jake." He shrugged, turned up his hands. "That's all I know."

"That's it?" She stared at him. "Did you ask her how she'd heard about this? Did you call the police to confirm? Look through the faxes?" Wordlessly, he shook his head and Hanna clenched her teeth. "Did you at least get her name and number?"

He looked away. "I forgot to ask for her number, but I think she said her name was Helen, uhm, Vaughn... something like that."

"Helen Vaughn?" Hanna knew David was relatively new at reporting, but this was beyond incompetence. Not only should he have gotten the caller's name right, but he should have had the correct spelling of it as well. Not to mention anything about a number, an address, notes on the interview. The five w's - the basics. Just where had he been during Interviewing Techniques 101? she wondered.

"Yeah. Helen. Or Ellen. Vaughn. I'm pretty sure of the last name."

"Wonderful." Gritting her teeth, she swept the phone in her hand and punched in the number for the Midland Police Service as she rifled through the faxed pages. Nothing.

"Yes, hello, this is Hanna Laurence from *The Post*. We've just received a call from a neighbour of the mayor's who said she heard a rumour that Mr. Marshall's daughter might be missing. Is there any truth to this? What can you tell me at this time?"

The neighbour - whatever her name was - had been right. Although not officially considered a missing person case because it hadn't been 24 hours yet, the Midland Police Service confirmed it was 'looking into the possible disappearance' of the mayor's daughter. She had last been seen by a neighbour as she was leaving her parents' house in her car at 12:30 p.m. that afternoon to go to work. Hanna tried to find out more but the dispatcher refused to answer any other questions until more information was known. She said thank you and hung up.

A cold weight lodged in her stomach. *The nightmare was starting again.*

"Her name is Ingrid Marshall," she said, looking up at David, her fingers icy against her throat. "Youngest daughter of Evan and Maxine Marshall. Last seen by a neighbour at about twelve-thirty this afternoon, could be the same one who called here a little while ago. She left her parents' house in her red Miata. Never showed up for work at Lakefield's Ani-" Hanna stopped, pressed her knuckles to her mouth. "Oh God."

Dr. Lakefield's Animal Clinic.

She felt the hairs at the back of her neck prickle as a pretty face swam up to the surface of her mind. The chubby blonde on the phone when she'd been by to see Kirk Andrews on Wednesday morning. The name tag she'd worn pinned to her shirt had identified her as Ingrid. Hanna swallowed hard as she thought of Kirk Andrews who worked at the same clinic. This was too much coincidence, she thought, and felt herself grow cold. Was Kirk the killer? Had he abducted Ingrid, taken her someplace and killed her - like he might have done with Lydia? And the others? But the evidence linking him to Lydia's murder was all circumstantial - sure, he had access to ketamine hydrochloride at his place of work; he had known Lydia first as a friend, then as a lover; he might have impregnated her and furnished her with the number of an abortionist; and he had lied about his relationship with her. But none of these things proved his guilt.

"Hey, are you all right?" David's voice sounded far away.

She blinked her eyes like someone waking from a dream. "What? Oh, yeah. Fine." She tapped her notebook with her pen. "Did you know she worked for your dad?"

"She's the blonde girl in the front office. I talked to her a few times."

Jake Belmont burst into the newsroom at that moment, his shirt sporting wet circles widening under his arms. "What the hell's going on?"

Hanna pulled him aside, quickly filled him in on what she had learned so far and added that she'd know a lot more if David had gotten the caller's name and number.

"All police agencies in central and southern Ontario have been notified to be on the lookout for her car," she concluded.

Belmont went to sit at his desk. "I hate to do this, Hanna, but I have to send you out there. You know what to do." Turning to David, he said, "You go with her and do whatever she says. I want shots of all the cops and people around the mayor's place, Hanna, and call me every half hour with updates. I'll stay here, check the local news, and try to set up an interview with the mayor and his wife for tomorrow. You'll be all right for that? Hanna?"

No. Not in a million years, she thought. She didn't think she could stand to see the same look on the faces of the mayor and his wife that she had seen on Albert and Cynthia Tomlinson's. The pain, the terror, the worry eating away at their souls. And underneath, something else. Hope. Always, there was hope. She had interviewed enough parents of missing kids and teenagers over the years to know that hope was the only thing they had left, the only thing that kept them going day after day. She remembered a woman she'd interviewed five years after her three-year-old son went missing from a crowded mall in the city, remembered something she'd said - "I would have killed myself a long time ago if it wasn't for hope." After all those years, she still hoped her son would come home.

Swallowing hard, Hanna nodded as she grabbed a handful of batteries out of her desk drawer and started out of the newsroom. She couldn't let herself think about these things right now; she had a job to do. But later… "My stuff's still in your SUV, right?"

"In the back."

She looked over her shoulder to make sure David was following, then pushed out the employee entrance into the parking lot. The air was as muggy as it had been that morning even though it was now past nine o'clock and the sun was starting to slip over the horizon. David got in her car while she grabbed her bag out of Jake's vehicle and threw it in her backseat. Then she drove off towards the Marshalls' home.

"Did you find her?"

Hanna held her cell to her ear as she watched David talking to a man on the front steps of his house, three doors down from the mayor's on the same side of the street.

"Not yet." She tried not to let her exasperation show in her voice, but it was easier said than done. She turned her back on David and gripped the phone. "But I've got him knocking on doors… all of them. He will find her, if it's the last thing he ever does."

"Easy, Hanna," Belmont said. "He's just a rookie. Don't give yourself any more stress than you already have. All right? So… tell me, what's happening?"

She filled him in on her interviews with neighbours and cops as she let her eyes roam across the street to the Marshalls' house, a rambling clapboard bungalow painted a pale yellow with white trim around the doors and windows. Climbing roses covered a trellis near the front door and manicured cedars lined the edges of the property. Three town police cruisers were parked in front, another in the driveway. The local news media vans and a dozen other cars littered the area. Reporters interviewed curious neighbours and pedestrians crowding the sidewalk across from the mayor's house.

"Call again when you know anything."

She promised she would, then signed off and looked back at David. He had crossed the street and was now talking to an old man in a tank top and bright red suspenders. She watched him scribble something down in his notepad and decided she might as well lend him a hand to speed things along. She headed for a small Cape Cod style house, climbed the steps to the veranda and knocked on the blue front door.

The tall, middle-aged woman who poked her head out had three jiggling chins and dark smudges under her eyes. "Yes?"

Hanna introduced herself and asked if she knew a neighbour by the name of Helen or Ellen Vaughn.

"You're from what? *The Post?* I called you guys already."

Hanna's heart did a little flip. "You did? Then you must be Helen Vaughn?"

The woman's face puckered into a frown, her eyes squinting. "Who? I don't know any Helen Vaughn, or whatever. My name's Yvonne Allen."

Helen Vaughn... Yvonne Allen. It took her but a second to figure out what had happened. David had mixed up the woman's first and last names, on top of everything else. She glanced at him down the street and caught him staring back at her.

"I'm sorry, Mrs. Allen," Hanna said and explained David's mistake. "We've been trying to find you so we can talk to you a little more. Would that be all right?"

Yvonne Allen opened her front door a few more inches, exposing the right side of a very fat body clad in a billowing red blouse and shorts the colour of lemon meringue pie. "Sure. Why not?" she said. "What d'you want to know? And it's not *Mrs.* Allen anymore, just for your information. I finally got up my nerve and turfed the bastard out last year."

"Oh. I'm sorry." Hanna pulled out her notebook and uncapped her pen.

"Don't be. God knows I'm not."

Hanna got the correct spelling of the woman's first and last names and asked, "How did you hear about the mayor's daughter?"

The woman looked down the street and motioned Hanna to come inside. "Maxine told me... that's the mayor's wife, you know," she was saying as she lead Hanna into a sparsely furnished living room with two bay windows overlooking the street. A large rocker faced the windows; a cup of tea sat on the carpeted floor nearby.

"She just came over, I guess that must have been around seven-thirty or so and asked if I'd seen Ingrid. She was pretty upset… went around the whole neighbourhood, knocking on all the doors. Asking if anyone had seen or heard from her daughter. Crying the whole time."

Hanna felt a stab of pain imagining Maxine Marshall running down her street, pounding on her neighbours' doors, tears streaming down her face. She blinked away the image and felt a crushing weight descend on her chest. "Had you seen her today? Ingrid?"

The rocker creaked and groaned as Yvonne lowered her bulk into it and motioned Hanna to a plaid love seat. "Yeah, around twelve-thirty or so. I said hi to her over the fence. Then a few minutes later I heard her start up her car and drive off. She works at that animal clinic every day for a few hours as part of some co-op course at school. When Ingrid didn't come home after work, Maxine started worrying right away. She said Ingrid always comes home around three-thirty, unless she had some plans or whatever, but she would always call. So when she didn't come home and she didn't call and it got to be later and later, Maxine finally phoned that doctor who owns the clinic and he said Ingrid had taken the day off. That wasn't like Ingrid, Maxine said, to take a day off and not let her know about it. So she called her daughter's friends, but no one had seen or talked to Ingrid today. And no one knew where she was. So finally, she called the police."

"Does Ingrid have a boyfriend, do you know?"

"I saw this guy a few times, but I don't know if they were dating or anything."

"Can you describe him?"

"Tall. Kind of cute. But I only saw him a couple of times."

"What about colour of hair? Eyes?"

"Reddish." She shrugged. "I don't know about his eyes."

Tall, kind of cute, with reddish hair. Could she be describing Kirk Andrews? Hanna wondered. "Did you notice what kind of vehicle he drives?"

Another shrug. "I'm not real good with makes, but it was a truck.

A grey pickup."

Hadn't she seen a grey truck somewhere just recently? And then it hit her. There had been a grey pickup, a Toyota she remembered, parked in Kirk Andrews' driveway the day she'd gone to his parents' home to interview him and other friends of Lydia Tomlinson's.

Hanna made sure to get the woman's telephone number, thanked her for her time and made her way outside to the street. A uniformed officer came out of the Marshalls' home and walked down the driveway to the sidewalk. Reporters immediately ran across the street and surrounded him on all sides, their microphones shoved in the air.

"...a search party," the officer was saying. "If the mayor's daughter doesn't turn up tonight, we'll be starting from here at first light, around six o'clock tomorrow morning, making our way along the route she normally takes to get to work at Lakefield's Animal Clinic. We're asking for volunteers... all you have to do is show up in the morning."

Several reporters broke in with questions, but the officer raised a hand. "There will be no comments at this time... all we can say is that we are investigating Ingrid Marshall's possible disappearance. We'll have more details at a later time. Thank you."

Hanna spotted David at the edge of the crowd and made her way over to him. "I found her," she said, inclining her head towards the Cape Cod house. "Just one thing... her name's Yvonne Allen, not Helen Vaughn. You mixed up her first and last names."

He slapped himself in the forehead. "God! I'm such an idiot."

"Don't beat yourself up," she said, hitting redial on her cell. "I've done a lot worse."

She handed him her camera while she waited for the call to go through, asked him to take some shots of the crowd and watched as he moved down the street. When Belmont answered, Hanna told him she had found the neighbour who had called the newsroom and explained what had happened with the name. She then filled him in on what Yvonne Allen had said, gave him details of the search and told him she was planning on taking part.

"That's great. I'll try to round up a couple of the others, but no matter what, I'll see you at six. Oh, and Hanna? I set up some time around nine o'clock tomorrow morning for you to talk to the mayor and his wife at their house. They remembered you when I told them you'd be the one doing the story... they said they wouldn't talk to anyone else."

On a professional level, this was heartening to hear but on an emotional one, it was heart-wrenching. She could already feel her stomach knotting in anticipation of the interview and knew it would affect her long after she had written the story.

"Hanna? You there?" Belmont asked when she hadn't responded. "Are you going to be able to handle this?"

She pulled herself back into the moment. "Yes. I think so."

"Good. Anything else going on there?"

"There are more people and reporters now, but nothing else seems to be happening. How long do you plan on keeping us out here?"

"Hang around a bit more, then call it a night. We'll pick up in the morning."

Hanna ended the call and tried Kirk's number, shuffling from one foot to the other as she listened to the phone ring endlessly. No one was home.

Spotting David in front of her car parked almost a block away, she walked over to him. She could feel exhaustion seeping into her bones as she asked him to call his father. "Find out if Kirk Andrews was at work today."

David gave her a questioning look, but said nothing as he took out his cell phone and punched in the numbers. "Dad? Have you heard about Ingrid? Yeah... it's terrible. I'm down here with another reporter right now... do you know if Kirk was at work today? Uh...no reason."

After a minute, David ended the call. "He came in this morning, but told my dad he had to rush out, some kind of emergency, and left around lunchtime. What's this about?"

"Nothing." Hanna shook her head. "Listen, we'll be heading back to the office in a few minutes. Would you mind getting a few more shots while I make another call?"

"Sure."

Hanna climbed into her stifling car, rolled down all the windows and contemplated what she knew so far. Ingrid had last been seen by Yvonne Allen, at around twelve-thirty. Kirk had left around lunchtime. Coincidence? Or something more sinister? She didn't know, but she had a hard time keeping her thoughts from spinning out of control as she tried his number again to no avail.

"Damn," she muttered as she disconnected and dialled Bennett's home number.

"Tim, it's me," she said when he answered. "I'm sorry I didn't make it out to your place tonight... something awful happened. It just slipped my mind."

"Marshall's daughter." He sighed. "Yeah, I know. My unit was called."

Hanna shut her eyes at this news. "Oh God, Tim. What's going on? Do you think it could be him? The Bay Killer?"

"I don't know, Hanna. I honestly don't know. But this is the mayor's daughter we're talking about and everything that can be done is being done. Unfortunately, that also includes checking into every possible scenario and any links she might have to the other victims. Which is why my unit was called in, as part of the investigation."

She told him everything she'd learned about Kirk in the last couple of hours.

"Hmmm," Bennett said when she had finished. "We'll check it out. I don't believe in coincidences, either. I'll be in touch with Midland and I'll let you know what happens."

"Okay."

"I know it's getting late now, but do you still want to come over?"

There was nothing she wanted more, but she'd gotten precious little sleep the night before and the earlier rush of adrenaline she'd felt barrelling down the street had long since gone. All that was left was total exhaustion; she could feel it in her bones.

"I'd love to say yes, Tim, but it's been an incredibly long day and I can't stop imagining the worst for Ingrid. I'd be lousy company... you'd hate me."

"I could never hate you, Hanna, but I understand. How about tomorrow night then?"

"Tomorrow," she said, grinning, "is another day. Expect me about eight."

Chapter Twenty-Five

THE HUMIDITY WAS thick enough to cut by nine o'clock the next morning as Hanna passed the throng of people jamming the sidewalk in front of the Marshalls' home and started up the driveway. She felt heavy and tired as she climbed the stairs to the porch.

An officer at the door studied her press card, then rang the doorbell and motioned her forward. She wished he'd turned her away because there was nothing she wanted more than an excuse to make a run for her car and go home. Instead she willed herself to be strong. As much as she hated to intrude on the Marshalls' at this most painful time, she knew a story had to be done. Ingrid had been missing for nearly a full day and the more time passed, the more her chances of being found alive were slipping away.

The door opened and Hanna swallowed hard as Maxine Marshall, in a ratty green sweatsuit and her ash-blonde hair dishevelled, looked at her with puffy, red-rimmed eyes.

"Oh Hanna, it's you. Please come in," she said, stepping aside to let Hanna enter an air-conditioned foyer decorated with antiques and Mexican tiles on the floor. The last time Hanna had spoken to Mrs. Marshall, the night of the victory party at a prestigious golf club after her husband had won the mayoral race, she had been carefully made up and superbly dressed, her hair perfect. She couldn't believe the changes she was seeing now. It was as if the woman had aged a decade overnight.

The mayor came into the foyer through an archway and joined

his wife, putting an arm around her waist. He was a tall man with a full head of steel grey hair and large blue eyes that appeared shadowed and haunted behind wire-rimmed glasses.

"Thanks for coming," he said, shaking her hand. "Hard to believe it's been a year."

"Yes." Hanna looked from one to the other. "Mr. and Mrs. Marshall, I'm so sorry about Ingrid. And I'm sorry to have to interview you at a time like this, but I… my editor and I want to do everything we can to help."

Maxine's eyes were pools of liquid. "It's… we understand. We hope a story can do some good." A sob broke the last word in two and Evan pulled her closer.

"I'll do the best I can, I promise you that."

"Thank you. And thank you for taking part in the search this morning… I saw you out there with your editor." Evan looked down at his wife. "It's too bad nothing came of it… but just the fact that so many people are trying to help is a big comfort."

Close to 100 volunteers had shown up at six that morning to take part in the search, but nothing of any relevance had been found along the route Ingrid normally drove to get to work. Not even a scrap of clothing or piece of paper, and Hanna felt their frustration.

"Yes," Maxine said, "it's been overwhelming."

Evan nodded, passed a big hand over his face. "We can talk in the living room, Hanna. We'll be comfortable there."

She followed the Marshalls into a room decorated in earth tones, her eyes pausing on a framed picture on the wall above a cappuccino-coloured sofa. It showed the mayor with a hand on the shoulders of two small daughters as they sat beside their mother who held a baby in her arms, the tiny face peaceful in sleep. Hanna swallowed around a lump in her throat as she realized that the baby was the couple's youngest daughter, Ingrid.

"I see you like our family portrait," Maxine said and moved closer, tracing the contours of the baby's face with her index finger. "Do you remember that day, Evan? The girls were so excited; they could hardly sit still long enough for the photographer to snap the picture. But Ingrid was so quiet - I couldn't believe she slept the entire time we were there. Remember, Evan?" She turned to her husband, tears streaming down her face.

"Oh, honey," the mayor said, guiding his wife to the sofa. "Don't think about it, Max, sweetheart. Please. It just makes everything worse."

"I can't help it," she said, her voice cracking. "What if something happened to her? What if this killer's got her? What if we never see her again?"

Hanna bit down on her bottom lip, feeling like an intruder as she watched the mayor draw his wife into his arms. He held her close against him as tears rolled down her face.

Hanna was filled with fear for this couple's daughter. She couldn't help thinking of Albert and Cynthia Tomlinson and how they had looked when she had interviewed them. Would it end the same way for the Marshalls as it had for the Tomlinsons? Would their daughter be found like the others, mutilated and dumped like so much garbage?

After a few minutes, Maxine managed to pull herself together. Sitting beside her on the sofa, the mayor opened a drawer on the coffee table and pulled out a couple of photo albums. "You'll probably need a picture of her," he said, looking up at Hanna and patting the space beside him on the other side of the sofa. "Here, come have a look."

She sat down beside him and he showed her pictures of his daughters blowing candles at birthday parties, opening presents at Christmas, hunting for eggs at Easter. Maxine cried silently, her hands clutching a tattered Kleenex in her lap.

The second photo album contained much more recent pictures of their daughters and grandchildren, including a graduation photograph of Ingrid taken just weeks before. She had long, wavy blonde hair and large blue eyes like her father, and Hanna could not take her eyes off the picture as she studied every detail of the girl's face and compared them to Lydia's and Tina's. But the colour of her hair and eyes seemed to be all she shared in common with the victims. Ingrid was a big, sturdy girl and quite a bit heavier than the others. Hanna knew it was irrational to hope that the killer, having preferred his victims thin and petite so far, wouldn't bother with someone who was overweight now. Even if she was blonde and blue-eyed. And irrational or not, she nonetheless clung to this hope.

It wasn't difficult to coax the Marshalls to talk about Ingrid. They were proud of their daughter and supported her decision to become a veterinarian. Evan talked about her love of animals and her need to help injured birds and stray cats and dogs she had found throughout her childhood. They described her as caring and loving - she had been an easy child and was an equally well-behaved teenager. She was close to her parents and extremely fond of her sisters, both married with children of their own. They couldn't believe something like this could have happened to their baby and implored anyone with any information whatsoever to do the right thing and call the police.

"It's not like her to just disappear like that," Maxine said as she dabbed at her swollen eyes. "She always made sure we knew where she was going to be. She was so responsible for her age. You could always count on her."

"Did Ingrid have a boyfriend? Someone she was seeing?"

Maxine shook her head. "No. She had a lot of friends, though. Both girls and boys."

"Were any of her friends people who worked at the clinic with her?"

"Sure. She was quite friendly with everyone."

"Did she ever talk about someone named Kirk Andrews?"

"Of course. She talked about him all the time. I think she identified with him a lot... he'd just finished the second year of the same veterinary program she'd enrolled in this fall at the University of Guelph..." Maxine twisted her hands in her lap. "I met him once when her car was in the shop and he came to pick her up. He seemed like a very nice young--"

"Excuse me?" A uniformed officer was standing just inside the room, the wide brim of his police-issue hat spinning in his hands. "I apologize for disturbing your interview, Mr. and Mrs. Marshall, but it appears we've found your daughter's car."

A stroke of luck.

The car was found parked behind two commercial-sized dumpsters located in the back lot of the IGA grocery store along Midland's commercial strip. One of the janitors, Mac Connelly, had gone out to get rid of two garbage bags. He never would have noticed the car had it not been for one of the bags hitting the edge of the dumpster and bouncing out. He walked around to the back and found the bag sitting on the hood of a red Miata.

"It was luck, plain and simple," Mac was saying, shuffling his dusty work boots on the cracked and buckled asphalt of the store's back lot.

Standing among weeds pushing out from the cracks in the asphalt, Hanna watched as two more police cars bumped their way into the lot. Uniformed officers seemed to be everywhere; one had even climbed into one of the dumpsters.

"How did you know the car belonged to Ingrid Marshall?" she asked, turning her attention back to the janitor.

"How could I not know? It's been all over the news, so when I saw the car, I ran inside, told the manager and he called the cops." He turned his head to spit on the ground.

"Did you notice anything unusual about the car?"

He frowned. "Like what? Blood on the seats or something? That what you mean?"

"Anything at all."

"No. No blood, nothing like that. Not that I could see, anyway. I never did get too close to the car, didn't even get the garbage bag off the hood, if you wanna know. I thought I'd better not touch anything... in case something did go down. Or whatever."

When she had gotten all the information she was going to get from the janitor and the police officers processing Ingrid's car for evidence, Hanna drove to the office as if on autopilot. She hated jumping to conclusions, but the fact that Ingrid's car had been found hidden behind dumpsters bothered her and raised more questions than answers in her mind. Was she really missing? Or had she stashed her car and been picked up by someone else? And if she had, was it of her own free will or had she been coerced?

This being Saturday, only a handful of vehicles, including David's blue pickup and Belmont's SUV, were parked in the lot when she pulled in at The Post. The building was quiet and cool as she walked into the deserted newsroom and settled in at her desk. Phone messages and press releases littered the top of it as usual. She pushed a few things aside, glanced at a few more and then found Belmont in the lunchroom to update him on the latest events.

"Well, I'll be damned," he said when she had finished. "That can't be good for this Kirk Andrews, right? I guess you didn't have any luck tracking him down?"

She'd tried reaching him earlier, to no avail. "No, and neither have the cops."

He took a last bite of his sandwich and threw the wrapper in the wastebasket. "File your story and get out of here, Hanna. David's got the weekend stuff covered, so there's no reason why you should be cooped up in here any longer than you have to."

"Thanks, Jake."

Hanna booted up her computer and spent a few minutes staring at the keys while she saw again Evan and Maxine Marshall's anguished faces. How was she going to write this story? Where was Ingrid right at this very moment? Was she alive... or dead?

Don't think, just write, she told herself. But of course that was easier said than done, and she spent several minutes trying to talk herself into it. Then almost of their own will, her fingers began to type and she was finally able to write the story of Ingrid's disappearance. She poured her heart into it and did not stop until the last word had been written. Then she sat back, reread her story and filed it over to Belmont's desk. He imported her text on to the front page, wrote in a headline and sent the page off to be pre-set.

After he left, Hanna dropped her head on folded arms and closed her eyes for a moment. She couldn't remember when she had felt more completely drained.

"So how goes the battle?" came a voice just behind her shoulder.

Hanna jumped and looked up into David Lakefield's suntanned, smiling face. "David! Where were you?"

"Out to lunch with my father. Anything going on?"

"Well, they found Ingrid's car. Did you hear about that?"

"Yeah. Dad told me." David circled around Hanna and leaned up against her desk, folding his arms across his chest. "What a lucky break. Did they find anything?"

She shook her head. "And no one can find Kirk either. Did he happen to tell your Dad why he had to leave yesterday?"

"Something to do with family, I think."

Hanna stared out the window a long time, lost in thought. She was startled when she heard David speak again.

"Do you think he could be behind Ingrid's disappearance?"

"I don't know… but let's just say that things aren't looking real good for Kirk."

David grinned. "The cops are after him, aren't they?"

"What's so funny?"

"Nothing." The grin vanished; a sheepish look came into his eyes. "It's just, well, I've known Kirk a long time. It seems unbelievable that he'd be involved in this thing… just look at the guy! He doesn't look like he could hurt a fly let alone a girl."

"Looks can be deceiving."

"I don't know… I'm having a hard time seeing it." David moved around Hanna's desk to his own and dropped into his chair. "So how's the investigation? Have they identified the girl they found Tuesday night yet?"

She shook her head. "Not officially."

David turned on his computer. "What's taking so long?"

"Pronounced decomposition," she said, grimacing. "She was under water for a long time. They'll have to use dental records to identify her."

"But they probably have some idea who she is, right?"

"They think it might be a girl by the name of Tina Joliet."

His eyes crinkled at the corners as they narrowed in thought. "Who was she?"

"She worked at a resort called The White Pine Inn at the Bay at the time she went missing. Twenty years old, originally from North Bay, she was three months pregnant. She'd just graduated from Tourism and Hospitality at Canadore College up there."

David's eyebrows arched. "No way! I just graduated from there myself this year."

She vaguely recalled Belmont mentioning this when he had hired David for the summer, but it had slipped her memory. In all the years she'd worked as a reporter, Hanna had met very few people who had studied journalism at the small northern college. At the time she was a student there, over a decade ago now, its journalism program had been one of the smallest in terms of enrolment figures in the province.

"I heard that's where you went, too."

"I did." She thought of something. "I know it's a long shot, but did you happen to know or have heard of Tina Joliet? You were both students there at the same time."

David thought a moment, then shook his head. "No. The name doesn't ring a bell. I know it's a small college, but most students tend to hang out with others in the same program as them. It was probably the same when you were there."

"Yeah... but we were all over the place doing stories for the college paper. I met a lot of other students that way."

"That's true. I met a lot of other people, too. But not this girl."

"So how'd you end up at Canadore, anyway?" Hanna asked, curious. "Most people have never even heard of it."

David shrugged. "My mom took some courses there a few years ago and really liked it. So when I decided to get into this field, it seemed like the logical place to go."

"Your mom lives in North Bay?"

"No, she's from this little town about 15 minutes away. Sturgeon Falls? She moved back up there after the divorce. I lived with her while I was in college." He grinned. "Saved a ton of money."

"I bet." Hanna looked around the office. "So what's going on this weekend?"

"Not much. The fair's on, some powerboat racing later. Tomorrow's dead."

So was any notion in Hanna's mind that she was going to get any more work done that afternoon. "Well, David, I'm out of here. But call me at home if there are any new developments with Ingrid... doesn't matter what time."

She scribbled her cell number on a slip of paper for him and grabbed her bag.

"Hey, Hanna?"

She turned around. "Yeah?"

"Sorry about screwing up yesterday. I won't be making that mistake again."

"Hey, don't sweat it. It happens to everybody."

Hanna could hear him laughing as she went out into the sweltering heat.

Her cottage was as hot as an oven when she let herself in a few minutes later. Pistachio gave a plaintive meow as she locked the door behind her and started peeling off sweat-soaked clothes. She skirted naked into her kitchen, downed two glasses of cold water, one right after the other, and filled her cat's bowls with food and fresh water.

In her bedroom, she slipped into an old, black bikini she never wore in public and made a beeline out the back door to her patio. Turning on the outside tap, she held the hose straight over her head and let icy water cascade over her until she was soaked and shivering, and completely refreshed. Then she dried off, made herself a salad and settled at the patio table to eat.

She had just raised the fork to her mouth when her cell chirped. "Hello?"

"We found him," Bennett said.

She sat up straight. "Kirk? Where was he?"

"Visiting his older brother in the Big Smoke. We finally tracked down his parents at home about an hour ago. There was some family emergency involving their eldest son, Kirk's brother, Derrick. Apparently, he'd tried committing suicide. A friend dropping in found him unconscious and called 9-1-1 and the family. That was yesterday morning. So he's got a solid alibi... he's been at the hospital with his brother the entire time."

Hanna sagged against her chair. Suicide, attempted or otherwise, was never an easy situation to deal with and her heart went out to Kirk Andrews and his family. She felt a mix of emotions: relief that he couldn't possibly be involved in Ingrid's disappearance and fear that a madman might be holding the balance of her life in his hands at this very moment.

"This doesn't bode well for the mayor's daughter, does it?"

A sigh whispered across the line. "Between you and I? No, it doesn't. But it still doesn't mean the Bay Killer's got her, Hanna. She might still turn up."

She said nothing, fear twisting in her gut.

"Listen," he said after a moment, "I have to get back to work, but we'll talk some more tonight. You're still planning on coming over, right?"

"Absolutely."

"Great. I'll see you then. Bye."

Her salad forgotten, Hanna stared a long time at the pines in her backyard. Lydia, Tina and Marianne's names paraded in her mind and she shuddered in the heat.

Would Ingrid's soon join the line-up?

Chapter Twenty-Six

THE SUN WAS still high overhead at 8:20 that evening when Hanna took a right onto Bennett's street. She drove past young maple trees planted in tiny, postage-size front yards of identical brick homes, her eyes squinting against sunlight for the number of his house.

She spotted his green Toyota parked in a driveway about halfway down the block. Pulling in beside it and shutting off her engine, she looked out her windshield at his house. The garage doors, the trim around the windows and the front door were painted a deep magenta - this and a wrought iron bench on the front lawn appeared to be the only differences between his house and all the others on the street.

Getting out of her car, Hanna cradled a bottle of wine as she walked up a curving cement path to a small porch. A mountain bicycle was propped up against the wall.

Pressing the bell and stepping back to wait, she felt a faint breeze swirl the thin cotton material of the raspberry-coloured sundress she'd chosen to wear.

When she heard the door open, she turned to look at Bennett silhouetted in the doorway and caught her breath. He was wearing a blue shirt over tight, faded jeans and his hair was wet from a recent shower. His slow smile made him look like an Adonis.

"Hi," she said, feeling her heart race at the sight of him. "Sorry I'm a little late."

"Not at all. Come on in," he invited, stepping aside to let her pass. "Am I imagining things or did I just feel a cool breeze there for a second?"

"Hard to believe… must have been 110 degrees in the shade today." She smelled apples and cinnamon and his spicy aftershave as she squeezed by him into a small foyer.

"Yeah and the worse part is, it's not over." He shut the door and turning, let his emerald eyes slowly travel the length of her. "Jesus, Hanna. You look... amazing."

"So do you," she said as blood rushed up to her face. "Nice jeans."

"These old things?" He looked down at himself. "Only clean pair left, but thanks. Can I get you something? A drink?"

"I brought some wine." She thrust the bottle at him.

He took it, thanked her and motioned her to follow him as he led the way into a white and blue kitchen. Hanna let her eyes trail along the room, glancing at charcoal sketches of buildings hanging on the walls of a breakfast nook tucked into the corner while Bennett made short work of pulling out the cork. Then he took down two long-stemmed glasses from a cupboard, poured the wine and handed her a glass with a flourish. "Voila, madame. Follow me... I think we'll be more comfortable in the rec room."

He led her through the hallway and down wooden stairs into a semi-finished basement. A computer, keyboard and printer sat on a worktable in one corner; a bookshelf held an assortment of mystery and horror paperback novels on the wall above. Mismatched easy chairs and a blue and brown plaid couch faced a large flat-screen television encased in a pine entertainment unit taking up most of one cinder block wall. A baseball game was underway on the screen, the sound turned down low.

Bennett folded his long limbs into a recliner. "It's almost over, bottom of the ninth."

Hanna settled on the couch and made appropriate noises, but baseball had never interested her. She was much more interested in him and took the opportunity to gaze at his face as he watched TV. She let her eyes trail along his features, admiring the way his hair curled over his forehead and around the top of his ears. But he looked preoccupied and worn out, and lines drew his mouth down.

She desperately wanted to cup her hands around his face, feel his skin against hers, kiss all his worries away.

Stop it, she fiercely admonished herself even as she remembered the taste of his lips on hers, the way his body had felt pressed against hers. She gulped down most of her wine and set the glass on the coffee table, aware of her heart pounding in her chest. She was more than attracted to him; there was no denying it. And while sex was definitely part of it, she knew there was a lot more involved. She was drawn to him in a way most people wouldn't understand - horror had brought them together, not love or infatuation or even lust. That had come after, she thought, tracing the shape of his lips with her eyes.

"You mind if I pick out some music?" she asked, unable to stand looking at him a moment longer without reaching out to touch him.

"Sure, help yourself."

Hanna studied his impressive collection of CDs. She picked out Coldplay's *Parachutes* compilation, one of her favourites, skipped over to the fifth track and returned to the couch as the first mournful notes of "Yellow" drifted out of the speakers.

"Great choice... I haven't listened to this in ages," Bennett said, clicking off the TV and turning to look at her. "So how'd it go today? I heard you had an interview with the mayor and his wife after the search?"

She could still see them sitting on their sofa, their faces pale and drawn, their eyes red-rimmed and desperate as they talked about their youngest child - a daughter who'd been missing now for almost thirty-three hours. "Yes."

"Hard, wasn't it?"

"It always is, Tim. Breaks my heart."

He patted her hand. "Tough jobs we have, but-"

"Someone has to do it." She smiled at him. "Lucky us."

He smiled back, then frowned. "I meant to ask you .. how'd it go yesterday? At the White Pine Inn?"

"Jody was great but she's taking Tina's murder pretty hard. Blames herself." She picked up her wineglass. "And you sure weren't kidding when you said Lydia and Tina could be twins. I nearly had a coronary when Jody showed me a picture of her. Jesus."

"I know. Eerie." He made a face, set down his glass.

"That's putting it mildly. Makes you think, though. Someone who looked a lot like those girls must have played a very important role in this psycho's life. Maybe his mother, his grandmother, a babysitter. I don't know. But it's scary, that's for sure."

He nodded and passed a hand over his face. "Talk to anyone else?"

"Yes," she said, unable to stop a mischievous grin from spreading across her face. "You'll never guess who in a million years."

"You don't mean... Benjamin Lachance?"

"The one and the same," she said and told him what she had learned during the interview.

"So what's your take on the guy?"

"Well, he's certainly tall, dark and handsome, Tim. And he knew Tina. He worked with her in the dining room, even admitted that he'd spoken with her a few times. But I don't know." She shrugged. "So, what happens next in the investigation?"

"Well, we're trying to track down Victor Lachance right now and we're planning on hitting the resort and talking to everyone who works there and everyone else who happened to vacation there around that long weekend. That's Monday." He shook his head, raked his fingers through his curly hair. "I don't know how we're going to do it. We're still working on tracking down employees and campers at Beausoleil. There's just too many people to talk to, not enough of us to do it and so little time. I just hope we uncover something soon - a solid suspect would be great - before another body turns up. Like the mayor's daughter."

Hanna's stomach tightened as she thought of Evan and Maxine Marshall again. "The cops were pretty tight-lipped out there today. How's that investigation coming along?"

"Grounded," he said, frustration in his voice. "The Midland cops talked to everyone who knew her, and nothing. It's like she just disappeared off the face of the earth."

"Something happened to her, Tim. I don't know what, but I am relieved that Kirk's not involved... any word on how his brother is doing?"

"He'll live. They had to pump out his stomach... he'd swallowed all kinds of pills, but they expect him to make a full recovery."

"What was the reason he tried to kill himself, did anyone say?"

"I think it was a combination of things. He'd lost his job and his girlfriend in the same week, and he was also struggling to stay off drugs. Kirk's mother said he'd been in rehab a few times over the years to deal with a heroin addiction."

Hanna wagged her head from side to side. "That's so sad."

"Not to change the subject or anything," he said, "but have you figured out what word *tatler* wanted you to rearrange?"

"No. It's been driving me crazy, but for the life of me, I can't figure it out."

"That's really too bad. The more I think of it, the more I think he's the link to this whole thing. We need to know who he is, where he is and what he knows."

"What's going on with E-Crimes? Have they gotten anywhere?"

"Still working on it... although I did hear they were getting closer." He drank the rest of his wine. "What about *tatler*? Has he sent you anything else?"

"No, at least not that I'm aware of," Hanna said, sighing. "But it has been a while since I've had a chance to check."

She grabbed her cell, logged on to yahoo and checked her mail. Fourteen messages had been sent to her since the last time she had checked. Going through them, she wasn't surprised to find a message from *tatler*, sent at 12:16 p.m. Almost nine hours ago.

"Open it," Bennett urged.

Words appeared in the message box. *Figured it out yet? Move them around and you get a different name.*

Hanna stared at the message, willing an answer to pop into her head. But the longer and harder she tried, the more frustrated she became. It just wasn't making any sense.

"I could be wrong about this," Bennett said, turning to look at her, "but he used the word 'name'. Could it be his name that he wants us to rearrange?"

Hanna looked back at the screen and suddenly, it all made perfect sense. "That's it!" she shouted, jumping up and grabbing her shoulder bag. She found a piece of paper and a pen and returned to the table. "You're right, Tim. It's his name. He wants us to rearrange the letters of his name. You're a genius."

On the piece of paper, she wrote down TATLER and together, they started to rearrange the letters to form a new name.

A few seconds later, a shiver raced down Hanna's spine and gooseflesh rose up on her arms. They had figured it out.

The new name was RATTLE.

Chapter Twenty-Seven

ALL THE AIR seemed to evaporate out of the room. Hanna struggled to find a breath, her heart knocking around in her chest as if it had come loose and was trying to get away.

"He knew about the snakes all along."

Bennett shot out of his chair. "Of course he did. Why wouldn't he? He knew about everything else… the locations where the victims disappeared from, the fact that the killer is a necrophile. This is all part of his little game, Hanna. I bet he killed himself laughing when he came up with that name."

He's right, she thought as she logged off the Internet, returned her phone to her purse, and tucked her legs under her on the couch.

"I just wish I knew what the deal with the snakes is, though," Bennett said. "What would possess this bastard to stick a snake in his victims?"

It was an issue she had thought about several times since she had overheard that conversation at The Loon. What had struck her the most wasn't that the killer had inserted something in his victims, but that his choice had been a snake. Why not a bird or a pop bottle or even a pair of pliers, like that serial killer in Florida had used? The answer was simple. Because it mattered to him. Somehow, snakes were significant for him.

Thinking about it now, Hanna sensed there was something else at the core of the matter. Something she was missing. And then an image came to her and she turned to look at him. "Are you Catholic, Tim?" she asked.

"No, my parents were Protestants. Why?"

"Doesn't matter. You know about Adam and Eve?"

He looked at her curiously. "Sure, doesn't everyone?"

Hanna smiled. "Then you know it was a snake that tempted them to taste the forbidden fruit in the Garden of Eden. I don't know what Protestants believe, but since the beginning of time Catholics have associated the snake with evil. My mom made us go to church every Sunday and there was this statue of the Virgin Mary where we always sat. I just remembered now that she was stepping on the head of a snake."

"So you think maybe this guy's religious?"

"Maybe. But I was thinking that this guy may have chosen the snake, either consciously or unconsciously, because it is the symbol of evil. I think he knows he's evil, deep down inside. He has to know. To kill and maim like he does..."

"That's interesting, I'll grant you that. But what would be his motivation?"

"I don't know. Maybe he knows he's a monster; maybe he's tortured by his own sick actions. Maybe using a snake is a desperate cry for help on his part; maybe he's trying to tell us something about himself. Maybe he even wants to get caught."

"That's a lot of maybes, Hanna. Who really knows what's way down deep in the psyche of a madman? Maybe it's just pure evil. Any way you look at it."

Hanna thought of Lydia, Tina and Marianne. She remembered the photographs *tatler* had sent her and imagined again all the vile things the killer had done to his victims after their deaths. *Pure evil. Any way you look at it.*

"I guess you're right," she said, closing her eyes.

"Hanna, can I ask you something?" Bennett asked, his tone hesitant as if he really didn't want to ask her anything but felt compelled to.

Curious, she opened her eyes. "Sure."

"How come you wanted to be kept informed with the investigation? It's always bugged me, not knowing."

Her anxiety level rose; she could feel her heart race inside her chest. She shifted on the couch, trying to get comfortable, and lifted her eyes to his. "In order to answer that question, I have to tell you a story, Tim. And it's not a pleasant one. Are you sure you really want to hear it?" He nodded and she took a deep breath. "Okay, here goes. A young girl meets a guy three years older than her. He's the friend of her best friend's boyfriend and he's tall, good-looking and older. Of course she says yes when he asks her out. They have fun at the movies and then he asks her out again. They go to the beach this time, swim around for a while and then he suggests they go for a drive. She agrees."

Hanna looked down, aware she was talking about herself in the third person. "It's a beautiful day in July. The sun is shining; the temperatures are climbing into the thirties. They drive around for a while and then he decides to park his truck in a government forest just off the highway. They start kissing and he fumbles with her clothing, trying to take it off. But she's not ready for that and she tells him to stop. Instead, he pulls out a Swiss Army knife, pushes her down and rips off her shorts. He doesn't care that she's crying, that she asks him to stop over and over again. He doesn't care that she's never had sex before, that she's a virgin. He holds her down and then he… rapes her."

She took a tremulous breath as memories of that day crowded in on her. She could still feel the heat of the sun as it slanted through the canopy of trees to beat against the windshield. She could still hear John Cougar Mellencamp singing on the radio about Jack and Diane. And even after all those years, she could still smell him, a sickly mix of stale sweat and beer that oozed from his pores as he hung above her, thrusting into her over and over again, the knife in his hand.

She swallowed hard. "And when it was all over, he got out of the truck, pulled up his jeans and laughed in my face. Like a maniac." She met Bennett's eyes. "It happened fourteen years ago next month."

She heard a low, guttural sound lodge in his throat and then he pulled her against his chest, hard. His heartbeat was loud in her ears, pounding in rhythm to her own, and she wrapped her arms around his waist as a tear slipped down the corner of her eye and coursed down her cheek to her lips. She tasted salt.

"Oh Hanna," he said in her hair, his voice strangled with emotion. "I'm so sorry."

She listened to the beat of his heart through the thin cotton of his shirt, then lifted her head to look into his eyes. "It's okay, Tim. It happened a long time ago."

"But I bet it doesn't feel like that, does it?"

A little sob tore out of her before she could stop it. "No," she whispered and looked down at her hands. "It always feels… like it just happened."

He took her hands in his and held them a long time. "So that's why you wanted to be kept in the loop? Because of what happened to you?"

She nodded. "Shrinks call it projection…when they found Lydia, I couldn't help thinking what if it had been me all those years ago?"

He stared at her. "How old were you when this happened, Hanna?"

"Fifteen," she answered.

"Jesus," he mumbled. "I hope you reported the bastard."

She gave him an are-you-kidding look. "I wanted to… believe me, there's nothing I wanted to do more than go after that piece of shit. I still think about it, you know, about how many others he probably went after… what I might have prevented. But you know better than I do what happens in a courtroom when someone is accused of rape, Tim. It would have been his word against mine. But it wasn't only that… at the time, I felt so ashamed. I didn't even tell my own parents until two years later."

"What did they say?"

Hanna swallowed hard. The rape had been the hardest thing she'd lived through. But her parents' reaction had hurt her more and even now, after all these years, there was still a part of her that bled a little every time she thought of it. But she no longer resented them like she once had, and hoped one day she would find it in her heart to forgive them completely for not being there when she needed them the most.

"They didn't believe me," she said, "or maybe it was that they didn't want to believe me, I don't know. My father never spoke a word of it… for him, it was like it never happened. My mother is religious and strict and I think, for her, it was all simply easier to just lecture me on the Ten Commandments. Like getting raped was me making a decision to have sex in the first place."

"Jesus," he said, continuing to rub her back. "I'm amazed you turned out to be such a well-rounded person, Hanna."

She smiled. "Well, I might be now but I wasn't always. I had a lot of problems with sex for a long time."

"No kidding. Something like that would put you off sex for good, I imagine."

She smiled again, but she couldn't look at him in the eye. "No, Tim. It was just the opposite, in fact. It's not something I'm proud of and it's not something I talk about very much. But after it happened, I started sleeping with any guy who was interested in me. Well, maybe not any guy, but you know what I mean. I dated a lot all through high school and college. I took a lot of stupid chances, went out with a lot of guys I wouldn't even give the time of day to now. And you know what?" she stopped, swallowed, and went on, "when I think back on it now, I think it was the only way I could try to protect myself. By giving myself to anyone who wanted me before they could just go ahead and take the only thing they really wanted from me in the first place. I don't know if I can really explain it, but it wasn't until my last year of college that it all caught up with me and I ended up seeing a therapist. And for the first time since it had happened, I started to feel better. I stopped blaming myself for what had happened and I stopped hating my parents for not believing me. And I stopped sleeping with any guy who showed me the slightest bit of attention. I finally learned to value and take care of myself by dealing with what had happened to me and by trying to put it where it belongs… in the past."

His eyes filled with compassion. "Come here." He rested her head against his chest again and used both hands to rub her back.

"Thanks, Tim. For listening and for not… judging."

"I'd never judge you, Hanna, and I'm here if you ever need to talk. You know that, don't you?" He lifted her chin, searching her eyes.

Nodding, Hanna felt pressure grating behind her eyelids. "I'm here for you, too, Tim. You must be going through hell right now."

He laughed, the sound forced as he raked his fingers through his hair and looked over at her. "I suppose I should have seen it coming… but I didn't."

"What happened?"

"I don't know. I came home Sunday afternoon and found Belinda upstairs packing a couple of suitcases. She said she had to leave right away to take care of her aunt who lives in Toronto. She'd apparently had a stroke the night before. So, the idiot that I am, I tell her how sorry I am, that I know how much her aunt means to her and I ask if there's anything I can do. She shakes her head, picks up her suitcases, goes down the stairs and opens the door. Then, all calm and cool, she turns to me and says, 'By the way, Tim, I won't be coming back here except to pick up my things. It's over between us. It's been over for a long time.' And just like that, she left. She didn't even bother to shut the door." He shook his head. "And you know what the funniest part is? She was right. It has been over between us for a long time. Hell, I can't even remember the last time we had sex or a two-way conversation, for that matter."

Hanna started to say something but he placed a finger against her lips.

"I know it's going to take a while for it to sink in, but in a way, it's not a complete surprise. I knew we had problems and that she was unhappy for most of our marriage. She hated the fact that I was a cop. But that was just the beginning. She wanted kids but she couldn't conceive, and I think she blamed me as well as herself for that. And adoption was out. She couldn't bear the thought of raising someone else's 'discarded' child - that's how she actually put it - and so she turned to her job at the Royal Bank with a vengeance. It wasn't unusual for her to work 70, sometimes 80 hours a week and it wasn't long until we became strangers." He shook his head, a sad smile turning up the corners of his mouth. "But I think the final straw for her came when we moved here five years ago. Not because she lost her job; she was able to transfer to the local branch. But it just wasn't the same. Her friends and family were in the city and we knew almost no one here. And so her resentment grew and she blamed me for everything."

"I'm so sorry, Tim," Hanna said, her heart breaking for him. She hugged him hard and it was her turn to rub her hands across his back.

"Fourteen years," he muttered against her shoulder. "Fourteen years and what do I have to show for it? A house, exactly like every other house on this goddamn block."

There was no bitterness in his voice, no anger in his tone. He sounded like a man who had always known, on some level, that it would all end up this way but had just now allowed himself to put it into words.

Hanna couldn't even begin to imagine what it would feel like to have someone walk out on her after so many years. "You don't sound angry," she said.

Bennett laughed, lifting his head to look at her. "Angry? Hell, no. This was a long time in coming, just like Belinda said. I just don't know why it didn't happen a lot sooner."

Hanna watched him pick up his glass and drain the rest of his wine in one gulp. He indicated her empty glass.

"More?" he asked.

"Tim, if you keep feeding me wine I'm going to have to crash on your couch tonight," she said, trying to lighten the mood with her words and a smile.

He smiled back. "You're damn right. You don't think I'd let you drink and drive now, do you? But seriously, you're more than welcome to get blitzed and stay over, if you want. I've certainly got the room."

She noticed his neck had started to redden the more he talked and she decided to tease him some more. "Hmmm. Now I wonder what your neighbours would say? My car is parked in your driveway, you know."

She was surprised when he laughed. "To hell with the neighbours," he said and pushed a lock of hair out of her eyes. Hanna felt a tremor spiral down her body as she locked her eyes on his. She held her breath, afraid to break the spell.

He searched her eyes for what seemed like an eternity and his hands came up over her shoulders to frame her face. Their lips met, as softly as two butterflies brushing wings, and Hanna sighed against his mouth.

They shouldn't be doing this, she thought. His wife had just left him and he was emotionally stunned - a man on the rebound. But her lips were on fire and she was drowning in his gaze.

She couldn't help herself. She pulled him closer, wrapping her arms around his neck, and deepened the kiss.

Just then, Bennett's cell rang and the sound shattered the magic of the moment into a thousand broken pieces at her feet.

Chapter Twenty-Eight

THEY BROKE APART and stared at each other as the phone rang again. Bennett snatched it off the coffee table, pressed the TALK button and barked out a hello.

Hanna watched his face grow more ashen with every second that passed, and all at once she knew.

They found another one.

It hit her full force in the middle of her chest. She felt an ache so profound it left her weak and gasping for breath. Oh God, was it Ingrid they'd found? Or some other poor unfortunate young woman?

Bennett disconnected and turned to her, his eyes reflecting all of her suspicions. It was like looking in a mirror into her own soul.

"Oh my God," she croaked, and the voice she heard was not her own. "Is it... oh God, is it Ingrid? What did they say?"

"Christ," he said through clenched teeth, combing his fingers through his hair, "there's been another one. They don't know if it's the mayor's daughter... they can't say for sure. I have to go. Now." A look of concern came into his eyes and he took her hands in both of his. "Hanna, are you all right? You're so pale."

"I'm fine." Air snagged in her throat.

"Well, if you're sure," he said, releasing her hands, "I really do have to go, Hanna."

He jumped up and was halfway up the stairs by the time she had grabbed her handbag and followed him up on shaky legs.

He had holstered his gun and was reaching for his leather jacket on the coat tree by the door when she came up into the hall. He shrugged it on and came to stand next to her. "I don't know when I'll be back, but stay here as long as you want, okay?"

"No, Tim, I'm coming with you."

"Hanna, please. I know how you're feeling, but there's nothing you can do," he said, his voice soft as he touched her cheek. "I'll see you later, okay?"

"Tim, no. Don't do this to me," she said. "Please. I need to come along. I need to do something. I'll go insane if I have to wait here."

A look passed between them, and then he nodded. "C'mon, then. Let's go."

The night was sultry with dead heat as they rushed along Highway 12.

At the cutoff to the 400, Bennett took the ramp and merged into light traffic heading north. A few minutes later he turned left onto a narrow side road, and Hanna glimpsed darkened homes as they flew by her window.

Rounding a bend in the road, the sweeping red and blue lights of several police cruisers parked behind a low building came into view. Bennett pulled up behind one of the cars, shut off the engine and turned to her, his hand on the door handle.

"Stay put. I'll be back as soon as I know anything." He jumped out of the car, slammed the door shut, and hurried down towards the scene.

Hanna studied the building directly in front of her. Small and rectangular in shape, it was covered with dirty, off-white siding. The windows she could see were tiny and grimy with years of accumulated dirt. Faint yellow light spilled out from them into the parking lot.

Looking to her left, she noticed a wooden sign planted in the middle of an overgrown flowerbed and squinted to make out the name. *Three Mile Marina and Cottages*, she read. A board with the word 'vacancy' painted on it had been nailed up permanently underneath the sign.

Getting out of the car to explore, Hanna walked around the

right side of the building and glimpsed a loose circle of tiny, run-down cottages. Two cars were parked near front doors, but no lights shone in any of the windows. Georgian Bay glistened darkly further down, and she could hear water lapping at the shore.

The entire marina consisted of the rental office-gas station-convenience store building they had parked behind and three rickety wooden piers, featuring no more than a total of thirty slips, laid out straight over the water in front of the building. Hanna counted a dozen moored boats, mostly of the fishing variety.

Down by the end of the furthest dock, a cluster of uniformed and plainclothes officers stood talking and peering over into the water. She could barely make out a small form on the pier and knew she was looking at the victim. Nausea rose in her throat as her eyes picked out Bennett's shape among the men standing on the dock. She fought a sense of déjà vu, thinking back to the day Lydia Tomlinson's body had been pulled from the bay.

Starting back towards the car, Hanna caught the sound of laughter drifting in the air. She felt empathy for the officers out on the piers, knowing that those who dealt with violent death day in and day out often felt a desperate need to joke about it. Some of the funniest things she'd ever heard had been told at crime scenes or at the morgue.

She climbed back inside Bennett's car as pulsing light cut through the darkness behind her. An ambulance pulled into the lot, its siren silent. Two paramedics stepped from the cab, unloaded a stretcher and started down towards the docks.

A half hour later, Bennett folded his long legs into the car and rubbed a hand over his face. "It's another one, alright. Number four. Jesus Christ, when is this going to stop?"

Hanna squeezed her eyes shut, her nails digging into her palms. "Is it Ingrid?"

She opened her eyes to see him shaking his head. "I don't think so. The mayor's daughter is overweight, isn't she? It can't be her. This one's real skinny, real small. She almost looks like a child. Christ."

Hanna said nothing, feeling relief for Ingrid's parents and sorrow for another set of parents somewhere out there who would soon be facing their worst nightmare.

"God, I know it sounds awful, but at least this one's fresh. We might get a chance to collect some trace evidence this time." Bennett rubbed the stubble on his jaw. "And we've got a witness."

Hanna stared at him, couldn't believe she had heard him right. Four dead women. Endless hours spent tracking down and interviewing campers, visitors and employees at Beausoleil Island. Hundreds of phone calls and hundreds of hours spent hunting down every possible lead that had come in, only to face one dead end after another. And now this. A witness. A miracle. Small, but a miracle nonetheless.

"Who is it?"

"A man by the name of Chad Morris. He's the groundskeeper for the marina here. Looks after the place, cuts the grass, does any odd jobs that come up. He lives about three cottages up from here. No wife, no family nearby. He's been doing this job for 20 years, ever since the present owners who live in Toronto bought the place back in the late 80s. He's the one who discovered the body, then called 9-1-1."

"Did he see anything?"

"Yeah, lucky for us, he was emptying the garbage when he heard a big splash coming from that direction," he said, pointing down at the dock where the body was found. "He looked up and saw someone in a boat just before it took off across the bay. He wasn't able to give us a clear description, but he was sure he saw a man. There's only that one lamp post out there, so there wasn't much light, but he says he's pretty sure the guy was dark-haired and was wearing dark clothing."

"Sounds pretty vague."

"Yeah, but that's not the best part." He looked at her, a glimmer of excitement in his eyes. "The best part is that he got the first three digits of the serial number on the boat. We'll pass this information along to the Coast Guard and the marine unit... and who knows? We might be able to nail this son-of-a-bitch after all."

"What about the victim, Tim? Any clue about I.D.?"

He shook his head. "But there's little doubt it's the same killer. The girl's got long, white blonde hair and blue eyes, like the others. But she's the smallest one yet; she can't weigh more than 90 pounds, soaking wet." He pressed his hands against the sides of his head. "The body's going to Toronto tonight. We'll know more after the autopsy."

Hanna watched as a uniformed officer tied one end of a roll of yellow crime scene tape around a tree. She followed him with her eyes as he roped off the parking lot and started down towards the docks. "Where exactly are we, anyway?"

"About fifteen kilometres south of Honey Harbour and the other two marinas where we found the bodies of Lydia and Tina."

A dark sedan pulled into the parking lot and parked beside the ambulance. Hanna recognized the two suited men who stepped out of the car; she'd seen them when Lydia's body had been recovered. They were with the OPP's Behavioural Sciences Section.

"There's Thompson and Jenkins," Bennett said, opening his door. "I'll be back."

They disappeared around the side of the building. A moment later, an older man dressed in jeans and a plaid shirt passed in front of Bennett's car, a bag of trash in one hand. He headed towards a dumpster near the road, and Hanna watched as he lifted the lid and tossed the bag inside. She wondered if this was Chad Morris, the witness.

Hanna stepped out of the car. "Mr. Morris?" she called as she walked towards him.

He turned a lined face her way. Red and blue light cut across sparse white hair and ruggedly handsome features, then retreated again, leaving him in shadows. "Yes?"

She stopped a couple of feet in front of him. "Mr. Morris, my name is Hanna Laurence," she said, offering him her hand. "I'm a reporter for *The Midland Post*. I understand you had quite a scare tonight."

He stared at her hand a moment, then looked away. "I have nothing to say."

He was gruff, distrustful and more than a little shell-shocked.

Hanna read all this in his voice, the stoop of his shoulders, the stoned look in his eyes, and withdrew her hand. "Mr. Morris," she tried again, her voice soft and soothing, "I know you've been through a very hard experience tonight and I know that as long as you live, you will never forget it. You're wondering right now if you'll ever be able to sleep again, having seen her out there in the water. She was like a little girl, wasn't she?"

Hanna looked off towards the docks. She felt angry and tired to the core of her being as she turned back and looked into his dark, troubled eyes. "Mr. Morris, I don't mean to upset you any more than you already are, but there have been others before her, and everyone is desperate for any information which might lead us to the killer. I need to talk to you, to understand what you saw and heard. I don't even need to use your name, if you want to remain anonymous. It's what you say that's important."

He met her gaze steadily then, his eyes wet with unshed tears. "Okay. Just a couple of questions, all right?"

She nodded and smiled. "It's a deal, Mr. Morris. Can I call you Chad?"

"Sure. So what do you want to know?"

"Would you like to sit down, Mr. Mor- I mean, Chad?" She curled her arm through his and led him to a nearby bench. "It's been a hell of a night, hasn't it?"

He dropped heavily, the wood creaking under his weight. "I think that's the understatement of the year," he said, passing a knotted hand across his face. "It was the worse thing I've ever seen... and I fought in 'Nam, you know. I still can't believe it."

Hanna sat down beside him. "Tell me what happened."

"I was emptying the garbage. It's one of the last things I do just before I'm through for the night." He stared at the ground. "It was quiet, no one was around, when all of a sudden I hear this splash. Like something heavy was being dumped into the water. I looked up in the direction the noise had come from and saw a man standing up in a small boat at the far end of the dock. The next thing I knew, he had taken off across the bay. But not before I got the first three numbers that are painted on the side."

"What happened after he took off?"

He twisted his hands in his lap, took a deep breath and closed his eyes. "I ran down there. That poor, little girl. Just floating there with her hair all spread out around her head. I started yelling and coughing at the same time, and then I... you know, I threw up on the dock." He looked at her, his eyes watery. "I knew she was dead."

Hanna blinked back tears, a stab of anger piercing her. "What did you do then?"

"I pulled her out of the water. She was naked and cold, so cold. Like ice, you know? Her skin was blue and her face," he looked away, choking, "ah Christ! I'm never gonna forget her face... it was all cut up like a butcher had gotten to her."

The words chilled her. Hanna clenched the muscles in her jaw, the image of yet another girl's battered face filling up her mind's eye. "Then you called 9-1-1?"

"No. I tried to give her mouth to mouth. I knew she was dead, but I tried anyway and I only stopped when something fell out of her mouth. It took me a while to figure out that it was a gag, all bloody. That's when I ran to the office and called 9-1-1."

Hanna briefly mulled over this information as she finished the interview by asking Chad about his duties and how long he had worked at the marina. When he was through answering, she offered him her hand as he stood up to leave. His grip was weak and she felt a slight tremor run through his body to the tips of his fingers.

"Thank you. I really appreciate your help, Mr. Morris. Will you be all right tonight? Is there anything I can do? Someone I can call for you?"

"No, there's no one... but I'll be fine. Won't be sleeping, though, I'm pretty sure."

He started off and waved a hand back at her without stopping his strides across the parking lot. Hanna watched him until he disappeared, then started back to the car, climbed in and turned on the interior light. She fished her notepad and pen out of her shoulder bag and, while it was still fresh in her mind, jotted down as much as she could remember of what Chad Morris had just told her.

Closing her notebook, she glanced at her watch and saw that it was just after one o'clock in the morning. She was tired, but sleep was the last thing on her mind as she pondered the information about the gag. As far as she knew, none of the other victims had been gagged. Then why a gag with this victim?

She was startled when the driver's side door clicked open and she turned to see Bennett bending his body to slide into the seat. He stared straight ahead as if in a trance, his face whiter than she had ever seen it. Dread filled her midriff, weighing down her limbs.

"Tim?" Her voice was squeaky and she cleared her throat. "What is it?"

"We need to head out to HQ. We have to go now."

"Oh. I knew I should have followed you up in my car."

He stared at her. "What are you talking about?"

"Well, it's just that I've had about enough of waiting around in the car, Tim. I was kind of looking forward to going home. I'm exhausted."

"Hanna, you don't understand. We both need to go."

Her mouth opened and closed. "But why?"

"We found something, Hanna. Something that involves you."

At nearly two o'clock in the morning, the Ontario Provincial Police headquarters were as quiet as a tomb. They took the elevator up to the second floor and a second later the doors slid open, revealing a shadowy corridor. Bennett led the way.

Hanna focused her eyes on his back as she followed, placing one foot in front of the other. The urge to turn around and run was strong, and she gritted her teeth to keep herself from bolting down the corridor like an animal startled by approaching headlights.

After dropping his bombshell, Bennett had told her he thought it best to wait until they got to headquarters to discuss what had been found. She hadn't pushed. They said nothing to each other on the drive to Orillia, preoccupied with their own thoughts. What in the world could they possibly have found? The question whirled around in her head as rustling corn fields rushed by her window, and it was all she could do not to scream.

Now, walking behind Bennett, Hanna had no idea what awaited her behind one of these closed doors and could only pray that it wouldn't be as bad as she imagined.

Bennett stopped in front of a door, turning to her before opening it. "Ready?" he whispered, reaching to squeeze her hand. "Remember I'm right here, okay?"

She looked down the corridor and swallowed hard. Words stuck in her throat, blocked by her fear. She could only nod when she glanced back into his face.

Pushing the door open, he motioned her into the room ahead of him. It took her eyes a moment to adjust to the light after the darkness of the corridor. The two detectives from the Behavioural Sciences Section were sitting at a long table. They both rose and came over to her as Bennett stepped inside the room and closed the door behind him.

"Hanna," one of them said by way of a greeting. "I wish we were meeting under better circumstances. I'm Detective-Inspector Chris Thompson." He indicated the overweight detective at his side. "And this is Detective-Sergeant Connor Jenkins."

Offering a grim smile and a beefy hand, Jenkins steered her towards the table. She glanced at Bennett as she sat down and it was then that she noticed the charts, maps and crime photographs tacked up on the wall where he was standing. The faces of Lydia, Tina and another girl she assumed was Marianne Legault stared back at her and Hanna was startled to realize that this was the CIB's investigation room.

Unable to tear her eyes away from the battered, smashed faces on the wall, she took in every gruesome, heinous detail of their mutilations, knowing each cut, wound and deformity would be imprinted in her mind for the rest of her life. She was numb to think that the madman responsible for these deaths could be filled with so much hatred towards women that he was capable of such overt savagery, such overkill.

It wasn't until Bennett sat down beside her that Hanna was able to tear her gaze away from the wall. At the same time, she realized

Thompson was speaking to her.

"...no way to prepare you for what we have to show you, Hanna," he was saying, his sky-blue eyes on her. "I don't want to spook you, but I'm afraid this piece of evidence we uncovered tonight puts you right in the middle of this insanity. But don't worry, we'll get an officer to swing 'round your place every hour or so for the next few days."

Was he talking about police protection? Fear spiked in her gut, making her nauseous. "Please," she said, "can we get this over with?"

Hanna thought she had steeled herself for whatever they would show her, but when Thompson pulled a plastic evidence bag out of the pile of folders on the table and held it up for her inspection, she thought she might faint. Vertigo swept over her in waves as her eyes lit on the mess inside the bag - a piece of cloth so saturated in blood and water, a pool of pink liquid sloshed in the bottom. She could vaguely make out something else inside, a strip of something pinkish-red covered in what looked like words.

Blinking a few times, she leaned over the table until her face was just inches from the bag. And then she saw what it was. A newspaper clipping, the words bleeding off the paper. But not enough that she wasn't able to recognize her own words staring up at her.

Like all sexual predators, he feels secretly powerless. Only rage and violence can help fend off those feelings of inadequacy and insecurity. Ritualized killings and mutilations make him feel powerful – if only until the next time.

She froze in place. Sweat poured from under her arms, coating her sides with ice as she read the words she had written in her weekend column and glimpsed her head shot at the top. She tasted bile as it washed up the back of her throat.

"Oh God," she whispered as a movie began to play on the screen of her mind. She saw her own lifeless body lying in a heap as the killer bore down on her, a hissing snake in his hands and a maniacal smile on his face.

Then black water swallowed her whole and she felt herself falling, tumbling, drowning in darkness.

Chapter Twenty-Nine

LIGHT FILTERED THROUGH the blackness like sunlight through fog, slowly dissipating the greyness that enveloped her mind.

Opening her eyes, Hanna realized immediately that she was still in the investigation room. The photographs of the slain girls stared down at her from the wall, their faces so bruised and torn and smashed they no longer resembled anything human.

Like a butcher had gotten to her.

She sat bolt upright, Chad Morris' words sending icicles of fear rippling along her spine. And then she remembered everything at once.

Moaning, she wrenched her eyes from the photographs on the wall. But it was no use. She could still see them lined up in the mirror of her mind, their faces so pretty and *alive* in the before shots and so brutalized and *dead* in the after shots. And though she knew that she did not fit the killer's victim profile, at least physically, she could not stop seeing her own picture up there with the others. Would she become this madman's next victim?

Number five.

A bubble of hysteria rose up in her, bursting out of her mouth in a stream of laughter that soon turned into whimpers. She could not help the tears that squeezed out of her eyes.

In the next instant, she felt herself pulled against a strong, hard chest and heard Bennett's familiar voice murmuring soothing words in her ears. She held on to him like her life depended on it, her cheek pressed tightly against the leather of his bomber jacket.

When she could trust herself to speak, she lifted her head and stared up into his face. "I'm sorry," she said, her voice a raspy whisper. "I didn't mean to lose it like that."

"Shhh," he said, tightening his grip on her. "I'm just glad you're all right now."

"We all are."

She instinctively stepped away from Bennett, embarrassed to realize that Thompson and Jenkins had also witnessed every second of her breakdown.

Thompson came around the table and led her to a chair. "It was only for a few seconds there, Hanna, but you fainted. Has this ever happened before?"

She shook her head. "No, not that I'm aware of."

"I was worried about how you'd react. I know it was a horrendous shock for you to see that evidence and to know that it had been stuffed in the latest victim's mouth. But as far as figuring out what this means, I'm afraid we're drawing blanks." He paused, raking his fingers through his hair. "Is this guy targeting you? Or is he trying to send you a message? Is the killer the same guy sending you the e-mails? We have so many questions and so few answers at this time, Hanna. But we will do everything we can to keep you safe."

She nodded again, but it was from reflex only. Would she become this madman's next target? Would she have to look over her shoulder from now on? Oh God, she thought, this can't be happening.

How would they keep her safe from this maniac? He had murdered a girl in North Bay. Then he had come here and abducted three women from local, public places, killed them with an injection of ketamine, raped them repeatedly, mutilated their bodies and faces, and dumped their corpses in Georgian Bay. Hanna thought of Pickton and all the serial killers who had fooled the world a long time before they were caught. She had little doubt that if this monster really wanted to get her, he would find a way.

It was too much to think about now and she closed her eyes tightly. She was beyond exhaustion. The events of the past two weeks were finally catching up with her and she still could not believe all the things that had happened in such a short period of time. Three victims. A young girl still missing. More pain and tears from those left behind than she cared to remember. Strange, disturbing photographs depicting nefarious acts of necrophilia. Unsettling interviews with the patients from Rolling Sands. Flashbacks from the hell she'd lived through 14 years ago. Weird dreams, haunting images filling her every waking moment. And now a clipping of her column, soaked in the latest victim's blood. It took every ounce of her self-restraint not to break down again.

Taking a tremulous breath, Hanna looked up at Thompson. "Killers settle for different types of victims all the time, don't they?" She swept her arm at the wall of horrors, hating the fact that her voice was on the verge of hysteria. "He's been after blonde, blue-eyed women. But that doesn't mean he can't change his mind, does it?"

Thompson exchanged a look with Jenkins. "Hanna, you have to understand that it's rare to see a change in a killer's pathology. While it's true that some killers 'settle' for a different type of victim than the one they usually go after, it's very uncommon. Victim profiles are intrinsically tied to their signature. This guy prefers young, single, blonde, blue-eyed women and so far, all of his victims have fit this description. Substituting a different kind of woman, one who was older, for example, wouldn't fulfill his need, his signature."

"But that's not a guarantee, is it?"

"No," he answered, his voice sombre. "But to put it colloquially, Hanna, you're not his type. You're a brunette, your eyes are dark brown and you're also older and a professional. His victims have been young, too young to be anything but students in high school or college, or in Tina Joliet's case, a recent graduate on her first job. Plus, there's the pregnancy and abortion issue. Lydia Tomlinson had been pregnant the year before and had an abortion just before she started college. This has since been confirmed by her doctor. Good detective work finding that number, by the way, Hanna." He smiled at her briefly. "Then we come to Tina Joliet, who was three months pregnant at the time of her murder. And Marianne Legault, we just

246 • *Sonia Suedfeld*

found out, already had a baby."

Hanna' eyes widened in surprise. "What?"

"She gave birth to a baby girl last summer just before starting her senior year. After she was murdered, Marianne's father committed suicide, leaving her mother to care for the baby. But she was in no shape to take on this responsibility; she's been in and out of mental institutions since all this happened. So the baby was taken into foster care."

Hanna wrapped her arms around herself. Would this nightmare never end?

"We still don't know about the young woman we found tonight, but pregnancy or abortion seem to be a trait the others shared in common, in addition to physical characteristics. Hanna, I have to ask you, have you ever been pregnant or terminated a pregnancy in the past? Are you pregnant now?"

She instantly flashed on the time when she'd been seventeen and worried out of her mind that she was pregnant. She had never been so happy as when her period had finally come, a week late. "No, no, and no. Thank God."

He nodded, looking relieved. "It would be highly unlikely that you would become a target." He paused as if gathering his thoughts. "You read the profile report, Hanna. A serial killer like this can change his MO over time, but his need will remain the same. He can kill 30 people, using a different method every time, but his signature will stay the same for every single killing. For that reason alone, I'd be surprised if he came after you. I think it's more likely that he's trying to send a message to you and through you, to us. Maybe you hit a raw nerve with your column, and now he's out to play games with all of us."

Hanna was too tired to contemplate the reasons behind a killer's sick actions. "You said an officer would swing by my house once in a while. Starting tonight?"

"No. Inspector Bennett thought it best if you stayed with him tonight, just until we can arrange for your protection in the morning. Is that all right?"

Hanna looked at Bennett, who smiled at her. "Yes, that's fine."

"Do you have any holiday time coming up?" Thompson asked. "The best thing would be for you to go somewhere and not tell a soul, just until things settle down."

"I'm not scheduled for holidays until August, but I'll give it some thought."

"You do that," he urged. "In the meantime, try to get some sleep, Hanna. You look as if you haven't slept in days."

She smiled grimly. "I *feel* as if I haven't slept in weeks, never mind days."

It was just after three o'clock in the morning when they set off for the drive back to Midland. The highway was free of other vehicles and Bennett drove 30 kilometres over the speed limit, zooming like a bullet through the darkness.

When they arrived at his house, he led her straight to the kitchen where he took down a bottle of Glenfiddich and poured them each an inch of single malt scotch.

"Sip slowly," he said, handing her a glass. "Swirl it on your tongue."

She did as he said, then swallowed. The fiery liquid coursed hotly down to her stomach. "Thanks, this is just what I needed."

"How about a shower, too? It might help you relax. C'mon, I'll take you up."

Taking her scotch along, Hanna followed him to the guest room on the second floor. He made sure she had towels, soap and shampoo in the adjoining bathroom, then hesitated in the doorway, watching her as she sipped from the tumbler again. "All set? Need anything else? All right then. I'll be downstairs if you need me."

After he left, she pulled off her dress, unhooked her bra and slipped out of her panties. She left her clothes on the floor and stepped inside the small bathroom, glancing at herself in the mirror above the sink. She was startled to see how pale her face looked.

Sighing loudly at her reflection, she drained the rest of the scotch, turned on the shower and climbed into the stall. The water had never felt so good and she let the spray pummel her back a long time without moving. But she could not stop seeing the blood-soaked clipping of her column in her mind and she could not believe that the killer had stuffed it in a gag inside the latest victim's mouth. She remembered writing it. When had that been? Tuesday. The day of Lydia's funeral.

A powerful urge to cry overcame her and Hanna felt a sob work its way up her throat. Tears flowed down her face, mixing with the water tumbling over her, and she cried for the young woman they had recovered just hours ago. She grieved for the years she wouldn't be able to live, for the pain and sorrow her family and friends would feel for the rest of their lives, for all the love and laughter she'd never experience. She thought of Lydia, Tina and Marianne and cried harder. She saw their before and after pictures on the wall of the investigation room, their faces unrecognizable after the monster had finished with them. She thought of Tina's unborn baby and Marianne's little girl, doomed to a life of foster care, and bashed her fists against the tile, outrage bubbling inside her.

Skin broke over her knuckles; blood mingled with water. Hanna saw again the bloody water in the evidence bag, the pictures on the wall, the photographs she had been sent and she screamed, crumpling to the floor of the shower stall, clutching her bleeding hand to her chest. She couldn't stop crying; the well of tears inside her would not dry up.

A noise made her look up. The door of the stall was sliding open.

Another scream died on her lips when she recognized Bennett's face in the mist. "Shhh," he said over the noise of the water. "It's okay, Hanna, it's okay."

He turned the shower off, lifted her up in his arms and carried her to the bed. He lay down beside her, pulled a comforter over their bodies and held her tight against his chest. He smoothed her wet hair away from her face and dried her tears with his hands.

In time, the tears stopped and she became aware that her wet, shivering body was pressed into his hard, warm one, that her breasts were flattened mounds against his chest, that her head was cushioned in the crook of his neck and shoulder. She became aware of the galloping of his heart, the way he smelled, the way he held her. The way her own heart was responding, her breath quickening, her senses stirring.

Hanna felt him harden against her, and she looked up into his face, her dark eyes searching his with a ferocity that took her breath away. She stared into his jade green eyes, lifted a hand and placed it against the rough stubble of his face. She heard him groan, saw his eyes darken with desire as they came to rest on her mouth, and then slowly, he bent his head and crushed his lips against hers.

The kiss awakened something inside her, some primitive need that left her aching. It moved through her like a powerful tidal wave, pushing aside all her fear and anxiety and every doubt she had ever had. It made her forget everything that had happened in the last few hours, erased everything except this need to be taken, transported, renewed. Loved.

She wanted oblivion. She wanted to forget. She wanted to lose herself in the sensations of making love with this man.

"Hanna?"

Her name on his lips. A whispered song. An invitation.

She didn't answer. Instead, she cupped his beautiful face with both hands and returned his kiss with all the passion she had kept bottled up inside for so long.

"Hanna." This time, her name on his lips came out strangled. He shifted his body away from hers, looking into her eyes. "Hanna, oh God, we can't do this. You've had a shock tonight, you know. You're tired and in a vulnerable place right now."

Placing a finger against his lips, she pressed her body closer to his. "Tim, I want you. I've wanted you for so long," she whispered as she rained kisses across his throat. "No regrets, not now, not tomorrow. Not ever. Okay?"

Searching his eyes with her own, she could see a battle raging inside of him. He wanted her as much as she wanted him. It was easy to see that. But he was also weighing the consequences in his mind, worried that nothing would ever be the same between them, and she loved him for that.

Hanna kissed him again, her tongue darting out to lick his lips. His heart jumped under her palm.

"No regrets." He moaned, his arms sliding all the way around her. "Oh God, Hanna, you have no idea how long I've wanted you, too. How many times I've dreamed of touching you." He stroked the side of her face. "But are you sure?"

"Shhhh, Tim. I have never been so sure of anything in my life." Her flesh was on fire, her mind filled only with the hardness of him as he nuzzled her neck, licked the hollow where her collarbones met and kissed the valley between her breasts.

Warmth flooded her body as her hands roamed over him, unbuttoning his shirt and tugging it off before moving on to his jeans. She fumbled with the zipper, lost in the sensation of his touch, his smell, his weight on her. He helped her, twisting his body to slip the jeans and boxers off and then he was naked and rolling on top of her, and she heard him groan as all the parts of their bodies touched for the first time.

Skin glided over skin, and Hanna forgot who she was. Time no longer existed. Her past was gone, her future non-existent. All that mattered was Bennett's body against hers.

Framing her face in his hands, he kissed each of her eyelids, her nose, her cheeks and finally her mouth. He wrapped his arms around her, drawing her close, and she could feel his erection pushing against her stomach. She grabbed her shoulder bag from the end table and out of her wallet pulled a condom packet she had tucked there a long time ago and forgotten about until now.

Unrolling it slowly over him, she pulled him on top of her and wrapped her legs around him as he entered her, his mouth on her breasts. She moaned, her eyes closed, her breath coming in harsh, little bursts as he slipped in and out of her. Hanna arched her back, her body quivering under his touch, her hips grinding into his. Then she cried out, calling his name, and he drove into her faster and deeper, again and again, and she heard him groan against her throat as he came hard, his eyes tightly closed.

"Hanna." Her name on his lips, a breathless whisper against her neck.

Time passed, yet their bodies remained entwined a long time on the narrow bed. Her heart continued to pound, her senses throbbing with pleasure. Making love with Bennett had been everything she had dreamed it would be - mind-blowing, breathtaking, deeply satisfying. But she had never guessed it would be this powerful, this humbling; the emotion brought tears to her eyes and she wondered if the experience had been the same for him.

He lifted her chin with the tip of a finger. "Hanna? Are you all right?" He searched her eyes, his voice husky as he wiped her tears with a thumb. "I didn't hurt you, did I?"

She smiled. He thought she was crying because he had hurt her. "Oh Tim, no," she whispered. "I'm all right. In fact, I'm more than all right. I feel wonderful."

"Me, too," he said, trailing his fingers through her hair. "Any regrets so far?"

She stared into his eyes. "None. You?"

He shook his head, touched her cheek with the tips of his fingers. "I never knew... I mean, it's been so long... you overwhelmed me."

Heat rushed into her face. Not from embarrassment, but from pure pleasure. She had overwhelmed him just as he had overwhelmed her; nothing he could have said would have made her feel more wonderful than she felt at this moment. "Oh Tim, thank you."

He looked puzzled. "For what?"

"Nothing, everything."

He kissed the corner of her mouth. "So it really was okay for you?"

"I think I may have felt the earth move," she said, grinning.

Bennett laughed. "So you wouldn't mind if we tried to make it move again?"

"Mmmm. Exactly when did you have in mind?"

He growled deep in his throat. "How about now? And all night long?"

"Then let's not waste any time." She inclined her head towards the window, where the first faint light of dawn was just starting to bleach the darkness out of the sky, and climbed on top of him. "Night's almost over."

Chapter Thirty

THE SMELL OF brewing coffee wafting up the stairs woke Hanna from a deep sleep. She took one look around the room and heat flooded her face as she remembered making love with Bennett until the room had been bathed in bright, morning sunshine.

She smiled now as she remembered the things he had told her. That he had been attracted to her from the very beginning, way back when she had just started working at the paper and had interviewed him for the first time. That he had dreamed of her many nights, and that she was beautiful and smart, and a damn good writer.

In turn, she said he had the most beautiful eyes she had ever seen on a man. She told him about her own attraction for him, about all the times she had wanted to grab him and take him to her bed. She told him she loved his smile, his strength, and respected his ability to push on in his work when everything seemed to be falling apart.

Throwing the blanket aside, Hanna noticed crusted blood on her knuckles and everything else that had happened the night before came rushing back. She remembered pounding the tiled walls of the shower stall with all her might, as if it had been the killer's face she was hitting, over and over again. She fingered her bruised hand as other images came, one after the other, like slides projected on a wall. The blood-soaked newspaper clipping of her column. The pull of the blackness as it had sucked at her. The before and after photographs of the slain girls on the wall of the investigation room.

Lydia, Tina, Marianne. And now a fourth. The smallest of the victims.

That poor, little girl, Chad Morris had said, just floating there with her hair all spread out around her in the water. Her skin blue, cold. Her face all cut up.

Like a butcher had gotten to her.

A shudder rippled across her torso as the quote came to her again and she sat up abruptly, glancing at the bedside clock. She was surprised to realize that it was past noon already and that she was, despite the images taunting her mind, starving.

The aroma of coffee hit her again as she padded naked into the adjoining bathroom and took a quick shower. She slipped into her underwear and sundress, rinsed her mouth out with some Listerine she found in the cabinet and styled her hair using only her fingers.

Rounding the corner into the kitchen, Hanna stopped in her tracks when her eyes lit on Bennett standing with a spatula in one hand and a cup of coffee in the other. He wore only a pair of white and blue boxer shorts and her heart lurched at the sight of him.

Turning and spotting her, he broke out into a slow, sexy smile and crossed the floor to her. He took her into his arms and planted a kiss on her mouth. "Hi, sleepyhead."

Hanna's gaze fell on the table in the breakfast nook. "Oh Tim, you shouldn't have gone to all this trouble. Everything looks amazing."

The table was set with matching place settings and laden with platters of bacon, scrambled eggs, and fresh fruit. Hanna's mouth watered and her stomach growled.

"Sounds like someone's hungry. Go ahead, have a seat," he invited, handing her a mug of steaming coffee.

"Thanks." She sat down at the table, stirred sugar and cream into her cup and watched as he piled a mountain of eggs and bacon on his plate.

She helped herself to eggs and fruit. "Mmm, these are delicious." The eggs melted on her tongue and she tasted fresh parsley. "What's your secret?"

He didn't stop chewing. "A little cream, butter. Parsley. Salt and pepper."

"Well, I'm impressed. I didn't know you could cook like this."

He gulped coffee and winked at her. "Lots of things you don't know about me."

"Like what?"

He caught her hand in his, brought it to his mouth and kissed her fingers. "Like… right now I'm thinking of how beautiful you are and how alive you make me feel. How long it's been since… well, since I've been happy." He looked down, his face flushed, and noticed her knuckles. "Does it hurt? I should have gotten you a Band-Aid last night."

"No, no. It doesn't hurt." She leaned over and planted a long kiss on his lips. "You make me feel the same way, Tim."

He rested his forehead against hers and sighed deeply. "I wish I could spend all day with you, Hanna, but I have to go in to work. I'm sorry."

She nodded and kissed him again. "It's okay."

"What about you? Got any plans for today?"

"Not really. I thought I'd go home and take it easy."

"Have you thought about what Thompson suggested last night? Taking some time off? I think it might be a good idea to lay low for a while."

Hanna was quiet as she turned back to her eggs, worried that he would consider her decision foolhardy. "I've thought about it," she finally said, "and I know you agree with Thompson, but I think I need to see this through. I can't drop this story and let someone else at the paper take over now… It would just kill me."

He covered her hand with his and smiled, surprising her. "I knew you were going to say that, Hanna. I'm starting to get to know you pretty well, don't you think? So I've got a few ideas for you, some suggestions I hope you'll take seriously. Okay?" He waited until she nodded and then went on, his eyes fixed on hers. "First off, I want you to scramble up your routine as much as possible. If you normally go grocery shopping on Saturday afternoons, I want you to go on a Wednesday night instead. Also, look around you. Be aware of everything going on, try to live in the moment. If there's one big difference between killers and their victims, then that's it. Killers live entirely in the moment and they're always aware of every detail. So keep your eyes and ears open, okay? And don't leave work after dark, unless someone else is staying late, too. And if, for whatever reason, you so much as get an itsy-bitsy creepy feeling that something's not quite right, I want you to call 9-1-1. All right? And always lock every door and window in your house when you're home… I don't care how hot it is, get yourself a couple of fans or something."

Hanna licked her lips. "Okay to everything."

"Good," he said, walking over to the counter where he took something out of a drawer. "One more thing… take this and don't ever hesitate to use it, if you need to."

Hanna stared at a key chain with a small, lipstick-sized tube attached to it and instantly recognized what it was. "Pepper spray? Isn't that illegal for me to have?"

He waved a hand in the air. "Just promise me you'll use it, if you ever need to."

She took the chain from him, located her shoulder bag and clipped it to her set of keys. Then she raised herself on tiptoe and kissed him again. "I promise."

Later when she got home, Hanna made a circuit of her sweltering cottage, checking windows and locks in every room. Satisfied that everything was secure, she turned on all the fans she owned, and headed to the kitchen.

An OPP cruiser slowly drove by as she sought refuge in her backyard where perennials poked through a rough cedar fence all along the edge of her property. Blues, purples and pinks bloomed around lush greenery like splashes of paint on canvas. Hanna could just barely make out the back of the cottage in the next row as she sank into her wicker chair on the patio.

She couldn't stop thinking about the night before, couldn't help grinning as she remembered how she had felt lying in Bennett's arms. He had awakened something in her that would not go back to sleep, something that had been buried inside her for far too long.

Some of the walls she had erected around herself had come down during the night past and she was filled with an incredible lightness of being, as if all the heaviness she had carried around in her heart for years had suddenly, magically lifted.

It might have sounded like a cliché, but Tim Bennett was so different from every other lover she had ever had that she still couldn't quite believe it. And it went far deeper than physical parts fitting together so perfectly for the first time. It was as if she had found in him the other side of herself, the part that had been missing for so long.

And it felt so good, so right, that she hugged herself and laughed out loud, startling a fat blue jay into taking flight.

Chapter Thirty-One

HANNA STARED INTO the unbroken blue of the sky. A seagull screeched overhead and she jumped up, suddenly in the mood for a long walk on the beach. Slipping on her one-piece swimsuit under shorts and a tee shirt, she locked up her cottage, pocketed her keys, and walked down the path between her house and the neighbour's. It was so hot, she felt as if her blood was boiling as she hurried down the path, sweat coating every inch of her skin.

A couple of minutes later, she spotted Georgian Bay sparkling ahead like a blanket of diamonds. Her bare feet sank into fine, hot sand as she left the path and jogged down to the water's edge. A few sunbathers and families with small children dotted the beach; a trio of teenagers in the water tossed a yellow ball to each other amid yells and laughter. A sailboat was a tiny white dot on the horizon.

Cool water lapping at her ankles and a slight breeze fanning her hot skin, Hanna walked along the edge of the beach until she came to a rounded point where huge rocks formed a line out into the bay. Beyond it lay a small, deserted beach in the shape of a jagged semi-circle - a place she had discovered shortly after moving into her home. Here, there were no cottages breaking the line of pines and no one lying on the sand. Only seagulls moved about on the beach, watching with beady eyes as she approached.

Stripping off her tee shirt and shorts, Hanna dove into the water. It was cool against her skin; she felt it like a caress as it swirled around her. She swam out until her feet could no longer touch the bottom and then turned around for the swim back to shore.

Climbing out and drying her face with her tee shirt, she sat down on the sand and looked out at the bay. She had no idea how long she stared mesmerized at the moving, glittering water and it was only when pangs of hunger rumbled inside her that she finally got to her feet.

Rounding the beach, Hanna spotted dark, foreboding clouds rolling in from the west and she wondered if they were in for an electrical storm. The air was so laden with humidity, she knew only thunder and lightning and rain would be able to break the heat wave that had been scorching many parts of the province for almost a week. She couldn't wait for it to hit, leaving in its wake some much needed relief and cooler temperatures.

She was sweating again as she came off the path into her street. The OPP cruiser drove past again and she waved to the officer behind the wheel as she started up her driveway and let herself in her cottage, locking the door behind her. She went directly to the kitchen, turned the fan to its highest setting and spread cream cheese on a dozen wheat crackers. She ate them at her kitchen table, washing them down with a cold beer she found tucked in the back of her refrigerator. She thought of Bennett again and their lovemaking the night before and the memory of his body pressed against hers brought a flush of remembered passion to her face. But it was impossible to think of him and not the case - the blood-soaked clipping of her column loomed heavily on her mind and she shuddered to think of the killer reading her words, hate and violence burning like fever in his eyes.

Inevitably, her thoughts turned to *tatler* and she knew she should be checking her e-mail. But it was the last thing in the world she wanted to do - the images he'd sent her festered like open wounds in her soul. She feared another would all but break her, cause something in her to shatter into a million pieces that could never be put back together again.

Downing the rest of her beer, Hanna reluctantly dragged herself into her living room and settled on the sofa with her laptop. Turning on the computer, she logged onto the Internet and downloaded her messages. As she had feared, *tatler*'s name stared out at her from the list and several minutes passed before she could make herself click on the entry.

There were two words in the message this time: OKANIMA MINISS. Hanna noted them down in her notebook and reminded herself to contact George Jackson for a definition. Then she clicked on the attachment and her eyes closed as the first line of the image appeared on her screen. She could feel herself tremble like a leaf in heavy winds as she steeled herself for what she was about to see and slowly opened her eyes.

One glimpse and the image seared into her brain like a prod used to brand cattle.

There was only a face this time, a young woman's face, her skin so pale and thin, bluish veins stood out at her temples and jawline like worms under onion paper. Pale hair formed a cloud around her face and a few loose strands curled around a small, upturned nose. A grey tongue protruded from colourless lips; a rivulet of dark fluid ran from a delicate nostril. But the eyes - oh God, the eyes - were milky blue like winter skies, wide open and filmed over in death and Hanna knew she'd be seeing those eyes in her nightmares for the rest of her life.

As much as she knew that this was a photograph that should never have been taken, of things that should never have happened, she could not drag her eyes away from it, even as she wished it would just vanish from the screen. Nausea rolled like a wave in her stomach and her breath was coming in short, raspy gasps. She struggled to draw air into her lungs; her windpipe felt tight and constricted as if a fist was squeezing it closed. And above the sound of her wheezing, she could hear someone sobbing, and realized with a start that the sounds were coming from her.

Several minutes passed before she was able to sit up, wipe away the tears on her face, and look back up at the screen of her computer.

The jungle animals of her screen saver were marching among trees and vines and flowers. With a stroke of a key, they disappeared into the netherworld and the face that was imprinted in the mirror of her mind returned, filling up the screen. She stared into the lifeless eyes and they seemed to be accusing her even in death.

Unable to stand the sight of those dead eyes a moment longer, Hanna saved the image to her hard drive and closed down her mail program.

Almost immediately, her cell rang and she spun towards the sound, her heart in her throat. She snatched the receiver in one shaking hand as she sank into the sofa.

"Hello?" Nothing came out and she had to clear her throat several times before the word could slip off her tongue.

"Hanna? What's wrong? You sound terrible."

The concern she heard in Bennett's voice started the tears again, but she managed to choke them back. "I got another one. Another picture from *tatler*." A sob bubbled up in her throat. "Oh God, Tim, it's just a face…"

"Take it easy, Hanna. It's all right… I've got good news. The E-Crimes Unit finally traced him."

"Oh." She surprised herself by laughing out loud as a brief stab of elation crossed her chest. "Oh my God, Tim. That's great. Where?"

"You won't believe this… they traced him to Rolling Sands."

She breathed in sharply, her eyes widening, and let out a gasp. "Rolling Sands?"

"Yeah. That's where it's coming from, but we have no idea who's been sending them. Whether it's a staff worker or a patient or whatever. But we're heading down there now to talk to the administrator and you can be damn sure we'll get to the bottom of it."

Hanna locked on the word patient and immediately saw the faces of Raymond Fortin and Mick Keating in her mind's eye, the two patients she had interviewed for the Reflections story. It was a very long shot, but could either of them be *tatler*? But how? She knew patients at the maximum security hospital for the criminally insane did not have access to the Internet. Yet, a part of her wondered how difficult it would be for a devious mind hell-bent on playing macabre games to get that access. Or was she crazy to even think of it?

Nonetheless, she told Bennett everything she knew about both men, including the reason she had been interviewing them and the threat Raymond had made to her the second time she had run into him while interviewing Mick Keating.

But Bennett, as she had suspected, was dubious. "I'll keep that in mind, but you know and I know that it's highly unlikely these messages are coming from these patients. They don't have online access for reasons everyone can understand. Can you imagine these guys roaming the Internet? It'd be like handing them victims on a silver platter."

"I agree and you're right. They don't have access… but with technology these days, who knows? Maybe, somehow, one of them was able to get access. I'm sure there are ways."

"I'll keep it in mind, okay? Can you describe the image you got?"

Hanna closed her eyes and the deathly-pale face appeared in her mind in all its ghastly details. "She's young, Tim, maybe twenty to twenty-five, but she could be younger. I could see bluish veins showing at her temple and around her jaw and there's a line of blood running out of her nose. Her tongue was hanging out of her mouth and there was this cloud of hair around her face, very pale and fine. But it was her eyes I'll never forget. They were this incredibly watery blue. I had the impression of the colour of the sky in winter, when it's so washed-out it doesn't even look like it's got a colour at all. Milky, you know?"

"Hmm… sounds like the girl we pulled out of the water last night, Hanna. But I wonder why he sent a picture of the actual victim this time and not just more disgusting pornographic images that he must have downloaded off the web like the first two?"

"I don't know, but as terrible as those earlier images were, this one's worst, Tim. I can't describe it… it's almost like… I don't know." She stopped, words failing her.

"Any words in the message, like the last ones?"

"Yes, two this time. Okanima miniss." She spelled them for him and added, "I was going to try to reach Jackson to see if he can look them up in that dictionary of his."

"Phone him right after I get off the phone with you. I'll be in touch in about an hour. We really need a lead on this newest victim… so far we've got nothing. The Missing Persons registry isn't listing anyone fitting her description. We're drawing blanks here."

"Okay. I'll call him right away."

"Thanks, Hanna. And could you do me a favour and send the picture out to the E-Crimes Unit? It might help with identifying her when the time comes."

"Sure."

"And Hanna? Everything's locked up tight at your place? You're all right?"

"Yes."

"Good. I'll call again as soon as I can. Bye."

Clicking off, Hanna reached for her laptop and composed a brief note for the E-Crimes Unit, attached the image she had received, and sent the message on its way to OPP headquarters in Orillia.

George Jackson answered his phone on the first ring, his voice ragged and scratchy with sleep. " 'Lo?"

"Mr. Jackson? It's Hanna Laurence, from *The Post*. I'm so sorry to be calling on a Sunday afternoon, but I was wondering if you might be able to look up a couple of words for me in your Ojibway dictionary."

"Sure. No problem. What are they?"

Hanna said the words as best she could without knowing their proper pronunciation and spelled them for him.

"Miniss? I don't know about the first word, but miniss is an easy one to translate. It means island."

She grabbed a notebook and flipped to a blank page. "Island. You're sure?"

"Absolutely. But the first word… I'll have to look it up. Just a moment." There was a pause, followed by the sound of pages flipping. "Well, according to this, it means bones."

A shiver shot through her. "Bones?" she repeated, her fingers icy against her throat.

"That's right. Bones."

"Island. And bones. What do you think this means?"

"Well, there is an island by that name. Bone Island. Just up the bay."

Hanna could no longer sit still. She thanked Jackson for his help, hung up the phone and stood gripping the edges of her desk. She was so strung out she could literally feel her body vibrating with tension.

If Jackson was right, the killer had abducted the victim recovered the night before from Bone Island.

The name alone was enough to send a chill running down her spine.

Chapter Thirty-Two

IN ALL THE years Hanna had covered crime, she had never come across a case that had inspired her to feel as much revulsion and frustration as this one. She felt as if bugs were crawling relentlessly along her bones as she paced in front of her desk.

She had no trouble imagining Raymond Fortin as *tatler*. The man was not only as smart as a devil, but God knew he had also derived enormous pleasure of out needling her both times she'd met with him. The only thing she didn't know was how he could have gained access to the Internet.

Mick Keating, on the other hand, didn't seem to fit the image she'd constructed of the type of person *tatler* undoubtedly was. But something about the arsonist continued to gnaw at her and she remembered what he'd told her just after Raymond had so rudely insinuated himself into their interview: that he was a voracious reader of history. And not just Ireland's history, as Raymond had been quick to point out. What was it he had said exactly? That Mick knew more history, including local history than anyone else in the entire institution. He'd called him a 'walking encyclopedia of historical facts'. Would it be all that far-fetched then to presume that researching the original names of three of the abduction sites would have been child's play for him?

Then, if that was the case, why not go a step further and presuppose that *tatler* wasn't just one of the two, but actually both men working together. If Mick possessed historical name facts, then perhaps Raymond had been the one with the computer knowledge required to send along the images.

Hanna stopped pacing, sat down heavily on the sofa and let out a loud, exasperated breath. She might be close or she might be chasing her own tail like a dog, there was no way of knowing. She could only hope that Bennett and his team of detectives were right now getting some answers to the questions bouncing around in her head.

But there was one thing she now could be certain about. If *tatler* was Raymond Fortin or Mick Keating or both of them working together, then the killer on the loose out there was definitely someone else. She had always believed this and remembered mentioning it to Bennett after she had received the first of the depraved images. Why she had believed this, she didn't know. It had only been a feeling at the time, an intuition.

Yet she couldn't begin to understand what possible connection could exist between *tatler* and the killer, although she knew there had to be one. How else would *tatler* know such crucial details as the killer's necrophile status, not to mention the locations where the victims had been abducted from? The knowledge *tatler* had possessed all along proved that a relationship had to exist between him and the killer. But not only did she think the two had to know each other in some way in order for the information to have been passed along, but she was beginning to suspect that the killer had no idea that *tatler* had been playing games of his own by sending her clues after the murders. Had he known, she was positive he would have used whatever means were available to him and put a stop to the messages.

Hanna was startled by a loud meow and glanced down to see Pistachio looking up at her. Picking him up, she scratched his chin and looked into his yellow cat eyes.

"So if *tatler* is Raymond or Mick or both of them," she mused out loud while the cat stared back at her, "and they of course are locked up at Rolling Sands and have been for years and years, then how in the world would they know the killer?"

Pistachio blinked and meowed again and the answer was suddenly in her head.

It was so obvious; she jumped off the sofa, spilling the cat to the floor. "Visitors," she yelled and laughed when Pistachio scurried out of the room, no doubt thinking she was losing her mind. "The killer's got to be a visitor! Of course!"

She should have thought of it right away. The killer had to be someone who had visited either Raymond or Mick or both at Rolling Sands in the last couple of weeks. All visitors were required to sign in at the desk, no exceptions. There would be records of their visitors, if she was right about this, and she willed Bennett to call so she could pass along this information, as well as the tip about Bone Island, and see where it lead.

But Bennett would undoubtedly already have thought of checking visitor lists for both patients, she thought. It was his job to think of these things. Just in case, though, she decided she would bring it up anyway when he called.

Going into her kitchen, Hanna was startled to see how late it was; the clock on her microwave oven read 7:34 p.m. and she was hungry again. Heating a can of chicken noodle soup, she ladled some into a bowl, dumped several crackers and slices of cheese on a plate and carried both to the table. Pistachio was sitting on one of the chairs and meowed incessantly until she gave in and shared the cheese with him. He nudged her hand with the top of his head, showing his gratitude, and devoured the cheese in a matter of seconds, then meowed for more.

Hanna gave him another slice and started eating while her mind returned to the case.

She knew better than to try to force all the elements of the case into a picture that might be untrue to reality. A cop she'd once interviewed in Toronto had told her that the surest way to make sense out of a mystery was to do nothing. Eventually, he'd said, the pieces of the puzzle would all come together. But she couldn't just sit back and wait for that to happen. She *needed* to do something, if only to keep her sanity.

What did she know so far? There was a psychopathic signature killer on the loose who had killed and mutilated four young women in the space of less than three months. All the victims not only resembled each other, but they had all been taken from public places - Marianne from a library in North Bay, Lydia from a campground at Beausoleil Island, Tina from the White Pine Inn at the Bay, and the latest victim recovered the night before from Bone Island, if the information tatler had sent earlier was correct. And there was no reason to assume it wasn't, given how the last two clues had been right.

Though they had checked and rechecked carefully, police had found resemblance and pregnancy to be the only connections among the victims so far. They were all young and beautiful with long, blonde hair and blue eyes, and while it was too soon to know about the latest victim, each of the other three had pregnancy in common. Lydia had terminated an unwanted pregnancy; Tina had been three months pregnant at the time of her death; Marianne had been the mother of an infant girl. Hanna felt a familiar knot of rage as she thought of their cruel fates, and she pushed her bowl away, too horrified to finish eating.

What else did she know? Each had been killed shortly after abduction with an injection of ketamine hydrochloride. A massive dose like each of the victims had been injected with would have caused fatal respiratory malfunction within seconds of the drug entering their blood stream. Each had been stabbed and raped repeatedly after death, and Marianne was the only victim whose face had not been butchered senselessly. Only one victim, Lydia, had been found with a part of her body cut off and kept as a souvenir - both Tina and Marianne had not suffered this further indignity. Hanna shuddered as she thought of the most heinous atrocity inflicted on at least two of the victims' bodies - the insertion of a Massasauga rattlesnake inside Tina's and Lydia's vaginas. It was too soon yet to know about the newest victim recovered the night before, but Marianne seemed to be the only one who had not been mutilated in this sadistic way.

And then there was Ingrid Marshall who was still missing and whose fate was still unknown. Thinking of her tied up Hanna's stomach in knots. She remembered the hollow desperation she had seen on the faces of the girl's parents and prayed that the Bay Killer had not taken her. She could not imagine a worse fate for Evan and Maxine Marshall.

"Christ," Hanna muttered, getting up and pouring herself a couple of ounces of vodka in a glass. She didn't bother with ice or mix, and downed the cold, fiery liquid in three gulps. Her eyes teared and her stomach was on fire, but at least it helped ease some of the tension in her back and a little of the nausea crawling in her guts.

Filling her glass with water this time, she forced herself to go on. What did she know about the monster who had been capable of all that evil? According to the profile she had read, this 'monster' wasn't a monster, at least not in the true sense of the word. He wasn't some creature with horns on his head; he was a human being with a heart and a mind like everyone else. Except he wasn't wired in the same way most people were. He did not feel disgust or remorse for what he had done. He did not feel pity or empathy for others. His was a world governed by rage and sadistic fantasy. He did not care that the families and friends of his victims would struggle with the savage murders of their loved ones for the rest of their lives or that they would wake in the small hours of the night drenched in cold sweat, haunted by nightmares too horrendous to imagine.

And he was dangerous. Not only because he didn't live by the same moral codes that ruled the rest of society, but because he had chosen watery graves for the corpses of all his victims. They had all been found dead beneath the water, Hanna thought again, and water had always been a friend to murderers. Not only could bodies vanish never to be seen again, but water didn't leave trace evidence.

She knew he probably looked no different than lots of other young men in their twenties or early thirties and she knew he would be clever enough to function normally in society. He would have no problem holding down a job and was probably employed in a professional capacity. He either owned or had access to a boat and was intimately familiar with Georgian Bay. He would live alone or have some place private enough to carry out his sick fantasies. He would own a freezer, large enough to hold a body.

She shuddered as other equally disturbing images came at her from the recesses of her mind. The pictures she had seen of the victims on the wall of the CIB's investigation room, their faces butchered in death. The newspaper clipping of her column in the bottom of the evidence bag, her words soaking in the latest victim's blood. The face on her screen, the dead eyes.

Hanna dropped her head in her hands, willing the images to go away. Her back and armpits were clammy with perspiration and the booze made her feel dizzy.

What else? What about the killer's rage? Where was it coming from? No doubt it had its roots firmly planted in his childhood, like most serial killers, but she could not imagine what kind of abuse or trauma he might have suffered at the hands of a parent or other trusted adult that could be the cause of all this rage. She thought again of his choice of victims. Had his mother been blonde and blue-eyed, or perhaps someone else who had abused him? Was he directing his rage at this person onto the victims he had chosen?

Of course he was. There was simply no other explanation for it.

Few understood the criminal mind and Hanna was as baffled by the actions of serial killers as anyone else. She understood the notion that the true nature of serial killers, sexual sadists and child molesters seemed to be rooted in the brain and not the groin. Scientists had long speculated and debated on the possibility of a missing genetic code that predisposed an individual to feel no empathy or remorse; others believed in a present gene that predisposed an individual to commit acts of violence and murder.

Either way, treatments didn't work. For these types of people, rehabilitation was simply out of the question. The only way to be sure they would never offend again, short of capital punishment, was to lock them up and throw away the key.

Hanna wondered about the basic human personality. Did each human being have at birth a set of character traits that never changed? Or was a person's socialization and environment factors to consider as well?

Nature versus nurture, she thought and sighed long and loudly. She had wracked her brains for over an hour, yet she was still no closer to the truth.

That police officer was right, she decided as the first signs of a headache mushroomed in her head. It would have been better to have done nothing. At least she wouldn't have wasted all this time thinking about a case that seemed to be going nowhere.

"Goddamn it," she mumbled and pressed her fingertips to her temples.

It seemed the more pieces of the puzzle she had, the more fragmented the puzzle seemed to be, the pieces floating away and dancing just out of reach in the shadows.

"We're still haggling with the administrator… it seems these bastards have more rights than the rest of us," Bennett complained when he called a few minutes later.

Hanna's headache throbbed. "So you're no closer to learning anything, then?"

"Not right now, but as soon as the search warrant gets here, we'll be ripping this place apart." He cleared his throat. "Any luck with Jackson?"

She told him what she'd learned during her conversation with the parks superintendent and smiled when she heard him whistle through the phone line.

"Bone Island… well, I'll be damned. I'll pass this along, get a couple of detectives to check into that right now."

"One more thing, Tim. Check visitor lists for both patients for the past couple of weeks, if you haven't already thought of it. It seems to me that if Raymond or Mick is *tatler*, then the killer probably visited them a few times to pass along information."

"It's one of the first things we plan on checking out." His voice dropped. "But enough about that. How are you?"

"Well, I've got a headache, but I'm fine. Why?"

"I don't know… I guess I just miss you, that's all."

A warm flush crept into her face. "I miss you, too."

There was a sudden commotion in the background. She could hear two or three voices all talking at once.

"I have to go, Hanna. I'll phone when I know anything, okay?"

"I'll be here."

Replacing the receiver, she turned to head to the bathroom and tripped over her handbag lying on the floor next to her desk. Out spilled pens, some loose change, business cards, her wallet, a makeup compact and a bunch of other odds and ends. The only thing left in the bag was her digital camera and she remembered the pictures she had taken on the boat ride with Jake and Trish on Friday. She had forgotten all about them, but seeing her camera now reminded her that she still had to go through them and choose one to go along with the story about Jody Adamson's and Benjamin Lachance's reactions to Tina's murder. A story she still hadn't written, she berated herself.

Setting her camera on the coffee table, she finished picking everything up off the floor and put her handbag by the front door. After a trip to the bathroom, she sat down on the sofa and picked up the camera for a look at the photographs.

Turning it on, she accessed the display feature and clicked through the photographs until she came to the one of the cottage Jake's family had once owned. Set back from shore, it seemed to have been built on a platform of pink and grey swirled rock. Bent white pines surrounded the little wooden structure and Hanna closed her eyes as she imagined herself standing on the dock as the colours of a beautiful sunset bled into Georgian Bay.

Someday, she thought wistfully, someday. She leaned back and worked Bennett into her fantasy. He would stand behind her with his arms wrapped around her waist as they watched the sunset together. They would share a bottle of red wine and -.

The doorbell rang.

Hanna's eyes snapped open. "What the hell?" she muttered and got up off the sofa, depositing the camera on the coffee table. She glanced at her watch and saw that it was half past nine. A little late for visitors to be dropping in unexpectedly, she thought as the bell rang again. She moved to her front window, looked out and breathed a sigh of relief when she saw David Lakefield standing at her door.

She unlocked the deadbolt and opened the door. "David! What

a surprise. What are you doing here?" she asked, stepping aside and motioning him to come in.

He did, smiling. "I was in the neighbourhood… had to cover a basketball game down at the public school and I thought since I was already here, I'd stop in to say hello."

"Well, hello then." Hanna gestured at the sofa and David sat down. "Can I get you something to drink?"

"No, thanks," he said, looking around. "Nice place you've got here."

Hanna wondered how he had known her address. "Thanks," she replied, sitting in one of the matching wing chairs opposite the sofa. "How'd you know where I lived?"

He smiled again and gave a small shrug. "Jake's got that sheet with all our addresses and numbers on it… I happened to glance at it earlier in the week."

"Oh." She made a mental note to talk to Belmont about it. She couldn't explain it, but it made her uncomfortable to think that anyone could have just walked over and glanced at the sheet on his desk. She searched for something to talk about. "How was the game?"

"Fine. Just a bunch of old guys shooting a ball at a basket. Nothing too exciting. Oh, I almost forgot. I've got some news… about Ingrid."

Hanna sat on the edge of her chair. "She's been found?"

"No, unfortunately. I ran into Kirk Andrews just a few hours ago… so we started talking about Ingrid's disappearance and he told me something interesting. Apparently, he ran into her on Friday around lunchtime, just after he got the news about his brother. He said he stopped at the IGA for a can of Coke and saw Ingrid standing against the side of the building. He thought that was strange… she was supposed to be at work… so he went over and asked her what she was doing and she told him something that got me thinking."

"What? What did she say?"

David leaned back against the sofa, crossed his legs again and smiled. "She said she was waiting for someone to pick her up."

Chapter Thirty-Three

HER EYES WIDE, Hanna stared at David. "Who? Did she say
who was picking her up?"

"No, unfortunately. Kirk said he was so upset about his brother,
he didn't even think to ask. He said he just mumbled something
and took off. Do you think whoever she was meeting had anything
to do with her disappearance?"

Hanna didn't know the answer to that question, but she seriously
doubted Ingrid would still be missing two and a half days later if
whoever had picked her up on Friday was a friend or a relative.
"Yeah… it seems more likely than not, now doesn't it?" She stood.
"I think I'm going to have a drink, David. Can I get you anything
while I'm up?"

"Just water, thanks."

Hanna returned with some lemonade for herself and ice water
for David and caught him looking through the pictures on her
digital camera.

"Sorry, I didn't mean to snoop," he said, setting the camera
down on the coffee table. "So what's the latest news with the
investigation? What's going on?"

"You probably heard that they found another victim last night.
Number four."

"Yeah, I heard about it on the news today. Apparently, there was
a witness?"

"That's right. Poor guy, he was so shaken up about it."

"You were there? Last night?" He looked at her with interest, his cerulean eyes bright and sharp. "Did you interview the guy?"

She nodded. "He reminded me of my dad a little. He seemed like such a nice man."

"Poor guy. Do the cops have any idea who the victim is?"

"No. But that reminds me," she said, glancing at her watch to see that it was now 9:59, "I wanted to catch the news to see if they've got anything. You don't mind, do you?"

David shook his head and Hanna clicked on the television. They sat through a commercial for Ford trucks before the familiar theme music for the national 10 o'clock news broadcast came on. The top story involved a horrific accident that had claimed the lives of nine people, two of them children, after an oil tanker had overturned in the middle of a major highway in Toronto and plowed into several cars.

How awful, Hanna thought, watching a mother screaming for her dead child. She wondered how many people throughout the country were watching this story at this very moment and how many of them were going about their business like nothing had happened. She remembered an old newspaper saying - violence and tragedy only count when it touches home. A plane crashing in Bangladesh, killing several hundred people, won't have the same impact - won't move the heart - as surely as the death of someone you know.

The accident story wrapped up and then the words 'Serial Killer Strikes Again in Cottage Country' were superimposed over the silhouette of a man brandishing a syringe as the anchor introduced the second story. "Here's Tom Hanley with the latest."

"The body of another young woman was recovered late last night at Three Mile Marina and Cottages near Severn Sound in cottage country after Chad Morris, an employee of the marina, witnessed her body being dumped from a small boat," reported an off-camera voice over a shot of evidence technicians and divers working the scene at the tiny marina.

Then Chad Morris appeared, his face pale and gaunt, and Hanna's heart went out to him. He repeated almost word for word what he had told her the night before, and gave the numbers and a description of the boat he had glimpsed just before it disappeared into the night. The reporter repeated the numbers and confirmed that the OPP's Marine Unit and the Coast Guard were now patrolling Georgian Bay, on the lookout for the boat.

"This latest victim, who remains unidentified at this time, was found just several kilometres from where the bodies of Lydia Tomlinson and Tina Joliet were recovered earlier this month near Honey Harbour," the reporter continued. "She is believed to be the Bay Killer's fourth victim, according to Detective-Inspector Tim Bennett of the Ontario Provincial Police's Criminal Investigation Branch."

One by one, the photographs of the slain women were shown, and Hanna was once again floored by the similarities she saw in each of the faces.

"With the help of ViCLAS, the OPP's Violent Crime Linkage Analysis System, investigators were able to link the unsolved murder of 17-year-old Marianne Legault of North Bay in April of this year to those of Lydia Tomlinson, 19 of Waubaushene, Tina Joliet, 20 of North Bay, and this latest victim recovered last night." The reporter went on to say that all the victims were believed to have been killed with a fatal dose of ketamine hydrochloride and mutilated before the killer dumped their bodies in Georgian Bay.

He described the victim recovered the night before as being between 18 and 24, petite with long blonde hair and blue eyes, and urged anyone with information to contact police immediately. "Back to you, Rob," he said, signing off.

"Thanks, Tom. In a related story," the anchor said, "the 18-year-old daughter of Evan Marshall, the mayor of the nearby community of Midland in cottage country, is still missing more than 58 hours after she was last seen leaving her parents' house to go to work early Friday afternoon. Rumours that she has become the Bay Killer's fifth victim are flying rampant in the town. With more, here is Ellen Harrisburg."

A pretty, 30s-something redhead appeared on screen, Evan and Maxine Marshall's rambling house visible beyond her shoulder. "This is the house 18-year-old Ingrid Marshall has slept in every night of her life until last Friday when she disappeared. Hundreds of volunteers turned up early Saturday morning to search the route she normally drives to Lakefield's Animal Clinic where she works, but found nothing. It was only a couple of hours later that her car, a red Miata, was found hidden behind dumpsters in the back lot of a grocery store along Midland's commercial strip."

A shot of the IGA's back lot came into view; police officers and cars everywhere. "Police dusted for fingerprints and carefully searched the car, as well as the entire area where the car was found, but found no evidence to explain the girl's disappearance. Police refuse to give credence to rumours that the mayor's daughter might have fallen victim to the Bay Killer who has so far abducted and killed four women in less than three months."

The shot of the store's back lot faded away and was replaced with Evan and Maxine Marshall standing together in front of their home. Hanna slid across her chair until she was perched on the very edge, her heart breaking all over again at the sight of the naked pain on their faces and the desperation in their eyes.

They held Ingrid's graduation photograph between them and talked about their daughter's love of animals, her plans to study veterinary medicine and her caring ways. Return Ingrid to us unharmed, they begged, and Hanna noted how many times they mentioned their daughter by name. She knew they were appealing to the killer, if he had indeed taken her, to see her as a person. Seldom will murderers use their victims' names for it is far easier to kill people who have been stripped of their identities.

In conclusion, the reporter gave all the particulars of Ingrid's disappearance, including her description, and urged anyone with information to call the police.

"Wow. Pretty heavy stuff. Did they find any evidence? With this latest victim?"

Hanna shuddered as her mind filled with the image of her newspaper column floating in bloody water, but that wasn't the kind of evidence David was asking about. "Nothing, as far as I know. They only did the autopsy today. But because she had just been dumped, there's a good possibility they might find something.

A hair, maybe some fibres."

David frowned at her. "Are you okay, Hanna? For a minute there, you looked as if you might be sick."

She smiled thinly. "I'm fine. It's just… well, they did find something."

"Oh?" An eyebrow arched. "What?"

"Keep this to yourself, okay? A clipping of my weekend column was found in a gag inside the victim's mouth."

"Oh my God! No wonder you looked like you were going to be sick." He stared at her. "You must be terrified. Maybe you should stop covering this story."

"David, I appreciate your concern. Really, I do. But I'm not backing off this story… it's gotten way too personal for that."

"I don't know. If it was me, I'd be hiding out for a while."

Hanna smiled, reached for her lemonade and took a sip. "That's what the cops want me to do, but I can't. I have to see this through. It's all about to end soon, anyway. There's reason to believe the killer's decompensating, and the cops were finally able to trace *tatler* today, so we'll be getting answers to a lot of questions soon."

"Tatler? What are you talking about?"

It suddenly occurred to Hanna that she had only told Belmont and Matthew Henry about *tatler* and the images she had been sent. No wonder David was looking at her like she was speaking in tongues. "That's right… I never did tell you about *tatler*, did I?"

As generally as possible, she described the images she had been sent after all three of the local murders. She explained that the Ojibway words accompanying each of the pictures had been clues pointing to the locations where the victims had been abducted. She watched David's face register surprise, disbelief and anger.

"So just a few hours ago, they were finally able to trace the messages to an actual location. You'll never be able to guess where in a million years," she said and paused for a bit of drama. "Rolling Sands. Can you believe it?"

"Oh my God."

"Isn't it something? I could hardly believe it myself, but it's all starting to make sense to me now. I don't know if you knew, but I interviewed two patients there last week for a story Jake wants me to do for the magazine this month. I'm starting to suspect that one of them is the bastard, or maybe it's even both of them working together. The only thing is, patients there don't have access to the Internet, so unless he broke into an office or something, I can't figure out how he could have done it."

"I can't believe this," David mumbled as Hanna's cell rang.

That'll be Bennett with some news, Hanna thought, snatching up the phone. "Hello?"

"Hanna, hi. It's me. Are you sitting down?"

"Just a minute." She covered the mouthpiece with her palm and told David to make himself at home; she would only be a few minutes. Then she walked into her kitchen and perched on the edge of a chair, already dreading what he was about to tell her. "Okay. I'm sitting."

"Good. I can't talk long; we're just wrapping things up here at Rolling Sands. And before you ask, yes, I do have some news about that, but first things first. Your tip about Bone Island checks out big time. I didn't know this when you told me, but it turns out we'd gotten a call earlier today from a man in Toronto who claimed he'd been trying to get a hold of his girlfriend and hadn't been able to reach her in the last three days. This guy, his name's Paul Alexander, said his girlfriend is a fashion designer who went up to her parents' cottage in the Muskokas last Monday for a week. Guess where the cottage is?"

"Bone Island," she answered, feeling suddenly cold. "Oh God."

"This guy said he talked to her the day she left as well as Tuesday, Wednesday and Thursday, but when he called on Friday, he wasn't able to reach her. Ditto for Saturday. At first he said he wasn't all that worried because Caitlyn - that's her name, Caitlyn Smith - often 'goes off to Pluto' when she indulges in her hobby. Those were his words, not mine. He said he didn't really start to worry until today, when he was watching the news at lunchtime. Then he picked up the phone and called us. Apparently, his girlfriend fits the description of the victim to a T."

"Oh God," Hanna said again.

"So we found out exactly where the cottage is and a couple of detectives went out there to check it out immediately. They found the place unlocked, but undisturbed like someone had just up and left. Then they searched the grounds and the beach around it and found a tube of paint half-buried in sand."

"Her hobby… she was an artist." Hanna felt faint with nausea. "How old was she?"

"Twenty-three. An only child. Her boyfriend said she was working on putting together an exhibition of her paintings next month at one of those prestigious galleries in Toronto; she was that good." He sighed loudly. "He must have taken all her other equipment if he took her from the beach… we were lucky to find the paint."

Hanna closed her eyes tightly. She could imagine Caitlyn Smith in her mind's eye, a very petite blonde with sparkling blue eyes. She had come up from the city to spend a quiet week painting at her parents' cottage on Bone Island, surrounded by Muskoka's unique beauty. Then a few days ago, she had set up on the beach to paint. For the last time.

"Hanna? You still there?" Bennett asked after a long moment of silence.

"Yeah. Tell me about Rolling Sands."

"I can't really say too much right now. We're almost done here, just wrapping up a few loose ends… but I was thinking," he said, his words rushed, "I could be at your place in less than an hour and tell you all about it in person. I mean, if that's all right."

Despite the heaviness in her heart, Hanna smiled. "It's more than all right, Tim. I can't wait to see you."

"I'll be there as soon as I can."

"Tell me one thing before you go, okay? Was I right? About *tatler*?"

He chuckled. "Can't even wait less than an hour, can you?"

"No. I can't."

He laughed some more. "Yeah, you were right. Raymond admitted everything, but even if he hadn't, the evidence we recovered in his cell or whatever you call the box he lives in is more than enough to prove he's the sender. And he was sure fixated on you. We found boxes full of clippings of your stories. Looks like he saved everything you ever wrote since you started in Midland."

Hanna's skin crawled at the thought of Raymond reading and saving her work. "So was it just Fortin or was Keating involved as well?"

"At this point, it's hard to tell. But Keating's apparently quite knowledgeable about all kinds of things and we think Raymond probably used him to get information about the Ojibway words he sent you."

"Did you find out how he got access to the Internet?"

"There's still some question about that… but apparently, the staff teacher for the Education Centre was in the habit of ducking out early for long lunches and Raymond seized the opportunity to use the computers during his absence. That's why all the messages were sent to you around lunchtime."

"Well, I'll be damned. So much for maximum security."

"Yeah… especially for a guy like him, you'd think they'd keep a closer eye on things up there. I take it you researched the guy?"

"Yeah."

"Did you know Rosalynne Parkes was only 21 when she died? And that he beat that poor woman to death with his bare hands?"

An image of what her body must have looked like rose in Hanna's mind. "Yes."

"Her skull was pulverized… fractured into some forty-odd pieces, if you can imagine it. She had more broken bones than Humpty Dumpty after his fall."

"Jesus."

"But the worst part was that poor kid they found. Barely four years old."

"What kid?" She had found no mention of a child in all the research she had done.

"Their son. Raymond met Rosalynne when she was 17 and it wasn't long until he got her pregnant. Of course, with Raymond being in and out of jail so much, the kid barely got to know his father and he sure wasn't around to support them. So Rosalynne got herself into prostitution. The day of the murder, Raymond had just got out of jail, and he went up to the apartment where they lived and walked in on Rosalynne and some guy. That's when he lost it… and his son, that little boy, witnessed his own father beating his mother to death during a violent psychotic episode. He was found hiding beside the doorway to the livingroom where it happened in a severe catatonic state. Social Services took him away, got him some help. And eventually, he was adopted."

"Jesus, Tim. That's just awful."

"Yeah… makes you want to cry, doesn't it?"

"And never stop." Hanna combed her fingers through her hair, blinking back tears as she thought of another little boy who had suffered unspeakable abuse at the hands of his parents. The last story she had ever done in Toronto. "So what happened to that little boy after he was adopted? Do you know?"

"Those records are sealed. All I know is that he was adopted into a good family."

"Makes you wonder what happened to him… how he turned out."

"Yeah… wait a minute." She heard muffled voices and the sound of a chair scraping against linoleum. A moment later, Bennett came back on the line. "We'll talk some more when I drop in later, Hanna, okay? Right now I have to go."

"Okay. Bye."

She was thinking of four-year-old boys when fireworks exploded in her head, bright orange and blinding yellow fusing into the most brilliant of reds, and then there was only darkness as she crumpled to the floor.

Chapter Thirty-Four

LIGHT SEEPED THROUGH the blackness in Hanna's mind. White-hot bursts kept going off like flashbulbs somewhere at the base of her skull. Pain flared, diminished, flared again as the darkness retreated further away.

Hanna opened her eyes. And saw only darkness.

She blinked, felt the flutter of her eyelashes on her cheeks and against her lids. Her eyes were open, she was sure of that. But still she couldn't see. Everything was black. And there was something else, too. Something crammed in her mouth. Was she blindfolded and gagged?

Panic swept over her like a tidal wave. She couldn't breathe; her chest burned as if it was on fire. Her throat closed down, squeezing her windpipe. And her head. It hurt so much. Like every headache she had ever had put together and multiplied by a hundred.

Oh God.

And what was that sound? Like the thud of water hitting up against something hard. Bouncing, slapping wet sounds. But there was another sound as well, a roar like the buzz of a hundred thousand angry bees. A motor? And that rocking, rolling motion under her body…

Oh God. She was on a boat.

Hanna struggled to breathe. Don't think, she shouted at herself in her head, just breathe! One, two, three. That's it. Slow and easy. *Don't think. Don't think. Don't think.*

Then a boom of sound exploded over her head. A second later, a blinding flash of light penetrated through the blindfold, and Hanna flinched in the instant before she realized that the sound was thunder and the flash lightning. A storm, she told herself, it's nothing but a storm.

The first drop of rain hit her in the face, then everywhere as a deluge of wind-driven water fell from above. Her clothes, her hair, her skin were soaked in seconds.

Oh God, she thought, hysteria closing in. What the hell is going on? Why am I gagged and blindfolded? Why am I on a boat in the middle of a storm?

But she already knew the answers to those questions and the truth was worse than she could have imagined in her lifetime.

Fear struck then, sharp and icy, and out of nowhere her mind filled with the faces of Lydia, Tina, Marianne and Caitlyn after the monster had finished with them.

The Bay Killer.

He'd butchered them all, one by one. Abducted, killed, mutilated, tortured, raped, stabbed, beaten and dumped in Georgian Bay.

Hanna remembered the terror she'd felt after she'd seen the clipping of her column. But it had been nothing compared to what she was feeling now.

This was beyond fear. It was terror, white and numbing, and she felt a cold trickle of urine run out of her body.

Oh God. Oh my God. The Bay Killer.

A strangled cry escaped from the depths of her being, loud and chilling as it rose above all other sounds, even muffled through the gag, and pierced the night. Something hard slammed into her head and she went down to that dark, dark place once again.

Hanna woke to searing pain. An ache throbbed steadily at the back of her neck and a new, pulsing pain spread from her left temple to the back of her eye. It hurt just to breathe.

What was happening?

But before she had finished asking herself the question, the answer was in her mind and everything came back to her. The gag, the blindfold, the storm, the boat. Cold, numbing fear splashed over her and she felt her breath clog in her throat.

The Bay Killer. *Oh God. Oh God.*

But there was something she wasn't remembering, something she felt was vitally important. A flicker of memory teased her mind as pain continued to pound in her head. Her wrists hurt and her breath came in gasping spurts, but she didn't notice. Fear gripped her like a straightjacket, wrapping around her tightly, and Hanna bit back a sob.

She was no longer on the boat; that much she knew. There was no rolling motion under her body, no sound of water slapping against a hull, no rain pelting her face. She could still hear thunder clapping somewhere in the distance and the spattering of hard rain against a window, but nothing else.

There it was again, that flicker of a memory, and every muscle in her body tensed as she strained to remember. But it was useless and she cursed in frustration.

She smelled urine close by, and another fainter, metallic smell that she knew was blood. There was no mistaking that distinct smell and she sobbed at the thought of all the victims being butchered in this very room, wherever she was.

She blinked open her eyes and tears leaked across her face and into her ear. At the same moment, she noticed something across the room, a rectangle that glowed briefly as lightning flashed then grew black again, and she realized the blindfold was gone.

When her eyes had adjusted to the shadows, she was able to see the room she was in. It was long and narrow, perhaps thirty feet in length and half that in width. The small window she had glimpsed seemed to be the only one in the room and it was situated in the middle of the far wall, high up near the ceiling. A dresser, a table and some chairs were arranged around the room, and something large and rectangular - a couch? - was pushed up against the wall in the darkest shadows at the far end of the room.

Hanna looked down at herself and gasped. Her hands were bound in front of her with duct tape, as were her ankles, and she was lying on her left side on a prickly, striped blanket atop a narrow single bed flanked on both sides by end tables. She thanked God she was still wearing clothes as she recognized the tee shirt and shorts she'd thrown on over her bathing suit when she had decided to go for a walk on the beach.

That was this afternoon, she thought, as thunder crashed outside. Or was it? How much time had passed since she'd been brought to this hellhole? Was it still Sunday?

She remembered she'd been at home. Then what? What had happened after that? She'd opened another one of *tatler*'s ghastly images. The girl's face now rose hauntingly in her mind and she recalled the conversation she'd had with Bennett about her.

Tatler! Something about him gnawed at her and suddenly she had it. He'd been traced, Bennett had told her. To Rolling Sands, home of the criminally insane where both Raymond Fortin and Mick Keating had been locked up for years. The police had gone there, she remembered now, to search the place and check visitor lists for both patients.

C'mon, she urged her brain as she struggled to remember everything that had happened between then and the time she'd found herself gagged and blindfolded on a boat. But her mind remained empty and she was so frustrated she wanted to scream.

Thunder boomed again, louder than before, and in the brief flash of lightning that appeared at the window, Hanna caught a glimpse of the wall directly in front of her. It appeared to be covered in some kind of busy, floral wallpaper. Or was it? She couldn't be sure, but she could have sworn she'd seen a face up there, several of them in fact.

Lightning alternatively bathed the room in light one second and doused it in darkness the next, and Hanna stared at the wall, her entire body tensing with repulsion as she came face to face with horrors that should never have happened. To anyone, anytime.

Oh God. Oh God Almighty.

Eyes looked out at her from what looked like four large framed collages hanging among the garish red roses of the wallpaper. She glimpsed pictures, newspaper clippings, trinkets and jewellery, and realized with a shudder that each of the collages represented a victim. She knew many serial killers collected souvenirs from their victims, but seeing those collages made her nauseous. She could imagine the killer applying a drop of glue to a picture, a lock of hair or a pair of panties as he arranged his treasures into a collage of unspeakable horror. The detail, careful arrangement of the items and expensive frames told her he had not only spent a great deal of time and money making them, but that he had also enjoyed himself immensely.

As repulsed as she was, Hanna couldn't deny a morbid curiosity. She wanted to see the collages up close, needed to study the items that had belonged to the victims. But most of all, she needed to look at the newspaper stories he had cut out to see if her byline was at the top. She didn't doubt she would see her name there, and she was filled with rage to think that she had been used by the killer; that she had been part of the whole evil drama he had orchestrated from the beginning. She had been his public relations officer, his messenger of hate and violence and carnage. Her words had reported what he had done; they were a permanent record of his depraved acts.

She felt sick to her stomach and her muscles screamed in agony as she slowly twisted her body into a sitting position, swung her bound legs to the floor, and froze.

Suddenly she knew. She remembered everything.

She'd been looking through the photographs she'd taken on the boat trip with Belmont when the doorbell rang; she'd been dreaming of being with Bennett at the little cottage that had once belonged to her editor's family. She'd unlocked and opened the door, smiling as she invited David Lakefield into her home.

Oh God. Oh please God.

Had she invited one of the worst, most depraved serial killer the country had ever seen into her own home? What other explanation was there? One minute she'd been on the phone with Bennett in the safety of her home and the next she'd found herself gagged and blindfolded on a boat. Nausea rolled through her stomach as disbelief mingled with white-hot fear. Was David Lakefield the Bay Killer?

She'd sat across from him in her living room, she'd watched the news with him, she'd brought him a glass of water. And he had hit her with something in the head, took her on his boat and tied her up here in this vile-smelling room. It had to be him.

The knowledge stole her breath away. She raised bound hands to her face and wept, her heart hammering at break-neck speed.

David Lakefield, who worked with her and whose desk was nearest to hers in the newsroom. David Lakefied, who had just graduated from the journalism program at Canadore College in North Bay and whose mother lived nearby. David Lakefield, whose adoptive father was the owner of the area's best veterinary clinic where ketamine was readily accessible.

David Lakefield, the Bay Killer.

Something else tittered at the edge of her mind. The conversation she'd had with Bennett on the phone. Raymond Fortin had raped and beaten his common-law wife to death in front of his four-year-old son 20 years ago. A son who was later adopted by a local family. A son who had grown up to be a depraved killer?

He was 24 now; he would have been only four 20 years ago. And he had been adopted. She had to be crazy to even consider it, but had David been that little boy? Could it be? It made sense; pieces of the puzzle were finally clicking into place.

But if she was right, if Raymond Fortin was David Lakefield's biological father, how had he managed to maintain contact with his son all those years? Especially since he was locked up in a maximum-security hospital for the criminally insane and David had been adopted?

She could kick herself for not thinking of asking Bennett who else had visited Raymond in the last few weeks, besides herself. Was David's name on Raymond's visitor lists? It would explain how Raymond had known her address. David had told her he'd seen the sheet on Belmont's desk and must have told his real father. She squeezed her eyes shut and wished she could talk to Bennett now that she believed she knew the Bay Killer's identity.

Thinking of Bennett brought physical pain. How long ago had she spoken to him? An hour? Two? A day? She remembered she had talked to him around 10:30 p.m. Sunday evening, just after she'd watched the news with David. He had told her he was just finishing up at Rolling Sands and would see her in about an hour. Hanna had no idea what time it was now, or even what day it was, but she prayed he would have been by her house by now and, discovering her gone, would have become suspicious.

Please God, she prayed with her eyes screwed shut, let that be so.

But even if he suspected something was wrong, how in the world would he find her? *She* didn't even know where she was. A wave of hopelessness washed over her and she felt the sting of fresh tears in her eyes.

The only thing she knew for sure was that she was more terrified than she had ever been in her life. She didn't stand a chance against someone as sadistic and barbaric as the Bay Killer; someone who had killed and decided he liked it so much, he had done it four times already. Would she die here like all the others and someday someone would find her body dumped in Georgian Bay?

Her tears flowed freely as she thought of David Lakefield. Where was he now and what was he doing? Getting his syringes and his snakes ready? Her teeth chattered violently and she bit down on her tongue, tasting blood.

Hanna felt a lump as her forearm grazed against the still-damp fabric of her shorts and she wrenched her bound hands across her stomach, reclining back on the bed as her fingers found the pocket opening. Jamming them inside, she encountered something that was hard and cold to the touch.

Her keys!

Triumphantly, she pulled them out as lightning popped again and her eyes alighted on the tiny lipstick-size tube of pepper spray dangling on the keychain.

Hanna broke down in tears again, silently thanking Bennett over and over again in her head as her fingers closed around the tube. She pressed it tightly against her chest.

Now at least, she might have a chance.

Chapter Thirty-Five

PRAYING SHE'D HAVE enough time to free herself, Hanna began gnawing at the duct tape binding her wrists. Thunder boomed overhead and lightning flashed on and off at the window. Time passed as she frantically worked and after several minutes, her jaws began to ache and tears born of frustration threatened to spill again.

No! She wouldn't cry anymore; she'd done enough of that already to fill a small ocean. She thought of everything David Lakefield had done to his victims, all the pain and horror he had single-handedly wrought in the last few weeks, and she felt rage.

Betrayal, too. He'd been right there under her nose the whole time, playing her like a fiddle, the rookie reporter eager to learn and tag along, asking questions and offering to help. But what he'd really been was a cold-blooded murderer who had stayed a step ahead of the investigation all this time. A heartless killer who had even helped her cover the story of Ingrid Marshall's disappearance, and this fact blew her mind because she knew now that he was most likely directly responsible for it.

Bits and pieces of the conversations she'd had with David at her home and the one that had followed with Bennett on the phone came back to her. She had told David about the clipping of her column found in the fourth victim's gag, something she now knew he had done to terrify her as much as to warn her off. Then she had told him about the two patients she had interviewed at Rolling Sands and the fact that *tatler* had been traced by the police to the maximum-security hospital for the criminally insane. She recalled seeing the shock and disbelief and anger on his face. She thought he had been reacting to the depravity of the images *tatler* had sent her, but she knew now that he'd been expressing his shock and rage at the discovery of *tatler*, his real father. And then later, when she'd been talking to Bennett on the phone, he'd overheard them talking about Bone Island. He had heard her ask if she'd been right about *tatler*; if *tatler* was Raymond or both of the patients she'd interviewed. He'd heard them talking about the fact that Raymond's own small son had witnessed his mother's murder 20 years before. And although Hanna had been careful not to use Bennett's name, he must have figured she was speaking with someone connected to the investigation. A cop who would be at her house within the hour.

Time had been running out for David; they had been so close to learning the truth. So he'd grabbed something, hit her on the head and taken her to this godforsaken place.

You goddamn son-of-a-bitch, Hanna screamed inside her head as her teeth ripped through layers of stubborn duct tape, finally tearing a gash through it. She clamped her teeth on a loose piece and with a violent twist of her head, ripped it all the way through.

Scrunching her face from the pain, she tore the rest of it from her skin, balled it up, threw it under the bed and rubbed her raw wrists. Then she started on the tape binding her ankles, teasing the edge of it with her long fingernails until a flap lifted. Using both hands, she ripped it all the way around, gritting her teeth as she felt another blast of pain.

Free at last, she lifted her hands to the back of her head and felt a lump the size of a small egg. Her fingers moved around to her left temple and came away wet with blood. She felt a gash about two inches long up on her forehead, just slightly above her eyebrow.

Removing the tube of pepper spray from the keys, Hanna uncapped it. Pointing the nozzle away from herself, she clutched it in her hand as she stood on shaky legs and moved around the bed to the opposite wall where she had spied the outline of a door.

But she knew before her hand closed around the knob that it

would be locked. She tried it anyway, and as she had feared, the door was locked from the outside. There was no way out; she was a prisoner.

She stilled the rising panic in her chest with a few slow breaths and turned around as a burst of lightning lit up the window and thunder crashed outside again. She walked across the floor to stand beneath it.

It was smaller than she had thought at first, maybe a foot from top to bottom and about four wide. Could she squeeze out of there? she wondered. Could she even break the glass?

Leaving the window, Hanna decided exploring the room might offer some other alternatives. And even if it didn't, she'd know every inch of it and might even gain some understanding of the monster that had used it for his sick fantasies.

Licking dry lips and adjusting her grip on the tube of pepper spray, she edged along the wall to where the collages hung a foot apart in their neat, expensive frames.

Lightning blazed through the room and Hanna was able to read a name she didn't recognize at the top of the news clipping stuck to the collage representing Marianne. She also took in a necklace of glass beads, a photograph of Marianne alive and smiling, strands of golden hair tied with a bit of ribbon.

A picture of Tina Joliet was stuck in the middle of the second collage, her head thrown back in laughter, her long blonde hair like a halo around her face. Diamond earrings had been stuck through the front of a pair of pink panties and three silver rings overlapped each other next to a clipping of a newspaper story.

In the next collage, Hanna noticed the story she had written for Lydia's funeral. A pair of black thong panties lay next to a lock of hair so pale it appeared silver. And in the top corner, something shrivelled and leathery lay stretched and pinned down at the corners and Hanna instantly knew she was looking at the square of skin that had been excised from Lydia's lower calf.

Oh God. The missing tattoo.

Hanna swallowed repeatedly to rid her mouth of the bitter taste of bile as she stared at the tattoo of a butterfly. The pain in her head drummed steadily; her eyes stung from tears and the strain of having to adjust over and over again from bright light to sudden darkness.

One more, she thought as she moved to the last collage on the wall – this one undoubtedly a shrine to the victim they had recovered Saturday night. Hanna remembered her name was Caitlyn Smith as lightning struck again, and she was surprised to see only three items glued to the collage. A tiny paintbrush, a flattened tube of oil paint and a ring sporting the biggest diamond she had ever seen. An engagement ring?

Just then, Hanna heard a noise and froze.

Cocking her head to the side and listening hard, she realized the sound had always been in the room with her. She had simply not picked it up because of the sound of the rain beating steadily against the window. But now, halfway down the length of the room, she was as conscious of it as she was of the heinous collages hanging to her left.

A steady whirring was coming from the end of the room. An electrical sound. Constant, it never varied in pitch or intensity and Hanna felt a shiver like a cold hand at the base of her spine.

She knew that sound. A steady buzz. A sound like a thousand flying insects batting their tiny wings all at once.

Rooted to the spot in front of the dresser, her eyes bore into the shadows at the end of the room. Only one thing could be that shape and size. A freezer.

Oh Jesus God.

Her heart thudded so loudly she could hardly breathe. She was frozen where she stood and her head felt like a giant balloon swaying at the end of her neck.

Then in a burst of motion, she crossed the floor to the freezer as vile images tumbled in her mind. The hand not gripping the tube of pepper spray reached out to grasp the lid and she let out a little cry of surprise when it started to lift up. It wasn't locked.

He kept them here when he wasn't using them, she thought with a shudder as she swung the lid up. Cold air hit her in the face; a foul odour stole up her nose. It was the smell of rotting meat, of things that had been frozen and thawed and frozen again.

Hanna gagged, felt her stomach clench as she thought of Lydia and Marianne and Tina and Caitlyn. Their faces floated in her mind, their features blurring into each other, and she imagined their bodies stiff and silent in this cold, cavernous space.

Oh God. Oh God. Oh God.

A whisper on her lips, the words came from a place she had long forgotten. *Hail Mary, full of grace, the Lord is with thee…*

Standing on the very tips of her toes, Hanna took a deep breath and held it as she leaned over to peer into the depths of the freezer. Even when the lightning flashed, she could see nothing but shadowy lumps down in the bottom. Balancing her stomach on the ledge, she reached a hand inside and touched something that was frozen stiff and ice cold.

She recoiled in horror, but forced herself to move her hand around, and that's when she felt it. Something that was soft and flowing.

Hair.

A scream rising up in her throat, she tumbled backwards out of the freezer. The tube of pepper spray fell out of her hand as she landed with a thud on her bottom. Barely conscious of a brief stab of pain, she patted the floor all around her with her hands, desperate to locate the tube.

There's a body in the freezer. Oh God.

No! Don't think about that, she repeated over and over to herself as she moved in ever-widening circles. Don't think, just find the pepper spray.

Tears of frustration and fear were leaking out of her eyes when her hand finally brushed against the metal of the tube. She snatched it up quickly, positioned it in her hand so that the nozzle pointed away from her, and stood up again.

She lifted the hem of her tee shirt and wiped her eyes and in that instant, a pretty face rose in her mind's eye and she knew whose hair and body she had just touched.

Ingrid's.

Everything David Lakefield had told her about Ingrid meeting someone at the IGA on Friday came back to her and she knew that he'd been that someone, that he'd picked her up and brought her here to this hellhole in the middle of God-only-knew where. And it was here that he had killed her and carried out his depraved fantasies with her corpse. Just like the others. And now here she was, a frozen cadaver in a freezer, victim number five.

So I was wrong, Hanna thought, tears rolling down her cheeks as she thought of the girl's parents. Ingrid was victim number five; I'm meant to be number six.

Jesus God.

Hanna crumpled to the floor on her knees as the enormity of her situation slammed home. She was going to die here, injected with a lethal dose of a powerful drug, and her body would become a revolting plaything, something David would periodically haul out of the freezer and use as part of his twisted sex games. And eventually, when her corpse became too fetid or mangled to use, he'd dump her in her watery grave and go after another innocent young woman. And the cycle would go on and on, a never-ending loop of evil and perversity, because no one suspected who the Bay Killer was.

Hanna screwed her fists into her eyes, retched sobs bubbling into her throat. She was the only person alive who knew that David Lakefield was the Bay Killer and when he decided to come after her and finish what he'd started, there would be no one.

She cried hard for herself and the others and almost didn't hear the sound of a key fitting into a lock. She only had enough time to stifle her sobs and scramble into the shadows before the door swung wide open.

Wearing only a pair of tan shorts and leather sandals on his feet, the Bay Killer stepped into the room.

Lightning flared at the window, illuminating his features, and Hanna bit down on her tongue. There was no mistaking those cerulean eyes in that tanned, smiling face and the dark hair that curled across his forehead. She was staring at David Lakefield.

Whistling a tune under his breath, he moved into the room

and as he turned towards the bed, she saw something gleam in his hand.

A syringe.

Oh God, she thought, squeezing herself into a tight ball between the wall and the freezer. Her heart slammed against her rib cage, beating so fast and so loud she was afraid he'd hear it all the way across the room. She could feel her eyes as big as saucers in her face, the rush of blood in her ears, the panic swelling in her chest. Terror was like ice in her veins, white noise in her head.

"Fucking bitch!" he bellowed, his rage at discovering her gone from the bed so palpable she could feel it like fingers of fire from across the room. "I'm gonna find you, you goddamn little bitch, and when I do…" His words dissolved into peals of laughter.

Hanna peeked around the freezer, saw him kneel by the bed and lift the blanket to peer underneath, and knew this was her chance. Her only chance.

It was now or never.

Adrenaline burst through her system as she clambered to her feet, the tube of pepper spray gripped tightly in her right hand, and lunged across the room. A guttural growl escaped her lips and she saw him turn towards the sound, surprise on his face.

She landed on him, toppling him backward to the floor, and the syringe arced out of his hand onto the bed. Grabbing his jaw, she pushed down hard on the nozzle of the tube in her other hand. A small cloud of spray found his eyes and he screamed, his hands instinctively going up to his face, and she sprayed him again and again.

His hands clawing at his eyes, David Lakefield howled in pain as Hanna rolled off his body, grabbed the syringe from the bed and ran out of the room into a narrow hallway lit only by a couple of light fixtures mounted on the walls.

There was a door at the far end of the hall and she ran to it, swinging it open. Towels and blankets and bed sheets stared back at her from floor-to-ceiling shelves and she cried out in frustration, looking back to see if David was coming after her.

But the hallway was clear and she started running in the

opposite direction, her heart slamming against her rib cage. She glanced into the open doorway of the room she'd just escaped and caught a glimpse of a hand coming out of the darkness at her.

Hanna screamed as she felt it graze her arm and grab on to her tee shirt, pulling her back and slowing her down. She turned and blindly stabbed at his arm with the syringe, but David swung his arm back as if to knock her to the floor, and in that split second before his arm came down, she felt the needle plunge into his chest.

Air whispered out of his mouth as his hands clutched at his chest and his knees buckled to the floor. All Hanna could see of the syringe was the depressor sticking out below his right nipple as she backed away. She couldn't believe she had stabbed him, couldn't grasp the fact that she had embedded the needle deep in his flesh.

She took another step backwards and watched as David clutched the depressor in both hands. With his eyes scrunched shut, he let out a blood-curdling scream that raised the hairs at the back of her neck, and started to pull the needle out of his chest. She heard the suck of air as it was wrenched free, saw the trickle of blood run down his stomach. She watched him fling the syringe against the wall in a burst of rage as he struggled to his feet. Hanna turned and ran down the hall as if a legion of demons was at her heels.

She was vaguely aware of a darkened living room to her left and a tiny kitchen to her right as she reached the door at the end of the hall. Wrenching it open, she glanced over her shoulder and saw David using the wall to drag himself as he stumbled after her and she wondered how much ketamine had been injected into his system.

Slamming the door shut, Hanna careened down the steps, tumbling headlong to the muddy ground. Rain plastered her hair to her head and her clothes to her body, as lightning zigzagged and thunder roared across blackened skies. Turning to look back at the prison she had just escaped, she gasped.

No! It couldn't be!

But it was. There was no mistaking the little cottage that had once belonged to Jake's family, the one that sat on a ledge of grey rock surrounded by bent pines and the waters of Georgian Bay. The same one she had dreamed about, the very one she had snapped a picture of when Jake had showed it to her on the boat.

And now it was David's little cottage of horrors. A place of death and desecration, when it had only ever been meant to be a place of refuge and recreation, and Hanna wondered how it had come to belong to his family.

A tiny, isolated islet in the middle of nowhere. Despair washed over her as she turned to face the darkness that was Georgian Bay. She had freed herself, attacked a madman and escaped alive only to find that she was as much a prisoner now as she'd been inside the cottage - she was trapped on an island with a psychopath.

There was no escape.

Sobs tore out of her throat as she looked around, her tears mixing with the rain streaking her face. There was nothing but the storm, the cottage, the rocks, the trees and the tumbling, black waters of Georgian Bay all around her. She looked for his boat but the dock was empty. Maybe there was another dock around the other side of the island. She peered through the rain and the darkness, twirling helplessly around and around, her wails snatched by the rain-driven wind as soon as they left her mouth.

Lightning briefly illuminated the island over and over again and Hanna abruptly stopped spinning as she caught a glimpse of the cottage.

The front door was wide open, faint light spilling out onto the porch steps. Terror washed over her in waves. Her eyes frantically scanned the darkness in front of her, her heart leaping into her throat. Where was he? Why couldn't she see him?

She twirled around and screamed. David Lakefield was no more than thirty feet behind her, crawling on his hands and knees, his eyes empty sockets in the darkness.

Hanna took off running in the opposite direction. She felt wet sand and rocks under her sneakered feet as she ran blindly in the darkness and then she was airborne, flying for a breathless moment before smashing down to the ground. Pain flared up her left side; air whooshed out of her lungs.

She lay stunned, rain splashing on her face, and extracted her arm out from beneath her. Checking it for broken bones and discovering none, she scrambled to her feet and started running again. The ground was rocky here and boulders the size of small cars appeared like hulking beasts in the darkness. Using her hands and knees against their slippery surfaces, she slid once or twice before hauling herself up and struggling back to her feet. She had only taken a few steps across a boulder when she fell face first again, scraping her elbow and cheek against the rock.

Tears of pain and frustration squeezed out of her eyes as she tried pushing herself to her feet again. But she couldn't. Only one of her feet obeyed, the other seemed to be stuck. She reached around with one hand and felt the hard, slick surface of rocks on either side of her left ankle. Her foot was wedged in a crevice between the large boulder she was on and the one next to it. She wriggled her leg around and back and forth, but it would not budge.

Hysteria swelled in her chest and her breath snagged in her throat as thunder boomed overhead. She looked back over her shoulder as the lightning struck and saw David crawling towards her. He was no more than fifteen feet away now and Hanna choked back a sob, desperation closing around her like a cloak.

She strained and pulled at her ankle, her eyes never leaving the dark, crawling mass that was David, and felt her skin tear against the jagged edges of the rocks. There was no pain, only terror as the mass got bigger and bigger, growing out of the darkness.

When she felt a hand on her ankle, she screamed in terror, her blood turning to ice in her veins. She felt his hands on her legs, her back and her hair as he used her body to drag himself up the boulder, his weight crushing her stomach and breasts and face into the hard rock. Struggling to breathe, Hanna twisted her head to the side as lightning sliced the sky in two and she saw the madness in his eyes, the foam around his mouth, the black blood trailing from the wound in his chest. His hands circled around her neck, squeezing down, down, down.

Her fingers pried at his hands, but she couldn't breathe. There wasn't enough air. Her mind was a tunnel and she felt herself floating along it towards a pinprick of light that grew brighter as she got nearer. Memories came out of the blackness at her and through it all, she could hear a roaring sound like a truck lumbering on the highway or a helicopter hovering in the air.

A helicopter.

Her eyes flew open and closed again, blinded by a sudden shaft of light cutting through the rain and the darkness from above. She was dying; the light was sucking her up into another world.

No! She hadn't imagined it, that brilliant light. Or had she? Her eyes fluttered open again and it was there, a shaft of light sweeping away the darkness.

So dazzling, she thought as her eyelids struggled to stay open, so many powerful beams crisscrossing the darkness. And so much noise; her head pulsed with the roar.

Growing dimmer now, the light and the noise, fading away. Her eyelids fluttered closed; her mouth slackened.

In the next instant, she was choking and convulsing on the boulder as air rushed into her lungs and her fingers went up to her throat.

The hands were gone.

She sputtered, coughing and gasping as if she had forgotten how to breathe. Sweet air rushed into her lungs, and she smelled the scent of rain as light exploded around her. Looking back over her shoulder, she saw a tiny figure running drunkenly down the beach, swaying and stumbling in the rain, the light following. Then a new sound pierced the night, rising above the roars all around her, and she saw flames flashing out of the darkness.

Hanna watched as David Lakefield jerked in the light, fell to his knees and crumpled to the ground.

Epilogue

THE FIRST STARS of evening shone like jewels as dusk rolled its blanket of midnight blue across the sky. A crescent moon hung like a sideways smile in the gathering darkness, casting its reflection on the calm waters of Little Lake.

"What a perfect night," Hanna sighed, leaning back on the sleeping bag she had spread on the grass of a rolling hill overlooking the tiny lake set in the heart of Midland.

"Hmmm," Bennett agreed, "the perfect end to a perfect Canada Day."

They had spent the day at Little Lake Park enjoying the many festivities taking place. They'd played some volleyball on the beach, strolled through the artisan booths, and enjoyed some folk music. Hours later, famished and thirsty, they'd washed down jumbo hotdogs and greasy French fries with several cups of cold Canadian in the Rotary Club's beer tent. The day had been bright and sunny and perfect, with none of the humidity that had plagued the region in the last few weeks.

"And the best part hasn't even started yet," she added, looking over at Bennett in the gathering twilight.

He wiggled his eyebrows like caterpillars and smiled down at her. "You got that right, sweetheart. Just wait till I get you home…"

She burst out laughing, causing a sharp pain to radiate from her rib cage up to her shoulder. "Ow…I meant the fireworks, you goof."

"It still hurts, doesn't it?"

"A little…but only when I laugh."

He pulled her to him, hugging her close.

A little more than a week had passed since that dark, terrifying night when David Lakefield had mashed her body into the boulder with his own, trying to choke the life out of her with his bare hands. But for Hanna the memories were still as raw as the bruises that covered her sides, ankle and neck in ugly purple and yellow splotches. Those and the gash on her forehead that had taken twelve stitches to close would eventually heal, but she knew there were other wounds inside her that never would.

Hanna flashed back to Ingrid's funeral held a few days before. It had been one of the saddest and largest she had ever attended with more than 500 people turning out, including every politician and police officer for miles around. Following the tearful service, Ingrid had been buried just a few minutes' walk away from where they were sitting now, at the end of the park in St. Margaret's Catholic cemetery, overlooking Little Lake.

Thinking of Ingrid's final resting place made Hanna shiver. She didn't want to think about how close she'd come to dying, to becoming the Bay Killer's sixth victim. She felt her heart thud at the thought of her body lying in the cold, dark ground, forever silent and still, like those of Ingrid, Caitlyn, Tina, Lydia and Marianne, and anguish tore at her soul.

At times, it would hit her like this, like a blow to the gut, and she thought the pain would eat her alive. But most of the time, all she felt was a strange and comforting numbness like a favourite blanket wrapped tightly around her and she could pretend that the things that had happened that terrible night were not real. She had almost been killed and mutilated by a deranged serial killer, and this was not something anyone was ever prepared to face. She kept waiting for it to fully hit her, and she did not know how she would feel when it finally did. Angry, yes. Traumatized, for sure. But for now, she felt only the barest shadow of those emotions. The rest of her remained hollow, empty.

"It's okay," Bennett whispered into her hair and Hanna realized she was crying. "It's okay… everything's all right."

"Oh God, Tim," she whispered back as tears blinded her, "I keep thinking if it hadn't been for that picture, I'd be lying over there with Ingrid right now."

He tightened his hold on her, and when he spoke again, his voice was rough with emotion. "Sweetheart, don't think about that."

She had pondered the question of why she had taken the photograph of the cottage that had once belonged to Jake's family so many times in the last week, she had thought of little else. And she had found no answers and certainly no reasons why she had snapped it that day. Was it fate? She didn't know. But she did know one thing with absolute certainty. She would be dead and floating under a pier somewhere if she hadn't taken that shot.

The photograph had saved her.

Bennett had explained everything to her after David Lakefield had been shot in the leg and arrested that night on the island, after she'd been rescued from the boulder and taken by chopper to Soldiers' Memorial Hospital in Orillia for treatment. She could still hear his voice inside her head and remembered the intensity of his eyes on hers.

"We found hundreds of pictures in Raymond Fortin's cell… pornographic images of every kind imaginable, as well as the ones he sent you. Plus a few others, including one that showed a cottage built on a small island surrounded by water. At first, it meant nothing to us. We just shucked it into the boxes with everything else to be sorted through later. Then, when we were finished at Rolling Sands, I headed out to your place like we'd agreed. But as soon as I pulled in your driveway, I knew something was wrong. Your front door was open halfway, every light was on and I could hear your cat meowing up a storm. So I got out my gun and went in, but of course, the place was empty. I found your phone lying on the floor and a baseball bat nearby. I checked it out, found a small spot of blood on it and called the cops in Midland. Then while I was waiting them to show up, I noticed there were two glasses on the table and I suddenly remembered our conversation on the phone earlier. When I asked you if you were sitting down, you said "Just a minute," and I heard some muffled talking before you came back on. I don't know why, but at that moment I knew that whoever had been there was responsible for your disappearance. So I searched your place carefully, found nothing. I was just standing there, wracking my brains, when I happened to notice your camera on the coffee table. So I had a look, and you already know what I found. The same picture Raymond had in his cell.

"I was stumped. Why in the hell would you and Raymond each have a picture of what appeared to be the same cottage? It didn't make any sense. But then I had an idea. If anyone knew what the picture was about or why you had taken it in the first place, it would be your editor. But I couldn't remember his name, so I called the Midland OPP again, got his name from them, and looked up his home number. When I got him on the line, I told him about the picture and, of course, you know what he said. That the cottage had once belonged to his family and that you had taken the picture the day you took that boat trip with him to the White Pine Inn.

"I knew that picture was more than coincidence. I asked Jake if he could help us find the cottage and he said he'd be at your place in 10 minutes. Then the cops arrived to process your house and I called HQ, briefed them on what was happening, and from their end, they arranged for the Coast Guard, the Marine Unit and the CFOPP helicopter to be on their way. When Jake arrived, we hopped into my car and drove like hell to a designated spot just off Highway 400 between Waubaushene and Honey Harbour, where the chopper picked us up. About 20 minutes later, Jake spotted the cottage from the air, and we got in close and shot Lakefield in the leg as he tried to run. And the rest, as they say, is history."

Overcome with gratitude and passion and a million other emotions, Hanna had pulled him down on top of her in the hospital bed and rained kisses across his face, all the while murmuring, "You saved my life… you saved my life."

For that and many other reasons, Hanna would always be grateful. A man like Bennett came along only once in a lifetime.

"It's okay, baby, it's all right," he murmured as he wiped tears from her face. "You don't have to worry about Lakefield ever again. He'll die in prison. The only question is whether it'll be from old age or another inmate doing him in."

"I know." Hanna was quiet a moment, then her brow furrowed. "But there's still something bothering me. Why did he take Ingrid and that other girl, Caitlyn? There was nothing linking them to pregnancy or abortion like the others… I don't get it."

"Killing was a mission for him," Bennett said. "Right around the time David met Marianne in North Bay, Raymond Fortin renewed his acquaintance with him after 20 years of no contact. And as you can imagine, having his real father in his life after all this time caused all sorts of nasty, long-suppressed memories to surface, and he couldn't handle it."

"His real mother's murder," Hanna murmured, nodding.

"Exactly. David didn't start out as a psychopath, he started out as an innocent child, same as everyone else. But then one night, at the age of four, he witnessed his own father brutally beat his mother to death. He saw all that blood, all that evil unleashed, and a part of him died along with his mother that night. Another part of him, another personality if you will, took over for him, blocking what had happened so that no memory existed in his mind. And it worked. For 20 years, David functioned very well and his life was as stable as anyone else's, except for his adoptive mother being very religious and strict. Born again Christian, bordering on the fanatic. But apart from that, he had a pretty normal childhood."

"Then Raymond came back into his life and all hell broke loose."

"That's right. At this point, David was finishing his last year of journalism at Canadore. He was doing well; he was saving money by living with his adoptive mother in Sturgeon Falls just outside of North Bay. Things couldn't have been better for him. And then Raymond reared his ugly head, and as you said, all hell broke loose. Literally."

"How did Raymond connect with him? How'd he know where to contact David? I mean, he'd been adopted so he had a different name and everything."

"Raymond never lost contact with David. After he was found not guilty of murdering his girlfriend by reason of insanity and sent to Rolling Sands, Raymond had nothing better to do than keep track of his son."

"But aren't adoptive records sealed?"

"Sure, but a little bribery money can go a long way, Hanna. He told me when I talked to him that it was the easiest thing to do. He contacted someone he knew from before, and within weeks, he had all the information he needed. From there, it was easy to keep tabs on David, find out where he went to school, what he was doing with his life."

"But why did he wait 20 years before getting in touch?"

"I don't know. But he did tell me this... he sent David a letter at Canadore College on the twentieth anniversary date of his mother's death, the exact day it happened in fact, February 28. He didn't have a copy of the letter and we never found one among David's belongings, but Raymond told me it basically recounted everything that had happened, in graphic detail. Not just the murder, but the fact that his mother was a prostitute, too."

Hanna shuddered and thought there was no limit to Raymond's monstrosity.

"My guess is that's when David's mind begin to shatter, and he started remembering," Bennett went on. "That was the big stressor that started the ball rolling. He came unglued, his world tilted upside down."

"And he went after Marianne."

"Yes, shortly after. That's when he embarked on this mission of his. He wanted to get rid of girls who had, according to him, sinned by engaging in the pleasures of the flesh outside of wedlock. Just like his real mother, who had been seventeen and living on the streets when Raymond met her and got her pregnant. And who was, like the victims David went after, a blonde and blue-eyed girl... a girl who tried to support herself and her small son by selling her body for money. He already had all these issues with religion, sex, and abortion from his adoptive mother, and then Raymond came into his life."

"And the monster inside him was born."

"Exactly." Bennett stretched out his legs and leaned back on an elbow. "And Marianne was perfect. It didn't matter to him that she'd chosen to keep her baby... quite an honourable thing to do for such a young girl. No, for him, she was a slut and she had to go. So he met up with her outside the library that night and persuaded her to go with him to his car where he injected her with ketamine he stole from his adoptive father's clinic. And after he had his fun with her body, he dumped her in a river a few miles out of town."

Hanna drew her knees to her chin. "Then he graduated, came out here to work and went after Tina. I still can't believe he lied to me about knowing her."

"Lying is nothing for these guys, Hanna. You told me yourself how small Canadore is, how easy it would be for him to have met her. And you were right. She won this award through her program; he interviewed her for the college paper and they became friends. She thought nothing of telling him about being pregnant. And why not? That's what friends do… tell each other their news, their troubles. So he arranged to pick her up after work that Victoria Day weekend and took her back to his cottage, where he killed her."

Hanna rubbed her hands up and down her legs, thinking how easily it could have been her. "And then two weeks later, he abducted Lydia."

"Right." Bennett shook his head. "I imagine he must have laughed his head off when we were looking at Kirk as a suspect. You have to admit the guy was perfect. Not only did he have a relationship with Lydia, got her pregnant and provided her with the name of an abortionist, but the poor guy worked at the animal clinic and had all the access in the world to ketamine. What a joke that must have been for David… he probably thought we were the biggest fools on the planet. Kirk, too, for that matter. After all, David had known Kirk ever since he came to work at the clinic and they were quite friendly. Kirk told me he'd been down in the dumps for months after his break-up with Lydia and ended up telling David all about it one night when they were hanging out together at the clinic. He even showed him a picture of her. So when David needed another victim, he thought of Lydia."

"But how did he know she was camping on Beausoleil that weekend?"

"He happened to come into the clinic just after Kirk learned about the trip. He seemed pretty upset so David asked him what was the matter and Kirk told him."

"And Ingrid and Caitlyn? Why did he go after them?"

"By the time David got to them, he was starting to decompensate in a big way. The need to kill was stronger than his need to pick out victims that fit his criteria perfectly, like the first three had. With Ingrid and Caitlyn, it was enough that they were blonde and blue-eyed. Like his mother. The rest didn't matter so much anymore."

"I keep thinking of Ingrid… waiting for David to pick her up that Friday afternoon. An older man showing interest in such a young girl… that holds a lot of appeal."

"Yeah, she was an easy target. Plus, she already knew and trusted him… he was her boss' son. But with Caitlyn, it was different. She was the oldest of his victims and engaged… she had a career and a life. She may have looked young and been the smallest of the victims, but she wasn't a little girl anymore… she wouldn't have gone willingly with him. David didn't talk much about her. All he said was that he saw her painting that day while he was out cruising and decided she would be next. But it's my guess she was the most difficult to abduct."

"You know what's strange? David visiting Raymond, sometimes two or three times a week. Like a dutiful son." Hanna shook her head. "It boggles my mind."

"For you and I, but for David, it went a lot deeper than that. Raymond was the only person in the whole world who understood him. You have to remember, the need to brag about their kills is very strong for a lot of murderers. But by talking to Raymond about what he'd done to his victims and bringing him pictures, not only of his victims but also of the cottage where he killed them, David wasn't only bragging as one killer to another, he was really seeking approval and acceptance from his real father."

"That's really twisted, but you know what's worst? The pride Raymond must have felt." Hanna couldn't help the shiver that raced down her spine. "The bastard must have loved hearing all about the details, especially the snakes."

"Hey, that reminds me, we finished processing the cottage yesterday. Remember I told you about the snake farm we uncovered in the shed behind the cottage? We found more than 50 snakes, some dead and some alive, that he hunted and captured. And it turns out that's where he carried out the mutilations on his victims... the laser light picked up so much blood, it must have been a bloodbath in there. That's also where we found his stash of ketamine, some suturing material from the clinic, knives and, get this, a whole trunk of women's things."

"Jesus," Hanna said, grimacing as an image of David prancing in nothing but heels and blood came to mind. "How did he ever manage to avoid discovery? His adoptive father came to use the cottage every once in a while, didn't he?"

"Yes, but he cleaned up after himself very carefully... there were no visible signs of blood. Plus, the shed was always locked, as was his bedroom and the freezer in it... I don't know why it was unlocked when you were in there. Maybe it was deliberate... so you would find Ingrid. And the collages were easily taken down and hidden away."

Bennett's last word was drowned out by loud thudding as fingers of colour bloomed across the sky and arced down like petals to fall into the lake. The fireworks had begun.

They settled into each other's arms, watching together as the darkness was banished again and again by bursts of red, blue, yellow, white and green light popping across the skies. Only when the last and most spectacular firework had faded did they turn to one another, the roars still ringing in their ears, and smiled at each other.

"Ready?"

Hanna knew Bennett was only asking if she was ready to leave, but looking into his eyes, it suddenly seemed to her that there was a lot more she could read into those green depths and in that one simple word. A lot of love and hope and promise. A lot of healing. She wanted that more than anything in the world and she prayed she was ready for all of it.

They rose, gathered their belongings and followed the crowd to the parking lot. Getting in the car, Bennett turned the engine over and the song that poured out of the speakers made Hanna's heart pump a little faster. Turn the page, sang Bob Seger and The Silver Bullet Band, and she knew it was an omen. God only knew she had turned more than a page in her life in the last few weeks, and was now ready to turn a few more.

Maybe even a whole chapter, she thought as Bennett leaned over and kissed her.

About the Author

Originally from Georgian Bay, Ontario, Sonia Suedfeld is a former newspaper reporter who now lives in British Columbia with her husband, two sons, and three cats. She can often be found behind the counter of her store, Everybody Loves Candy Shoppe, where she writes crime, mystery and mainstream fiction in her spare time. Over the years, several of her short stories have won awards and been published in anthologies, chapbooks, magazines and online. *Dead Beneath The Water* is her first published novel.

Acknowledgments

While researching and writing *Dead Beneath the Water*, many experts, friends and loved ones came to the rescue. Each deserves my thanks and gratitude - this novel couldn't have been written without their help and support.

In particular, thanks are due to Detective Staff Sergeant Kim Peters, who was at the time of research the Unit Manager, Provincial ViCLAS Centre, Ontario Provincial Police headquarters in Orillia, Ontario. Not only did he answer all my questions about ViCLAS and the OPP's Behavioural Sciences Section, but he also explained the roles these units play in the investigation of murder.

Thanks also go to Rick Kotwa, who was at the time of research the Superintendent, Corporate Communications Bureau, Strategic Services, Ontario Provincial Police headquarters. He provided anecdotes and information on police investigative procedures in matters of violent death, especially when it involves cases where human remains are found.

For information and advice pertaining to forensic evidence, medico-legal autopsies, cause of death findings and coroner investigations, my thanks go out to Dr. Jim Young, who was at the time of research the Chief Coroner for the province of Ontario at the Office of the Chief Coroner in Toronto, and Dr. Steven Lintlop, who was the head of the Toxicology Section at the Centre for Forensic Sciences in Toronto.

For answering my many questions about ketamine hydrochloride, dosage, and toxicology testing, thanks are also due to Brendon Lalonde and Rachelle Wallage, who were at the time of research forensic scientists in the Toxicology Section of the Centre for Forensic Sciences in Toronto.

Many friends and family members found time to read early drafts. For all the comments and insight, thanks to all of you. Special thanks also go out to my father-in-law Peter Suedfeld, who has always been there with encouragement and support along the way, and to Arthur and Stanley Coren of Blue Terrier Press, who took a leap of faith with me and made a lifelong dream come true. As always, support, love and kind words came from my husband, Michael, and my sons, Kaleb and Jordan. Thanks guys, for everything.

Any errors are entirely mine.

CPSIA information can be obtained at www.ICGtesting.com
Printed in the USA
LVOW062254010312

271215LV00001B/1/P